INTO THE CHURN

HAYLEY REESE CHOW

WHIMSICAL PUBLISHING

INTO
THE
CHURN

HAYLEY REESE CHOW

WHIMSICAL PUBLISHING

Whimsical Publishing

Copyright © 2023 by Hayley Reese Chow

ISBN: 978-1-7780044-8-3

Edited by Micheline Ryckman & Deborah O'Carroll

Cover Art by Gabriella Bujdoso

Graphic design and map by Micheline Ryckman

For my mom, who always believed I could.

CASOLLA SYSTEM
SAM HART · LOCAL ASTRO 101

OBRONE
OCEANIC EARTH ATMO

WORM GATE
BETA3

CASOLLA
22 UNINHABITED
MOONS

DRIETIS
DRY ATMO

CRION
ICY, AIRLESS

STAR CV-11
ZAO.

24 SPACE
STATIONS

BELETHEA
UNSTABLE ATMOSHERE

CHAPTER 1

WITH EVERY STEP, Ezren breathed in another lungful of restored sanity. With every leap, she bounded away from the underground cage of Tuzuno outpost. And with every gust of wind lashing her heavy topsuit, she could pretend that she was free here in Belethea's rocky landscape. A wild laugh gurgled up, and she flung her head back and howled with the frenzied storm curling around her.

The navy-shaded funnel cloud above her whipped at the castle of thunderheads towering over the jagged cliffs on the horizon. Ezren's weather map beeped in her goggs, warning her of the maelstrom's vicinity, its red-stained radar image updating every six minutes next to her green vitals readout. Eh, she still had another 146 seconds. At least. Ezren breathed in the tangy scent of the charged air, digging her boots into Belethea's mauve dirt, its scant layer of hardy weeds rippling against the craggy surface.

Even from four clicks out, the storm hurled dust and rock chips at her in between rumbles of thunder, warning her to go back to her underground home where she belonged. After twelve downside days in a row, she was just about sick of Tuzuno's narrow tunnels. And the truth was, if you couldn't handle Belethea's stormy temper, then you didn't go topside at all. Which was also why she was out here alone.

Well, that and the fact that even though the newly-risen sun would shine for the next six hours, it was nearing the middle of the night. But Ezren would take a topside run whenever she could get it, and she wasn't about to waste a second of decent conditions. She and the other terraformers had worked hard for sufficient O2 to enjoy these stretches of atmospheric calm, so surely someone should enjoy it.

Her long, powerful strides devoured the mossy rock plateau stretching before her. Sweat beaded under the goggs strapped around her helmet, soaking into the compression liner of the clunky, old-fashioned topsuit that anchored her in Belethea's lower grav, her emergency pack cinched around her shoulders and waist.

The goggs beeped again, and Ezren's eyes flicked back to the radar. *Mother suns.* She'd have to turn around now if she didn't want to get stuck in a storm den and endure one of her mother's multi-day rants on topside safety.

With a reluctant huff, she turned back toward the metal-cased dome now 4.73 miles behind her down the incline. *Ugh.* It really bothered her that she wouldn't be able to get up to double digits today. But... then again, she did still need to finish that mother-shafting history report.

The wind was howling so loud now, Ezren almost didn't hear her goggs chirp with the message.

Incoming call from Micah: Accept?

Did that girl ever sleep? Ezren blinked twice, and Micah's overly bright voice crackled in her ears. "Why didn't you tell me you were going topside, you surface rat?"

"Surface rat gonna surf." Ezren laughed dryly.

"Are you tracking this storm?"

"You could say that; I'm practically in it."

"Ooh, perfect!" she squealed. "What if I told you I got a storm truck, six trays of algae bombs, and four instrumentation birds to set off?"

"You lucky sneak! Where'd you steal those from?" Ezren's mouth widened in a smile under her dented helmet.

"And just why would I give away my secrets?"

"Fine, be that way, as long as you let me in on the heist." She mentally flicked her coords Micah's way, the neurochip in her goggs chirping confirmation. "Come get me!"

"Only four miles out? Tsk, tsk, Ezzy, are you going soft on us?"

"It was a short window!" A boom of thunder vibrated through Ezren's suit, but she could just make out the black storm truck already charging toward her across the incline, careening around the wart-like boulders peppering the stony slope.

"You gotta be in top shape if you're going to place in the race royale tryouts."

Ezren groaned. "Seriously, can't you even go fifteen minutes without mentioning that stupid race?"

"Not this week. Didn't I tell you? Belethea's team is holding open tryouts for the first time ever, and they start in 79 hours and 42 minutes." The skid of the truck's wheels on rock crunched through her comms. "This is a huge deal."

Micah probably *had* already mentioned the tryouts, but all her BRR gossip tended to go in one ear and out the other. Not that Micah seemed to mind repeating it—constantly. Still, Ezren couldn't help but smile at her friend's unbridled enthusiasm. "Well, my fingers are crossed for you, M. I know how much you love the race royale."

"Massive understatement, Ez. The BRR is my life. It's the whole reason I took this internship in the first place."

Ezren let herself skid down a gravel-slicked cliffside, her

feet steady on the familiar terrain. "Oh, c'mon, interning at a planet engineering research outpost on one of the first-ever half-terraformed planets is way crisper than that ridiculous publicity stunt of a race."

The storm truck roared up the serrated incline, its shock-hardened bumper careening into a boulder twice its size. Micah flung open the door, her signature pigtail buns a luminescent shade of green and her blue multi-lensed goggs glinting on her forehead. Her eyes—gold today—glared at Ezren from her heart-shaped face. "Get real, Ez! There are teams from all three habitable planets *and* all twenty-four space stations. It's the one thing literally everyone in the system can agree on but you."

"Yeah, yeah." Ezren shooed her with a hand. "Move over, I'm driving."

Micah had been interning at Tuzuno research outpost for a couple of months now, but her driving skills still left much to be desired. In fairness, the fickle storms, unforgiving terrain, and low grav made for a steep learning curve.

Micah scuttled into the passenger seat while Ezren slammed the door shut, mentally linking her goggs to the driving AI. "Well, if anyone can make it, you can." Ezren adjusted the six-point harness to her slight 5'2" frame. "They'd have to be scabbed to turn down your application."

She slammed on the accelerator, the storm's debris of rocks bouncing off the truck's metal casing. The holo-projection on the armored windshield showed the funnel clouds multiplying above them. Ezren had to get to the top of the ridge before the wind devils touched down if they were to deploy the goods.

Micah let out her oddly deep belly laugh. "I wish, girl. I have many assets"—she brushed a speck of dust from the storm-tracking arm bracer she'd designed herself—"and I may eat, sleep, and breathe the BRR fangirl life, but I was not cut out to run, drive, and fight my way across a hostile environment." She paused, jolting against her harness as Ezren adjusted the magnetic balance that kept them from bouncing off the surface. "But you, on the other hand..."

Ezren snorted, swerving to avoid a small avalanche while she cut her way up the spiral rock ridge as fast as she dared. "Have you cracked? I'd rather die than squirm under a million hovercams." Her skin prickled at the thought of it. "Besides, don't they have some ridiculous academic standards or something? You know my test scores are borderline at best."

"Oh, please, details. You'd be a perfect match. You're a born Obronian with the experience of a Belethean and a frankly unnatural love of exercise."

Ezren stuck out her tongue and blew a raspberry.

"And besides the obvious fame and fortune and my undying love, you'd get the chance to win the terranium prize for Belethea. Think of all the research you could do." Micah tapped on her storm tracker, a 3D holopro popping up from her forearm. "We have 185.3 seconds to release the microalgae into the atmosphere to maximize its chance of survival and spread the instrumentation as far as possible." She unbuckled the trays from the space at her feet, stacking them into a release box on her lap.

For a moment, Ezren's mind stuck on the thought of the terranium—the precious compound's unfathomable energy output powered everything from atmospheric regulators, to space stations, to intergalaxy cargo ships. It was the real reason every planet and station in the system sent their royalers into the BRR death trap.

A person-sized rock crashed against the broadside of the storm truck, sending them spinning and bringing Ezren back to reality. She fought against the pull of the collision, her mind racing as she reacted to the AI output to straighten the truck and continue the climb. "Don't try to sweet-talk me. Belethea's team is the worst." She slammed on the brakes and unbuckled, pointing to the narrow peak clawing the sky like a crooked finger. The wind screamed around the cab, the funnel clouds twisting dangerously toward the ground. If they touched down this close to them, even the armored storm truck would be tossed around like a pebble in the churn belt. "Give me the goods. I'll run them up."

"They're primed and ready to go, so all you have to do is pop the lid off." Micah shoved the box into her hands. "You have 58.2 seconds."

"Challenge accepted." Ezren flashed a grin at her and shoved out into the storm. Small chunks of ice pattered down from the violent sky while lightning and thunder held a lively argument in the illuminated heavens. Ezren snatched the tow hook from the front of the truck and clipped it to her pack's harness before scrambling up the spire.

In Belethea's low gravity, she dug her feet into the ground, dodging the largest of the projectiles and bracing as another knocked against her head, the outer shell of her helmet breaking off with a crack. *Mother suns.* That was the last fully intact helmet they had. Head ringing, she hugged the hard surface, one hand clawing into clumps of belweed as she climbed.

"I'm here," she called into the comms. The storm swirled furiously around her, tearing at the box in her hands.

"Are you sure you can't get any higher?" Micah asked.

Ezren ducked another rock that looked sharp enough to impale her. "I can if you're ready to pull me in."

"I'm ready."

Ezren double-checked her projectile radar, turned off her boots' magnetic lock, and then jumped off the cliff, spreading her arms and legs wide. Even with her heavy suit, the wind lifted her body like a kite, swirling her up with the rest of its debris. Her stomach wrenched as the tether yanked at her chest, fully extended from its storm truck anchor. In one smooth motion, she yanked the lid off the box, and the green and gray capsules whipped away like dandelion seeds.

"Deployed," Ezren said, her thoughts dashing away on the wind. A smile spread across her face as she looked out over the mottled purple-and-green curve of Belethea below, and she let out a triumphant whoop. Her body twisted among the frenzied clouds, and her racing heart soared, a wild laugh shaking her heaving chest.

Then, her harness tightened as the storm truck reeled her in. Another few moments and she was back in the driver's seat, adrenaline tingling across her sweat-dampened skin as they raced away from the storm.

Micah only shook her head. "It really is a chaffing shame."

Ezren couldn't dim her smile even for a moment; the rush was too fresh, her mind still fuzzy with the thrill. "What is?"

"Belethea has never won the race royale, but they've never had you."

Ezren shrugged. The race was a publicity event, a sham, entertainment for the masses. She cringed at the thought of her face plastered all over Virtual Society with comments and jokes and ridiculous holos. Out here, with the dirt under her feet, she could ignore all of that. This was the real work, the real Belethea.

And they would have to take her away kicking and screaming.

"You're going to be late again!" Sam shouted, his voice cracking, while Waffle, their short-legged capybog, trilled her disapproval.

Ezren raised her heavy head, blinking her bleary eyes in the harsh electric light of her room. Her vision focused on Waffle first; the genetically engineered mix of a dog's half-flopped ears and a capybara's resting bored-face stared back at her. Groaning, she pawed the bedside table for her goggs on their charging rig. What day was it, again? She wrinkled her nose, and then the realization hit her like a Belethean tornado. All three of her alarms were going off. That meant...

She leapt out of bed with a swear. "Asdef! Professor Holland is going to kill me."

Sam sighed, his bright blue gaze hooded. "That's what I was trying to tell you."

The tiny round hummingbot chirped on his shoulder. "Well, it's understandable. She didn't get in until three hours ago."

"Again?" Sam tsked with an unsympathetic smirk. "Mom's going to fritz."

"Wow, thanks for selling me out, Giles."

Ezren grabbed a long, chunky sweater off the clothes-strewn floor and threw it on over the tank top and tights she'd slept in. Then she snagged her pack and her goggs from her desk, littered with about a dozen other electronic trinkets, cups, and exercise bands. She dashed in and out of the tiny, shared bathroom, pausing only briefly to knot her mousy hair atop her head. Oh well, at least she didn't get a grade for personal appearance. She lunged into their living room and dashed to the cramped kitchen, turning on the sink to fill the water bladder from her pack, willing it to flow faster.

"So how many tardies does it take before Holland kicks you

out?" Sam asked as he trailed after her, a slight limp in his step and Waffle at his heels, nubby tail wagging.

"Sam, shouldn't you be leaving for class already?" Ezren stuffed the bladder into her bag and grabbed a nutri-pack. "And did you take your meds this morning? Pain, cell regen, bone regrow, organ stimulant—"

"Of course. I'm not the irresponsible one here. In fact..." He projected the station time from the shiny green goggs on his forehead. "I still have five minutes before I have to leave."

Ezren frowned. That may have been a fact, but she knew the real reason Sam hadn't left was that he didn't want to walk alone. Even though, at twelve, he was more than capable of navigating the perfectly safe pedestrian corridors to get to his class.

"And all of *my* homework is already turned in."

Ezren gasped, standing frozen in her whirlwind. "Mother suns."

"What?" Sam tensed, his eyes wide. "What is it? Are you okay?"

"No, no, no!" Ezren lurched back into motion, barreling toward the door. "I totally forgot about the stupid history essay."

Clutching his chest, Sam puffed out a relieved breath through his cheeks. "Oh. Well, that's normal. Could you save the dramatic gasps for actual emergencies?"

Ezren stomped her feet into her battered mag-trainers. "Sam! Let's go!"

The door hissed open, and Ezren tried to will herself to be calm. She could do this. Being twenty minutes late wasn't the end of the world, but this essay was worth fifteen percent of her grade. She'd have to finish it on the way.

She mentally brought up the file and skimmed through what she already had. Honestly, she only needed a two-hundred-ish word conclusion on the origins of the Casolla system. *Okay, no problem.* She could do this. She pulled up her mental dictation program from the neurochip in her goggs.

Ugh. Something about the original earthen discovery of the wormgate tech, which brought the first hotshot astro-pioneers to our beloved Casolla, a gas giant with twenty-two moons in the perfect Goldilocks zone around star CCVII-Zao.

Sam greeted a passing researcher whom Ezren hadn't even noticed. "Ez, Tom just said hi. Have you gone into zombie mode or what?"

They wound through the underground corridors, a colorful holopro of a tropical forest lining the walls today while the clicks of Waffle's webbed toes echoed on the metal floor. A few families and researchers passed them, but as a rule, Tuzuno wasn't a very crowded outpost. One of the many things Ezren loved about it.

"Shh, I have to finish this essay."

"You're trying to think it out through your goggs?" Sam barked out a laugh. "Seriously, Ez, that's a new low even for you."

"Oh, hush, I'm almost done. Just make sure I don't run into anyone."

A seventy-one-year journey in cryosleep ended in years of station living while they tweaked the atmospheres of nearly perfect moons, Dreitis and Obrone, to exact earthen levels. Slap a few biodiversity domes on them to preserve the native microbial life, import their favorite flowers and beasties from back home, and the settlers flocked for the fresh dirt.

But they couldn't fix everything. Though Obrone was almost Earth-sized, oceans covered 95% of its surface. And while floating and underwater domes had been invented back on Earth, they cost a hefty chunk of creds to build and maintain.

The floor inclined to surface level, and Sam and Ezren

walked into the dome—the thriving greenhouse center of Tuzuno. Layers upon layers of greenery stretched out on clear racks above them, and a bright blue sky holopro coated the dome's rounded metal ceiling. It was pleasant, but Ezren still preferred when the weather was calm enough to unshutter the dome and reveal Belethea's own unique beauty. Those days were far and few in between, though.

Meanwhile, Dreitis had the opposite problem. Nearly one-fifth Earth's size, and with about 10% of its water supply, it topped its max population cap in no time. Which is what continues to drive terraforming tech today, specifically on Belethea, with its hostile and unpredictable weather patterns, and Crion, with its weak atmosphere and icy surface.

"Okay, well, good luck with Holland, Ez. I have a feeling you're going to need it." Sam gave her a little salute at the door to his class.

"Thanks for the vote of confidence, Samster. Have a good day, and I'll pick you up after physical therapy." She absently ruffled his dirty blond hair.

"Don't forget, he got bumped twenty minutes earlier today," Giles chirped from his shoulder.

"I won't forget!" Ezren was already turning toward her corridor, desperately searching for her last sentences.

So the wormgate travelers keep coming. Some convert their arks into stations and fall into orbit with the rest of us, while some pass through on their way to other habitable systems. The never-ending stream of travelers gives Casolla its diversity, while its unified dedication to discovery keeps its political mess at peaceable levels.

Done. She blew out a hoarse sigh of relief, skimming it over once more. It wasn't great, but it would pass... Probably. She was turning into her class's corridor when she bumped straight into a short, bearded man with square goggles wrapped around the bowler perched atop his bald head. With an indignant huff, he straightened the vibrant red cravat tucked into his matching paisley vest.

Ezren scooted back, her vision focusing and cheeks burning. "Oh my, Professor Holland, I'm so sorry."

Holland let out a slow breath, his lips pinched with exasperation. "Ms. Hart. You're late." He ostentatiously projected his empty inbox holo into the air between them. "And I didn't see your assignment in my messages this morning."

Ezren let her eyes go wide and her jaw drop. "You didn't? What? Are you sure? I could've sworn I sent it." She let her goggs flash her class folder screen in front of her. "Oh no! Look, it's still right here in my outbox." She mentally flicked it toward him and cringed with an apologetic grimace. "So sorry about that, Professor Holland."

Holland's squinty gaze narrowed even further. "Ms. Hart, may I remind you that I only require you to be physically present two days of the week. We're only five weeks into the semester, and this is your fourth tardy."

Ezren ducked her head with a wince, hoping she looked properly contrite. "I apologize, Professor Holland. I promise I'll try to do better."

"Furthermore, while your test scores are technically passing, I'm disappointed by your negligent dedication to your studies, which honestly surprises me considering your mother's reputation. Do you aspire to further education upon your graduation?"

Ezren shrank just a little more at all the "ations" he volleyed at her like little spitballs of disappointment. "Well, I did apply to Belethea Cyber University, so I could attend from here, and maybe have a chance at a scholarship." Then, they could put the money saved toward Sam's regenerative surgery fund. With enough money and a proper doctor this time, they could re-code Sam's corrupt regen cells, adding decades to Sam's prognosis and—

Holland snorted.

Right. First she had to deal with Holland. Swallowing, Ezren continued, "I've also been getting lots of hours in the lab, so I was hoping the experience—"

"I'm sure you'd eventually like to do something a little more challenging than data processing. Get your priorities in order, Ms. Hart, or even Belethea Cyber won't take you. For when they call me for a recommendation, I can assure you, I will be *perfectly* honest."

Ezren bobbed her head in a fervent series of apologetic bows. "Yes, sir, of course, your honesty is all that I could ask. I will endeavor to regain your esteemed respect in the future."

"All right, all right, enough of the simpering." Professor Holland straightened his vest over his round belly and nodded, his mustache twitching. "You still have ten minutes left to take the pop quiz that your punctual classmates have been working on for the last thirty."

Shoulders caving, Ezren felt the blood drain from her cheeks. "Yes, sir." Surely after this, the day could only look up.

CHAPTER 2

A SIGH OOZED out of Foster as he wondered for the fiftieth time why he was wasting his time here.

He ran another scan on the topsuit, his brow furrowing as he read through the notes. The armory reeked of oil and metal, the walls covered in suit gear—spare goggles, helmets, grav-boots, strips of nanitelattice—all of it battered and broken. He pinched the bridge of his nose. The team had been on break for two months, and the list of repairs was still longer than one of Sylvia's promotional VSoc rants.

The race royale models just weren't meant to last longer than two seasons; extended topside exposure was too hard on them. He could get them working, but they were still less efficient than the new designs. And of course, with the Belethea team's track record, they didn't have the budget for new suits every year, even though they hosted a training team of twelve. Which was still the smallest national team in the system.

His hand spasmed as he finished his sweep of the code, and he kneaded the twitching muscles absently. On the third read, the code was fine, so that meant it was probably a wiring issue somewhere. Not his specialty.

He sent a quick message to Bex.

FOSTER: HEY, I GOT ANOTHER SUIT WITH A WIRING SNAG. THINK YOU CAN TAKE A LOOK?

Bex's terse response came almost instantaneously.

BEX: SEND THE SCAN.

FOSTER: THANKS.

BEX: YOU COMING TO THIS TEAM MEETING?

Foster paused, twisting a scrap of broken wire between his fingers.

FOSTER: I HAVEN'T DECIDED YET.

BEX: IT'S IN NINE MINUTES.

He stared at the dark ceiling, jagged with exposed pipes, and snapped the wire in two with an impatient huff.

FOSTER: WELL, THEN I GUESS NOT.

It was their first team meeting of the season, but he couldn't imagine anything they could say that they couldn't send him in a neurochip message.

Bex didn't respond.

Foster projected his to-do list in the dusky lighting, his gaze moving to the next item. *Read through Vieve's suit logs.* His attention shifted to the rusted pile of parts peeking out from the dust cloth in the corner. Rubbing the back of his neck, he quickly swiped the words away and pulled up the next task. He blew out another slow breath and grabbed a scratched helmet from a hook on the wall.

BEX: SO ARE YOU OUT FOR THE SEASON, OR WHAT?

Foster bumped his forehead against the helmet and closed his eyes. That was right. He'd said that. That this was the last time. He was finally fed up—was going to cut loose and forge his own path. He'd said it many times actually. But... that had been before Vieve's accident. With her gone, Coach Bhatt retired to a different system, and his mother finally off his back, he'd effectively been cut loose. Free. But also directionless.

With nothing to anchor him here, it should've been the perfect time to step away.

And yet, without those forces of motion in his life pushing and pulling him in different directions, he seemed to have lost any kind of momentum, instead freezing in place exactly where they'd left him.

He looked at the message again, tempted to ignore it. But Bex was the only royaler still actually speaking to him.

FOSTER: EH. I DON'T KNOW.

He sat with the helmet in his lap for a few more moments, his mind blank. He'd just picked up the wrench when the door to the armory burst open. Sylvia stood there, her umber curls in a lion-like mane around her head while her rainbow-dyed eyebrows popped in stark contrast against her golden-brown skin. "Hello?! Mandatory team meeting in five minutes?!"

Foster held up the helmet, prepared to use it as a shield if need be. *Bex, you traitor, you didn't have to sic Sylvia on me.* "But is it really mandatory if no one takes attendance?"

She rolled her eyes and shifted the monstrous teal purse on her shoulder. Though at twenty-five, she was only six years older than him, her lifted chin and unblinking glare sparked with the natural authority of someone used to being obeyed. "There's only nine of you. Who needs to take attendance? You're coming even if I have to drag you down there myself."

She reached out to grab him, and he quickly stood from his stool, holding his hands up in surrender. "All right, all right. I'm coming. Calm your fritz, Syl." He put the helmet and his tools back where they belonged before shutting down his server stack. "What's the deal, anyway? Can't I just catch the highlights later like I usually do?"

"No, the Calderon operations exec is here, and I think Warner Calderon himself is even popping in with a message. He asked for every one of you to be there in person." Sylvia's gaze rolled over his grease-stained jeans and dingy tee. She fished a black and teal team shirt out of the depths of her purse and threw it at him, followed by his worn bomber jacket from the door hook. "I think he's introducing the new coach today."

Foster grimaced. Did everything on this chaffing team have to be fodding teal? He pulled the shirt over his head and shrugged on his jacket. "Ah. Do you know who it is?"

"I guess we'll find out," Sylvia said, not looking at him.

Foster raised a brow at that. As the team's social manager, there wasn't much that got by Sylvia. Even if she didn't know, he'd make a heavy wager she had a good guess. But why wouldn't she tell him?

They walked down the corridor, past the training rooms, and down the stairs to the lounge on the first floor. Holo-projectors, bean bag chairs, and overstuffed sofas littered the space. A full kitchen took up one side, and a skimpy offering of cheap plastic-wrapped snacks dotted its counters. The rest of the team was already there, clumped in pairs or small knots across the room. The aching familiarity of their presence almost made Foster turn around, but Sylvia blocked his exit with a firm look.

He knew all eight of their faces, their names, their stories— had spent the last year training with them for twelve hours a day. But only two of them caught his notice. Simon Grady—his contemptuous dark eyes passing over Foster from under his meticulously styled curls—and the hulking mass of muscle that was Lucian Talmadge.

Talmadge pointedly ignored Foster's presence, laughing too loudly with his friends at the holopro game in the corner. Foster honestly couldn't believe that sack of pus had the stones to come back after what happened. But even as he thought it, he knew Grady was probably thinking the same thing about Foster.

And deep down, he knew the three of them were really

only seeing the gaping person-sized hole that would never be filled again.

"Ah, good, I do believe that's all of you."

Foster looked over to where a live holopro of Warner Calderon, founder and organizer of the Belethea Race Royale, CEO of Calderon Industries, and the owner of the Belethea national team stood in front of the room in a spotless navy three-piece. At 102 years old, he almost certainly never went topside anymore, but his old-fashioned brass goggs still nestled in his thick silver hair like any true Belethean.

"I'm afraid I don't have much time." His voice was well-oiled and smooth, as if he had rehearsed the words many times, practicing the correct emotions in the mirror. "But I wanted to be here to once again express my condolences over the loss of Genevieve Navarro and my thanks for your passion and dedication to this beautiful and important challenge. Also, although he's indisputably earned his retirement, I know we'd never truly be able to replace your esteemed coach, Neel Bhatt."

An uneasy shuffle rippled around the room. While Coach Bhatt had been old enough to retire, there was a strong rumor that Calderon had forced him to resign after Vieve's accident. Not that he'd ever admit that, of course—couldn't risk bad optics over something as trivial as the truth, after all.

"Unfortunately, with the budget cuts and withdrawal of key sponsors, I'm afraid we were unsuccessful in finding a seasoned applicant."

The unease burgeoned into mutters of concern, the tension in the room weighing down the air. Foster glanced at Sylvia, but she hadn't even flinched. Whatever was coming, she'd expected it.

Calderon held up an appeasing hand, a smile stretching between his ruddy cheeks. "Not to fear. Luckily, your social manager, Sylvia Long, has agreed to take on the challenge."

All eyes turned to Sylvia, and she met them with a tight smile. Foster pressed his lips together to keep from gawking. Sylvia was a fantastic social manager, and she'd even been on the team during her age window... but she'd been a bottom-of-the-barrel royaler. Usually, the coaches transitioned to the race royale after decades of experience in a sister sport of martial arts, auto racing, or any other endurance challenge. Sylvia had nothing. Was this guy serious?

But Calderon had continued on without pause. "After her past three years working under Coach Bhatt, I know she's more than prepared for this role. But my operations executive, Gustavo Harland, will also be assisting her in team administration."

A short man in a stiff gray suit gave a tense bow from beside Calderon's holopro. His slicked-back hair gleamed in the glow of the ceiling's recessed lights, and his black goggs hung from his neck. "It's nice to meet you all. I look forward to working together."

Calderon nodded approvingly and turned back to the room. "I'm afraid that's all I have time for, but I leave you in good hands, and I can't wait to see you uphold Belethea's oldest and most glorious tradition." He knocked his knobby fists together three times in the race royale's signal. "Into the churn!"

"Into the churn," the room echoed dutifully.

With that, the system's third-richest man disappeared in a blink.

Harland immediately stepped into the now empty space in front of the room, raising a placating hand to quell the bubbling disquiet threatening to evolve into an uproar.

"Quiet, quiet now." Harland folded his hands behind his back, his posture straight and uncompromising. "I understand this will take some time to process, but we're on a tight schedule, and we have a few topics to cover. Although Coach Bhatt leaves big shoes to fill, Coach Long and I are highly motivated to get this team in shape and earn back the respect of the Casolla system."

Foster stifled a snort. The flat words fell across the room like a lukewarm bucket of water. If that was his attempt at motivation, the guy had some work to do. Foster tried to make eye contact with Sylvia to see if this guy was serious, but her neutral gaze remained fixed on Harland.

"I know it's been a policy in the past to keep all eligible prior athletes and recruit to fill the open slots. But this year, we've taken a 60% funding cut, and our popularity is down by..." He glanced at Sylvia.

"Seventy-two percent," she said.

Harland nodded grimly. "So we have to make some changes."

Wow. He'd known they'd take a hit after the BRR committee shut down the Belethean team for the investigation, but those numbers were catastrophic. Foster understood better than anyone that while royale teams played at being symbols of nationalistic pride, they were a business at heart. And if Belethea's team wasn't turning a profit, they would be shut down—confirming Belethea as the pathetic joke the system already thought they were.

The other royalers traded dark glances, and Harland projected a holo into the room with a twist of his hand. The words *Belethea Race Royale Open Tryout* circled him in fat, teal letters. "As you all know, we're holding open tryouts in three days." He crossed his arms. "But this time, we only have four slots, and all prospective royalers, prior athlete or not, are expected to qualify."

For a beat, the room was dead silent, and Foster had to stifle a laugh at the absurdity of it. He was glad he came to this meeting after all. If nothing else, at least it was turning out to be interesting.

Talmadge spoke up first. He straightened to his full height, an imposing 6′4″ with a two-toned black-and-teal buzz cut. "Is this a joke?"

"No joke," Harland said. "In the past, Belethea has recruited athletes through a system of networking. We don't want athletes who are here because of who they know. We want Belethea's best, regardless of their resources or connections. Everyone earns their keep here, and everyone is going to work hard."

Oh, chaff. The indignation spreading through the room was too much. The laugh was bubbling up now, threatening to burst out of him. This was too good. Because, although Harland's delivery was absolutely terrible, he was right. Nepotism in the race royale community was notorious, and all nine royalers here had benefited in some way from that. Especially Foster.

Grady stretched his wiry body across the couch, his face a mask of nonchalance as he twirled one of his dangling earrings. "So you're saying we didn't earn our slots?"

Harland shrugged, apparently unaffected by the glares stabbing at him from every direction. "If you did earn your place, then you should have no problem proving it in open competition. The tryout will test athleticism, driving, and martial ability over the course of two hours. So with your experience, each of you will have a distinct advantage."

"It's a fair way to decide who gets the four spots," Sylvia cut in, moving to stand beside Harland. "And the open tryout has already increased our VSoc credit by 3%."

Foster regarded her carefully, trying to determine if she really backed this idea, and if so, why she was letting Harland run the show. Hadn't Calderon said she was the coach?

Cutting slots was a tough break, but the tryout itself wasn't a bad idea. He couldn't help but feel this would've gone over a lot better coming from her.

Still, the team met her words with a rebellious silence, although apparently no one had the stones to mutiny outright.

"I like it." Bex Gunderson stood from where she'd been crouched in the corner. Her one visible cold blue eye swept across the room while her white pixie cut obscured the other. "Will it be a solo race or doubles?"

The silence thickened. Partners were a requirement in the BRR, for reasons of tradition, safety, and publicity. But doubles partners weren't set in stone and often changed throughout the year based on growing abilities and relationships. Honestly, it was the lifeblood of the hologgers and the hardcore fanbase. But... they had an odd number this year.

"Doubles," Sylvia replied, taking a step forward. "In this race, you have to be able to work nicely with others. You can pick your partner, or if you want a promising rookie instead, we've got ninety-one solid recruits coming in. Some of them are pretty impressive and could give you a big VSoc bump."

A series of glances fired around the room as everyone mentally paired up. Foster could've guessed at least two of them. But he was still surprised to see Bex's silent message flash in his goggs.

Bex: You in?

Her blue one-eyed stare pinned him from across the room.

Sylvia squared her broad shoulders. "The tryout is in three days. Until then, the facilities are yours, but we won't have any official practices." She paused, looking from face to face. And maybe Foster imagined it, but he could've sworn she lingered on his. "And if you slack off, don't come crying to me when some rando embarrasses you."

Well, thanks so much for that, Syl. He had to laugh though.

At least she was being straight with them, and... she was also presenting him an easy out. All he had to do was walk away.

But was that what he really wanted?

This year would be different than the last one—than the last ten. For better or for worse... and most likely for worse.

So did he want to be a part of it?

In the end, it was Talmadge's mocking sneer that decided it for him. He wasn't sure what Sylvia's plan was, but if Talmadge made the team, he would make her year a living nightmare. Sylvia might annoy Foster from time to time, but she was like a sister to him, and he'd be chaffed if he let Talmadge walk all over her.

Bex crossed the room, a silent glacier amid the churn of agitated conversation. She leaned her tall boxer's frame against the wall. "Well?"

Foster folded his arms. Although he'd only doubled with her a few times last year, Bex was, without a doubt, the strongest choice here. She was smooth and capable... if a bit on the blunt side.

He shrugged, breaking away from her stare. "Sure. It's not like I have anything else to do."

CHAPTER 3

EZREN DRAGGED herself to the lab, sucking down a liter of caffeine-infused juice through the tube extending from her hydropack and feeling mildly triumphant. In the end, Holland had accepted the paper without a late penalty, and she'd passed the math quiz even with the limited time. Not by a lot... but still. And while she could've imagined it, she thought she'd seen a smirk of begrudging respect behind Holland's bushy beard. It was a well-timed victory, if only a small one, because the first round of application cuts was due soon, and she'd need at least a passing assessment by Holland to get to the second round. She did what she needed to do in order to get by, but the competition got steeper every year.

The lab's scanner glanced over Ezren's body with its green light before chiming its approval. "Welcome, Intern Ezren Hart."

"Thank you, nameless scanning machine."

The glass door hissed open, and she walked into the wide-open room of the lab. She breathed in the familiar, sharp scent of cleaning chemicals tinged with the smoky trace of burning gas. Her mag-trainers clacked on the cement floor as she weaved between the metal desks littered with computers, small machines, and endless drawers of tools. She nodded and smiled at the other researchers on her way to the assistant director's desk—her mother's desk.

Her mom's 3D blue-tinted holopro circled her as she flicked through tables of data, trying to decipher Belethea's baffling atmospheric patterns. Her oversized goggs dangled around her neck, and her long white coat hung to her knees on her short stature. The same diminutive stature she'd given to her daughter, but more graceful than Ezren's square frame. She tugged on the edges of her short brown bob, her intelligent cobalt eyes reflecting the storms she studied. The same eyes Sam had, just edged with lines drawn from years of laughter... and maybe a few of grief.

Ezren wrapped her arms around her mom's waist and laid her chin on her narrow shoulder, her strawberry-scented hair tickling her nose.

"Why, hey there, girlie," her mother said with a soft chuckle. "How was your day?"

Ezren gave the smallest of shrugs. "So far so good."

"Oh?" Her mother turned to raise an eyebrow at her. "And how was your late-night instrumentation with Micah?"

Ezren gave her a sheepish smile. "Great, actually. I'm looking forward to digging through the data."

Her mother shook her head, half-smiling as she turned back to her display. "I don't know what I'm going to do with you, Ezzy. You should really be getting sleep and focusing on your schoolwork."

"Oh, c'mon, Mom," Ezren said, stepping away. "You know this is so much more important. Most people focus on their studies so they can come to places like this to work, and I'm already here. How could I pass up this opportunity?" Not to mention, the extra pay helped to cover Sam's therapy and meds. Although the relief they gave him was temporary, even the low-end treatments were worth every spare cred they could scrape together.

Her mother pursed her lips. "Such a lab rat."

Ezren grinned, not missing the touch of pride in her voice. "What do you want to do for dinner tonight?"

"Oh, I'm sorry, love. We've got a holopro-conference with the Station C9 team, so I won't be home until late again." She frowned apologetically. "Think you can manage without me?"

"You doubt this mac and cheese master?" Ezren flashed a double thumbs-up as she walked away. "Don't work too hard, Mom, you should really be getting sleep and focusing on my schoolwork."

"Yeah, yeah." Her mother waved her off with a broad smile. "Get out of here, you cheeseball."

For a moment, Ezren took in the expanse of wall that projected the immediate Belethea landscape. The teal sky swirled with navy clouds, a fine drizzle of hail pelting the poor weeds that so valiantly clung to the rocky soil. The weeds *their* research had successfully planted.

With a wistful smile, Ezren crossed the lab to the workbench she shared with Micah. Approaching from behind, she crouched low, rounded the table, and then popped up in front of her. "Boo!"

Micah didn't so much as flinch, but her eyes—bubblegum pink today—went wide. "Thank the suns, I've been sending you messages all day!"

"I was in class!"

"So what! This is *huge*." Micah bounced up and down on her toes, practically vibrating with excitement.

Ezren squealed softly, leaning closer to Micah's projected graphs. "Is it about the data? Are the birds still reporting? I knew that software mod would—"

"No," Micah snorted. "The birds went dead at T+136.5 minutes."

"Oh." Ezren drooped. "Well, at least that's a minute and a half better than last time."

"Forget that, Ez, this is *life-changing*." Micah swiped away the display and enlarged the message she had tucked in the corner of her holopro. "Do you remember how I told you about Belethea's open tryouts?"

"Um..." Ezren tried to focus on the wall of text. "Yeah..."

"Well, I sent in your application."

Ezren ran a hand over her face and let her eyes roll back in her head. "Oh, c'mon, Micah, how many times do I have to tell you I—"

"And you *got in*." Micah pointed to the glowing blue words: *Congratulations on this opportunity of a lifetime.*

Ezren paused, her brow furrowing. "But... how? I thought you said they're super strict about grades and recommendations." She scrolled through the message and found her holopro near the bottom... except it wasn't really her. Her mousy shoulder-length hair was blown into luxurious waves, her pale complexion had been smoothed, and her small dark eyes shone with some kind of bright make-up—like a bizarro Ezren. "And where did this picture come from?"

"Oh, don't worry about that, everyone tunes up their resumé holo."

Ezren's frown deepened as she skimmed the words.

As an athlete ambassador for Belethea, we expect our recruits to excel in both their physical and scholastic pursuits. Your record as a superb student and your impressive exercise hololog...

"You got my exercise log too? Wait... is that my application at the bottom? Micah!" Ezren covered her open mouth with her hand. "I'm not number one in my class, and those aren't my test scores. Where did you get those records?"

"So I might have combined our applications into one... but so what? Anyone can do that ambassador chaff. Everyone knows it's really all about the BRR." Micah grabbed her by the shoulders. "But you're missing the point, Ez. Out of thousands of entrants, they chose ninety-one people for the tryouts. And you're one of them. Fame. Fortune. We're talking about the *system's* favorite sport, Belethea's number one claim to fame— the Belethea Race Royale!"

Ezren's stomach churned, the sugared caffeine in her belly going sour with nerves. "There's no way, Micah. I can't do that. I don't know anything about the royale stuff, and these people are like celebrities." The thought of all those stares and hover-cams made her heart sputter. That was a world away from the quiet solitude of her daily runs.

Micah's unnatural pink eyes practically popped out of her head. "Ez, you *can't* pass this up. Come *on*."

Ezren took a long drag from her hydropack and shook her head, the nerves bubbling into goose bumps under her sweater. She didn't know a whole lot about the royale, but she knew there was a reason that stuff was on the application. These people were expecting a beautiful scholar that she was definitely not. "No way. I really can't. I'm sorry, but that's not me, Micah. Maybe you can take my slot somehow."

A message popped up in Ezren's goggs.

Lutz: Ezren, could you come see me in my office? Thank the suns.

"Look, the race isn't for another three days, maybe you could—" Micah started.

"Sorry, Lutz is calling me," Ezren said, backing away.

Micah planted an elbow on the table and dropped her chin into it with an exaggerated pout. "You're no fun."

"That's what I've been trying to tell you." Ezren offered a weak shrug before crossing the lab to the closet that Director Lutz had managed to turn into a tiny office.

So what if she made the tryout? That didn't mean anything. Especially since Micah had blatantly lied on the application. Ezren took a deep breath to shake off Micah's ridiculous news before peeking in through Lutz's open door.

Inside, Lutz hunched over his display, caged in by the wires and hardware crawling from wall to wall. His gray hair spiraled up in chaotic tufts, and his wrinkled hands sifted through the holopro in front of him. Though he wore a vest and tie, stains marred his white lab coat, and a web of wrinkles crisscrossed his too-short pants. Ezren had to smile at the sight of him.

When her father had gone missing on Gobrion Station, and her family had struggled to pay their debts, it had been Lutz's idea to bring Ezren on part-time. It had opened her world and eased her mother's sleepless nights. He'd taught her so much in the last three years—six different types of modeling software as well as gobs of field tasks—and he was part of the reason she never wanted to leave this place. She would complete her university degrees online while continuing to work here, and then by the time she graduated she would have eleven years of planetary engineering experience—a shoo-in for a terraforming researcher slot. And it was all thanks to Lutz.

She knocked on the metal door. "Dr. Lutz? You wanted to see me?"

His brown eyes focused on her beneath his wild gray eyebrows and, strangely, his face fell. "Ah, yes, Ezren, please come in, and close the door behind you."

There was really nowhere else to go, so Ezren just closed the door and leaned her back against it. An odd buzzing started to vibrate in her stomach. Probably leftover from the royale business. Or maybe she'd hit the caffeine too hard that morning.

Lutz collapsed into his battered chair. He ran his hands over his face before frowning at her, expression soft. "I'm so sorry, my girl. I really don't know how to say this."

Ezren's brow furrowed. Oh, suns. What had happened? Was he sick? Was he leaving? Were they reassigning her mother? "What's wrong, Dr. Lutz?"

"Our budgets have been cut, and I'm afraid I'm..." His shaking hands fluttered from his hair to his vest, as if he wasn't sure where to put them. He swallowed before taking another deep breath. "We've lost your internship slot."

Oh. Ezren slumped, sitting quietly for a moment as she tried to process this news. Losing the pay from the internship was definitely a hit, but maybe she could get shuttle work or a janitorial job or something to cover it. The lost experience was a tougher break, but they would probably still let her volunteer.

Taking a breath, she sat up a little. Yes, it hurt, but the situation was still salvageable. It definitely wasn't good, but it could've been worse. And it only made sense, really. Their budget had been dropping for over a year now. She should've seen this coming. "I understand, sir. But I'd still like to do the work voluntarily. Casolla knows we're already so badly understaffed."

She flashed a smile at him, hoping to cheer him up. He didn't need to worry about her. They'd probably have to dip into the savings they'd put aside for Sammy's regen procedure for a little while, but she'd figure something out.

He shook his head. "I'm afraid it's even worse than that, my girl."

Ezren's stomach dropped another octave, banging against her full bladder. Definitely needed to cut back on the caffeine. "What do you mean?"

"They're pulling the plug on the funding for the whole Belethea terraforming project. The lab has maybe another year before we're completely shut down."

"But they can't do that!" Ezren's voice pitched up into a squeak. "We've made so much progress, and Dreitis and Obrone are literally overflowing with people. We're so close to perfecting the storm prediction algorithm before we can start the climate pacification research. We just need more time." Ezren attempted to pace in the cramped room, but there was nowhere to go.

Lutz held up a hand as if to calm her. "I know. I know. Making more space stations is just the more profitable solution right now."

"People weren't meant to live on stations. We need the ground under our feet." Ezren hated how her voice shook.

"Oh, my girl." Lutz stood and rested his hands on her shoulders. "If only they could see your passion." He chuckled even as his eyes glistened. "You might just be the one person who loves Belethea as much as I do. Perhaps your university research will be able to change things one day."

Ezren tried not to crumple as she thought of her pathetic university applications and her plans that had all been snuffed out in the last meager five minutes. What would her mother do when the lab shut down? Would they go back to Obrone? No, they couldn't do that to Sam. Maybe a station, then? Her heart wrenched at the thought of being trapped in a crowded metal box.

Lutz sank into his chair in a heap, his attention wandering back to his holopro. "Until then, I'm afraid we've done the best we could."

Ezren blinked away tears, thinking of the long hours Lutz and her mom and the others had put in. Thinking of all the work she'd poured into it herself—into the dream of creating another habitable world. Opening another planet to explore. And now, it was all for nothing. Because it wasn't *profitable* enough.

But she shouldn't have been surprised, really. Because in the end, it didn't matter how hard you worked. Sometimes your best just wasn't good enough.

CHAPTER 4

EZREN'S MAG-TRAINERS pounded into the metal of the underground corridor on her familiar loop. She blasted music through the neurochip in her goggs, trying to pull out of the horrifying tailspin Lutz's news had sent her into. Their extra income had vanished, the lab was closing, and the terraforming project was writhing in its death throes. While she'd certainly had worse days, this one was making an easy case for the top three.

Did her mom know? She had to, right? But she'd seemed so happy when Ezren had seen her that afternoon. Did she have a plan? Maybe she knew a loophole or a way to save the lab. Surely, there had to be a way. Something so important couldn't be wiped out so easily. Could it?

A message appeared on her goggs from Micah.

MICAH: I HEARD ABOUT YOUR INTERNSHIP. I'M SO SORRY, EZREN, BUT YOU HAVE TO LISTEN TO ME. THIS IS A SIGN. CASOLLA IS TELLING YOU TO GO TO THE TRYOUTS. EVEN IF THE BELETHEA TEAM IS CHAFF, ONCE YOU SHOW EVERYONE WHAT YOU CAN DO, YOU COULD TRANSFER TO OBRONE'S TEAM. AND THEY HAVE THE MOST BRR WINS IN THE SYSTEM!

Ezren turned a sharp corner, debating on whether to respond.

There was no way she'd make the team. And even if she did, the royale was a brutal race, and there were always a few fatalities every year. If Belethea's elements didn't get you, then the other royalers certainly would. *Suns.* She'd even heard that a Belethea royaler had died a few months ago in the *qualifier.* Not even the real deal.

Honestly though, it wasn't even the danger that bothered her. She could handle dangerous. What she couldn't handle was the swarm of hovercams and the interviews and the complete lack of privacy. She ran faster, wisp-light without her clunky topsuit, the nervousness giving her strength as her mileage ticked up to ten.

Ezren: It's not a sign, Micah. You're the fan. You go.

Micah: I AM going, but I can't compete. I've booked us two tickets on the storm truck Saturday at 0430. I'll get you everything you need; all you have to do is say yes.

Ezren slowed to a stop. There was really only one thing she could say to end this conversation without lying.

Ezren: I'll think about it.

Her calendar chimed with a reminder: *Pick up Sam.*
Asdef.

Ezren took off running again. She'd totally forgotten she was supposed to pick up Sam early today. Why hadn't she changed the reminder time? *Stupid. So stupid.* Ugh, Sam hated when she was late.

She pushed her burning muscles as fast as she dared in the narrow corridor, whipping around the sharp corners and dodging the occasional pedestrian. The holopro had shifted into a sunlit forest around her, and if she didn't think too hard about the metal under her feet, she could almost pretend she wasn't in the underground warren of Tuzuno.

Finally, she emerged into the brighter, open dome. Her gaze searched for Sam amid the neat, manicured park that sprawled across the center of the galleria. His usual bench next to the physical therapy office sat empty, so he must've started home without her. Which... could've been a good thing. She scanned the dome until she spotted his blue backpack cutting through the park's center, and Waffle happily snuffling at his heels. She even thought she could see him smiling as he chatted gamely with Giles on his shoulder.

She sagged with a huff, bracing her hands on her knees. After her rotten day so far, it was nice to have some good news. There'd been a time when Sam would've been anxious about going anywhere even with Ezren by his side. But today he was feeling good enough to walk home by himself, and he even looked happy about it.

For a moment, she watched him from a distance, wondering if she should let him finish the ten-minute walk home by himself. Then, she caught sight of the gangly preteen forms of Leon and Gert Vaughn lumbering along behind Sam. They hunched toward one another, giggling as they jogged to catch up to him.

Ezren tensed. *No.* How did those two trolls always manage to show up at the worst times? She started to run but knew she was too far away to catch them. She could already see the scene in her mind since she'd witnessed it so many times before. Gert would trip him, or Leon would bump Giles off his shoulder and say something obnoxious. It might seem like an innocuous joke to an unfamiliar eye, and maybe to a different kid, it would be. But something like that could make Sam withdraw for days, and those two knew it.

If they so much as touched him, she was going to tackle them and crack their heads together. It wouldn't help Sam, but it would make her feel better, and maybe it would make them think twice next time. If they ever thought at all.

Gert was reaching out now, and Ezren opened her mouth to yell at them to shaft off, knowing it would only encourage them, when someone else stepped into the path behind Sam. Ezren immediately recognized the styled sweep of his short dark hair, smooth olive skin, and crooked nose. She came to a screeching halt, her mouth clamping shut.

Davis Banda? What was he doing here?

With one strong shove, he threw Gert into the bushes on the side of the path and flicked Leon's forehead with a good-natured smile. "Haven't you two gotten a life yet? Get out of here, you mugs."

Sam looked over his shoulder at the commotion, and his face lit up. "Davis?"

"Hey, little man." Davis held out a forearm, and Sam knocked his own against it. Focused completely on Davis, Sam didn't seem to notice Gert and Leon scuttle by with rueful grins. Davis shot them a mocking glare, one of his eyes obscured by a transparent, red-tinted half-visor.

"What are you doing here?" Sam asked. "Ezren said you were going to school in Petraskis."

Davis slid the half-visor up to nestle in his dark hair. He'd always preferred the stations' lighter neurochip styles over the protective Belethean goggles. After all, he never went topside, so why would he need those anyway?

"I had a little time off, so I wanted to come visit." He looked around, and Ezren dodged behind a tree. "Is your sister around?"

Sam shrugged. "Dunno. She's late again."

"Well, I guess that doesn't surprise me," Davis said with a warm laugh, reaching down to scratch Waffle's ears.

Ezren couldn't help but notice how smart and professional

he looked in his dark blazer and black slacks—so different from the designer jeans and trendy button-downs he used to favor. As if all it took to grow up was a few months away from home.

Ezren untied the sweater from her waist and slid it over her tank top and tights. She combed her fingers through her hair and knotted it on her head again with some elastic. Her heart thumped in a way that had nothing to do with exercise, and she suppressed a groan. She was so not prepared for this today.

Ezren: Micah, Davis is here. Right now. With Sam.

Micah replied almost instantaneously, like she always did.

Micah: Oh yeah, I totally forgot he was coming back today.

Ezren: You knew?!?

Ezren was following behind them as they wove through the park, keeping enough distance so as not to be noticed.

Micah: Well, yeah, he posted something about it on VSoc. If you got on VSoc, you would know these things.

Ezren: Why didn't you tell me!??!?!?

Micah: Do I seriously have to answer that? You got selected for BRR tryouts!!! You may think Davis Banda's the shining star of Tuzuno, but I promise you he's small potatoes, sweetheart.

Ezren: We dated for two years, Micah! Two years is a lot of potatoes.

Micah: Which I totally understand, considering there's no one else to date here. But now he's an ex. And trust me when I say, you don't want any ex-potatoes!

Waffle stopped too long at a bush, busily chowing down on the grass in typical Waffle fashion, and Sam turned to wait for her. Spying Ezren, he waved an arm. "Oh, there she is! Hey, Ez, look who's here."

His hands shoved in the pockets of his slacks, Davis turned, meeting her gaze with his crinkled dark eyes.

EZREN: FESTERING SUNS. HE'S SPOTTED ME. OF COURSE IT HAD TO BE THE DAY I LOST MY JOB AND LOOK LIKE SOMETHING SCRAPED OFF THE BOTTOM OF A SHOE.

MICAH: WELL, IF YOU WANT TO IMPRESS POTATO-HEAD, YOU COULD ALWAYS TELL HIM YOU'RE TRYING OUT FOR THE BRR...

Ezren plastered a fake smile on her face and jogged to catch up with them. She dug deep for what she hoped was her most casual tone. "Hey, Davis, it's good to see you. Sorry I was late, Sam. It's been... kind of a long day."

"It's okay," Sam said, with nothing short of a miraculous grin. "Davis was telling me about his wormgate classes. They sound pretty crisp, actually."

Ezren fought hard to keep her smile steady, even as Sam's comment played on several of her already taut heartstrings. The one about how Davis wanted nothing more than to build wormgates and see the universe... to places she could never follow. But also the one where she hoped Sam dared to venture beyond Tuzuno one day. And what could she say when she was assaulted with that bittersweet flurry of emotion?

Something as bland as possible.

"That sounds just perfect for you, Davey. I'm so glad you're liking university." She kept walking to try to spur them along. If she didn't keep moving, there was a real possibility she would simply fall apart.

"University is great, but so is the city. I gotta say, I never really knew one place could have so many things to do and eat and see."

Ezren nodded, fighting the déjà vu that threatened to take

her back to their last conversation. The one when he'd told her about his big dreams, and she'd encouraged him to chase them. To leave her behind.

And he had.

"How wonderful. I'm so happy for you." The words were mechanical, but they were true, even if she was still sad for them.

Sam threw a ball for Waffle and then chased after her when she tried to run off with her treasure. Laughing, Sam stuffed a protesting Giles in his hoodie pocket and wrestled around with the plump capybog in the grass.

"It'd be better with you there though," Davis said, his smile softening.

Ezren scuffed her foot on the gravel path. "I like Tuzuno, and my mom and Sam need me here." But even as she said it, the words rang hollow now. Her job was gone, and Sam was twelve now, laughing and walking home by himself. In another year, even Tuzuno itself would be gone. In one afternoon, all of her reasons had evaporated.

He sighed. "Of course, I get it. But still, I had to ask." He flashed a wistful grin, and his fingers grazed her hand. "I miss you, you know."

And she wished he wouldn't. They'd made their choice. And it wasn't exactly a choice they could unmake. Even if she went to Petraskis, and they spent two or four or six amazing years together, she knew he was going through one of those wormgates. One day he would leave everything and everyone in the Casolla system behind for good. And her heart was here.

But if she wasn't careful, if his fingers lingered too long on her skin, or his familiar lips drew too close to hers, she was liable to forget all that. And that was a mistake she couldn't afford to make. She stepped away and forced her smile wider.

"I'm sure you've made lots of friends there. Micah says you post all kinds of great holos on VSoc."

Davis turned to where Sam lay on the lawn, looking up at the projected sky, the feigned breeze provided by the air cyclers blowing through the shorn grass. "It's a great place, Ez. I really think you'd like it if you gave it a chance. Get out of Tuzuno's little bubble and give yourself room to spread your wings."

Ezren regarded the confines of the dome circling them. Yes, it was a tiny bubble, but Petraskis was only a bigger bubble. The only real freedom was out on the surface—was through terraforming. But Davis had spent his first ten years on one of the stations. He was used to the confines of metal, the tight colonies of people stacked on top of one another. While Ezren dreamed of horizons and mountains, Davis dreamed only of more stars.

But she didn't really want to discuss this with him. She just needed him to leave already. "Aw, you know me, I can fly anywhere on the storm winds." With a lukewarm smile, she strode toward Sam and Waffle on the lawn. "C'mon, Sam, let's go! I've got work to do." She turned and walked backward, waving at Davis. "I'm so glad you've found a good fit, Davey. Give my love to your parents for me."

"It was good to see you too. If you're ever in the city, let me know, and I'll show you around."

Ezren shooed Sam toward their corridor, trying to ignore the old aches throbbing in her heart. "Sure thing." But the only thing she was really sure of was that she would never, ever, *ever* let that happen.

Ezren went through their evening routine mechanically, trying her best not to think about anything at all. She made instant macaroni for Sam, gave him his pain meds, and made sure he did his homework... which, of course, was perfect, as always. Really, it probably would've been more productive for him to do *her* homework.

She was nestled on their saggy futon, staring at the empty holopro of her biology assignment and listening to Sam snore from his closet-sized bedroom, when her mother trudged in through the door. Her shoulders were hunched and her face drawn as she set her messenger bag on the cluttered kitchen counter.

Even at a glance, Ezren knew that Lutz had given her the news. Rising from the futon, Ezren crossed the room to her in three steps and wrapped her arms around her middle from behind. She buried her face into her mother's back, breathing the sharp scent of acetone and algae that had soaked into her cardigan.

Her mother turned to fold Ezren into her arms. "I'm so sorry about your job, Ezzy. Lutz told me about it after you left. I'm sorry I didn't know, or I would've told you myself. I know how much it meant to you."

"Forget about that. What about the lab, Mom? What about the research?"

Ezren felt her mother's chest rise and fall with a sigh. "Well, we still have a year. So Lutz and I will have to try to drum up an alternate funding source."

"And if you don't?"

"Then we'll take that hurdle when we come to it, Ez." Her mother pulled back, looking into Ezren's face, her gaze deep and soft. "We've got to put one foot in front of the other. Day by day. Every step is a win, no matter how small."

Ezren nodded and hugged her mother tighter. It was something she'd said often after Ezren's father had gone missing. And while it was true, Ezren couldn't help but think it was one way of living in denial. If you kept your head down, then you didn't have to accept what you were marching toward.

"Try not to worry about it, sweetheart. This isn't the first time we've taken a funding cut. We'll figure it out like we always do." Her mother kissed the top of her head. "You just focus on school and getting enough sleep."

Though her mother tried to smile, Ezren could see the defeat in the lines in her brow. This was not just another funding cut. Still, she certainly wouldn't make herself another item on her mother's list of worries. She slipped into the room they shared and fell into a crumpled heap on the mattress. She couldn't lose Belethea to go live in a space box. Her brother was happy here—she was happy here, and she still dreamed of living under an open sky. Twirling through green fields without another soul in sight. A dream that had once seemed within her grasp now slid through her fingers.

A message from Micah scrolled across her goggs.

MICAH: STILL AWAKE? HOW WAS YOUR FAVORITE EXPIRED PRODUCE?

Ezren stared at the message, blinking as Micah's words echoed in her mind.

And besides the obvious fame and fortune, you'd get the chance to win the terranium prize for Belethea. Think of all the research you could do.

She sat bolt upright. This wasn't about fame and fortune... it wasn't even about Micah or even Ezren. It was about what was best *for Belethea.*

Maybe Micah had been right. Maybe this *was* a sign. She squeezed the bridge of her nose, inwardly quailing at what she was about to do. Leaving Tuzuno—leaving her family for the cams and the gossip and who knew what else. Not to mention Micah had falsified her application to a deadly inter-planetary publicity stunt the whole system took more seriously than life itself.

This was a *terrible* idea.

But it was the only way. Head down, one foot in front of the other.

EZREN: OKAY, I'LL DO IT.

And then Micah's voice was screaming in her ear, and even though it had been the third-worst day of her life and her sore muscles creaked and her numb brain sputtered with her caffeine crash, Ezren couldn't help but smile.

CHAPTER 5

FOSTER SAT in the mauve dust, twirling thin strands of belweed between his fingers and trying to look as unapproachable as possible. A scattering of press, support crew, and royalers milled about in front of the metal posts of the starting line, their voices a clamor over the audio channels echoing in everyone's helmets—the vigorous wind too loud for normal conversation, as usual.

Farther out, clusters of topjeeps lined the starting lane, with some braver souls even crowding around in their thinner, garden-variety topsuits, waving and laughing as they documented the event through their goggcams. The calm sky had decided to behave for the moment, but the teal clouds still twisted ominously above, the perpetual aroma of petrichor and electricity saturating the air. Threats of deeper storms rumbled over the rock spires in the distance, but their growls were relatively tame by Belethean standards.

The new royalers gathered in uncertain clumps, newly assigned doubles talking of strategy and nerves, or giving awkward interviews to the press. Nearly all of them had foregone the full royale topsuits for lighter, cheaper brands. While they didn't offer near the protection of the nanite topsuits, he didn't blame them. The nanites cycled through the bloodstream, harvesting energy from the user's cells to increase athletic performance and enable self-repair, extracting a steep toll on the body. They gave a big stamina boost, but without extensive acclimation training, they could easily do more harm than good.

It was one of the main reasons royalers had to be between eighteen and twenty-one. It was the only age window when they could wear the royale topsuits almost indefinitely. After that, the extended nanite drain could cause permanent damage to the user, and regen treatment didn't work well on full-grown adults. Besides, the new recruits didn't really need royale topsuits for such a short race. It would be more beneficial for them to wear what they were used to.

Still, it was a glaring reminder of how inexperienced these racers were. Anyone with actual topsuit training and talent had almost certainly fled to the stations to join the stronger, better-equipped teams.

The eight other experienced royalers stuck out in their fitted racing topsuits, moving through their familiar warm-up routines either in pairs or alone. A few paces off, Bex jogged across the rock-strewn plain, the short green weeds lashing at her shins. Teal bolts of lightning streaked across the sleek nanitelattice of her white topsuit. Every few paces, her fists snapped out in a wicked set of jabs, hungry for an opponent.

Sylvia climbed onto the top of a nearby jeep and paused for a moment, taking in a visible breath before projecting over the common channels. "Hey everybody and welcome to Belethea's first open race royale tryout! Today royalers will run, drive, and fight their way across forty miles of the rugged Belethean landscape and, as always, you can catch all the action straight through their goggcams."

"Keep your eyes on mine if you want to watch the winner," Talmadge called from near the starting line.

Foster resisted the urge to roll his eyes. Talmadge was definitely one of the better Belethean royalers, but he was nowhere near as good as he thought he was. Otherwise, he wouldn't have settled for the Belethean team in the first place.

Sylvia shot Talmadge a glare but continued with her professional cheerful tone. "For all the new racers, please remember, topside conditions are unpredictable and change quickly. If you get in a bad spot, find cover and send out a mayday, and we'll send a storm truck to pick you up as soon as possible."

A message from one of the offsite hololog reporters popped up on the main channel.

THE ROYALER REVIEW: HOPE YOU HAVE A LOT OF EMERGENCY STORM TRUCKS LINED UP FOR THAT RAGTAG LOT. LOOKS LIKE BELETHEA IS SCRAPING THE BOTTOM OF THE BARREL THIS YEAR. PERHAPS THE QUESTION WE SHOULD ALL BE ASKING OURSELVES IS: SHOULD THEY BE RACING AT ALL?

Foster winced. The question was pointed enough as it was, but to project it to the main channel? Brutal.

Sylvia continued, her eyes brighter now above an embrittled smile. "Also remember, since this is only a tryout, combat is only authorized in the brawling arena. However, if anyone would like to punch *The Royaler Review* in the face before we get started, please feel free."

A chuckle rippled through the crowd, and a smile tugged at Foster's lips. Whoever that hololloger was obviously didn't know Sylvia. If anyone threw chaff at her, she'd stuff it back down their throat until they choked on it.

"And we look forward to seeing you again at the finish line to announce this year's race royalers!" She curled her hands into fists and knocked them together three times. "Into the churn!"

"Into the churn!" the crowd echoed, their calls scattered on the wind.

Foster sighed, trying to remember why he was doing this again. When his mother had brought him to Naris Station five years ago to train with her team, it had been an easy decision. Although he hadn't been eligible until last year, being able to train with a royale team had been a unique opportunity. But his mother had wanted him to compete for Naris, and he'd wanted to make a difference for Belethea, the planet he'd grown up on. Belethea needed him. Had touted him as a wunderkind who could finally turn Belethea's luck around, and he drank in the attention at the time. Maybe he'd even believed it himself...

And it had all gone wrong from there.

Reality had bitten down with sharp teeth, opening his eyes to the truth he'd refused before. Belethea never stood a chance. They were a product of snowballing failure. Somewhere along the line, they'd placed poorly, lost sponsorships, equipment, and talent, and then placed even worse, continuing the cycle until Vieve's death had sent them into this sickening nosedive.

But even though she was gone now, he knew it was Vieve who held him here. Her unyielding drive to find the heart of the churn and stand on the podium—their shared dream of bringing honor to their planet instead of humiliation. Even if he didn't believe in that fantasy anymore, being here was the least he could do for her. His goodbye.

Sylvia leaned down and tapped him on the helmet, the tell-tale red recording dot gleaming in her purple goggs. "And here we have Foster Sterling, deep in concentration before the first royale of the season," she said in her overly cheerful VSoc voice. "How are you feeling before the big race, Foster? Today you'll be competing against ninety-one new recruits and eight of your teammates, and all but the top four will be leaving empty-handed. For those of you at home, this is the first time Belethea has required their royalers to defend their slots from new talent. Are you nervous?"

He stared at her for a moment. "No."

Behind her goggs, her glare intensified with warning. "Well, that's some cold hard confidence coming from a second-year racer. Any words for your fans out there?"

Thankfully, his helmet and goggs obscured most of his face, so although they could see his eyes, they wouldn't be able to make out the utter disdain oozing out of his pores. But if he didn't say something, Sylvia was liable to murder him on goggcam... which might finally give her the VSoc boost she was looking for. "Just hoping for a quick, safe race and a good start for Belethea this year."

Sylvia wiggled her hand in the universal signal for *go on.*

"And maybe we'll even find some fresh new faces to make it a little interesting."

Sylvia rolled her eyes but moved off to find a new victim, her voice still chirping through the feed. "There you have it, folks. As you know, Foster Sterling was last year's royale hopeful before the tragic loss of his partner derailed his quali-fying hopes. This year, he's teaming with mixed martial arts champion Bex 'Guns' Gunderson to get the team back on track." She hopped in front of Bex, halting her jog. "And how do you feel about your chances this year, Guns?"

"I'd feel better about them if I could warm up in peace," she deadpanned.

Cracking a smile under his helmet, Foster silently cheered as she turned and trotted off in the opposite direction.

"Well, they might not be winning Team Congeniality, but don't let them fool you, folks. Sterling/Guns is serious, and they're here to win."

Foster had to give it to Sylvia, she knew how to spin a holo. If it weren't for her expertise in the world of Virtual Society, their sponsorship numbers would be nonexistent. Not only were her own accounts popular, but last year she'd overseen the twelve accounts of the royalers as well. He didn't know where her dedication came from, but it earned her at least some of his cooperation. After all, if he had to do that stuff himself, they'd never get new gear.

Grady's tense voice interrupted Sylvia's cheerful broadcast, and the recording dot switched from red to blue. Still recording, but not live.

"Syl, there's only ten minutes till start, and she's not here. I thought you said this girl was supposed to be fodding blime. Who am I gonna double with if she doesn't show?" He pointed an accusing finger at the mob of new racers. "One of these randos?"

Sylvia straightened, but her gaze spun around the crowd too. "Calm your fritz, Simon. I'm sure she'll show. She was sparking thrilled when I offered the chance to race with you. Not only was she our number one recruit, but she seemed like a huge fan of yours personally."

Foster grimaced. The over-eager recruits were the worst. They always thought they knew everything and were always convinced *this was Belethea's year*. In short, they reminded him of how he used to be.

The racing official's voice projected into the common channels. "This is the five-minute warning; all royale doubles to the starting chute." With the announcement, a countdown appeared in the corner of Foster's goggs, along with all the other royalers.

Grady's whole body went rigid and beneath his octagonal goggs, a sheen of anxious sweat glistened across his dark skin.

"C'mon, Sylvia. I can't lose this for some rando we've never heard of who can't even be on time."

Sylvia shifted her weight from foot to foot, tapping her gloved fingers against her teal-and-gold helmet. "It'll be fine, Simon, we'll reassign one of the other recruits."

"But there's no time now!"

Foster had yet to move as he watched the spectacle, and Bex jogged up to his side. "You going to get off your ass or what, Sterling?"

Foster rose and dusted the dirt from the seat of his suit, a strange emotion roiling through him. As much as Grady had frosted him in the last few months, he really was a strong royaler. He brought good sponsorship numbers, and most of all, the guy wanted this. Foster's mother had always said drive was more important than talent, and Grady had both. If Foster was doing this to get Belethea back on the map for Vieve, maybe this was the right thing to do. Or maybe it was just an excuse to step back. Either way, it was a win-win.

"Nah, sorry, Bex. I think I'm out today." Bex didn't react as he walked over to Sylvia and the frantic Grady. "You might be able to double with Bex if she'll have you." Foster looked at Bex, and she shrugged, like he knew she would. The girl only cared about winning, and at this point, she had to see that Grady was just as good a bet as he was. If not better. "I'll wait for the new girl if she shows."

Grady froze, stock-still, as the clock ticked down to the two-minute warning. His fists shook, and Foster could practically see the conflict in his eyes. He didn't want to owe Foster, but at this point what choice did he have? "Your mom would kill you... and probably me too."

An unexpected laugh bubbled up in Foster. She totally would. "It's fine."

Nodding, Grady turned to Sylvia. "You good with that, Coach?"

Sylvia let out a huge breath and threw up her hands. "You know what, fine. Do what you want."

Without a backward glance, Grady and Bex jogged to the starting line, talking quickly through their starting tactics. But they'd been on the team together for a year, so this wasn't entirely new territory.

Foster sat in the dirt with a strange mix of relief and disappointment. The fans on the sidelines started to count down as the last minute ticked away, and a quiet anticipatory tension strung through the royalers.

Foster relaxed back on his hands and looked up at the strangely still Sylvia. He was a little surprised that she hadn't put up more of a fight about losing him. After all, he'd been the best royaler last year. Maybe Harland had convinced her he was just a product of nepotism that had devolved into unmotivated laziness. Maybe even Foster believed that.

He twisted his fingers into the weeds beneath his hands. "I guess that girl's not coming after all."

Sylvia's gaze sharpened on him. "Do you really not want to race?"

The clock hit thirty seconds, and Foster's legs started to tingle, his heartbeat speeding up in spite of himself. "I... don't know."

Twenty seconds until start time, Sylvia's electric-purple goggs scanned across the fans, the crew, and the press recording... until she stopped, and a smile shone through her eyes. "Well, you better decide pretty quick."

Hopping to his feet, Foster followed her stare to where a figure in a horrifically old-fashioned royale topsuit barreled across the plain toward them. She moved unnaturally fast for the obvious amount of bulky weight hanging on her limbs.

Pumping her arms furiously, the massive crack in her helmet glinted as she closed the distance. But her goggs couldn't hide the sheer determination in her night-black eyes, the crew and press scattering before her magtrain of metal-coated fury.

Foster's jaw dropped. *This* was the new girl? Casolla help him, she was a chaffing force of nature.

And she was tiny.

CHAPTER 6

THE STARTING gun went off as Ezren skidded to a halt in front of the only figure in a royale topsuit left in the flat starting area. Though she couldn't remember his name, her alleged partner cut an impressive figure in his form-fitting teal-and-black topsuit. His broad shoulders and a muscled chest balanced well atop long lean legs that probably put him around 6'—more than a full head over her. Though his helmet obscured everything except his clear goggs, she could make out the incredulous expression on his face. Yeah... he obviously had a little higher expectations than the rampaging mess that was her.

"Sorry... I'm late," she said, her chest heaving. "Are you... the guy?"

No response. *Suns.* Hadn't Micah said they'd doubled her with one of their better royalers? Maybe they'd changed their minds, because this guy obviously wasn't the quickest neurochip in the lab. But she couldn't blame them. Why waste their better bets on a nobody? Her gaze flicked to the royalers disappearing toward the rocky spires in the distance.

She turned to the curvy woman with the bright purple goggs and the word *Coach* projected across her suit. "This is the guy, right? Can we still race?"

"If you can catch up." Her deep brown eyes smiled at

Ezren from beneath her goggs. "Just make sure to turn on your goggcam and broadcast it for the fans. It's a royale requirement!"

The guy made a noise as if to say something, but Ezren didn't have any more time for words. She grabbed his arm and yanked him after the disappearing royalers. They could catch up, she knew that much... but there was still a lot about this thing she didn't know.

The guy followed behind her, his long loping strides matching her short fast ones. She switched to neurochip messages to save her breath.

EZREN: DO YOU KNOW ANYTHING ABOUT THE COURSE?

His head jerked toward her.

THE GUY: YOU MEAN YOU DON'T KNOW ANYTHING ABOUT THE COURSE?!

Ezren wrinkled her nose, trying to remember what Micah had told her in the storm truck, but she'd kept dozing off.

EZREN: I GET THERE'S PHYSICAL, DRIVING, AND COMBAT PARTS, BUT THAT'S BASICALLY ALL I KNOW. HOW LONG ARE THEY, AND WHAT DO WE NEED TO DO TO QUALIFY?

THE GUY: HERE.

A simple satellite holopro with a snaking red line overlaid onto Ezren's topological and meteorological readout.

THE GUY: THERE ARE FIFTY DOUBLES AND ONLY THIRTY VEHICLES, SO IF WE DON'T MAKE UP GROUND SOON, WE'LL BE CUT BEFORE WE EVER GET TO THE OTHER TWO LEGS.

Bounding over the rocky incline, Ezren pored over the map, comparing the weather, the elevation gains, and the destination. She glanced up at the mauve spires jutting into the sky, and the river that coursed between them, cutting through the landscape in a deep ravine. If they followed the red line, they would have to ford the river at its widest point and then climb their way out of the ravine, straight up the spire onto the plateau above. Although the course was technically the shortest route, whoever made it obviously had maximum suffering in mind... and they couldn't even have predicted the storm surge that would charge over that peak in 14.9 minutes.

Ezren: Do we have to follow this line?

The Guy: No, we just have to get to the vehicle checkpoint.

Ezren: You're sure?

Ezren glanced at him, but confidence radiated from his posture, his stare, and his every step. She still doubted his response time, but at least he thought he knew what he was doing.

The Guy: Yes.

Ezren: Then we're going this way.

Ezren veered off to the left, away from the paths of the other royalers.

The guy behind her only hesitated for half a second.

The Guy: Wait, what? Why?

Ezren: Weather, terrain, difficulty. All kinds of reasons.

He hesitated another moment.

The Guy: If you say so. This is your show.

If Ezren wasn't so focused on where to put her feet amid the field of moss-slicked stones, she would've looked a little closer at this guy. This celebrity royaler who was apparently just fine with trusting her decisions. Did he not care? Was that why they assigned him to her? She shook her head. It didn't matter. She just had to get through this.

After the sprint from the storm truck station, her muscles were already starting to burn as she leapt from boulder to boulder, but the unfamiliar terrain thrilled her. This was new ground she'd never seen before, peaks she'd never climbed. And if they didn't make the first cut, she wouldn't get to see more of it. That was reason enough to push harder.

They crested the ridge, skidding down toward the wide river at the bottom. According to her readouts, the river was shallow enough to wade across here, and while the incline on the other side was still steep, it wasn't the near-vertical the other royalers were traversing. That is, if her maps were accurate... If not, she'd totally chaffed them.

From the shore, she leapt as far as she could into the lazy river, and the water splashed up over her heavy suit, only to drift back down. Even though she'd lived here for nearly four years now, sometimes Belethea's 0.75 Earth gravity still struck her as oddly light. Maybe Obrone's 1.1 Egrav would always be her standard. Wading through the river in her heavy suit, she splashed more water through the air, laughing as the cool drops glittered in the overcast light.

THE GUY: ENJOYING YOURSELF?

Ezren turned to him with a sheepish smile he couldn't see. She'd almost forgotten he was there. She tried to move faster, but she could only wade so fast in her bulky suit.

EZREN: IT'S BEEN A WHILE SINCE I'VE GOTTEN TO PLAY IN WATER.

THE GUY: IT'S PRETTY COMMON IN ROYALES.

Ezren peered into his visor to try to get a sense of his expression but could glean nothing from the stormy green-gray eyes within.

EZREN: LUCKY YOU THEN.

They sloshed through the shallows to the steep incline on the other side, and Ezren immediately fell to all fours, keeping her body low to the ground. Sticking close behind, her double mimicked her movements.

The Guy: It seems like you've done this before.

Ezren grinned underneath her helmet.

Ezren: I've been lucky too. Can you get any live standings or anything through your chip to see where we are?

The Guy: No. No outside comms allowed during the royale. Just assume we're last.

Ezren's lips twisted at his negativity, but she said nothing. Still, she forced herself to move faster all the same. The incline steepened, and Ezren transitioned to a climb, her fingers feeling for handholds to push and pull herself—and her suit—to the top.

Above them, the clouds flashed, and the thunder boomed closer. To their left, she could count six funnel clouds whirling above, threatening to land. And worse, it looked like they were bringing hail with them today.

If they weren't off the peak by the time the funnels touched down, they'd have to wait until the storms passed. Which meant they had approximately 6.2 minutes to get up and get back down.

Ezren: Once we're up there, what do we have to do?

The guy climbed beside her now, silently keeping perfect pace, like a seamless shadow.

The Guy: Grab a vehicle, if there's one left, and drive to the brawl arena.

Ezren reassessed the map. Of course, the line they were supposed to follow was insanely steep. If they took anything with wheels, they'd be navigating switchbacks for ages.

Ezren: What kind of vehicle?

The Guy: There's a different mix every time. Probably jetbikes, quads, terrasails, and maybe a topjeep for whoever's first.

Ezren: One for each of us? Or to share?

She reached out a hand for another hold, and the rock under her foot crumbled away. Her stomach lurched, but before she could panic, the guy's hand snatched out, grabbing her arm. He steadied her until she got her footing, his gaze meeting hers as if to make sure she was okay.

The Guy: To share.

Her breath came fast now, arms shaking as they neared the top. The sweat slid around the edges of her goggs, but she just had to push a little farther.

Ezren: What's usually the last taken?

The Guy: Terrasails and jetbikes.

Ezren: And you know how to drive them?

The Guy: After years of training, I would hope so.

Ezren: Okay, we have 3.5 minutes to grab the terrasail before the funnels throw us off the top.

He paused in his climb, his head whipping toward her.

The Guy: There were a lot of things wrong with that statement, but mostly I'm concerned with your optimism. I doubt there'll be anything left.

Not bothering to reply, Ezren pulled herself over the top, and a scattering of different vehicles greeted her from the smooth plateau of purplish rock. The lightning lashed at the sky above them, followed by the bellow of thunder.

The guy's head popped up next.

The Guy: Well, I'll be chaffed. Nine left. Not bad, new girl.

2.1 minutes. Her head swiveled until she spotted the long

pole above the sleek board, the four thick all-terrain wheels strapped to the rock with stakes.

Ezren: There, the terrasails.

The guy hopped up onto the plateau, gesturing to a quad.

The Guy: Are you joking? Are you trying to make this *more* dangerous?

Ezren: The wind is a strong 45 mph, and when the storm bursts, it'll top 80. If you can drive, we'll fly down this mountain.

The Guy: You know these aren't meant to fly, right?

Ezren: Going down all those switchbacks would take too long. Besides... I saw it in a holopro once.

She knelt, unfastening the tethers and battling to keep the board from flying off without them. The board slipped from her hands, and she scrambled to catch it. The guy snatched the rear wheel, and he leaned in close to her, yelling this time over the crashing thunder. "This is a stupid idea!"

"This whole race is a stupid idea!" She climbed onto the board, latching her gravboots in place. "We have one hundred seconds!"

The guy eyed the funnel clouds descending on them and rolled his eyes, jumping up behind her on the board. His boots found the outer footholds immediately, and his long-fingered gloves clamped onto the boom beside hers.

"You'll have to lean into me!" he shouted, his body pressed against hers. His chest pushed against the back of her head, his legs against her legs.

Ezren's mouth suddenly went dry as it truly hit her what they were about to do. "Is this a bad time to tell you I've never terrasailed before?"

"All you have to do is hold on. And if you're the praying type... well, it couldn't hurt."

She found herself laughing instead, the complete absurdity of it all overcoming her. The thrill of the storm and the adrenaline and the open sky coursed through her electrified nerves, tingling across her skin. The clouds circled them in a massive cyclone, obscuring the empty expanse of Belethea's spiked panorama from sight. "Forty-five seconds!"

"Well, it's as good a day to die as any."

With that, he pressed the button to extend the sail, and they jetted off the mountain.

CHAPTER 7

WE ARE GOING TO DIE. It wasn't the first time in his royale career that Foster had thought this, but it was definitely the most convincing. The wind caught the thick sail, and the motor vibrated the board beneath their feet, their heavy suits the only thing keeping them upright.

The clouds swirled around them as they sliced through the roiling sky. The girl's small body, encased in its clunky suit, pressed against him, and his arms burned as he fought to keep them on course. Behind them, the thunder crashed, and the first drops of hail began to pelt his suit.

Not good. He could see through the gash in the girl's helmet to her brown hair beneath, and at these wind speeds, it wouldn't take a hail chunk larger than his eye to crack her head like a melon. He leaned forward, resting his chin on her head in a pathetic effort to protect her as Belethea's icy bullets pattered against the mesh of his racing suit. Far beneath them, quads and other royale vehicles crawled along the switchbacks—those that hadn't stopped to seek shelter, that is.

Her hands wedged between his, the girl jostled his elbow with her own.

FOSTER: WE DON'T HAVE TIME TO FIGHT THE SAIL.

Focus on keeping us upright and back to the ground. We can course correct later.

Another flash of lightning struck all too close, and he shifted his weight forward just a little. Chaff, they were high.

Foster: More.

She shifted aggressively forward, tilting toward the slope one hundred feet below.

Foster: Careful. If we descend too fast, we'll nosedive.

New Girl: And if those funnel clouds catch up with us, they'll suck us into the atmosphere. Better to crash and break from this distance.

Foster's heart hammered in his chest, and his quads strained as he stabilized the board. Break was never a good word. Although the regen tanks could work miracles on anyone under twenty, he didn't want to test their limits.

In a lash of wind, the whistling storm took on the intensity of a steam engine. The sky turned a sickly shade of green, and an explosive gust caught the back of their board, whipping them head over heels.

Every swear word Foster knew catapulted through his brain as he struggled to hold on, resisting the urge to brace the girl against him. Her old suit didn't have half of the reinforced nanite strength that his did, so he could only hope she could hold on without it. If she flew off now, he would lose her completely.

The board's sensors beeped frantically as they approached the ground at alarming speed, still tumbling.

Panic flooded his thoughts in an icy rush, and his hands tightened on the boom. "Push out!"

The girl reacted instantly, and together they shoved the sail away from them, slowing their frantic spin.

The board shot air toward the ground in its own attempt to

save them before the wheels crashed into the earth. Though his suit absorbed some of the impact, the crash still jarred every joint in his body, and the girl folded under the force, just barely holding on.

But they hadn't stopped yet. The board bounced again, and he pushed the boom out, letting the wind keep them upright. They skimmed the decline before the wheels skidded down again. His sensors had heightened to a shrill screaming as they warned of the tornadoes now eating into the landscape behind them. With the board once again under some semblance of control, they skipped along like a rock over a lake, still flying but maybe no longer actively cheating death.

One of the girl's hands came free, and her knees buckled beneath her—out of exhaustion or injury he couldn't tell—but this time he loosed a hand and wrapped it around her waist, holding her up.

FOSTER: ARE YOU OKAY?

NEW GIRL: FINE—FINGERS JUST SLIPPED.

FOSTER: ALMOST THERE.

Foster took her gloved hand in his and placed it back on the boom, squeezing to keep it there. He couldn't even imagine how exhausted she had to be in that suit. Her fingers were having to hold almost double her body weight onto basically a leaf on the wind, and her decrepit suit was barely assisting her. He didn't know where Sylvia had found this girl, but she had to literally be from a different world.

NEW GIRL: HOW MUCH FARTHER TO THE COMBAT ARENA? DO YOU THINK WE HAVE A CHANCE?

Foster pointed up ahead to the unnaturally round shape in the distance, maybe only another two miles out. If he squinted, he thought he could see a storm jeep tearing across the landscape. But no one else. That was a good sign.

FOSTER: ONLY A FEW MILES NOW. IF WE'RE IN THE TOP TWENTY TEAMS, WE'LL MAKE THE CUT-OFF.

NEW GIRL: AND THEN WE HAVE TO DO WHAT... FIGHT THE OTHER TEAMS? I SHOULD TELL YOU NOW, THE ONLY PERSON I'VE EVER FOUGHT WAS A KID WHO TRIED TO HIT MY BROTHER ONCE.

Even in her message, he could tell she was dubious. So this girl might've been a racer, but she apparently wasn't a fighter. That made sense. Most of the royalers had a specialty—the legs, the wheels, or the fists. At least now he knew she was mortal.

FOSTER: DID YOU WIN?

Her hand squirmed under his.

NEW GIRL: IT WAS CLOSER THAN I WOULD'VE LIKED.

He smirked under his helmet.

FOSTER: DON'T WORRY TOO MUCH. IT'S JUST A RING-OUT BRAWL. THE FIRST TEAM TO PUSH THE OTHER OUT OF THE ARENA ADVANCES. DOUBLE ELIMINATION.

NEW GIRL: IT TAKES A SHARP BREEZE TO PUSH ME ANYWHERE.

FOSTER: WE'LL BE FINE. IF WE GET THERE IN TIME, I CAN GET US THROUGH THE BRAWL.

EZREN: AND THEN WE QUALIFY FOR THE TEAM OR WHATEVER?

How did this girl not know about the royale? He thought Sylvia had said she was a fan.

FOSTER: THERE'S ONE FINAL SPRINT TO THE FINISH LINE. YOU KNOW, SINCE THE FANS LIKE A TIGHT FINISH AT THE END.

The land had flattened around them, the storm quieting and the hail finally easing up. His shoulders relaxed just a little; if they kept going like this—

A quad revved out of nowhere, broadsiding their board and flipping them sideways into the dirt.

The terrasail flew out of his hands, smashing against a boulder as Foster skidded into the ground in a flash of pain, his suit absorbing most of the impact. He searched first for the girl, but she'd already crawled to her hands and knees. At least that meant she was intact.

The quad turned sharply in front of him, and Lucian Talmadge blew him a mocking kiss. With her arms around his waist, Anna Lee fluttered her fingers at Foster.

Fury swimming through him, Foster surged to his feet, muted pain running through his back. "Are you out of your fodding mind? Brawls are limited to checkpoint only, asschaff. She's not even wearing a proper suit."

"Oh, c'mon, Sterling baby, what's a royale without a little scrap here and there?" Talmadge shrugged in his silver and black-streaked suit. "It's what she came for after all." With that, Talmadge revved the quad and took off toward the dome ahead.

Foster ran over to the girl, taking her by the arm and helping her to her feet. "Are you hurt?"

She shook her head, but another chunk of her helmet had flown off in the crash. "No, what about our terrasail?"

Foster looked at the ripped sail and the snapped board, the wind already trying to scatter the pieces. "It's crunched, but we've only got another quarter mile. Can you run?"

She straightened and blood leaked from a cut on her brow, the red visible beneath her goggs. He winced; it looked bad enough for a healing patch and probably had a concussion to go with it. He peered into her midnight eyes for a better diagnosis, but she met his stare with clarity.

"Yes."

Without another word, she took off at a stumbling jog.

With the retreating storm's gusting fingers still tugging at them, he kept a hand close to steady her.

As they ran, another quad raced by them, thankfully not veering to run over them this time.

The girl didn't turn to look at them, but she tried to pick up her pace as they blurred past.

Sweat trickled down Foster's furrowed brow. Honestly, he was relieved two racers had passed them. That meant they wouldn't be fighting Talmadge and Lee. And no matter what place they finished, if Sylvia didn't take this girl on, she was out of her mind.

Finally, they stumbled into the open doorway of the temporary dome that denoted the checkpoint, and Foster turned to the race official in the orange topsuit. "Sterling and..." Chaff it. He didn't even know this girl's name. But she quickly filled in the awkward pause.

New Girl: Hart.

Sterling nodded gratefully. "Hart/Sterling checking in."

The figure nodded, a broad smile behind their clear face shield. "Checking in as team four, your first opponent is waiting on the right ring. This is a lightning round, so helmets and boots stay on for this one."

Foster grimaced. They were earlier than he'd thought. Which meant they'd probably be facing a more experienced team. He glanced at the girl... Hart. She straightened, flexing her fingers, but at least the cut on her head had stopped bleeding. She was small, and in that suit, she'd be a goner almost immediately, but even so, he hoped she'd been modest about her skills.

They stepped into the meager shelter, and he quickly scanned the two brawl rings under the metal umbrella frame. Two officials hovered over each circle, and a scattering of topjeeps edged the outside, the red rings of recording goggs glowing around the arena. Only a handful of fans had ventured out this far, but he had to hand it to Sylvia that there were any at all. The open tryout really was a stroke of genius.

He returned his gaze to the rings—mere squares of rocks in the sand beneath the cheap metal dome—just in time to see a teal topsuit leap across it. Lucian Talmadge stood in the center, barking out a deep laugh as he and Anna traded feints with Roche and Zuniga, the other Belethea royalers.

Foster exhaled through his nose. Well, at least they wouldn't be fighting Talmadge. He turned to the right ring, and his eyes met the cool hazel glare of none other than Simon Grady. Bex turned from watching Talmadge's brawl to face Foster with her white brows drawn low over her hard stare.

Well, that settled it then.

They were totally chaffed.

CHAPTER 8

EZREN STOOD in one corner of the makeshift ring marked only with a diamond of large stones. Around them, a scattering of media and fans recorded the royale with staring red eyes from the storm jeeps walling in the spartan, mossy field. Ezren's stomach twisted and tangled as she tried to shake off the toll of the race's first two legs. She jumped in place to keep her taxed muscles from stiffening, even as her swollen knee complained beneath her—a casualty of the quad that had rammed them earlier.

There was a part of her that still couldn't believe Micah had talked her into this. And yet here she was, about to fight professional royalers, their sleek topsuits rippling with self-repairing nanites. What she wouldn't give for that kind of top-of-the-line gear to use at the lab. While she was appreciative of the little boost her old suit gave her, with the strength enhancement from the more efficient nanite models, they could instrument even the higher category storms closer to the churn belt.

She swallowed. And now she had to *fight* one. Couldn't she just sit this out while this guy—something Sterling—took care of it?

But then again, could he really take on two of his team-mates at once? When she'd shown up late, she'd assumed the coach had assigned her one of their benchwarmers. But the way he had kept control of the terrasail said otherwise. Who was this guy and why in Casolla had he risked his qualifying slot for her?

Whatever the reason, they'd come too far to fail now. Her hands curled into fists as the straight-backed girl—Gunderson, they'd called her—gave her an icy blue death glare. Her partner stood casually beside her, slinging his own chilled glower at Sterling.

"So what do you need me to do?" she whispered to Sterling.

While Ezren bounced on her toes, Sterling maintained a placid calm. "Don't do anything. We're going to lose this one."

"What?" Ezren stopped, mouth agape. "I thought you said you were going to *take care of this.*"

"It's double elimination, this is the second-strongest team out here, and they will be clawing for a win. It's wiser to save our energy and beat team three, which will lose to the strongest pair in the other ring."

"We're not even going to try?"

In the adjacent ring, a teal figure skidded across the flat ground but managed to stay in the boundary to the cheer of the crowd.

Sterling's eyes flashed with something like amusement. "Just trust me on this and step out of the ring." He shrugged. "Easy."

Ezren blinked, her mind sputtering, even as the referee lifted a yellow flag. Gunderson brought her fists up, and Grady crouched ever so slightly. Then with the blast of a horn, the green flag rose, and Grady rushed toward Sterling.

With a lazy smile in his gaze, Sterling took one lackadaisical step out of the ring, and a red flag went up with a deep, reverberating horn. Grady pulled up short of the line, glaring at Sterling. The wind whipped the crowd's jeers around them, the fans drumming their feet against the storm jeep hoods and honking the horns. The two royalers were so close their helmets almost touched, in what was obviously a very personal kind of standoff, their stares conveying messages Ezren couldn't read... not to mention what they were probably sending over chip comms.

But, in whatever kind of silent drama unfolded between them, Grady had completely ignored her right next to him, and she couldn't pass up the opportunity. She couldn't just give up. She wouldn't. So, with a quick crouch, she launched her hard armored shoulder into Grady's back.

He was shorter than Sterling, probably 5'10" tops, but he was way more solid than she'd been expecting. Still, she only needed an inch to get him out of the ring. And caught off balance as he was, she got it. Another deep horn went off, and a cheer surged around the arena.

A mix of emotions flashed behind Sterling's goggs—shock, bemusement, and then something like annoyance.

STERLING: THAT WAS NOT SMART.

Grady turned toward her, blinking quickly with surprise. And then, strangely, he laughed.

She didn't really have time to think about it with the patter of feet sounding behind her, and she turned just in time to duck a well-aimed punch to her head. But she wasn't fast enough to dodge the whirling kick that struck her directly in the diaphragm.

The air ripped from her lungs, the force of the blow sent Ezren staggering, until she collapsed flat onto her back, well outside the ring. Trying to reinflate her chest, she gasped through her helmet, new pain blossoming from her ribs.

Another horn blasted, and the two royalers raced from the ring with the circle of fans cheering them on. If they even spared her a backward glance, Ezren couldn't see it.

Sterling crouched over her, his eyes crinkled in smug amusement. "I told you to step out."

Ezren tried to collect the thoughts that had spilled out with her oxygen supply. "If you hadn't given up... maybe we could've won."

He offered her a hand. "Maybe, but I'm telling you, it wasn't worth the effort. We'll be quick in the next round and make up the distance."

A horn blared in the other arena, and then another right behind it. Once again, a deafening roar echoed through the stadium, and the victors—the ones who had hit them with the quad—swaggered toward the exit, waving ostentatiously to the crowd. There were two ahead of them now. They had to make this fast, or they'd never catch up.

"I'm not sure I can survive another of those kicks." She grabbed his wrist, her fingers not even going all the way around it, and he pulled her to her feet.

"Which is why I told you to step out. In this race, you need to conserve every ounce of energy."

Ezren made a face; there was a reason this guy had been stuck with her, and while she wasn't sure what it was yet, his game plan wasn't exactly giving her a warm fuzzy. Holding back for the possibility of saving energy later didn't sound like a good bet to her, but before she could think of a response, a pair of Belethea royalers stepped into the arena.

She drew in another ragged wheeze from her crumpled diaphragm. If she didn't get her breath back, she'd be no use in the next fight. "Well, it looks... like you're going to have to burn that... energy anyway."

"Nah, this is not the same thing," Sterling said, his arms loose at his sides.

One of the figures nodded to him, an odd waver to his deep

voice. "Step aside, Sterling, you know you don't really want this. Let it go."

Ezren grimaced. Sterling had been hauling some serious ass to step away now, but she didn't know him from her neighbor's turtle. These were his teammates. If they were able to convince him to "conserve" a little more energy, she would be totally chaffed. The flag went up, and Ezren tried to straighten, pain rattling through her chest. Just how hard had that girl hit her?

Sterling shrugged. "Maybe. But I'm so used to winning."

The horn blew, and no one moved. Ezren swallowed. What was she supposed to do? Should she charge like the others had?

"What's happening?" she gasped out.

"Just wait, they'll—"

As if of one mind, the two figures rushed across the dirt arena. The first charged straight into Foster, while the second's elbow crashed into Ezren's helmet, sparking pain exploding through her rattling head. Ezren staggered backward, her heels on the edge of the ring as she swayed, fighting the black that edged her vision.

Her opponent tensed, chambering the final blow, when Foster swung the second royaler around, using their momentum to fling them into their partner. Ezren watched, her head throbbing, as Foster followed with a fast double kick to the sound of two consecutive air horns nearly drowned out by the cheers.

And then, Sterling was there beside her.

"Let's go, Hart."

"What just happened?" She squeezed her temples in a vain attempt to steady her vision.

He gently guided her by the arm, a lazy smile in his voice. "In case you missed it, that was the *royale* part of the Race Royale."

His words cleared Ezren's head like a cold breeze. "That

means we're through, right? Then why are we wasting time?" She lunged forward, pushing the pain out of the way and forcing her feet to move. "Where do we go? What do we do? Are we behind?"

"Cool down. We've got six miles left, and like I said, just assume we're last." His eyes crinkled. "You're not a very good listener, are you?"

"No more talking," Ezren said, her breaths harsh now. She needed every scrap of focus to push her legs. They could make it. But even from a distance, she could see the two other teams ahead of them, the nearest perhaps only five minutes away—but with only six miles to go. That was an eternity.

She pushed herself harder, and the dark gray spires of the finish rose in front of them, the crowd lining the final stretch. Somewhere, her mom and Sam and Micah were watching her goggs feed. Depending on her. For them, she could go faster. Their cheers and faces blurred as she focused on the team in front of them. Even Sterling was breathing hard now, his long strides digging into the dirt.

The two nearest Belethea royalers—the same showboating fritzers who had wrecked their terrasail—jogged down the long chute before the finish. They waved and posed for the hover-cams, arrogantly unaware of Ezren and Sterling bolting behind them, their steps masked by the howling wind. When the larger guy finally turned to check over his shoulder, it was already too late. Ezren and Foster were past them and over the finish line.

"And team number two is... Hart/Sterling!"

A euphoric rush of relief swept through Ezren. They had made it.

And then she promptly bent over, lifted her helmet, and vomited into the dirt.

CHAPTER 9

FOSTER LACED his hands together on top of his head, sucking in deep breaths through his helmet. Well, that was not the race he'd expected to run. In fact, that was unlike any race he'd *ever* run. With Bex, he'd planned a relaxed, easy lope from start to finish. It wouldn't have taken a lot of effort to qualify if they'd started on time. Then for that brief moment, he thought he wouldn't be racing ever again.

Now here he was, lungs burning after a—no kidding—six-mile sprint to the finish line. And this no-experience, heavy-suited late-starter had come in *second*. He'd known when he'd seen Talmadge that they were near the front. He could've told her as much, but it wouldn't have made a difference. This girl did not pull punches, she did not step back, and she would've powered to the finish even if she'd been in first. And there'd been a part of him that had wanted to see what she could do. What *they* could do.

Now she was crouched in the dirt, dry heaving in front of dozens of flashing goggcams. Even as the next team finished behind them, the bloodshot recording eyes didn't move from their chosen prey.

The press was going to eat this girl up.

He stepped in front of her, shielding her as best he could

from the handful of fans and reporters jockeying for an interview. Above them, the slate clouds churned into a dangerous navy, and Foster's suit clung to his damp skin. Talmadge, not taking third place well, stormed past him into the small metal dome of the storm truck outpost Sylvia had rented for the tryout. Anna Lee followed more slowly behind, hiding her teary face with a hand before she too disappeared into the dome's airlock.

The girl—Hart, he reminded himself—straightened, her eyes widening at the sight of the crowd around them, as if she hadn't noticed they were there. They pressed in closer, flinging questions at her.

"Hart, can we get your first name?"

"How'd you get on a team with Foster Sterling?"

"Where are you from?"

"Come talk to us, Hart!"

"I... I... um..." she stuttered, cringing away from them.

Foster: You don't have to answer any of those questions.

He touched her back to try to shepherd her toward the dome.

Foster: You probably want to at least get cleaned up first.

She bobbed her head and followed his lead into the airlock.

The storm truck outpost was little more than a giant garage, but with some good holopro work, the ceiling had turned into a wide blue sky streaked with wisps of clouds, and an expansive spring garden spread before them. Clumps of violet, red, and cornflower blooms swayed in the tiniest slip of a breeze, at great odds with the storms brewing outside. Long refreshment tables stretched across the faux-garden, and a few of the reporters from better-known holologs had been allowed in to talk to the finishers. An upbeat melody rocked through the buzz of chatter as the trainers and organizers milled about.

Foster pulled off his helmet with a sigh of relief, tousling the short damp waves matted to his head. He pulled the teal goggs from his helmet and slipped them around his neck.

"There's the locker room." He pointed out the door. "And then you'll need to check in at the med table."

Foster half expected her to sprint at full tilt toward the locker room, but she lingered, kicking at the projected dirt floor.

She carefully pulled her maimed helmet from her head, wincing as she tried to avoid the cut in her brow. Fully revealed, her black coffee eyes, underscored by dark circles against her pale skin, darted around the room. Her round lips pursed, and she rubbed at her nose with the back of her glove. Here, she showed none of the confidence and daring she had on the surface. In the light of the afternoon, she seemed small, and, well... kind of cute.

He felt a strange reluctance to abandon her there—like their morning ordeal, their dance with death, had looped them together, and to walk away would be to break that delicate thread.

"Do you have to check in at the med table too?" she asked, her fingers tracing the cracks in her helmet.

"Yeah, I just got to get out of this suit first. Otherwise, they might try to medicate me for the smell."

Her shoulders relaxed with a soft breathy chuckle. "Okay." With the unspoken agreement that she would meet him there, she moved off toward the girls' lockers.

Foster watched her go, a limp in her step as she favored one leg, and once again found himself wondering where she'd come from. He turned and headed to his own locker room, mulling over the mystery that she presented. Talent like that didn't just pop out of the ground like belweed. She was strong, and she knew Belethea's temperament even better than he did. That took experience. But the royale community was a small one, so how had she ducked under the radar?

Walking into the locker room, he nearly ran into Grady lumbering out of it. Their highest maintenance member had seemingly donned his hololog-ready style in record-breaking time. Not one of his lush black curls looked out of place beneath his octagonal goggs. He wore a long-tailed coat over his high-necked button-up, and gold glinted from his ears, neck, and fingers. Foster tried not to wrinkle his nose at the hint of his spicy cologne.

Grady stopped, his eyes sharp but also curious. "Who *is* that girl?

Foster stifled a laugh, but he couldn't stop the smile that curled his lips. "Of all people, I thought you would know. She was supposed to be your partner."

He straightened his cuffs and shook his head. "She's got to be from one of the stations or something. Or maybe even sent by your..." He didn't finish the sentence, but he didn't have to.

Foster raised an eyebrow. Someone sent from the stations by his mother? Well, that was certainly an idea. "Not a stationer. This girl knows Belethea like you know your face in the mirror. And besides, my mother has the team she wanted. Her hands have been long washed of Belethea. I really can't see her going through the trouble to send a girl like that here for any reason."

"I could see your mom sending you a replacement partner," Grady said coolly.

Foster's shoulders tensed at the barb, and he shouldered past him. "But she wasn't supposed to be *my* partner."

"Well, something's not right about her. And I'm sure we'll find out what it is soon," Grady called as he left the locker room.

Foster huffed out a long breath. If he didn't hurry, Grady or someone else would scare this girl off before he got his own answers. He rushed through his shower before pulling on a surprisingly grease-stain-free pair of cargo pants, a t-shirt, and his usual bomber jacket. He passed a hand through his brown hair, still wavy with the damp, and called it good enough. After all, if he tried too hard, someone was sure to notice.

He strolled back out into the main room, more crowded now with the finishing royalers and their families, and found that Hart was already at the med table. She wore a baggy, over-sized sweater over a pair of leggings and gray mag-trainers, her wet hair hanging just past her shoulders.

He chuckled to himself as he thought of Sylvia's inevitable reaction to her style choices. But at least no one recognized her as the mysterious Hart racer without her gear, so none of the vultures had descended on her yet.

She nodded as the trainer ran the laserstitch over her brow, knitting the skin back together with quick swipes. Another trainer rolled up her legging to assess her swollen knee. But her eyes scanned the room, crinkling into a smile when they alighted on him.

He pulled up a chair next to her and sat down. "So how bad is it?"

She shrugged her boxy shoulders. "Nothing to write home about."

"Oh, yes," the trainer interrupted. "Just a four-inch facial laceration, a second-degree concussion, and a hairline fracture of the patella."

"But you said you can fix it, ri—"

"There's the girl of the hour!" Sylvia said, sliding into the seat beside her, her goggs glowing red as she captured the moment. "Ezren Hart, are you ready to be the first and only new recruit of the season to sign on with the Belethea Race Royale Team?"

Foster's attention snagged on the name. *Ezren Hart.* So her name was Ezren.

Not waiting for an answer, Sylvia projected a wall of text toward her, the fine print of the contract scrolling by. Ezren's gaze darted to Foster, and a part of him wanted to throttle Sylvia for ambushing her so publicly.

"Well, um, I think I need to have my mom look over it and—"

"Of course!" Sylvia waved the words away with a smile. "It's just a formality, really, spelling out practice schedules, mandatory promos, and our academic reqs. But you're such a big fan; I'm sure you know all that already."

Foster rubbed a hand over his jaw. A fan? That's right, Sylvia had mentioned that'd been on her application. But Ezren hardly knew anything about the race royale. Had she said that to increase her chances of getting in?

"And showing up late!" Sylvia laughed ostentatiously for her VSoc audience. "I have to admit, you had me worried there for a second, but what a dramatic entrance that turned out to be. The fans loved it."

"Oh, suns." Ezren winced, looking like she was about to bolt at any second. "I'm *really* sorry about that. It's just the storm truck was weather-delayed... so we got in later than we—"

"And just where are you from again?" Sylvia leaned forward.

"I—"

"Stop!" Talmadge barked, stalking toward them from one of the back rooms. He pushed his goggs up onto his buzz cut head and flashed a huge triumphant grin. "I checked her VSoc references. This girl is not who she says she is."

The rest of the reporters in the room flocked to Talmadge

in a mad rush, and he made sure to look at each of them as he barreled closer, drinking in the attention. Foster leapt to his feet, getting between Ezren and the tension that rippled from Talmadge's rigid stance. He didn't know what was going on, but Talmadge rarely had anything good to say.

While the newer racers drew closer with wide eyes, the experienced royalers kept their distance. Once he got going, getting in Talmadge's way was like trying to stop an avalanche and would probably result in the same amount of pain. Meanwhile, Ezren's already pale complexion had gone nearly sheet white.

FOSTER: DON'T WORRY ABOUT HIM. HE'S JUST LOOKING FOR A LITTLE ATTENTION TO BANDAGE HIS BRUISED EGO. I'M SURE HE HAS NO IDEA WHAT HE'S TALKING ABOUT.

Still, the reporters revolved around him all the same. Talmadge might not have been as popular as Grady, but he'd been favored to win here—which made this drama irresistible.

EZREN: BUT HE'S RIGHT.

Foster whipped his head toward her and, sitting up a little taller now, she met his gaze with the smallest of nods. Doubt started to worm around in his stomach. No way. Had Grady been right? Had his mother sent this girl? Was this how she was trying to keep him racing? His whole body tightened at the thought, heat burning across his skin. And without thinking, he took a step away from her.

Talmadge holo-projected her tryout application to its maximum size—the picture and the words in a huge sphere nearly as tall as Foster.

The full-body holopro drew his attention immediately. It was definitely her... but it was what Sylvia would call a "fan face." Her skin had taken on a richer, healthier tone, the bags disappeared from her eyes, her mousy brown hair had been dyed in fiery tones of red and orange, and a sleek topsuit hugged her body, showing off her muscular physique. The angle of the holopro even made her look taller. Now, this looked like a royaler, born ready to take VSoc by storm. If the figure didn't have her name above it, he might not even have recognized her.

And that wasn't the only thing. Skimming her profile, her answers gushed with an enthusiasm and tone that didn't at all jive with the direct, unostentatious girl he'd raced with for the last few hours. So had she done this to try to get accepted?

"Those test scores," Talmadge announced, pointing to the nearly perfect numbers listed underneath her picture, "don't belong to the girl called Ezren Hart. She's faked the records."

Foster snorted. Test scores? Really? Everyone knew that was just a formality levied by the board of education to keep kids from dropping out of school to be royalers. But still, he let out a tense breath of relief. Something was going on here, but it didn't have anything to do with his mom. He glanced at Ezren, her eyes wide, and took a step forward. "Look, kin, do we really have to do this here in front of—"

"No, he's right." Ezren popped out of her chair. "And everyone deserves to know."

Foster ran a hand over his face. This girl really didn't know when to stay out of it.

"Those aren't my test scores, and that's not a real holopro of me."

"Disqualified!" Talmadge shouted, stabbing a finger in her direction as if he had any kind of authority to do that.

An audible gasp ran through the crowd, and Sylvia shot eye-daggers at Talmadge. Because, when it came down to it, this was a royale coach's dream, and Foster was 99% sure that Sylvia would take this girl even if she turned out to be an alien. If he had to guess, he'd bet Sylvia was sending her a flurry of messages saying as much at that very moment.

Ezren's hands twisted in her sweater sleeves, her gaze moving around the room. "You see, I wanted—"

"Step back, fritzer!" A girl with twin hot-pink buns and sea-green eyes elbowed to the front of the crowd with a strange, square-headed dog at her heels. "If you want to point fingers, I'm the one who fudged the application."

A small, middle-aged woman and a thin preteen boy who both looked a little like Ezren trailed the pink-bun girl, their faces creased with uncertainty—her mom and brother, maybe?

Ezren groaned even as a little smile eased her frown. "Oh, Micah..." Her mom crossed the room to put a comforting hand on her shoulder, and her brother stood beside her, his bright blue gaze combing the crowd while the stubby dog-thing sat at his heels.

The new girl, Micah apparently, marched right up to Talmadge and planted her fists on her ample hips. Although she was on the taller side, she had nothing on Talmadge's towering frame and had to crane her neck to stare up at him, her goggs glowing red as they recorded. "Those are my test scores, I modified the holo, and I sent in the application on Ezren's behalf because I knew she wouldn't." The girl crossed her arms over her low-cut shirt and turned to the reporters. "And you're welcome, by the way," she sniffed, her pink skirt, striped tights, and knee-high boots cutting a rather intimidating image. It was immediately obvious that if anyone could steal the stage from Talmadge here, it was this girl. "She's the best recruit Belethea has seen in years, and if you don't take her, you're absolutely out of your mind."

Ezren's cheeks glowed scarlet, and she buried her face in her hands while Talmadge's fists turned white-knuckled at his sides, his eyes practically bulging.

The ridiculous image was the last straw for Foster. Unable to hold it in anymore, he burst out laughing. The sound broke the icy layer of tension, and the media seized the moment, surging forward and shouting questions.

"I don't care if she's fodding superhuman. She's a liar, and she's ineligible!" Talmadge yelled over them. "She's scratched from the race."

Grady's smooth voice cut through the crowd. "Oh, stop your crying, T. You're just saying that because you're desperate to qualify."

The reporters swung around to where Grady stood with a cocky smile, his own hovercam hanging in the air above him. A vein pulsed in Talmadge's temple, and he stepped toward Grady, his chest puffing out. "This race was a shaft, and you know it. Why don't we have a bout right here and see who really deserves to go?"

In the midst of the clamor, Foster slipped over to where Sylvia stood chewing furiously on her lower lip. "She's the real deal, Syl."

"I get that, Foster, but she did cheat. People aren't going to like that," she hissed through her flexed jaw.

"And you'd prefer to have an asschaff like Talmadge on the team instead? He fodding hit us with his quad today. Is that really better than an embellished application?"

Grady and Talmadge drew closer to one another, and Sylvia's full lips twitched, the gears in her head almost visibly spinning. "But she's a novice. You think she's a better bet than Talmadge? Can we even train her in time?"

He glanced over to where Ezren swayed uncertainly on the edge of the crowd. Anxiety tightened her face as Micah prevented her from intervening in what was about to turn into a Talmadge-Grady smackdown. He couldn't believe he was about to say this. "Bring her on, and I'll train her."

Sylvia turned to him with a smug grin on her face. "Done."

Foster's brows knitted. Had he just been played?

Sylvia hopped up onto a table, her goggs recording again, and sliced through the noise with a shrill whistle. "Everyone just chill your chips!" The crowd paused, turning toward her. "I'm sure we can sort this out. What matters most is that Ezren Hart kicked some serious ass today, and if she's willing, we'll work through whatever chaffing paperwork we need to bring her on." She smiled at Ezren, protectively sandwiched between Micah and her family. "So what do you say to that, Ezren?"

Ezren took a deep breath and looked at her mom and Micah, silent chip messages obviously coursing between them. A bubble of hushed whispers rippled through the room, waiting for Ezren's answer. Even Foster's muscles tensed. If she said no, he would probably never see this girl again. And he was surprised to find, for whatever reason, that bothered him.

Then finally her gaze met his, and a message dinged into his goggs.

Ezren: What do you think? Should I do it?

If she'd been anyone else, he would've told her the truth. Would've told her what he had tried to tell himself. It's not worth it. Walk away. But this girl didn't seem to walk away from anything, and he definitely didn't want her to walk away from him.

He held her gaze.

Foster: Yes.

She swallowed and turned back to Sylvia. "If you want me, I'd be proud to race for Belethea."

CHAPTER 10

EZREN STOOD outside the wrought-iron gate to Belethea's race royale training campus, the busy street buzzing with auto-cabs behind her, and a darkening sky holo-projected on the dome above. A mass of people pushed through the sidewalk, jostling her to get past, and she edged closer to the gate. *Ugh.* She'd almost blissfully forgotten the crush of these big city bubbles. Well... as big a city as Belethea had to offer.

She took a deep breath, intensely regretting her life choices up to this point. Apparently, her performance at the tryout three days ago had caused a Virtual Society storm. Coach Sylvia and Micah kept telling her it was a good thing, but she really couldn't see how arriving late and then getting caught lying on her application could earn her any points.

Thinking back on it, she couldn't shake the guarded stares of the royalers—like she was something other. Like she had already betrayed them. Especially that guy, Lucian Talmadge. She shuddered. But then again, his resentment was under-standable. If she hadn't shown up, he would've qualified, and Sylvia had publicly chosen a new recruit over him.

Ezren cringed at the embarrassing confrontation and his resulting rejection. But he'd really brought that one on himself, hadn't he? Not that it mattered. Micah had said he'd already somehow managed to squirm his way onto a station team. Her stomach flopped. If he'd tried to run her over with the quad when she was a stranger, he'd definitely be out to get her now.

She sucked in a deep breath and let it out slowly, trying to cleanse her useless worries. The only reason she hadn't tucked tail and ran at the finish line had been Foster Sterling. He'd said she should come...and she had the strange feeling she could trust him. Not that he'd contacted her since.

Maybe she'd misread his message somehow. Was he being sarcastic or something? She thought about his hooded eyes meeting hers, the permanent frown line between his brows, and the pout of his lips. He'd definitely seemed serious. Maybe even too serious.

Then again, he hadn't even told her his first name. She'd had to pick it out from the barrage of the reporter's questions at the finish line.

But it was too late now. She'd signed the contract. The one that had promised her special tutoring to bring up her grades, the one where she agreed to maintain the image of a Belethean athlete or some such chaff, and most importantly, the one that promised a stipend of a whopping 1,500 creds a month—roughly three times her internship pay. And there had been talk of performance bonuses, fundraising opportunities, sponsorships, and more.

Money that they could put toward Sam's regen treatment, and a spotlight that she could use to raise money for Tuzuno's terraforming lab.

That's why she was here. Even if the other royalers hated her, even if she had to jump through their chaffing hoops, and study, and train till her limbs fell off. She would do it.

But she really hoped at least one person was on her side.

With a final deep breath, she sent a message to Sylvia.

Ezren: I think I'm outside.

No sooner had the message left her chip than Sylvia whipped open the gate with a wide smile. Her dark brown curls fanned out around her head while a long-sleeve dress flowed along her curves. "Ezren! It's so good to see you again. It was getting so late we were afraid you wouldn't make it." She pulled Ezren into a tight hug and looked around her. "Where's your luggage?"

"Uh, right here." Ezren shifted the oversized rucksack on her shoulders and then frowned at Sylvia's horrified expression. "I... um... don't exactly have a lot of stuff."

Sylvia's gaze raked over Ezren's baggy sweater and leggings before recovering her smile, though a little weaker than before. "Oh, that's all right. We'll get you some new things anyway." With another wave, she beckoned Ezren inside. "Welcome to the home of the Belethea race royalers."

Ezren took a step and stopped. She wasn't sure what she'd been expecting, but the squat four-story metal-and-glass building with an unadorned green yard definitely wasn't it. It looked like it could be an office building rather than an athletic training center. Micah had said Belethea was a small, low-ranked team, but with all the hype of the BRR, surely they had more space than this?

Sylvia turned, sensing her hesitation. "You okay?"

"Yeah, just, uh... is this the whole... campus?"

Sylvia offered a warm smile. "Ah, yeah, it's not much to look at, but good old Carmella Hall has everything you'll need to get into royale shape. It was built by Warner Calderon himself after the original Belethea race."

"Who?"

Sylvia's smile fell even as she barked out a dry laugh. "Are you really from here?"

Ezren's cheeks prickled with heat. "Sorry, history's not my best subject."

"Well, you know the race royale was based on the original terranium rush when it was first discovered here eighty years ago. Every space station, ship, and planet sent a team to stake a claim to its fortunes. Of course, there was no way around Belethea's churn belt back then, so they had to run, climb, drive, and fight through the storms to Belethea's equator. Warner Calderon won and later started the race royale to avoid all-out war. That's why the race is so important to international relations. The winning nation gets export rights to the terranium for the following year."

"Yeah, I guess that all sounds familiar," Ezren said as they walked into the foyer of the building, the information already leaking out of her other ear. Honestly, it sounded as boring as the first ten times she'd probably heard it, and she still thought the original racers had to have been completely insane to try to traverse Belethea's wicked cummerbund of nearly impenetrable storms.

Sylvia arched one of her rainbow eyebrows. "Which is why royalers are also considered to be junior ambassadors. Which is also why we'll be making sure you keep up your studies to show the world you really are worthy of being here."

Ezren cleared her throat, her itching hairline forewarning an outbreak of nervous sweat. "Right."

They seemed to be in some sort of open lounge with holo-projectors and couches littering the room, along with a few virtual gaming areas and holo-pool tables. But Sylvia didn't linger as she led her to the carpeted stairway in the corner.

"Anyways, this is where you'll spend most of your time. My office, the armory, and the training sims are on the second floor, the exercise rooms are on the third, and the bunks are on the fourth. I've just sent you your schedule, and if you have any questions, just let me know."

Ezren's goggs chirped with Sylvia's message, and she quickly scanned through the list of activities.

0530 *Lights On*
0600 *Morning Training—Physical*
0800 *Breakfast*
0900 *Science*
1000 *Math*
1100 *Coding*
1200 *Lunch*
1230 *Afternoon Training—Driving*
1400 *History*
1500 *Language*
1600 *Foreign Relations*
1700 *Evening Training—Sparring*
1900 *Dinner*
1930 *Virtual Society Maintenance*
2000 *Tutoring*
2100 *Personal Time*
2200 *Lights Out*

"We actually have a bedtime?"

"Beauty sleep is mandatory," Sylvia said with a smile.

"This is no joke." Ezren's mind stuck painfully on the 0530 lights-on time. "Is this every day?"

"There are only 270 days left until the BRR. Trust me when I tell you our schedule is gentle compared to some of the other teams."

Ezren scrubbed her sleeve across her forehead. Right. Although Sylvia had been nice enough not to say it, the unspoken words hung between them. Ezren had a long way to go to even have a chance of catching up with the others.

"Which reminds me, you'll also be on a strict diet here, prescribed for optimal physical enhancement."

"A diet?"

"No calorie restriction, of course," Sylvia assured her. "After your physical scan, we'll be able to measure your perfect blend of proteins, carbs, and fats. But we do prohibit sugar and caffeine while you're here."

Ezren muffled a horrified squeak with the sleeve of her sweater. She would have to ration the meager stash of contraband she brought with her until she found a way to smuggle more in. Seriously, when did they get to the good part of this deal?

They reached the fourth floor and walked down a quiet, carpeted hall dotted with doors before stopping at the second on the left. With a chirp from Sylvia's goggs, the door slid open. "And here you are."

Ezren's mouth dropped at the sheer amount of space. The room had a narrow bed, a desk, a small loveseat by the window, a dresser, a sink and mirror, a closet to one side, and there was still extra room on the plush carpet. "Wow."

Sylvia rested a hand on her hip with a grin. "Yeah, these rooms were meant to fit four royalers, so I guess a small team has its perks. Since it's already late, we'll have to do intros tomorrow. We'll meet at five till six on the front lawn. The lights cut out in ten minutes, so you'd best go ahead and get all your things sorted. I'm the room right across from you if you ever need anything."

Ezren nodded, the hugeness of this new life crashing into her. "Yeah, got it. Thanks."

"Okay, see ya tomorrow. So great to have you on the team." Still smiling, Sylvia wiggled her manicured fingers and the door slid shut.

Ezren slung her bag to the floor after the long day of storm trucks and magtrains and trying to find her way in a strange and crowded city. The room was oddly quiet. No Sam muttering in his sleep or Waffle snoring. No Mom puttering around the kitchen before crawling into bed late and stealing the covers.

She was alone.

Her eyes burning, she leaned against the door and scrolled through her messages for something familiar, steeling herself for the next day's overwhelming to-do list.

There was Mom's, of course.

MOM: DID YOU GET IN OKAY? LET ME KNOW YOU MADE IT. REMEMBER EVERYONE AT TUZUNO IS CHEERING FOR YOU!

EZREN: YEP! THIS PLACE IS HUGE! CAN'T WAIT TO GET STARTED TOMORROW.

So it was a total lie. But sometimes she had to tell her mom exactly what she wanted to hear. That morning, her family had beamed enormous, proud smiles when they'd packed her into the storm truck, and Ezren wanted those smiles to last as long as possible. The only alternative was to heap worry on her mom's already overflowing plate. Something Ezren absolutely would not do.

She slid down the door until she was sitting on the thick carpet with her knees to her chest. Too tired to do anything else, she opened Sam's message next.

SAM: HEY, YOU LEFT YOUR SPARE GOGGS HERE.

Ugh. Of course she had.

EZREN: ASDEF. I KNEW I FORGOT SOMETHING. MAYBE YOU CAN MAIL THEM MY WAY SOMETIME. ALSO, I SENT A NOTE TO DR. TANAKA TO ADJUST YOUR PAIN MEDS. DON'T LET MOM FORGET TO PICK UP THE NEW PRESCRIPTION TOMORROW.

And then there were a couple from Micah.

Micah: I'M SO JEALOUS. REMEMBER TO TAKE DETAILED NOTES. AND PICTURES. AND HOLOS. I WANT TO KNOW EVERYTHING. CAN I POST TODAY'S VIDS ON MY HOLOLOG?

Micah: OKAY, SORRY, BUT I COULDN'T WAIT. I POSTED IT ALREADY. FORGIVE ME?

Ezren: GOT IN LATE, BUT SURE, POST WHATEVER.

Micah's hololog had totally skyrocketed after her face-off at the tryout had gone viral, and Ezren was pretty sure Micah was more stoked about Ezren being here than she herself was. And even though it was late, Micah's response chirped immediately in Ezren's goggs.

Micah: EEE! SO CRISP! IN A LIVE CHAT NOW, BUT TOMORROW—MORE DETAILS.

Then, Ezren hovered over the one message chain she had been ignoring for the last two days. The three messages from Davis Banda. Even looking at them made her eyes sting a little more. But she couldn't avoid it forever. Especially not with him so close.

With a groan, she pulled her mag-trainers off and chucked them across the room toward the bed. At least there'd be no one to complain about her mess. Thank the suns for small favors. She looked up at the plain white ceiling, trying to find an excuse to procrastinate a few moments more. Finding none, she took a deep breath and opened the first message.

Davis: I CAN'T BELIEVE YOU DIDN'T TELL ME YOU WERE TRYING OUT FOR THE ROYALE TEAM. I SAW YOUR FACE ON VSOC NEWS AND NEARLY SPAT OUT MY COFFEE. AND IT WAS GOOD COFFEE! HOW DID THIS HAPPEN? SO YOU'RE MOVING TO THE CITY? WHY DIDN'T YOU TELL ME? THIS IS AWESOME! CONGRATS, EZ!

Davis: C'MON, EZ. YOU CAN'T LEAVE ME HANGING

LIKE THIS. NOW I HAVE TO STALK MICAH'S HOLOLOG FOR YOUR NEWS, AND THE BRR FANDOM IS JUST WAY TOO WEIRD FOR THAT. THEY'RE ALREADY FRITZING OUT OVER YOU. WHICH I GUESS IS EXPECTED. HONESTLY, I DON'T KNOW WHY I'M AT ALL SURPRISED. WITH ALL YOUR SURFACE TIME, OF COURSE YOU'D BE PERFECT FOR THE ROYALE. I GUESS I JUST NEVER THOUGHT IT WAS SOMETHING YOU WANTED. WHAT WAS THE TRYOUT LIKE? YOU KNOW, IF YOU'RE MOVING TO CARMELLA HALL, I'LL ONLY BE A FEW BLOCKS AWAY. I COULD SHOW YOU AROUND, AND WE COULD HANG OUT SOMETIME. IT'D BE CRISP. BUT YOU GOTTA ANSWER ME BACK FIRST!

DAVIS: OKAY, SO I THINK I GET THAT YOU'RE IGNORING ME, BUT SINCE I'M STILL STALKING MICAH'S HOLOLOG, I KNOW YOU LEFT FOR THE CITY TODAY. I WOULDN'T HAVE MESSAGED AGAIN, BUT YOU LOOKED A LITTLE SCARED IN THE VID. I DON'T REALLY KNOW WHY YOU'RE DOING THIS, BUT I KNOW IT HAS TO BE BIG TO GET YOU TO LEAVE TUZUNO. I JUST WANT YOU TO KNOW I'M HERE FOR YOU IF YOU NEED ME, EZ.

That last one almost did her in. The lights winked out around her, but it did nothing to mute her goggs' holopro, and the message glowed in front of her like a bright window in the dark. Of course, Davis would've seen right through her. But couldn't he also see these messages were a bad idea? It only hurt more this way. And yet, she still thought out a response.

EZREN: HEY, DAVEY. I MADE IT TO THE CITY, AND I'M FINE REALLY. IT'S JUST KIND OF A BIG THING. LOOKS LIKE THEY'RE GOING TO KEEP US BUSY HERE, BUT MAYBE WE'LL CATCH UP SOMETIME. AND I'LL BE SURE TO LET MICAH KNOW HOW MUCH YOU LOVE HER HOLOLOG.

She regarded it for a moment. No lies, no false promises, nothing too personal. Hopefully it would keep him from sending another one. She sent it and closed her eyes, the weight of the day falling over her. She was mentally preparing herself for the task of going through her bag in the dark when another message came in.

She quailed. *Not from Davis. Please not from Davis.* She opened her messages, and Foster Sterling's name popped up on her holo.

Foster: WHY AM I NOT SURPRISED YOU WERE LATE ON YOUR FIRST DAY?

A knot unraveled in Ezren's chest. At least she had some kind of friend here.

Ezren: I MAY HAVE GOTTEN A BIT LOST WANDERING THROUGH THE CITY.

Foster: YOU COULD'VE CALLED SOMEONE TO PICK YOU UP AT THE STATION.

Ezren sighed. She'd thought about that... but she really didn't want to inconvenience anyone and give them another reason to hate her.

Ezren: IT'S ALL BLIME. I MADE IT.

Foster: WELL, JUST DON'T BE LATE TO THE FIRST PRACTICE TOMORROW. I DON'T WANT TO HAVE TO COME POUNDING ON YOUR DOOR.

Ezren smiled.

Ezren: 0600 IS KIND OF ASKING A LOT, BUT I'LL DO MY BEST.

Foster: SEE YOU BRIGHT AND EARLY THEN.

With that message, Ezren let herself flop onto the floor, spreading her arms and legs out in the largest bedroom she'd ever been in. It wasn't home, it wasn't her lab, and she wasn't sure when she'd have dirt under her feet again.

But she wasn't completely alone. And that made all the difference.

CHAPTER 11

FOSTER CUT the shredded nanitelattice away from the arm of the topsuit and measured the hole. With the first day of training looming on the horizon, he should've been in his bunk, but his hands and mind wouldn't stay still. So he'd retreated to his little cave to make some repairs.

Which was apparently way too predictable. The click of Sylvia's heels echoed down the hall long before her mass of dark curls popped through the door.

"Couldn't sleep?"

Foster fixed her with a bored look. Sylvia fussed over him more than his own mom did, but he really wasn't in the mood for her mothering. Although he'd only known her for a year, he couldn't help but wonder if she considered him her special project or something.

He offered only a grunt, but she smiled anyway. She crossed the room and picked up a discarded oil rag, wiping at a stain on the counter.

"So I've noticed you've been ignoring my VSoc update messages."

He laid a length of nanitelattice over the hole, drawing the lines for the patch. "That's not unusual."

"Is it because of all the talk about Vieve? Or the rumors about you and the new girl?'"

He entered the patch code into the topsuit interface through the neurochip in his goggs. "Listen, Syl, you know I don't care what you post on VSoc or any of the other five hundred accounts you keep for us. All I ask is that you leave all the fan badgering where you find it."

She rolled her eyes. "Okay, you're not getting it. Yeah, we all know you're one of the most talented royalers we have; your mom is a Belethean household name, and you're easy on the eyes. You should be chaffing VSoc gold! But the way you present yourself..." She plucked at his holey t-shirt, wrinkling her nose at his baggy plaid pajama pants. "Sweetheart, we have *got* to work on your image."

"Isn't that your job?"

"I'm trying, Foster." She tossed the rag into the soiled bin. "I've painted you as an up-and-coming star, the brooding lone wolf, the betrayed son, the mourning boyfriend..."

He stopped, shoving down his irritation. "You were always good at spinning chaff."

"What else am I supposed to say?" Her face tightened, sharpening her tongue. "That you're lazy and you're shaft at working with others? That you're the son of a Belethea legend who abandoned us for another team? That your teammates blame you for Vieve's death?"

He flashed a false smile. "You mean they wouldn't go for that?"

"Ugh!" She reached out as if to strangle him. "I know you want to win! But this is part of the game, Foster. No fans—no sponsors. No sponsors—no money. No money—no chance."

He ran the software, and it beeped at him with an error. Shaft it. "Fine. I get it. What do you want me to do?"

"Are you going to ask Ezren Hart to be your partner?"

Sylvia watched him closely with a shrewd gaze. "She's fresh, motivated, likable... she could be a game-changer for you."

He scoffed. It's what they always said about the newest, hottest recruit. It's what they'd said about him. Still, his eyes stuck on the suit on the workbench. It was the smallest one they had, and he'd still have to mod it to her size. Though it was an older model, it was light-years better than the one she'd worn at the tryout. And honestly, he'd been looking forward to seeing what she could do in it.

But Sylvia was asking the question he'd been purposely pushing away. He scanned his code piecemeal to root out the snag. "She won't want to be partners with me."

"And what if she does?"

There it was. Syntax error. A clumsy mistake. He fixed it and ran the code again, the nanitelattice humming as it knitted itself into place. "And what if she does?" he parroted.

Sylvia watched as the edges of the fabric wove together. "Well, if you do, you need to play it carefully. I thought the application scandal would be a black mark for her... but her friend, Micah, is some kind of fan-whisperer and is trying to spin her into an underdog hero. She's talented, and I think the fans will take a shine to her." Sylvia smoothed her rainbow eyebrows with a manicured finger. "But she's new and she seems... I don't know... flighty? Like she's one word away from walking out the door."

Foster chuckled. "If she's going anywhere, she'll definitely be running."

Sylvia smacked his shoulder lightly. "I'm just saying... be careful with her. If you're her partner and she leaves or gets hurt or whatever—"

"Then they'll blame me like they always do. So what?"

"I'm just saying play it safe. Fabricated relationship drama only. I've been looking at the numbers, and I don't think the team could survive another scandal. Talmadge is still running his mouth to whoever will listen, and the sponsors we have left are... on edge."

He laughed dryly. "Honestly, Syl, I thought you knew me better than that. If you're worried about drama, talk to Grady." The nanitelattice finished its repair, and he ran another diagnostic on it. A green shimmer ran over the scales of the material. All clear. He shook out the suit and held it up. The patch was just barely visible, a thin outline amid all the others, like a spiderweb of fault lines.

"Is that for her?" Sylvia asked softly.

He shrugged and folded the topsuit, stashing it neatly on the shelf with the others. "Or anyone else."

Sylvia straightened with a sigh. "I guess all I'm saying is if she does choose you, don't shaft it up."

His right hand spasmed, and he squeezed it with his left, turning toward her. "Maybe we should just hope she chooses Grady instead." But even as he said it, something in him tightened. What if she *didn't* choose him?

A frown dug into the corner of Sylvia's mouth. "Hope isn't exactly something we have in huge supply here."

"But we have plenty of shaft-ups," Foster countered with a smile, kneading his hand.

With a shake of her head, Sylvia walked out the door, heels clicking. "Go to bed, Sterling."

Foster scanned the armory for any other loose ends that needed his attention. As always, his gaze stopped at the crumpled suit in the corner staring at him from the shadows. He exhaled, the fatigue finally settling heavy on his shoulders.

"Ah, fod it." With that, he turned and followed Sylvia out the door.

As it always did, morning training came way too chaffing early. Foster leaned against the smooth cement wall of

Carmella Hall in his teal and black Belethea warm-ups. The dark sky had lightened to navy, but the air still had a brisk chill that raised goosebumps underneath his jacket.

He scratched at his five o'clock shadow with a yawn, watching Grady and Bex stumble out of the sliding doors onto the short green lawn, bleary-eyed and grumbling.

But Ezren wasn't with them. Although he'd been half-joking about pounding on her door to make sure she was awake, maybe he should have. It was five until six now, and if Sylvia had been taking notes from the last coach, Ezren would already be forfeiting her free hours on Sunday.

FOSTER: HEY, ARE YOU COMING?

No answer.

Another minute ticked down, and he was about to run up to the fourth floor when the door slid open, and Ezren sprinted out. She looked almost identical to the last time he'd seen her. She wore the same oversized crimson sweater that hung down to her mid-thigh, and her legs nearly blurred in her black tights. But this time, she had her hair piled into a bun on top of her head.

The human whirlwind skidded to a stop only a few feet from where Foster stood, and she bent over for a minute to catch her breath. Foster checked his goggs—seventy-two seconds left.

"Cutting it a little close?" he asked.

She made eye contact and smiled before pulling a mock grimace. "There may have been a small skirmish with the snooze alarm."

Her gaze swept over Grady's raised eyebrow and Bex's flinty stare, and her smile fell. The fans may have forgiven her after the Micah-girl took the fall for the bogus application, but between that and the tryout fiasco, she hadn't earned any points here. It used to be that once you were a royaler, you had a spot for all three of your eligible years, and the new recruits were often friends and family from the junior circuits. Now, with a stranger among them, that veneer of safety had been stripped away.

The door opened again, and Sylvia walked out with a too-bright smile. "Good morning, everyone!" She strode over to Ezren and pulled a set of warm-ups from the massive purse on her shoulder. "Here ya go! Sorry I forgot to get them to you last night."

"Oh, thanks," Ezren said, accepting the bundle. "I was a little worried for a second I didn't get the memo."

She pulled the pants over her tights, the bottoms eclipsing her mag-trainers. Without any hint of surprise, she doubled and then tripled the waistband until they weren't a trip hazard. Then she yanked her sweater off and tossed it to the ground, revealing her small, muscular frame for just a moment before pulling the jacket over her tank top. Her hands disappeared in its long sleeves, but she didn't bother to cuff them up.

Foster considered the possibility that her usual oversized sweater was, in fact, a normal-sized sweater. Did all of her clothes swallow her that way?

He turned to Sylvia. "Don't they make smaller sizes?"

Sylvia cocked her head, frowning at the fashion disaster before her. "The extra-smalls were out of stock, but we'll be sure to tailor it."

Ezren's eyebrows rose, as if the size hadn't even occurred to her. "Oh, don't worry. It's really not a big deal."

Grady strolled toward them, his fist-sized hovercam now humming above his shoulder. Resisting the urge to intercept him, Foster watched as Grady offered his hand with a smooth grin. "Hey, glad to see you made it. I know we had a rough start in the tryout, so I just wanted to introduce myself. I'm Simon Grady, your almost partner."

Foster's fists tightened at his sides, the sharp realization sinking in. He hadn't been the only one Sylvia had talked to yesterday. Ezren was strong, and she was VSoc's flavor of the week. Grady leeched off fan approval, and he consulted with Sylvia on VSoc strategy ad nauseam. There was no doubt she'd given him some version of the same speech he'd gotten last night. Ezren Hart was a smart move.

But Ezren didn't know that.

"Oh... uh, hi." Ezren pulled up her sleeve to shake his hand with a small bow. "I'm Ezren Hart from Tuzuno outpost."

"That's out in the rocks, right? Petraskis must seem like a pretty big step up. Are you loving it?"

"It's, uh... different."

"Sure is." His smile widened. "After a few days of civilization, you'll never wanna go back."

Sylvia clapped her hands together. "Now that we're all here, we might as well get started." Her gaze jumped between the four of them like she wasn't sure where to look. "I know it's really weird with just the five of us, but on the upside, it means we're going to get to spend more time together. I know the BRR qualifier seems far off, but nine months will go by faster than you think, and the pre-season exhibition is only ten weeks away. So it's going to go fast."

Ezren blinked, her brow wrinkling. "But we can qualify both teams, right?"

Bex rolled her eyes at the question, and Foster shot her a look. This was actually an improvement on Ezren's BRR knowledge from the tryout. It sounded like she'd at least been trying to read up on it, and in fairness, he wasn't sure Belethea had ever had two qualifying teams.

Sylvia brightened at the softball question. "Yes! You just have to come in the top fifty. And it'll be our last chance to nab sponsors and size up the competition before the final."

"*If* we get to the final," Bex grumbled under her breath.

"What about doubles?" Grady asked. "Are they going to be assigned like last year?" Grady winked at Ezren, and Foster's shoulders tightened.

Sylvia looked away, her lips flattening. "While I think doubles work best together when chosen by the athletes themselves, Harland has reserved the right to intervene for the good of the team."

Foster frowned, wondering what constituted *the good of the team*. Maybe that's why Sylvia had given them the "no drama" speech.

"But I'd prefer that no one pairs up before you all get to know each other, so we'll be delaying doubles announcements for at least a week. However..." She flashed a cheeky grin. "Feel free to spread whatever rumors you want on your VSoc."

"Hype is always good for business," Grady explained to Ezren with another smile that made Foster want to punch him in the face.

Sylvia tapped her cheek thoughtfully. "I think that's it." Her gaze scanned each of them. "Everyone good?"

Bex's blank expression hadn't wavered through this speech, and Ezren fidgeted with her sleeves, looking more like a lost puppy than ever.

But Sylvia plowed on. "Great!" Fishing a hovercam from her purse, she tossed it into the air, and its small red eye blinked on. "Well then, in true royaler fashion, let's start off the day with a good long run. Let's see who can clock in the most miles before breakfast, shall we?"

As if finally released from detainment, Bex ran off to the small path that circled the building. The drone tailed Bex while Ezren watched it with a skeptical grimace. Grady hesitated as if to wait for her but couldn't resist the pull of competition running away without him.

Apparently getting the hint, Ezren slowly jogged after him in her huge warm-ups, and Foster loped to her side. "Are you okay? I thought you'd be sprinting off with Bex."

Ezren craned her neck as though to look around the building. "Is there a hatch to the surface around back or something? It looks like conditions are pretty decent today."

"Nah, we run the quarter-mile track around the campus."

"And we never run outside?" she asked, eyes wide with horror.

He chuckled. "Um... no. There's not exactly time in the schedule for a field trip." Her shoulders caved in just a little, and he searched for some kind of positive spin he could put on it that wouldn't feel like a lie. He came up empty. "I guess that's not what you're used to?"

They turned the corner onto the rubber track, and she eyed the twelve-foot stone wall on her left. "I lived on Obrone until I was fourteen, so I miss the horizon."

Ah... so that explained at least some of her strength. The gravity on Obrone was 0.35 G higher than on Belethea—it made Obronian bones denser and their muscles stronger. "Trying to get back to Obrone one day?"

She shook her head fervently, picking up speed. "No, I love Belethea." She gave him a rueful smile. "I just love it a little more when I'm actually *on* it instead of in a bubble. But, one day, when the terraforming is done, we'll be able to run as far as we like." Her face glowed with hope, like she was trying to convince herself.

But with the amount of terranium Belethea needed to power their atmospheric regulators, that could be a long time coming. The thought brought a sudden realization that clicked into place like a missing piece. "Ah, so that's why you're doing this. So Belethea can use the terranium prize for terraforming."

He chuckled through his rough breaths. "Well, aren't you the optimist?"

"Maybe it won't happen." She widened her stride even as they rounded the sharp curve. "But I do know I don't want to give up until it does."

She was full-on running now, her face set with determination as they passed Simon and Bex. The projection of the rising sun bathed her face in yellow and red.

Sylvia's words echoed in his mind. *She could be a game-changer.*

And a seed of panic bloomed in his chest. Because he knew at that moment, without a doubt.

He was totally going to shaft this up.

CHAPTER 12

EZREN DRAGGED herself into Sylvia's VSoc consultation at the end of her first day, wondering what new variation of torturous humiliation she had in store for her. Between the tutors asking her questions with words and equations she'd never heard of, a driving sim she'd failed eleven consecutive times, and a sparring class that left her bruised and aching, she half-expected Sylvia to tear up her contract and show her the door.

Still, if she was planning on throwing her out, she certainly looked peaceful about it behind her tiny synwood desk in her houseplant-covered office. "How was your first day?"

Too tired to lie, Ezren crumpled into the chair and laid her forehead on her desk with a groan, her temples throbbing from caffeine withdrawal.

Sylvia laughed with a honking bray that Ezren couldn't help but chuckle along with.

"Well, at least you're honest. But don't worry too much; most of our new recruits feel like that the first week."

"So it gets better after the first week?" Ezren asked, her head popping up.

Sylvia wrinkled her nose apologetically. "Not really."

Ezren's head sank back onto the desk with a *thunk*. "Oh."

"So, during this time," Sylvia continued, her upbeat tone unaffected by the invisible storm cloud hanging over Ezren, "you and I will go over how your image is doing and what you would like to do with it."

Ezren let out another groan.

"Here." Sylvia flicked the holopro up to maximum height. "These are the accounts we've set up in your name." Ten different spheres swirled with words and pictures and gifs and vids—an amount of content Ezren couldn't even begin to understand. "Despite Lucian's persistent whining, we've done quite a bit of damage control on the whole falsified application front, we've amassed a decent follower size in the tens of thousands, and the fans have really responded to the dark horse image." She smiled up at the holopro like a proud mother of a newborn. "You'll have to thank your friend, Micah, for us too; she's been tremendously helpful with that."

Ezren's lips twitched in a smile. Thank the suns for Micah, but she was having way too much fun with this. "So what do we do now?"

Sylvia leaned forward in her chair and laced her fingers together, her long nails glinting in ten shades of blue. "Now, we talk about what you want to say, what you want people to know, and what kind of image you want to project. And then I take that info and spin it into something marketable. Think of it as me getting to know you and showing the fans your best side."

"Right, well, I'd really like to promote Belethea's terraforming efforts." She tugged her sleeves over her hands. "If that's okay, I mean." Doubt crawled through her. That was what she wanted to say, but who would listen? The fans were looking for some brilliant, glamorous wunderkind to represent Belethea... not a lab rat nobody from the rocks. All she could do was run, and with all those cams, it wouldn't take any time at all before they figured that out.

"No problem. That'll fit right into the quaint country outposter angle." Sylvia's lips pursed as she swiped through the holo spheres. "Oh, also, since your app photo was altered, we're using an image captured from the tryout."

With a flick of her hand, an image of Ezren and Foster sailing through the teal sky on the terrasail popped up on the holopro. Ezren's mouth dropped open. The photo had captured them from afar with the massive navy funnel clouds churning behind them, making their dark figures look fragile and desperate and... well, rather miraculous.

"But I'll be scheduling a smoothing appointment before the exhibition so we can get some close-ups. Oh, and before you ask about the dating rumors, we're playing it coy at the moment until the doubles announcements."

Ezren squinted at the holo, trying to keep the alarm from her voice. "Dating rumors?"

"They're mostly between you and Foster, understandably, but after we released the holos of you and Simon together from this morning, they've started to shift."

Ezren's throat tightened. They'd already released holos from this morning? She thought of Simon Grady's hand lingering in hers, his smooth wink when Sylvia had mentioned doubles, and she blushed. With his sharp cheekbones and full lips, there was no doubting he was incredibly handsome, but his words and gestures always seemed angled for the hover-cams, rather than the people in front of him.

Still, what would Davis think of those holos? Her heart squeezed, and she wanted to slap herself for the stupid reaction. Davis probably didn't care. He hadn't responded to her message yesterday, after all. "So what happens when doubles are announced?"

Sylvia's smile broadened, showing off her gleaming white teeth. "Well, that depends on you. Usually, we switch to a more focused narrative, but there are several that have been shown to be effective. The 'I swear we're just friends, wink.' The 'constantly on the rocks, but determined to get through this,' and the 'we're passionately in love and can't keep our hands off each other.' " She started ticking them off on her fingers. "Hate to lovers, friends to lovers, secret lovers, power couple... or we can always get creative."

"Oh." Ezren's cheeks heated in preemptive embarrassment, the warmth crawling down her neck. It looked like her mess of a personal life was going to be on display no matter what option she chose. "So do the doubles actually date, then?"

"Sometimes, but most teams actively discourage it. Doubles seem to work better without the emotional baggage. Even so, everyone puts on a show, of course."

"That seems kind of weird."

"That's what sells."

"Right." Ezren rubbed her forehead where her headache pulsed, as if trying to break out of her skull. "And what are we selling, again, exactly?"

Sylvia laughed. "We're selling you, love."

Ezren's hands dropped into her lap, the blood draining from her face. "M-me?"

Sylvia gestured as if she were painting the headlines in the air. "Fresh-faced and motivated, Ezren Hart—top recruit and best hope for the Belethea Race Royale team."

"Ah," Ezren mumbled. And she didn't know if she felt relieved or sickened.

Because that wasn't really her at all.

Ezren nearly ran to her room when the last tutor finally released her. The door hissed shut, and she let herself collapse onto her expansive floor. What in Casolla had she gotten herself into? She had an hour left before the lights went out, and she wasn't even sure what to do with her blessed freedom. Honestly, she probably wouldn't even have time to decompress in an hour. Above all, she really just wanted to go back to Tuzuno, slip into her bulky old topsuit, and race the storms. But that was a useless dream.

She thought she'd been busy before, but it had been a comfortable busy. A choice. Juggling a few balls she was familiar with. This was a new kind of busy. Aggressive, violent, and totally vindictive. Like someone had suddenly thrown a pair of chainsaws into her carefully crafted routine.

She checked her messages again, the ones from Sam and her mom sending a pang through her. Sam had even sent her a holo of Waffle diving happily in the pool during his new swim therapy, her four short legs pulling her plump body through the water. Ezren had answered most of the messages at lunch and dinner, but Micah had already sent her a fresh slew of questions and updates she couldn't handle right now. And then there was the one from Davis. Already numb from the disappointment of the day, she opened it without pause.

DAVIS: WOW, THAT'S REALLY CRISP, EZ. SERIOUSLY, I'M SO PROUD OF YOU FOR TAKING THE LEAP. HONESTLY, IT'S PRETTY AWESOME KNOWING WE'RE SO MUCH CLOSER. I KNOW YOU'RE BIG-TIME NOW, BUT I'VE ALSO HEARD THE TEAM GETS SUNDAYS OFF. IF YOU WANT TO GET OUT OF THERE, I CAN COME PICK YOU UP AT AROUND 0900. (I KNOW HOW YOU LIKE TO SLEEP IN.)

Ugh. It was only Monday, and she did totally want to get out of here, but while she'd love to see a familiar smiling face, she still didn't want his.

EZREN: THANKS, DAVEY, BUT LOOKS LIKE I'M ALREADY BOOKED. HOPE YOU'RE HAVING FUN BACK AT SCHOOL.

Read between the lines.

She tensed as her goggs chirped with his response. *Ugh.*

DAVIS: OKAY, I GET IT, BUT AT LEAST LET ME DROP SOMETHING OFF FOR YOU.

Drumming her hands on her stomach, she tried to stay strong. *Don't bite, don't bite, don't bite.* But she only lasted twenty seconds before curiosity got the better of her.

EZREN: WHAT IS IT?

DAVIS: IF YOU WANT TO FIND OUT YOU'LL HAVE TO MEET ME AT THE CARMELLA GATE AT 0900.

EZREN: YOU'RE SINISTER.

DAVIS: You LIKE IT.

Ezren groaned and rolled onto her stomach. That had gone entirely wrong. She was supposed to be firmly pushing him away, and now it sounded like they were flirting again.

Her goggs dinged, and Ezren squeezed her eyes shut, willing herself not to make things worse. But when she opened them, it was Foster's name in her messages.

FOSTER: DID YOU SURVIVE YOUR FIRST DAY?

EZREN: THE CLASSES ARE OVER MY HEAD, THE DRIVING SIM IS IMPOSSIBLE, A HALF-SQUISHED SHIPROACH COULD PROBABLY BEAT ME IN THE DOJO... AND SYLVIA SAYS SHE'S SELLING ME... SO I'M A LITTLE SCARED.

FOSTER: CAN'T BLAME YOU THERE. SYLVIA IS SECRETLY TERRIFYING... DID SHE MENTION ANYTHING ABOUT CHOOSING A DOUBLES PARTNER?

Ezren's heart sped up just a little, her mouth suddenly dry. Which didn't make any kind of logical sense. She only had two options for her doubles partner: Simon or Foster. And she really didn't need a week to know which of those two she'd pick if she had the choice. The only question was... would he settle for her? Not feeling brave enough to answer that question, she opted with something as vague as possible.

EZREN: YEP.

Foster: Do you think I might be in the running?

Ezren's pulse ratcheted up another notch. Well... apparently he was a lot braver than her. Or maybe he just didn't care about all the fake dating stuff. He was probably used to it by now anyway.

Ezren: Yep.

Three hollow knocks rang from the door, and Ezren stood to open it. The metal door retracted with a hiss to reveal Foster Sterling leaning against the door jamb, a battered bomber jacket thrown over a pair of sweats.

"Then we should probably talk."

"Oh... okay." Ezren retreated until her back reached the far wall of the tiny room, which had felt large just a second ago. This was where she got the easy letdown. Well, at least he'd come in person to give her the bad news. That was a decent thing to do... even though she would've preferred he rejected her with a chip message, so she didn't have to school the disappointment from her expression.

Foster ran a hand through his short brown waves. "How much do you know about me?"

"Um... not a whole lot, I guess."

He snorted. "Right. You said you weren't really into the royale." He stepped in, and the door slid closed behind him. "Well, I'm sure you'll find out soon, so I wanted to be the first to tell you. My last doubles partner was Genevieve Navarro."

Ezren's lips twisted at the familiar name. "The girl who died in the qualifier?"

Foster nodded, one finger drawing patterns in the dust on her desk. "A whip squall dropped out of nowhere, and we were separated in a scrap with Talmadge and Bex. When the storm let up, Vieve's helmet had been knocked off, and her head had been crushed by debris." He told the story mechanically, as though he'd repeated it a hundred times.

Ezren's jaw swung open with a wince, the shocking image sending a shudder through her. "Her helmet came off? In the scrap or in the storm? I thought the topsuits were designed to knit together into one piece."

"They are." His long finger continued its circuitous path through the dust. "But for some reason, her suit malfunctioned. We don't really know what happened, but it didn't even send out a distress call."

Ezren rubbed her palm across her forehead. She remembered Micah telling her about the royale qualifier accident, but they weren't all that uncommon. They lost a few royalers to Belethea's unpredictable storms every year. It was an inherently dangerous sport. It was also one of the reasons why people were so addicted to it. Still, she couldn't imagine something like that happening to a friend—much less someone you loved. Couldn't imagine a storm lifting and finding Davis's body there. Her eyes threatened to well at the very thought.

She blew out a slow breath, trying to find the right words for such a horrific loss. "I'm sorry that happened," she whispered, "to her and to you."

Foster looked at her then, his head slightly cocked, and his brow drawn low, as if trying to figure her out. "I wanted you to know why I might not be the best choice for you."

Ezren didn't really know what to say to that. She knew the kind of invisible wounds survivor's guilt could leave... and despite Foster's stoic recount, she imagined his were far from healed. "But that wasn't your fault."

"Maybe. Maybe not." Though his tone was casual, Foster's expression could've been cut from stone. "It's hard to know what could've happened if I'd stuck closer."

The heavy words sank into the empty space between them, and a part of Ezren wished she could reach out and hug him. If she'd known him better, she would have. "Well, I don't know about that, but... thanks for telling me."

His shoulders fell ever so slightly—from disappointment or relief, she couldn't tell. He nodded and turned to the door.

"I don't really think that'll affect my decision though," she rushed out, taking another step forward.

He turned back, a hint of a smile hiding in the corner of his mouth. "I know Sylvia had to warn you I'm not the popular one. Grady's strong, motivated, and a sponsor favorite. He would be the better pick."

"Not for me." She paused and her cheeks warmed, her gaze darting to the floor. "If I have a choice, I mean."

Foster's smile widened just a touch. "Well, okay then." A shaky relief shot through Ezren, stretching a grin across her face as he held out a hand. "Here's to team Hart/Sterling."

She took it, her hand sliding over his warm, smooth palm, her fingers barely able to squeeze around it. "I like Sterling/Hart better."

"It does have a ring to it." He slipped his hand from hers and opened the door. "Don't be late to training tomorrow."

Ezren tangled her fingers in her long sleeves as he walked down the hall. "Hey, Foster?"

He turned around, walking backward with his hands in his pockets. "Yeah?"

"Thank you."

He waved her off. "Go to sleep, Ezren."

She smiled as he walked away... until her mind flicked to Sylvia's talk about dating, and a kind of panic slid through her. Secret lovers. Friends to lovers. Hate to lovers. Lovers. Lovers. Lovers.

Suns. Had she just picked a doubles partner? Or a boyfriend?

CHAPTER 13

FOSTER KNOCKED on Ezren's door at 0545, just as he had every day for the last two months.

"Okay, I'm up," she called through the door.

And just like every day before, he could tell by her scratchy voice that she hadn't been up at all. She really wasn't a morning person. But at least she was quick. She must've slept in her warmups because it only took her five minutes to emerge, still rubbing the sleep from her eyes.

But this time, he had to do a double take, because this girl looked totally unlike the Ezren who had tumbled out the door the day before. The light acne that had dotted her forehead had disappeared overnight, her hair now sported bright highlights of magenta and tangerine, and he could've sworn even her eyelashes looked longer.

He cleared his throat. "I guess Sylvia finally got her smoothing session in last night."

Ezren stifled a yawn and nodded, turning down the corridor. "Do I look presentable now?"

He stole another glance at her rumpled clothes as she knotted her usual high bun and snapped her goggs into place. Her near-black eyes were the same, but the dark bags underneath them had somehow vanished. Her slightly crooked front tooth had been straightened and the coffee stains wiped to a snowy white.

It was still Ezren, she just looked... healthier. Like the best version of herself. He'd gone through the same thing when he joined the team, but it was still a disorienting transformation.

"I guess it depends on who you're presenting to."

She punched his arm ever so lightly, and he flashed a smile. Then, together, they walked the rest of the way to the training yard in a comfortable silence. As usual, Bex and Grady already stood in the fake sunshine, stretching and muttering to each other.

Sylvia sat in a chair in front of Carmella's double glass doors with her holopro at full scale and glanced up at them distractedly. "Oh, good. Now that we're all here, I wanted to start something new. Since you've all had time to adjust to your new schedules, we're going to start weekly competitions to add a little motivation to our training sessions."

Foster crossed his arms, unease tightening in his chest. "Why the change?"

"Well, the fans love a little inter-team competition and..." Sylvia paused, digging a few hovercams out from the purse beside her. "Harland wants more quantifiable stats."

With a swipe of her hand, Sylvia projected their individual rankings in front of her.

1. *Bex Gunderson*

2. *Simon Grady*

3. *Foster Sterling*

4. *Ezren Hart*

Based on how the training sessions had been going, Foster was sure none of them were terribly surprised at the standings, but Ezren went pale beside him. Foster's jaw clenched. Was this really necessary? He thought back to what Sylvia had said about changing doubles for "the good of the team," and he wondered if they would use this to justify their intervention. At least with the current rankings, the teams seemed to be in the correct order. But the thought still put his teeth on edge.

As if sensing his train of thought, Ezren edged just a little closer to him. He wanted to reach out and squeeze her hand but stopped himself. The last thing he wanted to do was weird her out. Especially after he'd seen that guy drop off a box for her almost every Sunday. And the last time it happened, she'd even hugged him.

One of the hovercams blinked on, and Sylvia let it whir into the air before continuing. "The winner each week gets their entire Sunday off, while the last two spend their Sunday doing extra drills."

Grady whispered something to Bex, and Ezren looked at her shoes. Was she worried? She still had a ways to catch up with her brawling, but her driving was surprisingly decent, and he was confident she could beat Grady and Bex in a racing challenge. He nudged her with his shoulder, and she grimaced up at him.

"I thought you liked doing drills," he whispered.

She elbowed him back. "I've already had to get extra tutoring the last three Sundays. At this rate, they're not going to let me out of here until the first exhibition."

"Today, the challenge is a race," Sylvia called. "Except this time, just like in the BRR, there are no holds barred."

Foster swore inwardly. He'd hoped they would have at least another few weeks before a competitive scrap. Ezren was improving, but she was no match for Grady, and especially not Bex.

"What's she mean by 'no holds barred'?" Ezren whispered.

"It means we're going to beat the chaff out of each other to get to the finish." He leaned closer to her ear. "What would you say if I recommended we just concede last place on this one and try again next time?"

Her eyes hardened. "No way. I need to get out of this place for a day."

Grady's voice cut through their murmurs. "What's the drill?"

"On Carmella's roof, you'll find three flags with numbers on them. The royaler who brings me the flag with the lowest number gets the most points." Sylvia stood from her chair, and a stopwatch flashed onto her huge holopro. "Without further ado, get ready." She tossed two more hovercams into the air, where they buzzed like metal hummingbirds. "And go."

Ezren took off before he could get in another word, her tights swishing in a teal blur. Foster swallowed a swear as he chased after her. She barreled in through the doors and up through the stairwell. At least one person followed behind them, but not too closely.

"Ezren." Taking the stairs three at a time, his arms pumped through the air as he and Ezren sprinted up the four stories. "We need to be smart about this."

But she didn't respond until they burst onto the garden roof, the fake blue sky shimmering above them. "There." She reached and snatched the red flag with the one on it nestled in one of the many colorful potted plants. An orange flag had a two in the far corner, and a yellow with a three stood in the other.

"No, grab the orange one!" he nearly shouted.

"What, why?"

"Just trust me, Ezren. You're not going to finish with the red flag. We just want to be not-last."

"So you're not trying to win?" She shook her head. "You take the orange one. I want to try."

"If we don't—"

But she'd already vaulted over the side of the building, just before something slammed into his back.

Grady's fist connected with his jaw in an explosion of pain. "You know, you'd rank higher if you actually tried for once, Sterling." With that, he grabbed the orange flag, and he too went over the side.

Fodding suns. Pain lancing through his face and back, Foster rolled to his feet and snagged the yellow flag. He had to reach Ezren. Springing over the roof railing, he turned off his mag-trainers and easily picked his way down in Belethea's low G. He landed just in time to see Bex tackle Ezren, taking them to the ground.

Bex's fist smashed into Ezren's face, one, two, three times—Ezren's nose crunching and blood streaming from her mouth while Bex seized the flag from her limp grip. Foster ran over, and grabbing Bex around the middle, pulled her off Ezren. Bex elbowed him in the gut, loosening his grip enough to turn toward the finish. But Ezren, face bleeding, didn't know when to quit. She barreled headfirst into Bex, snatching the flag back... and making the absolute worst move because she obviously couldn't help herself. Sylvia fled her seat as they rolled toward her, and sensing a weapon, Bex grabbed the heavy chair and whipped it down on Ezren's body.

With a sickening wet crack, Ezren's chest seemed to crumple under the metal, stealing the air from her lungs and leaving a scream frozen on her contorted face. Bex's cold gaze flicked to the flag, but Ezren's fist had only tightened reflexively around it.

Foster tensed with realization, and he whipped out a hand. "Bex, don't—"

Bex brought her heavy gravboot down on Ezren's hand with another gruesome snap. This time, Ezren managed to scrape up enough air to scream.

With quick fingers, Bex snapped up the flag from the bloody mess of Ezren's mangled hand and crossed the holopro line where Sylvia and Grady waited.

The race was over.

Foster ran across the grass, sliding to her side on the lawn. He scanned her crushed chest, and the fingers no longer bending in the right direction. "Ezren, hang in there. We're going to get you help."

Ezren bit down on another scream, eyes screwed shut and tears leaking down her cheeks while her breath escaped in erratic gasps. Still, she tried to whimper out something he couldn't decipher.

Sylvia rushed to her side, but Grady barked out a dry laugh. "Welcome to your first scrap, sweetheart."

Furious black edging his vision, Foster rose to his feet and stalked toward the expressionless Bex. "What the chaff, Bex? She was such a threat you had to use a fodding chair to drop her?"

Grady stopped him with a warning hand to his chest. "Back off, Sterling. It was no holds barred. Bex didn't break any rules."

"It's called a royale for a reason." Bex shrugged. "If she can't take it, she should leave now, before she really gets hurt."

Coming from anyone else, the words might've been a threat. But from Bex, they were just facts. There was no use being mad at her. So Foster turned to Sylvia instead. "Seriously, *Coach*, is this the kind of training we're doing now? She wasn't even wearing a topsuit."

Sylvia ignored him, pulling up Ezren's shirt to expose the purple already blooming over her ribcage. Her goggs shone a light along her body and chirped. "A few broken ribs, and a collapsed lung. Simon, can you get one of the airstretchers?" Ezren had stopped screaming now, but she let out a soft whine, her eyes still shut tight and breath rasping out in a wheeze. Sylvia touched her shoulder with a light hand. "You'll need a day or two in the med tank, but you'll be just fine." She came to her feet and lifted her chin. "Look, Foster, I know you're upset. But part of the royale is learning how to deal with pain."

Bex nodded at her with an air of approval in her squared shoulders.

"Wow. What a hero, Syl. I'm so glad you're looking out for us," Foster said.

Returning with an airstretcher hovering at his waist, Grady let out another dry laugh. "Oh, that's rich. Foster Sterling is worried about watching out for a teammate."

His words were a bucket of ice water, dousing Foster's temper in a moment. He opened his mouth to say something but closed it when Grady pressed the button for the stretcher to lower to the ground.

Ezren's eyes opened to puffy red slits, her cheeks wet with tears. "S-s-sorry."

"Don't worry," Sylvia said with a warm smile, the hover-cams circling them. "It was a great showing for your first real scrap, and we'll get you fixed up in no time."

Ezren's body trembled with shock as she found Foster's gaze. "Sh-sh-should've l-l-listened."

"It's fine. We'll get it next time." With gentle, smooth movements, he lifted her onto the stretcher. "I promise."

Ezren nodded as the stretcher rose in the air once more, her stare not leaving Foster's. "N-n-not... l-l-last."

"Just for starters." And strangely, he meant it. They could be better than that. They *would* be better than that. For her? For himself? For Vieve?

He wasn't sure.

CHAPTER 14

EZREN LAY on her narrow bunk dreading the Sunday of drills that lay before her, but simultaneously wondering if it was a better deal than spending the day buried in never-ending schoolwork. Then again, at least the essays and presentations didn't leave her in the med tank for two days. She flexed her hand. Even though it was good as new, she still winced as she remembered the snap of her bones—the overwhelming pain that had nearly short-circuited her senses.

Then she was hearing Sammy screaming all over again. His broken body. The blood. The bodies in the street. She sucked in a sharp breath. *No, don't go back there. You're safe. Sammy's safe. Mom's safe. Dad's—* She pulled in another breath. *I'm here on Belethea, in Carmella hall, and everything is fine.*

She ran a hand along her mended ribs, thinking of Bex's arctic expression before she'd smashed the chair down. Like Ezren didn't belong there. Like she was just another obstacle to be removed. Yeah, Ezren definitely knew to stay out of her way now.

And if a *teammate* had done that to her without batting an eyelash, what would an opposing royaler do? Especially one with a grudge.

Lucian Talmadge's furious scowl flashed through her mind,

and she clutched her hand into a fist. If she didn't get better at this stuff, he was going to tear her apart. But what more could she do?

She sat up, stretching her aching body still sore from the week of relentless sparring and sims. While she enjoyed the physical activity, the constant state of being behind made her head feel like it was going to implode. There was always something she should be doing. Books she should be reading, tests she should be studying for, driving sim hours that needed to be logged. With Sylvia and Harland checking her status every day, the pressure weighed on her heavier than her old topsuit, her place in last confirmed once again by a dismal jetbike sim.

She sighed and went through her messages again, lingering on the latest from her mom.

Mom: Just wanted to tell you not to worry, but Sam developed some minor necrosis in his left foot. Luckily we caught it in the early stages, so Dr. Tanaka's starting him on a new cell homogenization treatment, and his pain management plan's been adjusted. I know you're working hard up there, but I want you to know what a huge difference you're making to your brother. With all the extra money you're bringing in, we should be able to save up enough for Sam's surgery in the next three years! And Dr. Lutz wants you to know that you should absolutely not be spending your time on Tuzuno, but he used the donations you gathered to replace the cracked helmet. We're all so proud of you, baby, and can't wait to see you race again!

Then there was a follow-up from Sam.

Sam: No matter what mom says, don't worry, I'm totally fine. You getting into the Race Royale is the coolest thing that has ever happened to us, so

DON'T FRITZ IT UP! ALSO, DO YOU THINK YOU COULD SEND HOME SOME AUTOGRAPHED SWAG? EVERYONE IS ASKING.

Tears pricked her eyes with a mix of emotions. Necrosis was a common side effect of poorly aligned cell regen, but it still ached that she hadn't been there to help. Still, there was always the possibility of more serious complications that would be a lot harder to fix. The faster they could get Sam's surgery, the better.

Could she do more?

Her lips twisted as she thought about it. There were significant performance bonuses in the contract, but at this rate, they seemed hopelessly out of reach. Despite Micah's constant flood of optimism, Ezren's daily training struggle only drove home the reality that she'd probably never even *qualify* for the BRR, and her meager VSoc attempts to promote Belethea terraforming had so far gone largely ignored. Still, at least she'd made a small difference for the ones she loved the most. That made it all worth it.

And Sam thought she was cool. Which would probably never happen again.

A quiet knock on the door turned her head. That was weird —the lights had gone off twenty minutes ago. She double-checked the time in her goggs. Yep, it was 2232. Whoever was at her door was risking some serious Sylvia ire from across the hall.

She padded to the door and used her chip to open it. Foster Sterling silently stepped inside with two packs slung over his shoulder.

Ezren cocked her head. "What are you—"

"Shh." He hushed her, the door closing behind him. "We can't wake up the others."

She looked up at the ceiling, appealing the suns to cut her

some slack. "Oh, don't tell me the Sunday drills start now because—"

"No, we're going to get out of here."

"Out of here? And go where?"

He smiled, his eyes glinting in the luminescent glow of the goggs perched on his head. "Didn't you check the weather today?"

Ezren paused. She had, in fact, not checked the weather since she'd lost the sim race. It was just too depressing when she could never actually go out there. She pulled it up in her goggs. Air quality well above breathing standards, 2.28-hour clear window starting in another thirty-one minutes. Perfect.

"We're going out?" But still she hesitated. "What happens if we get caught after curfew?"

His brow scrunched like he'd never really thought about it. "I think you spend your Sunday doing laps."

Ezren nearly laughed. "I'm in."

"And maybe get your pay docked."

Ezren stopped mid-step. "Wait, what? I can't—"

"Relax." He put a hand on her back and herded her toward the door. "Trust me, you need this, and we're not going to get caught."

Still, she leaned against his hand, resisting the thought of the fresh wind on her face and the beckoning horizon—a brand new one she hadn't already memorized.

He bent closer to her, his voice low. "I promise."

Ezren took another deep breath, the solid weight of Foster's hand and the easy confidence in his voice quieting her doubts—leading her toward the escape she so desperately needed. She nodded. "Okay."

He rewarded her with another half-smile, before stepping into the hallway and gesturing for her to follow.

She stuck close to his heels as he moved through the

carpeted hall, down the back steps, and out the door with a rubber doorstop propping it open. Then they moved across the lawn to a shadowy corner of the wall. He produced a small stepladder from behind the square line of bushes and set it against the twelve feet of mauve stone.

Ezren snorted. "I can jump pretty high, but there's no way I'm going to be able to make that."

"Give me some credit." He knelt beside the ladder. "I'm going to give you a boost."

Ezren hesitated before stepping up the ladder and onto his shoulders. His hands closed around her ankles, and he stood. With Foster's added height, Ezren shimmied over the top of the wall and slid to the other side. In another thirty seconds, he was beside her on the sidewalk.

"I'm guessing this isn't the first time you've done this?" Had he and Genevieve snuck out too? Or his other doubles?

He shrugged and started down the sidewalk. "Going out after curfew is practically a royaler tradition." His gaze scraped across the few other pedestrians out late on the residential street. "And I'd be shocked if our beds are the only ones empty on a Saturday night. But I will say I don't think I've ever lost out on sleep to go to the surface."

Above them the fake stars sparkled in the projected sky, a silvery cloud drifting over them. Ezren chewed the inside of her cheek, part of her expecting Sylvia to pop out in front of her at any moment. "And no one ever gets caught?"

He chuckled at that. "Honestly, I think Sylvia likes the drama and exposure we get from hitting the clubs." He turned around a corner onto a busier road. Here the talk drifted from restaurants, and people crowded around doorways filled with music and voices. "It's good for business."

"Sometimes Belethea's royalers seem more like a business than a sports team." Ezren frowned as they skirted around a long line crawling down the sidewalk, the clubbers barely noticing them as they stood in their glittering long gowns, three-piece suits, and jewel-encrusted goggs. She'd always joked with Micah that the Belethea fashion was to put on as many clothes as possible. Nothing like the bikini and swim brief looks trending on Obrone.

He paused and looked down the rail street for the magtrain before crossing over into a rowdier, less polished crowd. "It's chaff, but it definitely is. That's why Calderon Industries owns it, after all. Even without us though, the BRR brings in spectators and teams from all over the system—along with the advertising, visibility, and influence that comes with that. Without the BRR, a lot of people think Belethea would just be a remote mining colony."

The depressing thought hung over Ezren like a fog, and she forced a rebellious smile to dispel it. "I'd still be here. Just me, the mining bots, and the storms."

A man in a ragged top hat and suspenders staggered toward them, and Foster put a hand around her shoulder, pulling her close, out of his path. Ezren's pulse tripped with the surprising ginger-mango scent of Foster's detergent that made her want to lean into his jacket.

"And who wouldn't dream of that paradise?" he laughed, releasing her.

He stopped in front of a yellow sign that warned: *construction ahead, no entry*. They posted the same one on all the dome streets to try to keep people from running into the holopro of the never-ending road on the hard dome wall. He opened the door next to it, and she followed him into the familiar metal box of an airlock.

She ran to the outer door and slid open the viewport. Outside, Casolla's spidery webs of volcanic channels glowed bright orange between the wisps of racing clouds in the night-darkened plain, the grass swaying like dancers in the oddly gentle breeze. She rested her forehead against the blast-proof plastic. "I've missed it so much."

"Oh, yeah, who wouldn't miss the death fields of Belethea?" Foster tossed her a topsuit from one of the packs.

Ezren's shoulders caved in at the thought. Belethea was a challenge, yes, but she had so much to give. The terraforming effort was closer than most people realized. They just needed one more solid breakthrough on weather mapping. If they were able to predict the storm patterns, then they could tweak the conditions in order to weaken or isolate them enough to keep them to the churn belt... or maybe even shrink it, so the settlements could branch out beyond the poles.

It was hard, dangerous work, but it would be worth it.

"Danger is everywhere." She thought of Sammy in the hospital bed, encased in a body cast with a cold machine pumping his heart and chest. "It's just something we have to be aware of." Ezren shook out the topsuit, finding that for the first time ever, it seemed to be exactly her size.

"Oh, c'mon, the danger's not what you like about it?" Foster slipped out of his bomber jacket and peeled off his t-shirt, revealing a muscled abdomen underneath.

Ezren stared for a second too long before turning her back to him, her ears burning. Oh, suns. Hopefully, he wasn't one of those that went full commando under his topsuit. The heat spread down her neck and into her belly.

Shaking her head, she pulled off her own chunky sweater and mag-trainers, and then, still in her tank and leggings, stepped into the connected boots of the topsuit. Once she had her arms in, the nanitelattice meshed together like an automatic zipper, fitting to her body perfectly. It had a weight to it, but compared to her old topsuit, it was as if she wasn't wearing anything at all.

She smiled at the wonder of it and peeked over her shoulder to see that Foster was already fitting his goggs over his helmet. He threw the other helmet to her, and she paused for a moment.

"Thank you. I really did need this."

He opened the door to the starlit darkness of Belethea, his stormy gaze locking on hers. "I know."

With that, Ezren hurtled into the blackness, running with her first step. Her stare latched on the highest point she could find, and she launched toward it, every stride new and free and strong. Obrone, Dreitis, Crion, and Casolla peeked in on her through the clouds, like old friends saying hello.

Foster trailed behind with loping steps, saying nothing as she bounded along. The huff of their breaths mixed with the familiar whistle of the wind in a comfortable silence that filled her from head to toe. No din of trains or people or music... just Belethea.

The lights of her suit illuminated the mauve dirt as she leapt from boulder to boulder, skidding across the emerald belmoss with a grin. All the fatigue and anxiety that had weighed on her in Petraskis couldn't keep up here—torn away by the heady thrill of discovery. Of freedom.

She raced Foster beneath soaring stone archways, weaving between twisting towers of rock warped and smooth from centuries of Belethea's cutting winds. Grinning wide, she let him catch her, his hands snagging her by the waist and whirling her around. His crinkled eyes shot wide as she seized his hand and slid down an incline until they tumbled into a heap, laughing until she could scarcely breathe. The light of the moons flickered through the whipping clouds above them, showering them in flashes of silvery light.

They ran and climbed and leapt until Ezren's goggs protested with a chirp, telling her they could go no farther. She turned, looking down on the metal bubble of Petraskis. Then she spread her arms and screamed, loud and long. Just because she could.

Laughing, Foster stepped up beside her, his gaze meeting hers before he turned and yelled with her. And together they howled at the Belethean sky.

Wrapped in her worn sweater once more, Ezren walked back to Carmella brimming with an exhausted euphoria that threatened to lift her to the projected midnight sky above. Neither she nor Foster had said anything after their run, and the quiet snuggled around them like a warm blanket. Foster's elbow brushed against her as they walked, and she couldn't help sneaking peeks at him.

The omnipresent line between his low brows had softened, and though he wasn't smiling, he had a relaxed, almost peaceful glint to his hooded eyes. A five o'clock shadow edged his sharp jawline, and he shot her the smallest of grins.

Her stomach flipped, and she looked away quickly, her own smile dancing between warm cheeks and her feet light beneath her in spite of the twelve miles they'd torn across Belethea. Closing her eyes, she imagined that unexplored open land, savoring the lingering intoxication of freedom. And Foster had brought her there. She could have said thank you a thousand times, and it wouldn't have been enough.

Now that she knew how to sneak out, she wondered how often she could get away with it. A clear night would be so hard to resist, even if it meant dozing off during tutoring the next day. But would Foster be up for coming with her again? Although running alone had always brought her a measure of serenity, sharing it with him had been so much more... well, *fun*.

She opened her mouth to say as much when a laughing gaggle stumbled out of one of the pulsing nightclubs lining the street, and the dry, musical tenor of one of the clubbers rang out over the clamor. It only took another second to spot the familiar figure in their midst.

Davis.

Her elation turned to stone in a second, her body suddenly all too heavy. She stopped short, willing herself to blend into the crowd, the wall, anything. She was small—forgettable.

But the broad-shouldered, six-foot-something royaler next to her definitely wasn't. Foster stopped beside her, turning to look her full in her wide eyes. "Hey, you okay?"

Ezren didn't get a chance to reply before Davis turned toward them. Even from afar, his gaze zeroed in on Foster before sliding to her. Then, of course, he smiled and started purposefully in their direction.

"Mother suns," Ezren swore. She clutched Foster's elbow in desperation, the flannel of his shirt soft beneath her fingers. "Look, can you do me a huge favor?" she whispered. "I just need you to play along."

The line between Foster's eyebrows deepened, and he followed her pointed look to Davis approaching them with his rolling gait, fully spiffed in a blue tailored suit with a fedora perched on his dark head. He looked good. Way too good.

"Wait, what?" Foster whispered, bending his head down to hers. "What do you want me to do?"

She moved her face an inch away from his and put on her best fake smile. "I'll explain later."

"Ez!" Davis called, weaving through the crowd to where they stood on the corner. "Hey! I can't believe I ran into you."

"Hey, Davis." Ezren slid her hand down Foster's arm to

lace her fingers with his and edged closer to him. From the corner of her eye, she caught a flicker of understanding quirk his mouth. "This must be a smaller city than I thought."

Davis stopped at arm's length and held out a hand to Foster. "Hey, I'm Davis Banda. Ez and I grew up in Tuzuno together."

Foster released Ezren's hand to shake Davis's with a short bow. "Ah, always nice to meet another friend of *Ez's*. I'm Foster Sterling."

Davis's smile only deepened. "Yeah, I know. Actually, it's really crisp to meet you. Since Ez's joined the team, I guess I've kind of turned into a royale fan myself. I've read a lot about you." He turned to Ezren. "But I've got to say, I'm a little disappointed. I'd hoped to show her the sights myself." He gestured to the glowing club behind him.

Ezren cringed. Why wouldn't he just give up already? Davis really could not take the hint, and apparently, Sylvia needed to feed the dating rumors a little harder. Luckily, Foster seemed to be more perceptive.

He wrapped his arm around her shoulders and pulled her against his body, back into his mango-ginger scent, now slightly tinged with salt. He flashed a roguish grin at her. "You'll have to forgive me for stealing her. I can't help but try to keep her all to myself."

Ezren had to stop herself from rolling her eyes. That was laying it on a bit thick. She shook her head at him with what she hoped looked like a flirtatious smile and not the brittle grimace she fought back. "Wow, you're quite the smooth talker tonight."

Davis held up two hands with a laugh. "No, man, I totally get it. She really is something special. Honestly, I'm glad she's found someone to keep her company while she's here."

Foster's smile fell a little at that, and Ezren slumped under his arm. That was the problem with Davis—it was just too hard to hate him.

"C'mon, Davis, we're leaving you!" one of the girls called from his posse, now across the road and headed into a different flashing establishment.

"Sorry, I've gotta run. But, Ez, if you liked those cronuts, I'll drop you off another box next Sunday, okay? I don't think I'll be making it out of bed any time before noon tomorrow." Backing away, he waved to Foster. "Nice meeting you."

As Davis jogged to his friends, Ezren couldn't help but stare at his back. He'd been completely unfazed by the fake boyfriend routine. Had he seen through her? Or were his feelings for her just that dead? She watched him laugh with a pair of girls in his group, and her stomach twisted in a way she wished it wouldn't. He stole a glance back at her, and she quickly looked away. Ugh. What was wrong with her?

"Well, that was interesting." Amusement lit up Foster's face in the orange gleam of the nearby club.

Ezren sighed, running a hand down her face as if she could wipe away the embarrassment. Then, realizing Foster's arm was still around her, she scrambled out from under it, her face burning. "Oh, suns, I'm sorry. I wasn't... ugh."

"So that was... your contraband dealer?"

She started down the pavement, shoulders sagging, the thrill of the run completely vanished. "My ex-boyfriend."

"Ah, I see." His smile fell away. "And you're trying to make him jealous or something?"

"No!" Ezren's eyes practically bulged out of her head, and she waved her arms emphatically. "No. We broke up months ago, but ever since I got here, he keeps wanting to hang out."

"Like as friends or..."

"It doesn't matter. Either way, I don't want to open up that can of worms." She wrapped her arms tightly around herself. "Ever. Again."

Foster stuffed his hands in his pockets. "That sounds... complicated."

"It's not," she said quickly. "Tuzuno is a tiny station, and we were the only two kids our age. Without any options, we were just a convenient match." She tugged her sleeves over her hands. "So we were together, and then when he left... we weren't."

"Fair enough." He cleared his throat. "I should warn you though, the probability of pictures of us showing up on VSoc with my arm around you are almost 100%."

She rubbed at her forehead, heat crawling down her spine. "Oh, I'm sorry. I didn't mean to make you look bad or anything. Suns. Especially when you were nice enough to bring me out tonight."

He laughed with a dry rumble. "No, that's not what I mean at all. That's totally fine by me. In fact, I've been meaning to ask you what you wanted to do about our 'social image' with the exhibition in a couple weeks. I'm surprised Sylvia's not hounding us about it already."

"Oh." Ezren scuffed her heels against the pavement as they turned onto the dusky side street behind Carmella. "I don't really know. I mean, I definitely want us to be competitive for sponsors... but it still seems kind of weird. How do you decide something like that?"

"Well..." Foster stopped and put his hands on either side of the wall next to her, pinning her in. Ezren leaned against the wall, eyes round with surprise and a sudden heat scorching through her whole body. He leaned forward with a smile. "It's all about what you're comfortable with. The more real we can make it feel, the more sponsors we'll get."

His minty breath blew warm on her cheeks, and Ezren's

heart pounded almost audibly in her chest. All thoughts of anything else that had happened that night flew out of her mind as her gaze flicked to his lips. Were they really doing this? A shock of anticipation tingled through her fingers. "Um... okay." The words seemed to catch in her throat. "Sponsors are good."

For a moment he stared at her, his stormy eyes glinting in the streetlights. Then, all too soon, he pulled away with a wistful smile, something almost like disappointment tightening his expression. "Eh, don't worry about it. We should just let it come naturally, and Sylvia can take care of the rest." He turned to continue down the walk.

Ezren took a long, deep breath to calm her racing pulse, her emotions snarled in a mess of confusion and, strangely, disappointment. Natural was good, right? She could be natural. In the last few months, Foster had been there for her every day—always there with a steady hand, a wry comment, or a knock on her door in the still-dark morning. He'd grown to be more than a friend. He was her double, her rock, and she couldn't risk messing that up.

Natural was easy, safe.

So why did her chest suddenly feel so hollow?

CHAPTER 15

THE BELETHEA ROYALERS gathered by Carmella's gates in their traveling finery—hats, long-coats, corsets, and ruffles—all in the various shades of the black and teal team colors, along with the tall boots that were in style. Foster tugged at the high collar around his neck, internally cursing the team policy that required formal dress to stand in front of the press for two minutes before traveling in a storm truck for twelve chaffing hours. *Seriously, Sylvia, why?*

Harland talked loudly through his goggs while Grady and Bex stood close together on the lawn in their matching top hats, each absorbed in their own holopros. Bex flicked through some kind of word puzzle while Grady's goggs projected an interactive comic. They murmured to each other occasionally, sharing a few grins, and although Foster knew Bex wasn't into Grady... or anyone else for that matter... they would still reel in the sponsors somehow. Grady always did.

Foster adjusted the flat cap on his head, feeling absolutely ridiculous. While he loved Belethea for the most part, he still wondered why they couldn't go for the more practical jumpsuit fashions that the spacers loved. Even the full-length robes of the Dreitians would be better off than the never-ending layers Belethea embraced.

The pinks and golds of a late sunrise streaked across the holopro dome, and the whir of magtrains and autocabs filled the air. He checked the time in his goggs again before glancing at Carmella's glass doors. At this rate, they were going to miss their scheduled storm truck. He knew Sylvia had deemed Ezren incapable of readying herself, but what could they possibly be doing in there?

Thoughts of Ezren drew his mind into the same spiral they'd whirled in since they'd snuck out that night. Although on some level he'd known that his feelings for Ezren simmered well beyond friendship, something about that night had brought them crackling to the surface. The smile that had lingered on her face, the way she'd fit so naturally under his arm, how her breath had tickled his cheek as he leaned toward her... And in his mind, he couldn't help but close that distance between them. Over and over.

But he couldn't. Not yet. He'd seen the way she'd looked at that Davis guy. Sure, they weren't together, but there was still something between them. Not to mention the fact that Foster hadn't gotten around to explaining the Vieve situation yet. He still needed more time.

"So..." Harland's oily voice brought Foster back to the moment. "How's it going this year?"

Foster stiffened. Harland had only graced them with his presence twice in the last two months, and Foster had managed to avoid him almost entirely. He could think of nothing he wanted to say or hear from this man. "Fine."

Harland nodded, running a heavily bejeweled hand over his slicked hair. "I know it must be hard with a new recruit as a double, but we appreciate all the effort you've put in to help her along."

Foster's fists tightened. This sounded like the buttering right before the bad news. Were they considering replacing her? "Ezren's trying to make up for years of experience in only a couple of months. She's not the strongest fighter yet..." *Make that rock bottom.* "But her driving skills are nearly as good as Bex's, and her physical scores have always been off the charts."

"Noted. But your fan support has dwindled to record lows." His vibrant green gaze sharpened. "It seems like they're angry you've replaced Genevieve with Ezren."

"That's not our fault. Talmadge has been working a smear campaign since the tryout." Foster's jaw flexed, and he kicked at the long belweeds growing up against the stone outer wall. The only reason they were even afloat was thanks to a herculean effort by Ezren's VSoc savvy friend. "Besides, Vieve's manic fans will be in mourning for the next decade. There'll be no pleasing them."

"Perhaps that's true, but it's hurting you with the sponsors, which you'll certainly need for new equipment and travel funds if you want to be competitive. It might be time to mix it up and see if things go better." He gestured across the lawn to where Grady and Bex were obviously pretending not to eavesdrop.

Foster stilled, his hooded stare boring into Harland. "Shaft off."

Harland folded his hands behind him. "It's just a friendly heads-up we're giving to everyone. If you like your double, we're giving you this last chance to bring up your VSoc numbers. How you wish to do so is completely up to you." With that, Harland walked over to Grady and Bex, presumably to give them the same news.

Bleeding chaff.

Foster looked away, grinding his teeth together. This shouldn't have surprised him. Harland had said as much earlier on, and suns knew his mother and all the other coaches switched up teams at the drop of a hat. Still, the unfairness of it rubbed him raw. This was their first real exhibition as doubles, and if they didn't make something happen—it would be their last.

The doors to Carmella hissed opened, and Sylvia strutted out like a proud parent. Her cape flowed behind her, and uncountable layers of ruffled skirts waved around her boots. At first, Foster thought she must have offed Ezren in the primping process, but then Sylvia turned with a hand on her hip and beckoned impatiently at the door.

Rolling her eyes, Ezren shuffled out after her, looking nearly unrecognizable. A magenta braid laced with flowers ran to an elegant bun behind her head, and a whorling gold design rimmed her eyes, making them shine like polished opals. She wore a low-cut corset, with black lace running up her arms to meet in a collar around her neck. A full skirt, short in the front to show off the laced thigh-high boots, rustled around her as she took quick unsteady steps.

This was a far cry from the sweatpants-clad Ezren who stumbled out of her room every morning.

Sylvia caught his eye, smiling at his slack jaw as she herded Grady and Bex toward the gate. "Okay, everyone, listen up! This is our first exhibition, so this is also our best chance to really show the sponsors what we can do. We have four station teams coming down to compete, so we want to keep their attention on us."

"And show them that we're the team worth backing," Harland added.

"Right, right," Sylvia said, dismissing him with a wave. "But before you get there, I want all smiles for the cams, do you hear me? Remember the social images we discussed and don't be afraid to give them something to gossip about."

Ezren sidled up next to Foster, and he struggled to find something to say. She looked... amazing. But she also looked like an entirely different person. She glanced up at him with a grimace, and he couldn't hold back a smile. Okay, still the same Ezren in there.

"If we pull in some creds, can we finally get a few topjeeps and jetbikes to train on?" Grady asked, straightening the bright teal ascot around his neck.

"If you can pull enough for a decent victory dinner, we'll be getting somewhere," Sylvia said flatly. "Just don't do anything stupid while we're at the outpost. It's a small place, so if you do, everyone will know."

Bex hooked her thumbs into her belt, a long, tailored men's coat swirling around the many buckles and straps that ran along her tight synleather outfit. "I'm so inspired right now."

"And here I thought we were supposed to win or something," Grady added with a laugh, not even looking up as he polished the silver buttons on his ankle-length black coat.

Sylvia glared at him. "There's more to winning than just the race." Something chimed in her holopro, and she gasped. "And we're about to be late, so hurry up and remember to smile." Bex favored her with a particularly grim look, and Sylvia shrugged. "Or, you know, whatever works for you."

"Ready?" Foster offered Ezren his elbow, but when she smiled up at him, he could see the nervous worry shining between her lashes. It made him hate this game of forced smiles put on for thousands of mindless, bulging eyes. It made him jealous of Davis Banda for getting to spend those years with her all to himself.

They stepped out of the gate behind the others, into the flash and glow of a pathetic scattering of reporters. Bex and Grady paused to pose for a few pictures—Bex popped a hand on one hip and propped her other elbow on Grady's shoulder, looking bored while he gave her the winning smile that had captured the hearts of so many fans.

The four reporters turned on Foster and Ezren next, but their chuckles dried up in an onslaught of sharp-toothed questions.

"Foster, is it true you're still hung up on Genevieve?"

"How are you feeling about Genevieve's death going into the new season?"

"Do you think it's too soon to be moving on?"

Ezren's smile stumbled beside him, her face a shade paler than it had been. "Uh... should I be doing something?"

Foster turned toward her, leaning his head close. "Don't worry about—"

Ezren pressed a kiss directly on his mouth, her lips cool against his own. Her eyes were closed as she balanced awkwardly on her toes, her body only inches from his, and for a beat, Foster froze.

What. Is. Happening.

When his brain jolted back to life, the shock of it nearly knocked him over. *Wait—What?* He stumbled half a step back, mouth agape, as she retreated with a scarlet blush. Had he missed something? The reporters erupted in a fresh series of clicks and frenzied questions Foster couldn't parse over the buzzing in his ears. *Do. Not. Fritz. Out.*

But he didn't have time to recover before Ezren took him by the arm and whisked him down the walk. From the corner of his eye, he could just barely see Sylvia applauding against the gate while Harland grinned smugly beside her. *Had they told her to do that? That couldn't have possibly been real... could it?*

They turned a corner, out of sight of the reporters, before Ezren released him, striding purposefully ahead while he lagged behind, a heated confusion scrambling his thoughts. *Wait. Stay blime. Just relax,* he reminded himself. It wasn't a big deal. It was just a kiss. It's not like he hadn't thought about it... *a lot.* It was just... not how he imagined it.

"Ezren," he called, catching up with her. "You... caught me a bit off guard there."

Ezren didn't look at him, her face oddly serious as she marched toward the storm truck station in her tall boots. "Well, Harland said if we don't start performing, we'll be separated, right? Didn't he tell you the same thing?"

"Uh... yeah." Foster tried to follow her train of thought, but his mind still stuttered over the quick press of her cool lips. Wasn't that what he'd wanted? So why had it felt wrong?

"So I talked to Sylvia, and she recommended we up the ante." Ezren turned abruptly in the street, earnest brows drawn low as a scattering of people streamed around them in the early morning light. "As much as I like Simon, I prefer to stay doubles with you."

Foster rubbed the back of his neck, not at all sure how to feel. She'd faked the kiss... but it had been to keep them together? "I... uh. Yeah, that's what I'd like too."

She flashed another smile that didn't reach her eyes, a professional one that nearly punched him in the gut. "Great, then we're on the same page." And though she put her fingers stiffly in his, she didn't meet his gaze.

How had their perfectly comfortable silence crumbled into a mess in less than three minutes? "Wait, Ezren." He cupped her hand in both of his. "This doesn't feel right."

She pulled away, her round goggs glinting in the holopro sunlight. "What do you mean? Don't you want to give it our best shot?"

He huffed in exasperation. Why did it feel like they were running in the wrong direction? "Yes."

Looking away, she pulled at the lace sleeves of her dress, as if trying to pull them over her hands. "Look, I'm sorry about the kiss. I probably should've warned you."

He ran a finger along the brim of his cap, resisting the urge to pull it over his face. Was it possible she could misunderstand him so badly? He had to get out of this conversation before he did more damage.

"No, there was nothing wrong with the kiss. Please, feel free to do it again... w-whenever." He scratched his head, the heat of embarrassment thickening his tongue as a plump man in a bow tie jostled past him. He stepped closer and put his hands on her shoulders. "Really, it's fine. I can just tell whatever Sylvia and Harland said must've really thrown you, and I don't want you to worry, okay? We'll figure it out. We're totally going to blow this exhibition out of the water anyway."

Ezren covered her face with her hands. "I'm sure you're right. Sorry, sorry, sorry. I'm really no good at this."

He pulled her hands away from where they had smudged the painted gold swirls around her eyes. "Stop saying sorry." He offered her his arm, and she reluctantly looped hers through it. "C'mon, if we hurry we can probably sneak a latte at the station before Sylvia catches up."

She groaned with a weak smile. "Nothing like caffeine to drown my mortification." He opened his mouth, but she hurried on, pulling him hastily along through the thickening crowd of commuters. "Might as well get going while we have the chance."

The crisis averted for a second, Foster let her drag him down the street, hoping they had left the awkwardness on the pavement behind them. Because the next time they kissed, he wanted it to be just for them—and he wanted it to be real.

The Chaymi Outpost was little more than a snowy dome stuffed underneath the outcropping of one of Belethea's huge cliffs on the edge of the churn belt. The research outpost had originally been built to study the cliff's strong magnetic patterns, but after the funding had run out, the large main house that had once sheltered scientists had been repurposed for royalers. The interior had been holo-projected to look like an old-fashioned lodge of some nature with high wood ceilings and disturbing animal bones hung on the walls. Fake fires crackled from enormous stone hearths and plush couches and chairs crowded around them. There was even a pair of tiny ark-cats watching the newcomers from a recliner, their six tails flicking idly.

The Belethean royalers stood in a loose knot, absorbing the quaint décor and exchanging awed smiles as they basked in the glow of the novelty. Ezren's eyes shone along with them, but she didn't meet Foster's gaze. Unsurprisingly, the twelve-hour ride in the cramped storm truck had done nothing for the weirdness between them.

Just chaffing great.

He'd been itching for a moment to themselves to talk it out, and the waiting was slowly killing him. With Sylvia and Grady's chaffing hovercams buzzing around their heads, he couldn't say a word without one of them blasting it across VSoc. And this wasn't a conversation he wanted the others to hear, much less the rest of the 'verse.

Foster's attention reluctantly slewed to the four station teams that had already arrived. Their half-visors illuminated their jumpsuits with artistically patterned holopros while they chattered in the lobby area over the beat of a poppy tune. They hardly glanced at the Beletheans as they entered, and the message could not have been clearer. The Beletheans were beneath their notice—not competition, not worth their time.

And the worst part was, he knew some of them. Wait, he knew *a lot* of them. The Naris Station shield flashed in the corner of the room, and he jolted to a stop. His shock seethed into irritation, and he snatched Sylvia's elbow, pulling her away from her conversation with the staff.

"You didn't tell me Naris would be here."

She looked at him out of the corner of her eye. "Would you have come if I had?"

"No," he said through gritted teeth.

Ezren shuffled to his side. "Is something wrong?"

Before he could answer, a silky, familiar voice cut in. "Oh, Foster, I was hoping to see you here."

Foster turned and came face-to-face with perhaps the second-biggest celebrity Belethea had to offer, a top-ten royaler in the BRR, and the coach of Naris Station.

He didn't even bother with a polite smile. "Mother."

Ezren looked from one to the other like she was putting together two pieces of a puzzle that didn't quite fit.

Greta Sterling wore a fashionable jumpsuit just like the other spacers, with a holopro of a stormy sea crashing across her neckline down to her ankles. Unnaturally young under her holopro, she had the same brown hair, sandy complexion, and green-gray eyes that she'd given to him. She twirled her fingers through her ponytail with a frown. "Surprised to see you're alive considering you never answer my messages."

She reached out to squeeze his shoulder, and he stiffened.

"I've been busy."

"So does that mean you've picked up your training?"

He adjusted the cap on his head, trying to act casual despite the bitterness that coated his tongue. "As a competing coach, I really don't see how that's any of your business."

With a sigh, her sharp gaze brushed over Ezren, Sylvia, and the rest of the team. "If you're going to waste your talent like this, I really don't know why you race at all."

The Naris royalers gathered behind her, whispering to one

another as they watched him with condescending smirks or, even worse, sympathetic frowns. Some of them were teammates he'd trained with when he was younger, and others were famous enough to recognize from VSoc. It looked like they had brought their full team of sixteen. He grimaced. Wouldn't it be nice to have that kind of travel budget?

"There will always be a spot on our roster for you though if you want to take this seriously," his mother continued.

"Well, uh..." Sylvia started, conflicting emotions flickering across her face. The internal war between her obvious admiration for *the* Greta Sterling, and the reality of this snide celebrity fritzing her team flashed in her brown eyes. She took in a slow breath before recovering her holopro-ready beam. "Thanks, Ms. Sterling, but Foster's quite comfortable with us."

His mother turned her glittering smile on Sylvia. "Yes, well I did say serious, not comfortable. If comfortable's what you want, I'm sure last place would be a great fit." Sylvia's expression wilted, and his mother's gaze turned to steel, the veins protruding from the clenched fists at her side. "Winning is hard."

"Too bad you wouldn't know," Foster said, stepping in front of the speechless Sylvia.

It was a low blow, and even though she didn't flinch, he knew it had cut her deep. Her features still smooth, she took a long breath before she spoke again.

"Lovely to see you, son. Please pick up on my calls one of these days." And with that, she turned away.

Her royalers turned to go with her, but one familiar redhead darted in a little closer. She squeezed his arm, her smile the only genuine one in the room. "Don't listen to her, Foster, you know how she is."

He tried for a half-smile and failed, a deep heaviness pulling on him from all sides. At least if he had to talk to anyone from Naris, Callie Phanik was probably the least annoying. "Thanks, Callie."

"You really should come check out the Naris training rooms sometime. The gear they give us hasn't even been officially released. Seriously, you'd love it," she whispered, the words falling out in an excited tumble. "Maybe you could enter one of our virtual royale tours coming up."

He repressed an eye roll as a stab of jealousy punched through him. She had to know that the Belethean team didn't have the creds for that. "Thanks, Callie, we'll see what we can do."

"We do all miss you though! We should hang out after the race." She waved at the other Beletheans. "Good luck out there."

For a moment, the Beletheans were quiet. Then Sylvia turned to them with a plastic smile that almost looked as if it were holo-projected onto her face. "All right, everyone, I've sent you room assignments, and they're keyed to your goggs. The magnetism in the area is high so our chip updates are spotty. If you need anything though, you can find me in room 204. Remember, just like the real BRR, this is an outpost-to-outpost race, with only the gear on your back. Race starts at 0500 tomorrow, and you have to be there at 0430, so get out of here and get your rest."

Grady and Bex took their cue, wandering off to find their rooms, but Foster stayed rooted in place, trying to filter the resentment and sorrow and bitter jealousy still rushing through him.

"So..." The suddenness of Ezren's voice almost made him jump. "That was your mom, huh? She's... not quite what I expected." But even as she said it, her gaze followed Callie as she bounced back to her teammates.

His hand spasmed, and he kneaded it with the other. "And what were you expecting?"

Her brow scrunched, wrinkling the golden ink there that had already started to fade. "I guess I thought she'd be a little like you?"

He laughed. He'd been expecting something about how kind and thoughtful she came across in interviews and holos. Then again, Ezren always surprised him. "I'll take that as a compliment."

"Do you miss it?" she asked softly.

"Miss what?" He shifted his bag on his shoulder and started across the lobby. "My mom? Do you really have to ask?"

"No." She fisted her hands in her skirts as she followed him. "Being on a winning team."

The words crashed into him, the shards of truth prickling him with shame. "Oh." He stopped, wanting to reach out and touch her. Yes, he liked to win, but he'd much rather be here with Ezren, even if they lost. Didn't she know that? The other royale teams still bustled around them, but maybe they could step away and finally sort this out. "I... uh..."

Her false smile broadened. "It's okay, you don't have to answer. Besides..." She headed toward the stairs with a wave. "If Sylvia expects me to get up before dawn tomorrow, I really do need my rest."

Foster's stomach sank as he watched her go. Although she'd only disappeared up the stairs, she already felt so far away. He internally banged his head against the wall. Somehow, in the space of a day, he felt like he was losing Ezren. And while there were a lot of things he didn't know, he did know he couldn't do this without her.

CHAPTER 16

EZREN WALKED into the small room where Bex was already unpacking her bag, making sure to give her a wide berth. The old scientist quarters boasted two bunks unfolded from the wall, a projected fireplace in the corner, and a holopro window that showed the snowy world outside. Though it was only 2030, the strain of traveling all day had bent their shoulders and wrinkled their clothes, and Ezren wanted nothing more than to collapse onto her bunk.

She found her way to the hall bathroom and, by some miracle, managed to squirm out of the corset Sylvia had stuffed her into that morning. The shower pummeled her body with steaming hot water, reminding her of the stiff awkwardness she'd been wading through all day. She winced as she thought of the reporters' questions about Genevieve, Foster pulling away from her kiss, and then that incident with his mom. Putting it all together made her realize how little she knew about him, even after they'd spent nearly every waking moment of the last few months together.

Groaning, she slid her hand over her eyes. Now what did she do? It seemed like since the *incident* that morning, she'd only managed to make things worse. Desperate for ideas, she read over the conversation she'd had with Micah that afternoon, wishing she could call her now if only just for a venting session.

Micah: So how excited are you for your first real royale?

Ezren: I kissed Foster Sterling, and he didn't kiss me back, AND the reporters caught it on cam. You can just bury me right now.

Micah: WHAT!?! You made the first move in front of PEOPLE?! Are you sure you haven't been replaced by an alien? I can't believe you did that! You've got some stones, girl!

Ezren: Well, Sylvia and Harland had just given me this pep talk about how we needed something to improve our image, and I was just so nervous, and then they were asking all these questions about Genevieve and... I think I lost my mind for a second.

Micah: So... you kissed him because the coach told you to? Or because of the ex-girlfriend questions?

Ezren: ...I don't know. But both of those sound like awful reasons.

Micah: Oh, they definitely are. But who can blame you? I'd take any excuse to kiss Foster fritzin' Sterling.

Ezren: But now I've made it all weird! He's sitting beside me now, and I can't even look at him.

Micah: Well, I did warn you when you were doubled with Foster Sterling. He and Genevieve were all over VSoc for a whole year. And they were STEAMY. Not to mention the fanart... but, I mean, she died a few months ago, so it makes sense he'd still be grieving.

Heat rushed to Ezren's cheeks at the thought of steamy

pictures of Foster, and she had to will herself not to go looking for them.

EZREN: OH, SUNS. YOU'RE RIGHT. AND I TRIED TO PUSH HIM INTO IT... OKAY. IT'S OFFICIAL. I'M THE BIGGEST ASSCHAFF.

MICAH: DON'T BEAT YOURSELF UP ABOUT IT. I MEAN, MAYBE IF YOU TWO AREN'T DOING WELL, MAYBE YOU *SHOULD* DOUBLE WITH SIMON GRADY INSTEAD. HE'S ACTUALLY A REALLY GOOD DRIVER, AND HE'S SUPER NICE TO THE FANS.

EZREN: ...BUT FOSTER AND I *ARE* DOING WELL.

MICAH: YOU JUST SAID IT WAS WEIRD.

EZREN: I GUESS SINCE HE NEVER BROUGHT UP GENEVIEVE, I KIND OF FORGOT ABOUT HER. IT WAS STUPID OF ME.

MICAH: SO WHAT ARE YOU GOING TO DO NOW?

EZREN: WELL, FIRST WE NEED TO NOT COME IN LAST. THEN I CAN WORRY ABOUT GENEVIEVE LATER.

MICAH: AS FAR AS PLANS GO, I GIVE THAT ONE A C-.

EZREN: DO YOU HAVE A BETTER ONE?

MICAH: NOPE! :)

Ezren closed out the messages with a long, slow breath of resignation. Maybe he really did still care about Genevieve, or maybe Ezren was just a charity case he felt sorry for. After all, she certainly wasn't up to par with his last team. So did he race for Belethea just to get back at his mom? Was this some weird revenge scheme?

She turned off the shower and dried herself before dressing in her usual tights and tank top. They were the clothes that took the least amount of effort in the morning, which meant she could sleep up until the last minute before jumping into her topsuit. Shivering, she pulled on her sweater too. Even after four years, sometimes she still missed the warmth of Obrone's sunshine.

Her breath clouded even after the hot shower, like the walls couldn't quite keep out the storm. She checked the weather: -50°F, 40% visibility, and precipitating. Ugh. If these conditions kept up, it was going to be a rough race tomorrow. She swept a laserbrush Sylvia had given her across her teeth before heading back to her room.

Stepping into the hall, she nearly bumped into Foster, his own hair still wet and steaming, and nothing but a towel wrapped around his waist.

"Oh, suns, I'm sorry." Heat rushed to her cheeks as her eyes darted to the towel and back up his muscular body. "Aren't you cold?" Even as she said it, she could see the goosebumps prickling his bare skin.

He shrugged. "It's only a couple steps to the room."

"You better hurry then before you freeze to death." Ezren wrapped her arms around herself and turned to go.

"Hey, Ezren?"

She turned by her door. "Yeah?"

"Are you—" He moved aside to let someone else pass in the narrow hallway, his bare chest coming within inches of her face. "Are you good for tomorrow?"

"Um, yeah." She shifted the bag on her shoulder, her face still on fire as she tried to keep her gaze on his. "Meeting at 0430 and race at five, right? My pack's all set, and my suit and helmet are ready to go. With any luck, I won't be late tomorrow."

Foster massaged one hand with the other. "Yeah, no, I'm not worried about that. I'll come by and get you. It's just... today was pretty weird, right?"

She leaned against the door, wishing she could melt into it and away from this conversation. "Yeah, I guess." She rapped her knuckles on the door frame. "First time I've been to another outpost with a bunch of royalers."

"That's not what I meant."

Another person passed by them, and they both pressed against the wall to let them pass. They were so close now, Ezren could feel the heat coming off his skin, and the urge to touch him nearly overwhelmed her. She *had* to get out of here.

"I know." She sighed, and her words flew out in a fast rush of air. "Look, it's my fault. I'm really sorry. I know the kiss thing was out of line. I really didn't mean any disrespect to... to Genevieve. I know how you felt about her. So let's just forget about it." Embarrassment threatening to swallow her, she opened the door in a desperate bid to end the conversation.

Foster jerked a step back, his dark brows shooting up. "You know how I felt about her? Who told you?"

She shook her head, waving her hands frantically. "It's really no big deal! I get it. And it's not at all going to affect our race tomorrow."

The line between his brows deepened, and Ezren slunk backward through the doorway.

He leaned toward her again, lowering his voice as a laughing gaggle of racers slipped by him. "Ezren, I'm not worried about the race."

Ezren thought back to Harland's warning about doing well. The one he'd given all of them. So apparently Foster wasn't worried about being split up. That made things pretty clear then.

"I just want to talk about Genevieve," he said.

Ezren sagged, a hole opening in her stomach. That was absolutely the last thing she wanted to talk about. She looked up at him with something between a wince and a smile. "Okay. But can we wait until tomorrow? I'm kind of tired, and I want to focus on the race."

He pulled away from her, his shoulders falling in defeat. "Okay. After the race." But his tense gaze held hers until she gave him a little wave and let the door hiss shut. Temporarily saved from further self-mortification, she drooped to the floor with one long exhale.

Bex looked up from where she lay on her back on the lower bunk, cold blue eyes assessing as her goggs holopro glowed above her. "Normally I wouldn't ask... but you're not having a lover's quarrel the night before the first big royale, are you?"

Ezren's brows shot up in surprise, and her face flushed once more. "Not lovers. Just doubles." Bex almost never spoke to her about anything, so for her to witness this was more than a little humiliating. Not that Bex's opinion of her could sink much lower.

Bex rolled onto her stomach, propping her narrow chin on her palm as she absently played a game on her goggs. A projection of colorful planets fell in front of her as her fingers darted between them. "Are you sure about that?"

Ezren stood and climbed the ladder to the top bunk. "I know how he feels about Genevieve. It just feels weird to be stepping into her shoes, I guess." Especially when everyone knew she'd never be able to fill them.

Bex shifted on the creaking lower bunk. "I don't know what you know about Vieve, but if it's from VSoc it's probably chaff. She was good at building a brand."

"I wish she could've told me her secrets," Ezren murmured. "So far I'm totally bombing the social image stuff." Yet another thing Genevieve had been better at than her.

"Vieve was good, but Sylvia didn't bring you on to replace her. Belethea needed someone fresh."

"Even though I'm chaff?" Ezren said with a laugh.

"Being new doesn't mean you're chaff." Bex's game chirped

with a high score. "You're allowed to be a beginner. Besides, everyone's trying to improve in some way."

Though it wasn't exactly a compliment, it was the longest conversation Bex and Ezren had ever had, and Ezren's eyes turned damp. "Thanks. That means a lot coming from you." Ezren paused, pulling the thick blanket to her chin. "So, then, are you trying to get better at something too?"

Only the upbeat jingle of the game filled the room, and Ezren realized she'd overstepped. Just because Bex had said something kind, didn't mean they were friends. She'd broken Ezren's arm, after all. Frowning at her own fritz-headedness, Ezren shifted to face the wall.

Below, the game chimed with a cheery "game over" before abruptly cutting off. Bex cut the lights and a dark silence filled the room. Ezren dangled on the edge of sleep before Bex's monotone voice rolled through the dark. "Still working on being a good teammate."

Ezren's eyes opened in surprise. "I think you're doing well," she whispered.

"Shut up and go to sleep already, Hart," Bex grumbled, a fondness softening the words.

Ezren smiled into the dark. It was the first time Bex had ever called her by name, and despite the cold winds raging outside, Ezren was warm.

Ezren sat up with a gasp, a barrage of panicked dream chaos blurring together into nothing. The bunk below her was dark and quiet in the cozy room. A driving ice storm still filled their holopro window while their faux fire crackled cheerily in the corner. She groped for her goggs on the wall-mounted charging rig and checked the weather out of habit: -66°, wind 75 knots to the northeast, 15% visibility, and 100% chance of precipitation in the next hour. She'd thought Tuzuno had bad weather, but this was a whole new level.

The royale topsuits would send out a danger alarm at -70°, but it would only keep them alive to -75°. There wasn't much margin for error. Hopefully, conditions would improve by the time the race started. She lay back down with a yawn, wondering how much time she had left to sleep.

Time: 0440

"What?" She jerked up and threw her blanket to the floor in a pile. Jumping down, she grabbed the topsuit hanging next to the bed. "Bex?"

Her gaze darted to the empty bunk beside her. Bex let her oversleep? Why? Ezren didn't even pose a threat to her this time! Ezren stuffed her legs into the topsuit. And what about Foster? Were things that off between them? Had he changed his mind about racing after seeing his mom?

"Mother suns," she growled to herself, jabbing her arms into the suit. She grabbed her helmet, strapped her goggs to them, and dashed out the door.

Running down the hallway, she tried to collect her sleep-heavy thoughts. Where had Sylvia said to meet, again? She tried to send a message only to remember the stupid magnetism interference. Oh, right, the lobby. She could check the lobby.

She bounded down the stairs and skidded around the corner, only to find two Naris girls in topsuits standing at the entrance to the airlock, gazing out at the whipping ice.

"Where is everybody?" Ezren huffed. "Am I late?"

One of them, the girl with red hair and freckles—Callie, if Ezren remembered her name right—turned to her with curious eyes. For a moment, she hesitated, and then she frowned. "They didn't tell you?" She pointed out at the storm. "The starting line's about two miles north of here. The racers left just a few minutes ago in the storm trucks, and... I thought I saw Foster go with them."

Ezren gaped at her for a moment. Had Sylvia said that? Had she really missed it? She still couldn't believe they'd left without her. Had Foster found a different doubles partner somehow? She pressed her hand to her mouth as if to keep the betrayal and shame coursing through her from escaping. Did they really think she was that incompetent? Maybe she was.

Callie looked at the dark-haired girl for confirmation, and she nodded. "The alternates are waiting here, but... I didn't think Belethea had enough racers for a bench."

Ezren bit the inside of her cheek so hard she tasted blood. "You said two miles, right?" She looked at the map in her goggs again. She had to try. If there was even the faintest chance he was waiting for her, she had to take it. "I can make that. Do you have the coords?"

"Uh... yeah." Callie pulled up her map and read off a sequence of numbers.

"Thank you so much," Ezren said, jamming on her helmet and mentally marking the coords on her map.

"Anytime." Callie smiled. "I hope you're able to catch them."

And with that, Ezren shoved open the heavy airlock door and ran out into the storm.

CHAPTER 17

"SO HOW LONG until they start now?" Foster asked.

The racers had all gathered into an empty lab space that had essentially been turned into a large staging area, or holding pen, for the racers. A holopro of the ice pelting down on the rocky landscape outside covered one wall, and an array of chairs had been set up for the racers while they waited for the weather to become survivable. The royalers buzzed around the cold breakfast buffet of synthetic meats, cheeses, and breads, or lay about the room, talking in muted murmurs as they waited.

Sylvia projected a message from her goggs. "They're saying another hour at least." She looked at the three Beletheans spread out on the floor and across the chairs. "Try to relax and save your energy."

"Well, at least E will be happy she got to sleep in," Grady said from where he lay on the floor, his head on his pack and his eyes half-closed while a comic holopro glowed in front of his face. He turned to Bex stretching out her hamstrings next to him. "Hey, Bex, could you wake me up when the race is about to start too? I could really use the extra Zs."

"Sure," she replied. "I'll ask Sylvia for a bucket of ice."

Grady didn't even flinch. "Now, now, save the violence for the scraps."

"I'm not even sure that would wake up Ezren," Foster said. "That girl sleeps like the dead. There have been days I've had to actually shake her awake."

"You mean sleeping beauty doesn't wake up with a kiss?" Grady smirked.

"Maybe she's just waiting for her Prince Charming," Sylvia teased, plucking a synth strawberry from her plate.

"Well, she's going to be waiting a long time on this team," Bex said under her breath.

"Yeah, yeah." Foster waved them off.

"Maybe you should go check on her just in case," Sylvia said, distracted by something on her holopro. "She was already asleep when I came around with the updates last night, so she probably still thinks we're meeting in the lobby."

"She's fine," Bex said. "I left a note directly on her chest."

Foster seized on the excuse. Maybe he could get some time alone with Ezren before the race to smooth things over, even just a little. He could explain about Vieve and his mom... that is, if Ezren didn't kill him first for waking her up before the absolute last second. "I'll check, just in case."

Grady made kissing noises as he walked away. "Don't forget the smooch."

"Oh, hush. You're just jealous," Sylvia said, smacking his arm.

"Well, of course," Grady replied.

Foster strode up the stairs and down the hall to Ezren's door. Swallowing the strange knot in his throat, he raised his hand and knocked. Then he laughed at himself. There was no way Ezren would wake up to that. He slid the door open and poked his head in the dark room.

"Ezren?" he whispered.

Nothing. He peeked into the top bunk and found that it was, in fact, empty. So she'd gotten up? That was weird. He turned on the light just to make sure before walking down the hall, his gut churning. It was almost 0530. He tried to imagine Ezren waking up to an empty room. She probably would've fritzed. And if she'd gone into the lobby and no one had been there, what would she have done?

He jolted into a jog, down the stairs and into the lobby where a cluster of Naris and Syndali Station royalers gathered on the huge sofas. He stopped short, surprised to see Talmadge among them with a smug grin on his face, his two-toned buzz cut gold and red now. Wow, so Syndali really *had* picked him up. He must've had some serious connections. Callie sat next to him, smiling and laughing with the others.

Foster jumped down the last few steps and bounded up behind them. "Hey, did you see a girl come down here? Magenta-brown hair, smallish, kind of pale."

They all burst into another round of laughter, and the hair on Foster's neck stood up.

Callie tried to get out the words through her giggles, and then finally had to take a few big breaths to get it under control. "Well... we may have had a little fun with her."

Foster's teeth ground together, his hands tightening into fists. "What do you mean 'fun with her'?"

"Oh, c'mon Sterling, you know that girl wasn't royaler material. Cal just sent her on a little extra conditioning practice," Talmadge continued, his arms and legs spread wide on the couch. "Unless she's an absolute fritzer, she's probably wandered back by now."

Oh, suns. Ezren never turned back from anything. "Where. Is. She?" Foster said, pronouncing the words slowly.

"Who knows," Lucian snorted. "She was heading to the starting line last we saw her."

Callie put a hand over her mouth, giggling through her fingers. "To be honest, I can't believe she actually went."

"You sent her into a whiteout by herself?" Foster lunged forward, barely managing to restrain himself from throttling Callie. "What the fod is wrong with you?"

She flinched back, her eyes wide as if he'd slapped her.

Foster's gaze darted to the forecast in his goggs: -67° and the storm wasn't supposed to slack off for another hour. He pointed a finger at Callie. "If anything happens to her, it's on *you*." With that, he ran to the holding area.

He careened into the quiet, knocking over chairs as he grabbed his helmet.

Sylvia jumped to her feet in alarm, drawing the curious stares of the other teams. "Foster, what's going on?"

"One of the Naris royalers sent Ezren out into the blizzard. We need storm trucks and the chip tracker on her now."

"What?" Sylvia's full red lips parted, her goggs flashing with text as she sent out messages. "I'll let everyone know, but most of the storm trucks are already at the first checkpoint, Foster. It'll take them hours to get back in this weather." She chewed on a knuckle. "And the temperature's almost to mayday levels. There's no way they're going to let anyone leave."

"What about her chip tracker? Can't we find out where she is, at least?"

Grady popped to his feet, his own goggs glowing. "The cliff's magnetism has been chaffing our readings all day." His narrowed gaze flicked back and forth as he read.

Bex projected a holo-map in front of her. "Yes, but it looks like if you go out a quarter of a mile from the cliffs, you might be able to get a patchy reading."

Foster shoved his helmet on his head and snapped his goggs around them. "On it. You all work it from here. I'm going to try to get a location."

"No way, Foster, you can't go out there," Sylvia hissed.

"And you can't stop me," he said, already jogging away.

"The temperature's still dropping, and if she's hurt, she needs help now."

He didn't wait for an answer before he ran out of the staging area, through the lobby, past the still-whispering spacers, and into the airlock. Without a second thought, he shoved open the door and stepped out into the storm.

The wind hit him first. At ninety-eight knots, it nearly knocked him off his feet. The cold was next, seeping through his topsuit and into his bones like splashing into an ice bath. The nanites in his suit churned through the threads as they leeched his own energy to generate heat and protect his skin from the melting ice.

But he was still freezing. He could barely see through the wind-whipped sheets of ice and snow crashing around him, the larger chunks splintering against his helmet. Even with his suit distributing the force, the blows sent jolts of pain radiating through his body. Ezren had already been out here for an hour? There was no way she was still standing. He grimaced as he started to bound laboriously through the knee-high snow. Just a quarter mile. He could make it a quarter mile.

The look on her face as she closed the door on him last night stuck in his thoughts. He should've busted into the room right there and explained everything. Cleared the air. Now she was missing, and he hadn't even gotten a chance to explain himself. He should've known better than to let things go unsaid. Wait till the race was over? He dodged a large chunk of rock hurtling over his head, and continued on, trying to stay low to the ground. Who cared about this stupid race? It was just an exhibition anyway.

And now here he was again, searching for his doubles partner. The memory of finding Vieve was enough to send nausea bubbling through his stomach. He wouldn't let that happen to Ezren.

His goggs beeped as the temperature dropped to -70° and started to chirp out the mayday signal. Fodding chaff, it was shafting cold. Ezren wouldn't just stay out here. She had to have gotten lost somehow with the false readings or gotten hurt. And honestly, the girl had such a good sense of direction, he had to expect the latter. His goggs chirped again. He'd made it: 0.25 miles. He crouched behind a boulder in the field of white, sending out a frantic message.

Foster: Ezren, where are you?

His goggs readout froze and stuttered as it tried to send out the message. *Error.* The temp dropped another degree, and his fingers started to numb, his breath coming in fast clouds that rushed away in the wind.

He staggered farther, a rock bashing into his shoulder.

Foster: Ezren, where are you!

More flickering. Chaff the fodding magnetic cliffs. Why would they make a research outpost here if they couldn't get any comms out?

Had he checked her suit before they left? No, he definitely had... but then they'd gone topside the day after. It had been a calm day, but what if something happened to it? He'd planned to check it again this morning for tears. In this weather, the smallest nick would mean death. Or, chaff, it could've been ripped in the first moment she stepped out the door. The horror of it sent him into a shambling run.

Foster: EZREN. WHERE ARE YOU!

Finally, his goggs chirped with her location. Not far. His legs jellied with relief. *Thank the suns.* He started toward her flashing dot, the wind lashing at his back. But... she wasn't moving... and she wasn't answering her messages. He started running faster. Something had happened. But that didn't mean she was dead. Maybe she was just scared, taking shelter, rolled an ankle. Surely it couldn't happen again. Not twice. Not to Ezren, he—

His goggs beeped in a series of urgent notifications—one of them Ezren's mayday—but in the rush of updates, he didn't pick up on the chunk of rock hurtling in his direction until it slammed into the back of his head.

CHAPTER 18

EZREN'S BROWS shot up as the notifications updated in a flurry of messages from Foster, followed almost immediately by his mayday signal. Her eyes widened in the darkness of the storm den she'd taken shelter in, squeezed in between the stacks of emergency supplies. He was out there in the storm? She leapt out of her heated survival bag and flung open the metal hatch above her.

The blizzard whipped in full force as she tumbled into the snow and debris. Checking her goggs, she calculated she had roughly five minutes to find him before her suit would start to fail. But if he was already out here... he had even less.

He was close though. She could reach him.

Ezren launched into the blinding swirl of white, her legs churning through the deep snow. The wind flung sharp rocks into her suit, and she lifted her arms to protect herself, praying to the elder suns it wouldn't rip as the cold already licked her skin while the nanites struggled to keep up. The temperature dropped another degree, and the alarms sounded in her helmet, urging her to go back. But her gaze stayed pinned to the dot in her goggs. The one that wasn't moving.

"Foster!" she shouted, the wind snatching away her voice. "Can you hear me?"

Her heart pounded in her chest, her breath coming fast as she ran through the snow, her heavy mag-boots sinking into the drifts. She should've been nearly on top of him now, but visibility was practically zero in the pelting snow. What if his location wasn't updating? She scoured the blinding white for footprints, her time ticking down on her goggs.

A chunk of rock bashed into her shoulder, throwing her to the ground. The beep of her warning alarm crescendoed into the cacophony of a mayday.

"Mother suns." Ezren clutched a hand to the rip in her suit. Although the auto-repairing nanitelattice already whirred under her fingers, the burning cold of the air seared her skin. Whatever time she'd thought she'd had was gone. "Come on! Cut me some chaffing slack!" she yelled to the sky.

But Foster was still out there. If she turned around without him, she was sentencing him to death. Period. His only hope was in the storm den, and he probably didn't have the locations uploaded to his goggs like she did, per her mother's long-standing requirement for surface runs.

"Foster!" Ezren crawled along the ground, fighting the furious wind. "I can't leave without him," she whispered to herself. "I won't."

As if hearing her, an update chirped through her goggs. Ezren flicked away the messages to home in on Foster's beacon. *There.* He'd moved. Just a little, but enough. She lurched off to her left, but after three steps, tripped over something hidden in the snow.

Swearing, she looked to her feet and caught a bright teal flash of a Belethean topsuit peeking out of the snow beneath her. "Foster!"

His motionless form sent a bolt of fear crackling through her. *No.* With her free hand, she dusted the snow from his prone body, looking for damage. Spidery cracks ran along his helmet, but other than that, she could see no obvious tears. The vitals displayed on his goggs were positive, but his eyes were closed.

"Foster! Wake up!" she yelled again, shaking his shoulder.

He winced and a tightness eased from Ezren's chest. At least he was responsive. She could work with that. But they had to get back to the storm den first. She checked the rip on her shoulder. Although it was still leaking cold air into her suit, at least it had stitched together well enough to cover her skin from direct contact. It would have to do.

She shoved her hands under his arms and around his chest. "Okay, Foster, this isn't going to be graceful, but it'll be fast. We're going to be okay."

With that, she dragged him over the snow and rock and dirt backward toward the storm den. Their mayday calls screaming in her ears, Ezren didn't stop once. Her arms, legs, and back burned as she pulled him over the snow-slicked terrain, his legs bumping over the rocks. Debris shot by overhead, but Ezren paid it no mind as her body began to shake, her teeth chattering furiously together.

But where was the hatch? Was her chip not updating again? What if she'd already passed it? Ezren's mind fumbled for possibilities, but her frozen body refused to respond. She could be dragging Foster into the middle of nowhere, but if they stopped moving, then they would certainly freeze out—

A hollow thunk sounded under Ezren's boot, and she let herself fall to the ground. With nearly unresponsive fingers, she pawed at the hatch, the seconds ticking away with the blinding snow. Finally, the embedded sensors registered her body heat and popped open with a hiss.

With a cry of relief, Ezren grabbed Foster and lowered him into the shallow bunker. In another fifteen seconds, she hopped in after him and yanked the hatch closed.

The dimly lit space was essentially no bigger than a six-foot metal cube, but it felt like a tropical oasis without the relentless wind. Still, their maydays continued to ring in the unheated bunker. Their body temperatures would need more of an assist.

"Foster... are you still... with me?" Her words were barely understandable between her clattering teeth. She might've imagined it, but she thought she heard him groan in response.

"Good, that's good." She ripped off her own helmet and then gently eased Foster out of his before scanning his head for damage. No visible injuries popped out at her, but that didn't mean he wasn't hurt. Two towers of tightly packed supplies crowded them from either side, but with the closing of the hatch, a strange exhaustion had started to wash over her. Even parsing through the equipment seemed like an unscalable task.

She seized the heating bag she'd been using and slid it over Foster's feet. "I know we haven't knownseach other all that long yet, but I hope you don'tsmind sharing withsme." Her words were slurring now, and if her mind had been clearer, she might've realized what that meant. But right now, all she could think of was getting warm.

Thank the suns the bag was wide, and she was small. She slid in next to Foster, shaking uncontrollably, and with the last bit of her strength, unzipped their suits, peeling them to their waists. Sensing their skin, the bag reacted with a soft green glow of warmth. Although their maydays still blared from their nearby helmets, her temperature mercifully ticked up even as her vision darkened.

"Izorry," she said to the motionless Foster. "Izall I can do now... More later."

With that, her eyes fell closed.

"Ezren. Ezren!"

Ezren blinked, trying to focus her blurry vision on the green-gray eyes in front of her. "Did I oversleep again?" she groaned.

"Not exactly."

Her gaze focused on Foster's face only inches from hers and then proceeded to trail down his shirtless torso, pressed decidedly against her sports bra. *Oh... my... suns.* What had she done? Her body went rigid with panic before it all came back to her. The storm, the cold, the heating bag still nestled around them.

"Oh, right." She turned away from Foster in a desperate attempt to regain her balance. Releasing a slow breath of relief, she swiped a clammy palm across her face, roasting in the pleasantly warm bag. There was an explanation. They were lying in a sack together for survival, and suns help her, she would not make this awkward. She swallowed, steadying herself, and faced him again. "Are you okay? Your helmet was all banged up. I'm sorry, I really shouldn't have fallen asleep with you like that."

"It's okay," he said, touching the back of his head with a wince. "Just a concussion probably."

"Oh, good. You know I—" Ezren bolted upright and scrambled for her goggs, ripping them from her helmet. "The race! Did we miss it? Asdef, Sylvia is going to kill me."

"No, Ezren. The storm is still going. From what sporadic messages are coming in, it looks like they're going to postpone it for another few hours."

"Thank the suns." Ezren flopped back down, looping her goggs around her neck and burrowing into the glorious warmth of the heat bag. Although it was really impossible not to touch Foster in the bag, she tried her best to lean away from him. "I guess we'll just wait it out here then."

Foster sighed and pinched the bridge of his nose, his goggs glinting from where they nestled in his hair. "Are you really going to make me ask?"

"Ask what?"

"Why the suns did you run off into a whiteout by yourself?"

Ezren turned away from him, her fingers fiddling with the splayed magenta strands of her hair. "The girls in the lobby said you'd already left without me."

Foster's body tightened beside her. "And you didn't question it? At all? You can read the storm patterns better than anyone. You had to have known it was suicide."

"The whole idiotic race is suicide. How was I supposed to know that would stop them this time?"

He raked an agitated hand through his brown waves, his voice lowering to a grumble. "I can't believe you thought I would leave without you. I always come to get you."

She shrugged, still not meeting the stare she could feel boring into the side of her face. "I was in a rush after thinking I overslept. I don't exactly do my best thinking in the morning... especially when I'm in the middle of a panic." She finally looked at him, her brow furrowing. "But why are you getting all fritzed with me when you turned around and did the exact same thing?"

He held her gaze now, his face so close she could feel his even warm breaths on her cheek. "I *always* come to get you."

And Ezren really didn't have anything to say to that. Something about it made her insides melt into a dysfunctional puddle of mush. "You scared me, you know? When I found you on the ground out there, I wasn't sure you were..."

He softened a little and shifted his head with a wince. "Yeah, I'll admit it wasn't the best thought-out rescue. But with the storm trucks out and comms down, there weren't a lot of options."

"I hope our messages went through before Sylvia pulled all of her hair out." Ezren stiffened, her hands clenching together. "And your mom. She must be so worried about you. You've sent her a message telling her you're okay, right?"

"Ha," Foster snorted humorlessly. "You obviously don't know Greta Sterling. I'm sure she didn't bat an eye over it."

But Ezren's mind was already spinning into overdrive. "And she'll think it's my fault. Oh, suns, if you're not going to send her a message, I will," she said, already silently dictating the words to her goggs.

Foster's hand on her bare shoulder stopped her. "Seriously, Ezren, don't."

Ezren blinked, frozen under his broad palm. "But... if it were my mom—"

"It's not. Look, Greta and I aren't exactly close."

"You call her Greta?" Ezren wrinkled her nose. "That seems a little... weird."

He removed his hand, and Ezren tried not to miss the feel of it on her skin. "Well, we're a bit of a weird family."

She propped her head on her elbow, silently encouraging him to continue. Anything to distract them from the situation.

Meeting her eager glance, he shook his head with a wry grin. "My mom spent most of the last fifteen years on Naris Station, training the team there, and my dad, well, I don't know if you've heard of Gerard Y from Belethea Badditude."

Ezren scrunched up her face, trying to pry the name from her memory. "Why does that sound familiar?"

"They were more popular a couple decades ago, but have you heard of that song, *Star Jungle*?"

"Yes. They play that song on every music serv."

"That's them. My dad's the lead guitarist."

"Well, that's kind of crisp," Ezren said, still trying to rack her mind for a picture of the guy. "Okay, so your parents were a top Belethea royaler and a rock star."

"Yep."

"Wow." Ezren chuckled. "That must've made for an interesting childhood."

"Not really. With my dad always on tour, and my mom living on the station, I was raised mostly by the nannies." Foster pillowed his hands beneath his head, and the bag rustled around him. "I think that's why I wanted to race for Belethea so badly when I was little. Somehow I thought maybe if we could prove we were more than some backwater planet, they'd come home."

"Oh." Ezren retracted all her thoughts of little Foster going to rock concerts and cheering at the BRR. Instead, a picture of a boy alone in a fancy house took over her mind. Although Foster seemed matter-of-fact about it, it sounded incredibly lonely.

"What about you?" he countered.

"What? What about me?"

"I saw your mom and brother at the tryout, but I don't know a lot about them."

Ezren shifted on the metal floor. "There's not a lot to say, really."

"Oh, c'mon, I told you about my dysfunctional family."

She rolled her eyes with a reluctant smirk. "My family isn't nearly as interesting as yours. No rock stars. No royalers."

"But you have a dog, right? That's better anyway."

"Waffle's a capybog—a genetic mix between a capybara and a dog." The smile pulled harder on Ezren's lips, the patter of debris drumming against the hatch door. "They were originally engineered to increase biodiversity on

Obrone, but they were so friendly people started breeding them as pets."

He snorted. "A capybog, huh? You should have brought her with you to Carmella. It would've been worth it just to see Sylvia wig."

"No way, I don't know what my brother would do without Waffle. She's even considered part of his therapy regimen ever since my dad..." Ezren swallowed, feeling suddenly warm. She couldn't remember the last time she'd talked about her dad, but in the dim lighting of the storm den, with the wind howling outside, the words seemed to flow from her tongue. "After my brother got hurt in a speedjet accident, my dad went space-side for a remote job to help pay for Sammy's regen surgery." She licked her lips, her gaze boring into the gray metal ceiling. "The surgery didn't go as well as we hoped, and Sammy was having a hard time, so my dad got Waffle to keep him company while he was away."

"That was pretty blime of your dad. Regen is rough. I could've definitely used a capybog during mine."

Ezren turned to him, her brows knitting. "You've gone through regen?"

Foster held up one hand and wiggled his fingers. "Yep. Racing crash. Lost my right hand two years ago. I was already talking to the Belethean coach, but when my mom fritzed and threatened to permanently bench me, it was kind of the last straw."

Ezren grabbed his hand, inspecting it. She could just barely make out the new, lighter skin from the old. "Wow, this is amazing work. Was your doctor here on Belethea? Do you still take the integration meds? Any pain?"

He raised an eyebrow. "I didn't know you were so interested."

Ezren released his hand with a blush and moved away

again. "Sorry, that was intrusive. It's just that Sammy's going to need another procedure in the next few years, hopefully with better matched cells this time." And if he didn't, the nonnative cells would eventually spread to his heart and cause mass organ failure. She quickly shoved the thought away. Not yet—they still had time.

"It's okay. You can look if you want." He placed one of her hands on his. "I was lucky. Full regen in six months, off integration meds in twelve, but it still hurts whenever I use my fingers too much. I got surgery on Naris, but I'll ask the doc if she has any Belethean contacts."

"That'd be incredible. Thank you, Foster." *Full regen in six months.* She couldn't imagine what that had cost. Sammy's recovery took three years for both legs, and that had nearly bankrupted their family, even with her dad's extra income.

"So is your dad still out there then, on his remote job?"

Ezren wrapped her arms around herself. It looked like they were going to talk about all her most hated topics today. If he could figure out a way to weave Davis Banda into the conversation, he'd have her top three. "I... uh... don't know."

"You don't know?"

"The money and the messages stopped coming a couple years ago. The company said he just turned in his notice and quit. They assumed he was going home, but there's no record of him buying tickets." She ran her fingers back and forth over the slick material of the warming bag. "For all intents and purposes, it seems like he just disappeared."

For a moment, Foster was silent, and Ezren could almost hear him thinking in the quiet. There was no shortage of people who booked passage through the wormgate under false names looking to start new lives. Especially those who had just completed high-stress remote tours.

Maybe, so far away from his family, he'd fallen in love again and decided to start a new one. Maybe he'd cracked under the strain of isolation. But one thing remained the same no matter how you looked at it—none of the options were good. If he'd wanted to get a message to them, he could have. But it didn't make her stop wanting to know what happened.

"I'm sorry," Foster murmured. "That must be shaft."

"But at least we have Waffle," Ezren said, trying desperately to retract the tears swimming in her vision.

Foster chuckled, his hand finding hers in the dark and giving it a squeeze. "Maybe we could at least include her in some of our publicity shots. I bet Sylvia would die."

Ezren laughed at the thought. "Waffle would probably be better at it than me. I haven't exactly been doing our brand any favors."

"Yeah... our *brand*... we should probably talk about that."

Ezren slapped her hand to her forehead. The suns were punishing her. For what, she didn't know. She hadn't even realized she had so many topics she wanted to avoid until today. "Look... I'm really sorry about the kiss," she babbled out for what felt like the tenth time. "After Harland's spiel, I panicked a little bit. I should've known you still need time, and I really didn't know the reaction would be so bad. I should've talked to you—"

"Stop." Foster propped himself up on his elbow, the heating bag falling away from his muscled chest, and his gray-green eyes piercing her.

Ezren quailed inwardly. This wasn't going to be good. How had she been so dumb?

"Yesterday, you said you knew how I felt about Vieve. What did you mean?"

Ezren swallowed, wishing she could edge farther away without getting out of the heating sack, her words babbling out in a nervous gush. "Well, Micah told me you two were head over heels. And I saw the VSoc articles. You were in love. I totally under—"

"Vieve and I were never in love. We didn't even like each other."

Ezren stopped, momentarily shocked into silence. "Um... What?"

"As the top royalers, Coach Bhatt assigned Vieve and me to be doubles. Vieve was super into VSoc, so she wanted to put on a show to up our popularity—off again, on again... We both would've done anything to win, but we were a bad match, even as doubles. It's one of the reasons things... went wrong."

Ezren stared at him, trying to process what he was saying. So... they weren't star-crossed lovers? It was all made up? Wow. This was why she didn't follow VSoc. But what did she say now?

"O-oh." She laughed and looked down at her hands to avoid his gaze. "I guess I'll add that to the things I totally got wrong." Maybe she could try to change the subject. "Speaking of getting stuff wrong, you know I think we could really increase the weather algorithm accuracy on these suits if we use Tuzuno's storm-tracking—"

"Is that why you've been so weird?"

"The weather accuracy?" She reluctantly met his gaze, still steady on her. "Well, it really just occurred to me, and I think Micah—"

"No, Ezren. C'mon. I'm talking about after the kiss."

Ezren took a long slow breath. There was no escaping this. She was totally and completely trapped. "I don't know. This is all so weird, Foster. I mean, after talking to Harland, it seemed like the right move for the VSoc thing. But you obviously didn't want to... so then I felt bad, and I got confused, and now I'm completely lost. As usual."

"I wasn't into it?"

Ezren threw up her hands, her exasperation overcoming her embarrassment. "Well, you didn't kiss me back. So what was I supposed—"

Then his lips were moving against hers, his bare chest pressed against her sports bra, and his hand warm on her cheek. And this was no friendly peck, no polite kiss for the cams. His mouth was hot and searching, and she responded in kind. Every hair on her body stood on end, her back arching into him, until just as suddenly, he pulled away.

She gasped for breath as his swirling eyes looked into hers. "I don't want to kiss you for the cams, or for our brand, or because fodding Harland says we should." His breath misted in the air between them, smelling of sweet mint. "But that does *not* mean I don't want to kiss you." He bent down and kissed her again, gently this time.

"Oh," she breathed, blinking rapidly, her thoughts and heart and stomach one huge fluttery mess.

"Forget about all that fake stuff, Ezren. I want us to be real."

Ezren nodded, her chest heaving as if she'd run a mile, and all the feelings she'd been trying to ignore crystallizing into a rush of elated relief. "I want that too."

Foster's face crinkled in a rare full smile Ezren couldn't help but return. He kissed her again, light and teasing, sending a pulse of electricity tingling across Ezren's lips. She wanted nothing more than to bottle that moment and save it for her stormiest days.

"So no more weirdness, right?" he asked, pressing his forehead to hers.

She shrugged with a smile, her cheeks flushing as she became hyperaware of his skin against hers. "Well, you already know I'm always weird."

"Definitely don't change that." He twirled a strand of her hair around a finger. "As long as you—"

The beep of their goggs interrupted him with a slew of backlogged messages slipping through a lull in the storm.

Ezren projected the first message into the air in front of them, and her eyes flew wide.

Her panicked stare met Foster's.

The race had started without them.

CHAPTER 19

FOSTER SAT in the back of the storm truck exhausted, sore, and, oddly, smiling. He'd never missed the first cut of a royale before, much less by an entire hour, and he knew as the race transport bumped through the icy landscape to the finish line that the irate faces of Harland and his mother probably awaited him. But with the hot weight of a warming blanket draped across his lap and Ezren curled against his side, he couldn't bring himself to care.

No one could've expected them to make up an hour, and, all things considered, they'd made incredible time. He'd thought Ezren had been fast in the first race, but that didn't at all compare to her now, after two months of regimented training and nutrition—she was a machine. And she was with *him*. He pulled her closer, pressing his lips to her hair, and she looked up at him with a tired smile, her eyes tight with worry.

He leaned close to her ear, the truck ridiculously loud as the hail and rocks clattered against it. "It's going to be fine."

"You don't think Sylvia will be mad?" she asked, raising her voice to be heard.

"No way. Trust me, she'll just be glad you're all right."

And that was the truth. Harland, on the other hand... But who cared what Harland thought. The guy wasn't the team owner, and technically he wasn't even the manager. He was just the operations exec. A person who had apparently always existed, but who'd never bothered to show his face before they hit rock bottom. Now he just popped in so... what? No one else died? Well, then he should be giving the Naris royalers fodding chaff for letting Ezren run out into a death storm.

And yet... somehow Foster still knew this wasn't going to play out in their favor. After ten years in the sport, there were some things he knew with a bitter certainty, and one of them was if something went wrong, it was always the royaler's fault. It was one of the reasons why Vieve's investigation had chaffed him so much. The investigation had reported that it'd been her fault for not checking her suit—her recklessness that had gotten her separated from her doubles partner. Then in two days, the investigators were gone, and they were all supposed to return to business as usual.

At least Bhatt had the decency to leave with his tail tucked between his legs. Not that it was his fault either.

The storm truck slowed as it approached the metal bubble of another, smaller outpost that served as the finish line. Royalers stumbled through two tall metal posts, their chests heaving through their dinged suits, and farther off, Foster could make out a last-leg scrap going on in the home stretch. Reporters and fans clustered in their storm trucks, cheering them on through their speaker systems as one of the royalers landed a haymaker, sending their opponent skidding across the icy ground. Now two on one, the other teammate didn't last three seconds before her attackers slammed her head into the ground and ran toward the finish line.

The spectators soaked it up with another clamorous roar. This was what they loved about the royales. Not the running, not the driving, not even the brawls. They loved the last-minute, out-of-the-blue scraps that could hit you at any moment. It was the reason you always had to be on your game. Foster glanced down at Ezren tucked under his arm. It was a part of the race she had yet to experience, and if he was being honest, he was glad he'd get another month or two to prepare her for it. She was strong, no doubt, but she didn't have that viciousness, that necessary paranoia to keep looking over her shoulder.

The truck rumbled to a stop and a cluster of reporters huddled around the vehicle, waiting for the failure story of the day and probably hoping they were in a suitably gory condition.

Foster unbuckled his restraints and paused with his hand on the door latch. "You ready?"

Perched on her seat, Ezren chewed her bottom lip. "I guess so."

"Just remember, it's going to be fine, and you don't have to answer any of their questions."

She nodded, and he flashed her what he hoped was a reassuring smile before he opened the door.

The questions lurched out in a furious rush as the bright lights of the recording drones buzzed around them.

"Foster Sterling, where have you been for the last eight hours?"

"Are you trying to get back at your mother?"

"Why do you keep getting separated from your doubles?"

Foster's gaze swept the crowd for any sign of Sylvia, Harland, or his mother. None. That was a relatively good sign. Hopefully, it meant they were too busy with Grady and Bex to care what the last-ranked Belethean pair did. Not looking at any of the reporters, Foster opened the door wide and offered his hand to Ezren. Mouth open, she goggled at the jostling crowd.

"Ezren Hart, were you trying to avoid the race?"

"How do you feel your chances are as a rookie?"

With the other teams here, their coverage was five times what it had been for their tryout. And even so, this was nothing compared to what it would be for the BRR qualifier.

Foster folded his arm around her shoulders, and the questions immediately changed.

"How long have you two been together?"

"Is Ezren the new Genevieve?"

He could feel Ezren flinch at that last question, so he gave her a squeeze as he shepherded her into the dome airlock.

The door hissed closed behind them, and a sudden silence cut through the chatter. Alone in the small metal compartment, Foster looked at Ezren, her dark eyes round and uncertain.

"You still with me?"

Her gaze sharpened, as if coming out of a daze, and she turned toward him with one of her wide smiles. "Definitely."

Leaning down, he kissed her softly just to be sure, wishing they had time for more. Suns, he would definitely be doing that a lot more often now.

She laughed as he pulled away, her cheeks flushed. "Sorry, I still can't get over how crazy people are about this race."

"You haven't seen anything yet." He led her through the inner door into the milling crowd of teams and support personnel. Gear booths, team tents, and food vendors littered the open space projected to look like a colorful tropical jungle. "Meet you—"

"Ezren! Foster!" Sylvia's voice shrilled through the crowd as she flung her arms around both of them. "How could you be so stupid? Holy chaff, I almost tore my hair out because of you two! And I chaffing love my hair."

Ezren's brows sloped up, her worry cresting again. "Sylvia, I'm so sorry, really, I didn't—"

"Don't *ever* do that again. Seriously, I won't survive," Sylvia continued her tirade as if Ezren hadn't spoken. "I think I've lost about ten years of my life. And you!" She reached up and clapped her hands around Foster's cheeks, shaking him. "I can't believe you went out there."

Foster said nothing, knowing from extensive experience that he had to let Sylvia get everything out before trying to get a word in edgewise.

"And then, did you decide to do the first leg just to worry me more? With the stupid slow chip updates, we were still looking for you in the storm den."

She let out a long breath as if the words had taken the steam out of her. She pulled them both closer. "I'm just so glad you're all right." Her gaze toggled between them, worry and relief mixing on her face. "But you should know—"

"Hart. Sterling!" Harland's voice snapped through the crowd as he strode toward them, attracting a few curious glances. Grady and Bex trailed behind, a stiffness to their steps. "Glad you finally made it. We're having a meeting." He waved them into one of the empty waiting rooms.

Foster's stomach sank, and Ezren's eyes grew round again. She frowned at Foster, and he rubbed a reassuring hand across her back before following her into the room. Colorful autumn trees rustled in the holopro around them, and a scattering of metal-framed chairs dotted the white tile. Inside, Grady leaned against the wall in his warmups, his face flat, while Bex stood rigid, her arms crossed and her expression unreadable, as usual.

"How'd it go today?" Ezren asked Grady as Sylvia and Harland filed in, but before they could close the door behind them, a familiar shout rose over the clamor.

"Hey, wait! Is Foster in there? I want to see him."

Foster ran a hand across his face. Of all the things, he really didn't need this right now.

"Ms. Sterling—" Sylvia started.

"No, this is ridiculous." His mother appeared at the doorway, a vein pulsing in her forehead. "This is *your* fault. Pairing my son with an incompetent and risking his life. What were you thinking? And you!" She turned to Harland. "This whole team is a hazard. They don't have a real coach, equipment, or enough capable athletes to fill the minimum roster. You tell Calderon he's out of his geriatric mind, keeping the team running in this state. And I don't want to hear any chaff about sponsors. Either give the team what they need or shut them down. This is how people die in—"

"Mom!" Foster crossed the room, shame and rage steaming through him in waves of heat. Her gaze snapped to his, eyes burning above her flushed cheeks. "Get. Out. If you really cared about the Belethea team, you wouldn't have abandoned us for fodding *Naris*."

"You can't be on this team, Foster. It's dangerous, and with your skill, you could do so much—"

"Dangerous?" He slammed his hand against the door frame. "Why don't you go talk to your own athletes? You know, the ones who sent Ezren into the storm in the first place?"

"I already—"

"I don't even care. Just keep them and yourself away from me and my team. Has-been chaffing sell-out." He didn't wait for a response before manually shoving the door closed.

Slowly, he turned around to the ashen faces in the room— Bex, Grady, Sylvia, and Harland all mirrored some version of shock. But Ezren, of course, looked like she'd been hit by a magtrain.

Grady broke the silence first. "So... how 'bout that team meeting?"

The dread in Foster only thickened. If Grady and Bex had done well, Grady would've said something already. And if he hadn't... He looked at Bex.

"We got knocked out in the brawl," Bex said, answering his unspoken question in her matter-of-fact tone.

"Knocked out? How?" That didn't make any sense. Grady was the wheels, and Bex was the fists... after the legs, they should've been a shoo-in.

"Talmadge was waiting for us, and he knew exactly what to do," Bex said.

Foster nodded, thinking of Lucian's cocky attitude that morning. He'd probably been training for just that moment. His fists tightened.

Ezren winced as she glanced between Bex and Foster. "Are you okay?"

Grady shrugged again, noticeably keeping the weight off his right leg and holding his left arm close like an injured wing. "It's fine. We were—"

"An absolute disgrace," Harland said coldly. "The worst performance in Belethean history. It's already blaring all over VSoc: Belethea's only double couldn't even finish in the first exposition of the year." He straightened his suit jacket. "From now on, Sterling and Gunderson race together."

"What?" Foster said, heat rising in him once more. "You have to be joking. We didn't even get a fair chance."

Sylvia wrapped her arms tightly around herself. "Maybe if we brought on a new coach or a few more teams—"

"We don't have the funds, and VSoc cred has hit rock bottom," Harland said, his face suddenly showing a network of weary lines. "We'll have to sell the new teams hard, and until the ratings rebound, we'll have to dock pay to fund the marketing campaign." He sighed, pulling at the loose goggs around his neck as if they were choking him. "Perhaps Greta is right. If we can't turn it around here, this might be the last of the Belethean royalers." His lips twitched with something like disappointment. "A sad way to go out." With that, he strode through the door, his usual indifferent mask piecing into place as the door slid shut behind him.

The autumn trees rustled around them with a gust of the air cycler, and Foster's gaze swept across the room. Sylvia swallowed, her brown eyes shining with suppressed tears, and Ezren stared intensely at her knotted hands, guilt almost visibly weighing on her.

Grady and Bex looked strangely unsurprised, their expressions impassive. Why weren't they protesting this shaft? Grady, at least, should've been upset, right? Unless... had they planned this somehow? Grady was always looking for a way to fod with him. Realization burned through Foster in a blazing fury, and he lunged toward Grady, slamming his hand into the metal wall next to his head.

"You threw the brawl."

A flash of surprise flickered across Grady's face before he looked away, his gaze hooded with calculated boredom. "Fod off, kin. I don't owe you any answers." He pulled a hovercam from his pocket, and it hummed to life in his hand.

"Oh, shut up, Grady." Bex took off her steel goggs and rubbed slowly at a scuff on the lens. "He didn't throw the brawl. Lucian's a lot stronger than he was last year, and he knew all of our soft spots. Besides, Grady was never the strongest fighter anyway."

"So putting him with Ezren, our *weakest*, is a good idea, how?" Foster nearly shouted. "They'll be destroyed."

Ezren's cheeks reddened, and she folded her hands behind her back. "Maybe... it's a good idea then." She absently kicked at one of the metal chairs, her attention stuck to the white tile floor. "To have the best fighters together. Whatever gives Belethea the best chance is what we should do, right?"

The air went out of Foster's lungs. Did she really mean

that? Hadn't they been a good team? Wasn't this something she wanted to do together?

Sylvia massaged her brow with one hand. "For the record, though I don't like Harland, I don't think this is a bad idea. The fans never really took to the Sterling/Hart combo, and we know Guns/Sterling is a strong team—one that doesn't threaten Genevieve's legacy."

Grady's frown deepened, and Foster longed to break something in the spartan room. How did that lie of a relationship still seep into every part of his life? Nothing that girl ever did was real. He could barely fodding stand her for suns' sake.

"Plus, Simon has always been a bit of an unpredictable wild child. Who better to be his double than the dark horse, herself?" Sylvia brought up her holopro, and Foster could nearly hear the whir of the gears turning in her mind. "I can already see how we're going to spin this." *Coaches couldn't keep apart passionate lovers* popped up in big letters on her holo, and a wave of nausea swept through Foster. "Don't you worry about the pay dock." She squeezed Ezren's arm. "We're going to have those points back in no time."

Grady's usual confident smirk returned as he tossed his hovercam in the air. Brushing by Foster, he offered a hand to Ezren. "I think Hart/Grady can give them a run for their money, E. I've always loved a dramatic underdog win. What do you think?"

Ezren blinked once, twice. Then, not looking at Foster, she reached out and squeezed his hand. "I'm in."

Grady lifted her hand to his lips, pressing a kiss to the inside of her wrist. "Then we'll give them a show, huh?"

Fury boiled in Foster's stomach. *What. The. Fod.* Grady was doing this to get back at him for Vieve. But why in the chaff was Ezren going along with it? Hadn't she just kissed him in the storm truck? Hadn't that meant something? He froze. Or was she still just playing this stupid game? He went to take a step forward, but Bex stopped him with a heavy hand on his shoulder.

"Let it go," she murmured.

"That looks perfect," Sylvia cooed, her goggs flashing red to capture the moment. Ezren blushed pink, and her gaze flicked nervously to Foster's.

"Now make sure you stick together for the rest of the exhibition." She shooed the two of them out the door and shot a warning look at Foster. "Stick to the script. I don't want to send any confusing messages."

"Are you sure this isn't weird, Sylvia, because Foster and I —" Ezren started.

"Don't worry, E, if you want the spotlight you've got to be creative," Grady said. "And if it's what the fans want, they'll roll with it so fast, you won't even miss a beat. I'll bet you a coffee that by the end of the week you'll be the darling of Belethea." Grady shot a smug glance at Foster as he took Ezren's hand and pulled her out the door. "Because I happen to be very good at this."

Ezren started to turn around again, but Sylvia shepherded her out of the foyer. "No coffee, Simon, you know we just—" The door hissed shut behind them, cutting off Sylvia's tired rebuke.

Foster stood frozen, feeling like he'd just been suckerpunched. What had just happened? "That was such a load of chaff."

"Not really. You're just thinking with your pants," Bex said.

Foster flinched away. "I am not."

"Are you sure?" Bex's ice-chip stare tore into him, a shower of projected golden leaves swirling across the wall behind her. "Because everyone here wants to do what's best for Belethea.

And everyone, even your little crush over there, knows that this is the way to go."

"Ezren and I were a good team, Bex. We just didn't get a chance to prove it."

Bex shook her head. "Take off your rosy goggs and take another look. She may have the talent, but not the experience. Zero. She can barely get out of bed on time for practice. Forget about knowing how to deal with the pressure or the stress of racing."

"But Grady is a flighty asschaff. He'll abandon her in a second. What's she going to learn from him?"

"What makes you think that? He and Vieve always did pretty well together."

Foster's mouth went dry. He had nothing to say to that.

"Look, you can still drool over each other off-cam, we're just asking you to do what's best for the team and give it a chance. Grady and Hart have similar styles. They both like to go fast. Not like us."

"Not like us?"

Bex's thin smile widened. "No, we like to kick ass."

Was that right? Were Grady and Ezren really the better fit? Foster pressed his lips together, trying to shake the sinking feeling that Ezren had just abandoned him somehow. Or that he'd abandoned her. How could he protect her if she wasn't his partner? Either way, he couldn't let her go just yet, so he'd have to keep moving forward and figure it out as they went. "Okay, whatever. I'll give it another shot, I guess, but I'm going to need a favor."

Bex crossed her arms. "Depends on the favor."

"You're the best brawler I know. Can you teach Ezren?"

Bex regarded him with cold eyes for a moment. "Maybe."

"Maybe?"

She shrugged. "If she's got fight, I'll show her how to use it."

"And what if she doesn't?"

"Then she's going to lose no matter what."

And then Foster remembered what he both loved and hated about Bex.

She was almost never wrong.

CHAPTER 20

EZREN SLID into the oversized med tub for the fifth time that week, the hot, nanite-infused water bubbling against her skin. Across the room, Simon's eyes had closed as the massage pod kneaded each of his muscles in turn. He might've even been asleep, and Ezren oozed out a jealous sigh. She made a mental note that their thirty-minute training recovery period might be a good time to snatch a nap if she chose the right post-workout therapy.

Exhaustion wrapped around her bones as she went through her messages, rapid-firing answers to her mom's daily check-in and Sam's request for juicy details to pawn off to his friends. She swiped away the invoices from his new therapist but paused on the latest update from the lab and its announcement of the latest research outpost shutdowns. Three of them. And Tuzuno officially had a vacate date that was only a month after the BRR.

Her heart turned to stone and sank into her gut. That was her home they were shutting down. Apparently her campaign to re-energize terraforming was going just *brilliantly*. Even after she'd changed partners to revive the team's VSoc cred and cover Sam's bills and do what was best for Belethea. Now Foster was gone, and everything was still crashing down on her.

Sylvia and Harland had flooded her chip with reassurances that changing doubles was the only choice, but then why did it still feel so wrong?

She took a deep breath. No, there was no point in looking back. The decision was made, and now she just had to keep working. There was still time. Her performance was improving, and with the new sponsors, they'd restored her pay.

Resolving to reattack the terraforming station closures at her next VSoc strategy session, she swiped it away with a scowl. She deleted ten different schedule changes from Sylvia and a sponsor update from Harland before clicking on Micah's latest message—a link to this month's Belethea hype holo.

Micah's cheery face filled Ezren's goggs, her pigtail buns a gold-streaked auburn and her irises glinting deep purple.

"Gooooooood morning, my Belroy boys and babes. Checking in today to bring you the latest upload on what our favorite four have been up to. It has been nearly two months since the outpost exhibition, and our pairs have been hard at it clawing their way back to respectability. Guns/Sterling has been flying through a whirlwind tour of the station's virtual royales and tearing it up." A holopro of Bex and Foster fighting their way through a multi-team scrap in what looked like a huge black sphere flashed across her goggs. "They've placed in the top five in their last six showings, and they even took bronze in the Ruelotte 5000." Another image of Bex and Foster popped up, the grim-faced pair knocking their arms together as they stood on a podium. "Meanwhile, although Hart/Grady is playing their cards closer to their chest, the climb in their reported sim stats has been pretty incredible. Like, I'm not sure Coach Long is giving them time to sleep. Not to mention..."

A holopro montage of Simon and Ezren flowed through her vision—the two of them racing playfully through the crowd on the street, the two of them giggling as they shared an illicit chocolate milkshake and then fleeing the scene as Sylvia barreled in, Simon ruffling Ezren's hair, the two of them strewn on the couch asleep, silly-dancing on the table in the kitchen— every single moment they'd posted for the fans in the last month.

"Just how cute are they?!" Micah squealed. "I absolutely cannot get enough! The dark-horse wild-child pair is absolutely my newest favorite team, and I can't wait to see them go head to head in a real race. All I can say is way to go Coach Long on the change-up. That's all I have for today, Belroy boys and babes, look out for another update next—"

Ezren silenced the holopro and leaned her head back, the hushed gurgling of the med-tub filling her ears. She tried not to think about Foster and Bex moving seamlessly through the pack of racers—a near-perfect team.

If she'd known she wouldn't see him for weeks, she would've tried harder to talk to him after the exhibition. She hadn't realized how serious Sylvia and Harland had been about trying to recoup the lost VSoc cred, until Sylvia used her own money to send Foster and Bex on the virtual royale tour to scrape up some good PR.

Messages to the stations were delayed, but they still should've been able to get through. She looked at the message she'd sent him over a week ago.

Ezren: So how's the tour?

No response.

Should she send another one? *I miss you,* she thought out. Then she remembered how Foster had practically spat out her name: *"Ezren, our weakest."* A hot blush crept down her neck, and she deleted the message. Maybe while he was on the station tour, he'd decided he liked having a stronger double after all. She'd known she wasn't a strong enough match for him. So did Harland and Greta and everyone else. It really was better this way.

She touched her lips, the water tracing the groove of her mouth. But what about that kiss...?

Could they still be together even while she was posing with Simon for their media shoots? Her cheeks burned even hotter as she thought about it. If it was her, she wouldn't want that. It really was easier just to forget about the storm den.

But that kiss...

She shook her head and another message from Micah chimed in her goggs.

Micah: Okay, seriously, tell me what's going on with you and Simon Grady! I NEED more details!

Ezren: It's just a show for the fans, Micah. We're friends, but there's nothing between us like that.

Micah: WHY NOT?! He's as fine as it gets, Ezren. And if it's really just a show, I want to see some lip-locking!

Ezren rolled her eyes. She'd specifically told Simon no kissing, and although he seemed a little disappointed, he made it a point that they really didn't need to kiss to set the fans on fire.

Micah: Is this about Foster, still?

Ezren sank lower in the water. She hadn't told Micah the full scope of what happened in the storm den, but she could swear the girl had some secret sixth romantic sense.

Ezren: I just want to focus on racing. That's all.

Micah: I'm telling you, Ezzie, Foster Sterling has way too much moody baggage. He's so not worth dealing with Genevieve's rabid fans. I mean, have you seen that Navarrling Forum? Simon Grady is a step up!

Ezren paused for a moment, considering the link floating in her goggs. She'd believed Foster when he'd said there wasn't anything between him and Genevieve, but... she glanced at Simon. There was definitely something weird going on.

She clicked on the link, and the first topic jumped out at her.

Belethea Royaler Investigation—The FACTS

She skimmed the rest of the article, her gaze hopping between bullets.

- *Genevieve Navarro died of debris trauma after being separated from her OTP, Foster Sterling.*

- *Authorities found no evidence of foul play and blamed "outdated Belethean equipment" for failure to send out an emergency signal.*

- *But teammates claim the suit was sent in for a routine tune-up only the week before.*

So what actually happened to Genevieve Navarro?!

Simon sat up from his massage with a yawn, and Ezren came back to reality with a jump.

"This schedule Sylvia has got us on is ridiculous." Simon stood, clad in nothing but a pair of compression shorts, and shuffled over to the med tub, his ever-present hovercam following close behind. Ezren moved to one side as he slid in. "How're we supposed to drum up more VSoc cred when we don't have a chance to go out on the town?"

Ezren cringed, thinking of running into Davis outside the club. That was one place she'd rather not be. "Well, we're doing pretty well, aren't we?"

"Better than expected, I guess, but since the Guns/Sterling virtual tour is racking up creds, I asked Sylvia if we could go on one too."

"Oh." Okay, so maybe there was another place she'd rather not be. "Can't we just race actual courses here on Belethea?"

"We could." Simon slid closer to her and put his arm around her shoulders. She smiled automatically as the hovercam flashed. "But we need to schmooze more people to snag more cred. And there are way more schmoozables on the stations than here on Bel."

Sliding away, Ezren suppressed the urge to make a face. Too tired to sneak out, she hadn't been outside of Carmella in weeks, and she was itching for open skies—not more boxes. "But I really feel like I've been getting better at driving. I was thinking maybe you'd be up for a race one of these days on real Belethean dirt."

"You have been acing the sims lately." Simon twirled a finger through one of his dark curls. "Maybe we could have a wheels exhibition or something. I'll talk to Sylvia about it. I bet you could even give Bex a run for her money now."

He offered her a real, perfectly symmetrical smile, and even if she wasn't actually interested in him, she could admit it was rather dazzling. "You must miss Bex. Has she always been your double?"

His face darkened, and he leaned his head back to look at the white ceiling. "No."

"Oh." Ezren cocked her head. "Did your double age out, then?"

He met her eyes with his hazel ones. "When we had more royalers, we used to mix up the doubles a lot more often. It gave people something to gossip about and let Coach Bhatt see who worked well together. Bex is an awesome double, but she can't stand the VSoc stuff, so she prefers to work with Sterling.

They're both pretty low-key, and Vieve and I were way more in tune." He cupped the frothing water with his palms. "But before the quals, she suddenly asked Coach Bhatt to reassign her to Foster. Said they might have a better chance. And then..." He let the water fall through his hands.

"You were together, weren't you?" Ezren murmured.

Simon ran a finger along one of his dangling earrings, not meeting her gaze. "Vieve was never one for labels, and she would never have done anything to hurt her royale chances. But I always thought we were... something."

"So that's why you and Foster are..."

"Sterling should've been there for her," he said, his voice rough and raw.

Ezren recognized the pain cracking his words—the shrapnel of guilt buried in a survivor. As though loosened by the hot water, the intrusive images of Sammy's broken body flooded her mind in a wash of frenzied sorrow. She reached out a leaden hand and rested it on Simon's arm. A lifeline to steady them both. She'd never be able to take away his pain, but she could feel it with him. Her breath came out in a tremoring puff of air, and the infected memory slipped out with it.

"When my younger brother was three, we were crossing the street on Obrone. He was between me and Dad, holding our hands. But then he slipped away, running ahead, just before a speedjet rammed through the crowd."

Simon stared at her, the water bubbling softly around them. "Is he okay now?"

"Nine people died, but we were lucky. Sammy lost his hand and both of his legs, but he survived, and regen therapy put him back together." She tried not to think of Sam's last scan. The one that showed the nonnative cells spreading dangerously up his legs. The one that said they didn't have three years to wait for his surgery anymore. She swallowed. She could get the money in time. She had to. "I still wonder why I didn't hold his hand tighter though."

Simon nodded, his eyes drifting down to the water. "I should've held her hand tighter too."

Ezren folded her knees to her chest, thinking of Foster running through the snowstorm to get to her. "We hold on as tight as we can."

But even as she said it, she knew it was a lie.

She'd let go of Foster, and now he was gone.

CHAPTER 21

FOSTER GOT OFF THE TRANSPORT, tired, sore, and sparking pissed. He stalked up to Sylvia where she leaned against her topjeep with a flashing holopro of their names and an infuriating smile amid the sparsely populated hangar. "Okay, we're here. Unlock my goggs, Sylvia. I'm not fodding around anymore."

"Oh, calm your fritz. It's a common practice on the top-tier teams." Sylvia shifted her teal purse on her shoulder as she mentally retracted whatever twisted parental controls that had restricted their goggs to basic functionality. "Harland thought it might help with your concentration to eliminate distractions. How'd it go?"

"You mean besides his constant whining?" Bex shrugged. "Meh."

Sylvia frowned, her bright holo dissolving under the drab hangar's weak electric light. "I guess you're not feeling relaxed?"

"Definitely fodding not," Foster growled at the same time Bex said, "Sure, whatever."

"Well, you finished great," Sylvia went on, turning to her bright purple topjeep. "And since you grabbed the earlier flight, you got here in time to see the race."

"What race?" Foster asked distractedly, scrolling through all his messages the controls had blocked. Mostly the usual check-ins from his parents... and there—from Ezren.

Ezren: So how's it going?

Ezren: Hope you're doing okay.

Ezren: I could definitely have used your wake-up call this morning. Why are mornings so hard?

Foster sagged with a flood of relief. Even after two months, Ezren was still... well, Ezren. And maybe she'd even missed him. Or was he reading into it too much? He started to think out a reply... but what could he say?

Sylvia opened the trunk of the topjeep. "The others are competing in a wheels race today."

"Well, that's way better than virtual racing," Bex huffed, tossing her bag in the trunk and sliding into the backseat. "Why did we get the lame gig?"

"Wheels race?" Foster's head jerked up. "Just the two of them?"

"Simon was able to get his street racing kin to compete too. They've gotten twenty jetracers together. Honestly—"

"Jetracers? Are you serious, Syl? Those things have practically no armor. Where are they racing?"

Sylvia laughed in her deep honking bray. "Oh, please, Foster, you literally compete in the most dangerous race in the system. The VSoc credit from the hype alone has been fantastic, and the city is fritzing over it. Besides, they're just racing around the dome."

"This sounds like one of Grady's half-brained ideas." Foster climbed into the front seat and slammed the door. "Has Ezren even driven a jetracer on the surface?"

Syl slid in beside him and the programmed topjeep pulled away from the bustling spaceport. "Yes, Foster. She's actually getting really good. It's part of the reason we're having this race.

She hasn't had a chance to show off her skills yet, and the sponsors will love it."

"Did anyone check her suit before she went?"

Sylvia wrinkled her brow, the answer plain on her face. "Well, I—"

Foster was already moving her out of the way as he got behind the wheel, switching from auto to manual. "Seriously, no one checked it?" He floored the gas. "What time did the race start?"

Syl grappled for one of the bracing bars as the topjeep rocketed across the surface, the skies surprisingly clear with patches of teal peeking through the navy blanket of clouds. "Holy chaff, Foster. Chill your chip. You know it's weather dependent. I'll check for updates."

Bex leaned forward from the backseat, her face expressionless as usual. "So how's the VSoc hole going anyway? Has Harland got the stick out of his ass yet?"

"Yes!" Sylvia's bright smile nearly blinded Foster in his agitation. "You'll have to thank Simon when we get there. He's a regular VSoc magician."

"Tell me you didn't actually say that to him. He's insufferable enough as it is," Bex said.

Sylvia went on as if she hadn't spoken. "Like we predicted, the fans have totally latched on to the dark-horse wild-child narrative, and the mystery relationship has got everyone talking about them."

What mystery relationship? Foster's hands tightened on the wheel. "Are they actually... together?"

Sylvia widened her eyes jokingly at Bex. "See, I *told* you it's magic. Even Foster Sterling is asking about them."

"They do look cozy." Bex projected a holo of a Belethea royaler news update with Grady carrying a laughing Ezren on his back, and the blood drained from Foster's face.

He opened his mouth to say something when Sylvia interrupted them. "Oh, it looks like they're nearing the last lap." She projected the course through her goggs—a red line that snaked in a wavy, uneven oval around the outside of the metal dome. "If you hurry, I think we can make it to the finish before they do."

Foster swerved, his jaw tight and his heart thudding as he followed the new directions. He didn't care what Sylvia said, the jetracers were banned from the royale for a reason. Bullet-shaped, they tore over the ground with the drivers lying prone on their bellies in the cockpit, while inches away, the concealed wheels maneuvered the jet engines across the rugged terrain.

They were fast, yes, but they didn't carry enough weight in the low grav, making them incredibly hard to control. That was the whole reason that Grady's parents shoved him into race royales in the first place after he broke his back in a jetracer pileup. The race royale might be the most dangerous official sport, but nothing was more deadly than the street jetracers. If they so much as got close to one another, you could practically guarantee they'd both go tumbling.

He slapped his hand on the steering wheel. "Shaft it, Sylvia. What's with the fodding VSoc stunts? When are we supposed to actually focus on training?"

Sylvia looked at him with wide brown eyes. "But Foster, everything's going well, and with Harland—"

"*You* are the coach, Sylvia. Not Harland. Fodding stand up for us, or we might as well not have a coach at all."

Sylvia sat in stunned silence for a moment while Bex looked back and forth between them. "See, this is what I've been dealing with for weeks."

"I—"

Bex's outstretched hand interrupted her. "There they are. Turn on the vehicle ID so we can see who's ahead."

Sylvia's holopro overlaid the puffs of dust in the distance, and Foster curved their topjeep toward the collection of trucks and protective pods that littered what he assumed would be the finish. The goggs zoomed in and ID'd Simon Grady as the leader. Unsurprising. A name Foster didn't recognize was drafting off his tail, but behind them was none other than Ezren Hart.

"Shaft it, she's in third," he seethed. She'd be right in the center of the final crush.

"Third is shockingly good. I thought you liked this girl?" Bex said as he veered to a stop along the virtual boundary. Due to the frequent nature of jetracer collisions, fans had to keep a wide berth from the actual racetrack. Still, they climbed onto the roof of the topjeep to get a better look, just like the rest of the spectators.

Sylvia said nothing as she projected the commentators' audio detailing the racers' tenth and final lap around the dome. Foster barely heard them as he watched the cars swerve across the rocky landscape. He may not have been a champion street racer like Grady, but even he could tell they were way too close.

"Only a mile left now, and it could be anyone's race," one commentator blared.

"Sylvia, they're too close," Foster said, sweat prickling his brow.

"What do you want me to do?" she asked, her voice high and tight.

"Can't you link to them or something?"

"You know I can't—"

But the commentators' screeching interrupted her as the jetracers made their final move. Ezren drifted around the inside curve, her nose just barely clearing a cluster of boulders. She pulled even with Grady in the last stretch as the racer behind them jockeyed to get alongside.

Foster's heart ratcheted into high speed. "That chaffer's going to—"

They were only two lengths from the finish when the rear vehicle lurched forward. Foster held his breath, sure they would hit Ezren, but Grady veered—on purpose or by mistake, it was hard to tell—and the jetracer clipped him instead. Ezren crossed the finish line first, but she didn't escape the tumbling cars behind her. In the space of a second, all three cars were rolling through the mauve Belethean dirt, metal and rubber flying off them.

Foster froze, even as the crowd roared and honked around them, the commentators screaming through Sylvia's goggs. All he could see was Vieve's shattered body rolling across the dirt, her blood carving a dark trail across the ground.

"Shaft, I can't believe she actually won." Bex's brows rose and an almost smile tugged at her mouth.

Foster broke out of his stupor, leaping back into the driver's seat with a growl. "Get off the roof."

"Wait, Foster!" Sylvia jumped down with Bex close behind her. "The other racers are still finishing! You can't just—"

Foster revved the engine once in warning to give them time to step back before slamming his foot into the accelerator, spraying rock and dust behind them.

FOSTER: EZREN, ARE YOU OKAY?

No answer. He craned his neck but saw no sign of flames.

FOSTER: EZREN!

Closer to him, the instigator of the wreck climbed out of his smoking pile of wreckage with a limp, his foot bent at an odd angle, and farther off, an upside-down Grady unbuckled himself from his own crumpled vehicle. Ezren's crushed racer leaned against a giant boulder, but no movement came from within. Was she trapped?

He skidded to a stop, placing the topjeep between the active finish line and her racer to give her a little extra protection, before scrambling out of his seat.

"Ezren!" He sprinted to the smashed driver's door on the far side.

He jerked on the handle, but it wouldn't give. With another panicked yank, the metal squealed open under his fingers. He crouched down to see Ezren hanging limp in her racing harness. Foster smashed the emergency release and the webbing retracted. Sliding her out, he carried her a few steps from the wreckage before kneeling in the dirt.

Her eyes were closed behind her goggs.

"Ezren, can you hear me?"

He inspected her helmet before gently removing it, laying her head in his lap. He was about to call for help when her eyes fluttered open. "Did I win?"

Foster wiped his face with a hand, his heart still sprinting, not sure whether to be angry or ecstatic. "Who cares if you won? Are you okay?"

She sat up, squeezing her temples. "Simon warned me about the Gs, but... mother suns..." Then, she stopped, her gaze locking on Foster's. "You're back."

Foster rubbed his neck, suddenly at a loss for words. The last time he'd seen her, two months ago, he'd been sure something was between them, but now... with Grady... "I'm back," he said lamely.

And then Ezren's arms were around his neck, her mouth was on his, and his hands were on her waist pulling her closer, closer, closer...

"Suns, I missed you," she whispered, pressing her forehead to his.

And after months of awful and the day from hell, everything was somehow blime once again. "I missed you too, Ezren."

Her brow wrinkled as the smile faded from her pale face. "But...where's Simon?"

Foster's mouth swung open, the jealousy resurging in a feverish rush. But before he could formulate a response, she was slipping away from him, going limp in his arms. That's when he noticed the massive shard of metal sticking out of the back of her shoulder.

"Can we get some help over here?" he yelled.

Then Grady was there, his hovercam following him as he scooped Ezren out of Foster's arms, cradling her to his chest. "You did it! You won! I knew you could, E. Don't worry, I've got the med truck on their way. We'll get you fixed up, stat."

Even from a distance, Foster could hear the crowd's cheers of approval.

Okay, maybe not so blime, after all.

CHAPTER 22

EZREN WOKE up dry-mouthed and groggy in Carmella's therapy room. The machines around her sat dark and silent amidst the white walls and tiled floors. Sylvia snored softly from the couch next to her, but other than that, the room was empty and dark. Her goggs read 0230, but she'd slept through another day. She frowned, touching the spot in her shoulder that had screamed with pain that afternoon. But only a raised scar remained from the gaping wound that had been there earlier. They must've given her a heavy dose of nanomeds for her to sleep that long—even by her standards.

Still, nothing hurt, and her head was clear. Sliding from the bed, she crossed the cold floor in her bare feet. She gently nudged Sylvia's shoulder and whispered her name.

With another choked snore, Sylvia turned away from her, curling tighter into a ball. Ezren smiled, grabbing the thin blanket from the therapy bed and draping it over her coach. She'd actually never seen Sylvia sleeping before. The woman seemed to run on VSoc cred and willpower. But if anyone deserved some rest, it was definitely her.

Ezren found her usual sweater and tights on the end of the bed and changed out of the loose pajamas before padding into the carpeted hall. As she meandered down the dark corridor, she scanned her messages—congratulations spilled in from everyone—Harland, Micah, Simon, Davis... and then a few worried lines from her mom that Ezren was glad to see Sylvia had taken care of in a group chat.

But nothing else from Foster after the race. Her memories from after the crash were admittedly a little fuzzy, but she could've sworn... She touched her lips. Had she dreamed that?

Maybe she had, or she could go knock on his door to see... She shook her head. It was two in the morning. That was ridiculous. She was about to head up the stairs to her own room when a light caught her eye from the armory. Someone was still up.

She poked her head in through the doorway, and her breath caught in her throat. *Foster.* He stood bent over the desk, injecting a syringe of nanites into a suit pulled taut across a metal frame. So he was there. Did that mean she'd really kissed him? Her cheeks heated as she frantically tried to sort out the tumult of emotions storming through her. Harland had been very clear that they were supposed to stay away from each other... So where did that leave them?

Only one way to find out.

She took another breath, about to say she didn't know what, when he looked over his shoulder.

His stormy eyes met hers, and he stilled. "You're awake."

She took another step into the room. "You're back early."

He faced her, tossing the empty syringe onto the desk and crossing his arms. "Yep."

Ezren twisted her hands in her overlong sleeves. Was he mad at her? He hadn't sent her any messages, after all. She shifted her weight from one foot to the other, trying to find something to focus on. "What're you doing up so late?"

He shrugged, his face blank and shadowed in the dim light. "Couldn't sleep."

Ezren peered around him to the suit. "Wait, is that mine?"

He swallowed, running a hand through his dark brown hair. "Uh, yeah... it was damaged in the race, and I talked to Micah about those weather upgrades you mentioned, so I was just... tuning it up."

"Really?" He'd remembered that? Ezren moved beside him to get a better look at it. She linked into the code, scanning the updates. "Wow, Foster, you must've been working on this all day." She looked at him, his mussed waves falling across his brow, close enough now that she could reach out and run her fingers through them.

"Well, Harland is sending Bex and me to the qualifier course tomorrow to train, so this is the only time I had."

Ezren's stomach dropped. "Already?"

"You should always have someone else look at your suit for you before you race, Ezren. Even Grady can do it." He scowled at the mention of Simon. "But don't let him drag you into any more of those stupid street races."

Ezren tapped her fingers on the table, trying to stifle the urge to take his hand. She didn't want Grady to look at her suit. She wanted Foster. And he was leaving tomorrow.

He peeked over her shoulder to inspect her back, where her wound had disappeared. His expression softened. "How're you feeling? Are you... okay?"

"Not really."

His brow furrowed. "What's the matter? Are you in pain? We can get you some more meds—"

"It's not the injury, Foster." She could see the concern swirling in his eyes, but how could she bridge the distance between them? It had to be now, before he slipped away again. "You know, it's a lot harder to wake up in the mornings when you're not knocking at my door." She offered a smile. "I even slept through the whole day."

Foster picked up the syringe again, twirling it in his hands, his words tinged with bitterness. "Oh well, I'm sure Grady could knock on your door if you asked—" Foster winced, and his hand spasmed, the syringe flying from his grip. "Mother suns."

Ezren grabbed his fingers, kneading them with her practiced hands, just like she had done so many times with Sammy's legs. "Simon is very good at racing and VSoc and getting sponsors and he's actually a surprisingly good friend." Foster tried to tug his hand back, but Ezren held on to it. "But I don't want Simon." His broad hand stilled in her grasp, but she didn't meet his gaze as she continued to massage his long fingers, the tremors smoothing under her thumbs. "There's only one person who I want to see knocking on my door in the morning, who I want to train with for fifteen-hour days and then sneak out with at night." The words rushed out of her—words she should've said weeks ago. "And I know I'm not the strongest racer yet, but I'm still working on it. So maybe I'll be good enough to—"

"Ezren." Then his hands slid around her cheeks, tilting her mouth to his, and he was kissing her. Kissing her. Kissing her. And she responded, her lips parting and their mouths moving together in a heated dance. He pulled her to him, folding her in his arms.

"You're more than good enough, Ezren," he murmured, his lips trailing down her neck. "Winning or losing or doing nothing at all. I want to be with you."

Ezren pressed her face into his chest, breathless as relief and bliss jolted through her. "I wasn't sure... after you left without saying anything..."

"Harland locked down my goggs." His hands around her waist, he lifted her onto the workbench, his tools skittering to the floor. He pressed his forehead to hers, the storm swirling in his irises. "So I changed the flights to come back early because I had to see you."

Her heart swelled, and she kissed him again. His fingers danced along the hem of her sweater, teasing the bare skin of her back as her fingers tangled in his hair. "Suns, I missed you," she breathed. "What are we going to do about Harland?"

But it wasn't Foster who answered her. "That is the question, isn't it?"

Ezren froze, and Foster turned to stone in her arms. Together they turned to see Sylvia Long, her arms folded, staring at them from the doorway.

Ezren leapt from the workbench, quickly yanking her sweater down. But as she looked at Sylvia's steely gaze, the words dried up on her tongue.

"So?" Sylvia prompted. "What's the plan? After all that VSoc work you put in, are you going to—"

"I don't care about VSoc, Sylvia," Ezren said, a certainty finally hardening in her gut.

She was tired of putting on an act for their show. She'd been playing their game for months now, but her brother's condition was slowly worsening, terraforming labs were still closing, and she ached for Tuzuno so much it hurt. But this— she laced her fingers with Foster's—was something real. Something she should have a say in. And something she wanted more than anything to hold onto.

"Foster and I are together." She glanced up at him, his hair mussed and a grin spreading across his face. "And we want to race together."

"Okay..." Sylvia raised a rainbow eyebrow, pointing to the two of them. "But let's be real. Are you serious, or is this just a fling?"

Foster glanced at Ezren and squeezed her hand. "We're serious."

For a moment, they all stared at each other, the tension pulling the air taut in the dim room. Then, Sylvia squealed, and Ezren just about leapt out of her skin. Sylvia clapped her hands, jumping up and down, before running over and wrapping them in a huge hug. "Why didn't you say something weeks ago! I'm so happy for you!"

Ezren exchanged an incredulous glance with Foster.

"You're not mad?" Ezren asked. "What about VSoc credit and sponsors and stuff?"

Sylvia threw up her hands. "Sure, those things are great, Ezren. But it's not as important as you two being happy. I didn't know you were actually into each other. It can be so hard to tell with you royalers."

The tension in Foster's shoulders eased, and his mouth curved into a smile. "Thanks, Syl."

Foster put his arm around Ezren's shoulders, and she leaned into him. "What about Harland?" she asked. "Foster and Bex are supposed to leave tomorrow."

Sylvia straightened, rising to her full, completely average, height. "You let me take care of that." She looked at Foster, her eyes strangely hard. "I'm the coach. It's my job to take care of the athletes."

"And you think Bex and Simon will be okay with this?" Ezren added. Even after weeks of training with him, she still had no idea how Simon would react. And Bex... The image of the tall girl bringing the chair down on her chest flashed through her mind again. She swallowed.

Foster gave Ezren a squeeze. "As long as Bex has a chance for a rematch with Lucian, that's all she cares about. And at the qualifier in a couple months, that's anybody's game."

Ezren stiffened at the thought of the qualifier. Was it really so soon? She wasn't sure how tough the top fifty would be, but Belethea hadn't qualified a team since Greta Sterling had come in 22nd thirty years ago. If Ezren lost, she'd be a failed experiment on the first truck home, and Sam needed that performance bonus now more than ever.

"But for right now, try to lie low for another day so I have time to break it to Harland. In the meantime, Ezren, you need to come with me for another dose of meds. And you"—Sylvia pointed to Foster as she ushered Ezren out the door—"need to go to bed."

For a moment, a swirl of thoughts clouded Ezren's mind: the relief of Foster's presence, how she would break the news to Simon, qualifying for the BRR... but one thought won out over all the others. She and Foster could do it together. Her heart stuttering, Ezren pulled away for just a moment, letting Sylvia go on ahead as she chanced a glance back at Foster.

But he'd already closed the gap, pressing his lips to hers one more time before whispering in her ear. "I'll be at your door in the morning."

And Ezren wasn't sure if she'd ever looked forward to waking up so much.

The next morning after Sylvia spirited Foster away on some anti-Harland mission, Ezren went to the training room to look for Simon. A small bubble of anxiety wobbled in her stomach as she searched. Although she was 99% sure he didn't have feelings for her, she knew he would go out of his way to lock horns with Foster, so she wasn't entirely certain how he'd take the news.

But instead of finding Simon in the training room, she found Bex. A broad-shouldered tower of solid muscle, her arms and legs lashed out furiously at the five padded training bots as if she had some personal vendetta against them. Even though Ezren had been working hard for months now, she probably wouldn't last two minutes against Bex. Even the thought of it sent a curl of fear spiraling down her spine. She shook her head, chewing her lip. *Still so far to go.* She turned to leave when Bex called out.

"Hey, Hart!" Bex turned to her, her blonde pixie cut artfully defying gravity, and sweat slicking her face.

"H-hey." Ezren walked over the black mats, her image reflecting in the mirrored walls. "Welcome back."

"I heard you and Sterling are a thing now."

Ezren froze, trying to keep her face neutral and failing miserably. "Oh, uh, yeah. He told you already? I was just looking for Simon to give him the news." She winced. "Is that... okay?"

"I don't know." Bex adjusted her gloves' straps. "You think you're good enough to race with Sterling?"

Ezren swallowed, her face heating. "I don't know. I guess we'll see."

"I'll tell you what." Bex grabbed a set of sparring pads from a nearby bench and threw them at Ezren. "If you can knock me down, I'll tell Harland you're a good match."

Ezren's eyes nearly bulged out of their sockets. Was this even a thing? Bex had at least forty pounds on her. Without her topsuit to narrow the strength gap, she didn't have a chance. But even as her adrenaline sparked through her fingertips, she put on the sparring helmet and pads. There was no way she could say no to this. If she was going to race with Foster, she wanted the team behind her. But that was an approval she had to earn.

The crack of bones echoed in her memory, but she shoved it away.

"Um... okay." She toed off her mag-trainers, kicking them to the side of the mat. "What happens if you knock me down?"

"Nothing." Bex slapped her gloves together, an excited gleam in her pale blue gaze. "I've got twenty minutes before lessons, so that's how much time you have."

Ezren took a deep breath. She could chaffing do this. She had to. If she couldn't, she probably wouldn't stand a chance at the qualifier. "Starting now?"

Bex bounced from foot to foot. "Let's go."

Ezren rushed Bex, trying to catch her off guard. Bex blocked her first strike, tapping her belly with a smirk. Grimacing, Ezren tried again with a spinning kick, and Bex danced away on light feet. Again and again, Ezren surged forward, and Bex saw through every feint, every strike, and every block. Then, after five minutes, Bex swept her feet out from under her and slammed her onto the floor mats in a flash of pain.

"Is that it?" Bex said, expressionless.

Ezren kicked out at Bex, and she hopped just out of reach. Rising to her feet, Ezren launched after her again, darting in and out. She landed a few glancing blows but didn't get close enough to take Bex to the ground. This time, Bex landed a roundhouse kick to Ezren's chin that sent stars spinning through her vision as she crumpled to her knees.

"Twelve minutes left, Hart."

Ezren wiped the blood from her cut lip and rose, trying to devise a different strategy. Bex was letting her overextend and then slapping her down. It was a pattern she needed to take advantage of. But she had to wear her down just a little bit more first. Bex might be stronger than her, but Ezren could outlast her. And more importantly, she wanted it more.

Three more times, Ezren tested Bex's reactions, watching her reflexes, and then crashed into the mat after a missed punch. Each time Bex threw her over her shoulder, Ezren got up slower and slower, her body stiffening with each new bruise.

But nothing was broken. *She* wasn't broken.

"Three more minutes," Bex said, her breath coming heavier now.

Ezren pushed herself up on shaking arms, her lips and nose bleeding freely as she came to her feet. This time she had to nail it. There wouldn't be another chance. She circled Bex with quick steps, peppering her seemingly impenetrable guard with a flurry of jabs. Bex answered with her powerful swings, slower than when they'd begun, but still crashing painfully against Ezren's forearms. Sweat rolled down Ezren's back as she dodged Bex's relentless onslaught, searching desperately for an opening.

But there was none to be found.

Time for plan B.

With an eye on the clock, Ezren threw a slow punch. Bex dodged, grabbing Ezren's arm and flipping her onto the mat.

With thirty seconds left and her chest heaving, Bex put her hands on her hips, standing much too close. "Well, at least you—"

Ezren grabbed one of Bex's ankles, hooking her leg around the other, and then used her free leg to kick upward into Bex's stomach. With a surprised grunt, Bex crashed to the mat next to her.

She glanced at her goggs. Bex lay on the floor, sucking in air from her crumpled diaphragm with two seconds remaining. Ezren sat up beside her, every inch of her sore and aching. She pulled the hem of her tank top up to wipe the blood from her face, the crimson staining the teal a rusty brown.

"So," she gasped. "Will you tell Harland?"

And then Bex started to laugh, a wheezing, almost silent

laugh, and Ezren's brow creased. Had she been teasing her? From the doorway, a hollow applause rang through the room.

"Chaff, E. That was pretty impressive for a half-pint," Simon said from where he leaned against the wall.

Ezren got to her knees, her ears ringing and nausea rolling her stomach. "Oh, Simon, I was looking for you to—"

"To tell me that you and Sterling are doubles now." He kicked at the mat with his designer mag-trainers, his expression unreadable. "Yeah, Bex told me this morning."

Ezren's face fell, looking from one to the other. Was this a set-up? Had this been some kind of hazing punishment?

Bex pushed herself onto her elbows, still laughing. "Shaft, Hart. Don't look so worried." She got to her feet and offered Ezren her hand. "We're blime."

Simon walked over and squeezed her shoulder. "Look, it's just, we all had our doubts when Sylvia brought on some wild rando from the rocks." He winked at her with a smirk. "And I mean even wilder than me. But you learned the wheels."

"And you've got the fight," Bex added.

"And you've always had the legs." Simon propped his elbow on Bex's shoulder like Ezren had seen him do a million times. He looked at Bex, and they shrugged together. "So basically what we're saying is, you're one of us now." He pulled her in under his other arm before rolling his eyes dramatically. "Even if you're with that chaffer, Sterling."

Ezren's eyes widened, strange tears swimming in her vision. "So you're not mad?"

"Get it in your head, E, we like you," Simon said with a soft chuckle. "Definitely more than Sterling." He winked at Bex, and she raised an unamused brow. "I mean, don't get me wrong, we're still going to beat your asses in the quals, but we think this would be a sparking year for Belethea to send two teams to the BRR. We're talking VSoc gold right there."

"Oh, shut up, Grady. We all want the same thing," Bex said, holding up her forearm. "Kick Lucian's ass."

Ezren sniffed even as a smile crossed her face. She knocked her forearm against Bex's. "And everyone else's too."

Simon ruffled her hair. "Atta girl, now you're sounding like a real royaler."

And for the first time, as Ezren stood grinning with her teammates, she felt like one.

CHAPTER 23

FOSTER WALKED through the hall of the qualifier outpost, the walls around him nearly blinding with their sponsored holopro ads and obnoxious team hype montages. He stopped at the fluorescent metal door ablaze with Belethea's lightning crest and knocked on the door to Ezren's room. Nerves tingled down his fingers while his topsuit pulsed through its warm-up routine—massaging and heating his muscles.

Inside, he could hear Sylvia's voice blaring with muffled commands, answered by Ezren's nervous laugh and a low mumble from Bex. Waiting for a moment, he raised his hand to knock again when, to his surprise, the door opened. For once, Ezren didn't look the slightest bit tired, and he could tell Sylvia must've already gotten to her. A wavy teal design edged her dark eyes, and her magenta-streaked brown hair swirled into a braid gathered at the base of her neck. Suns, she was beautiful.

He bent down, gently brushing a kiss against her lips. The touch of her skin sent an electric jolt through him he wasn't sure he'd ever get used to. "You ready?"

She inhaled shakily before blowing out a slow breath. "I think so. Do *you* think we're ready?"

He took her hand. "We're ready."

Bex opened the door wider, her white-blonde bangs

cascading down one side of her face, while a sharper, geometric design crawled up the other side, and Sylvia shooed them out into the hall.

"Save it for the cams, lovebirds! If you want to be more popular than Hart/Grady, you're going to need more holopro time."

"Ha!" Grady called, walking down the hall toward them. "Good luck with that," he chuckled, running one hand along his styled curls and clapping Foster on the shoulder with the other. Foster resisted the urge to punch him. The holos of Grady and Ezren were still all over VSoc, and it seemed there was nothing he could do to keep them from popping up on his feed. "The only thing that's saving our VSoc cred is that Grady/Guns is poised to be a Belethean record-breaker." Grady leaned on Bex's shoulder with a smug grin, and his hovercam circled them. "But we know that's because they're all just Grady fans."

Sylvia rolled her eyes and pushed him through the hall. "C'mon, Simon, if we stay here much longer you're not going to be able to fit that head into your helmet."

"Speaking of helmets," Foster said as they passed another cluster of royale personnel in the brightly lit hall. "Ezren and I finished integrating the updated weather algorithms into everyone's suits." He squeezed her hand, and she responded with a shy smile.

"The new code will automatically shift your course in accordance with the weather to give you the fastest route to the next checkpoint," Ezren added, her gaze darting across the bright holopros bulging from the wall.

"But I thought the weather was almost unpredictable, right?" Grady asked.

Ezren nodded. "Almost. But we've been making big strides at Tuzuno, and with the extra power boost from these royaler suits, the range is just about doubled. The prediction is 90% accurate for approximately two square miles and updates every five minutes."

"Impressive," Bex said, already projecting the recommended route from her goggs.

"Atta girl, E." Grady grabbed Ezren in a friendly headlock, and Foster smothered the jealous impulse to shove him off. "See, it's a good thing I convinced you to keep her, Sylvia. This is totally going to be our year."

"How's our stamina boost compared to the latest tech?" Bex asked, ignoring Grady.

Foster frowned, his jaw tensing. Although their sponsorships and VSoc cred had been doing surprisingly well with only two teams... they still hadn't put together enough to get the latest suits. "With our latest terranium boost, we're at about 98.5% of the performance of the CX-8s the Obronians will be wearing."

"Well, that's pretty close," Sylvia said brightly as she opened the door to the crowded central dome of the qualifier outpost. Royalers and their support staff milled in a rainbow of colors under the clear ceiling, the chatter nearly deafening.

Rows on rows of stacked seats jutted from the clear rounded walls, revealing the other packed temporary domes on either side—all translucent today for optimal royale viewing. Holopros of royaler faces, names, and logos popped up all over the crowd but, of course, none of them were for Belethea.

"It may sound like it, but 1.5% of a three-hundred-mile race is 4.5 mi. A twenty-minute difference, even if we're busting our asses in the final sprint," Foster replied as a qualifier organizer ushered them to the front of the airlock line.

"But the time difference between the first and last qualifying teams has been hours in the past. So it's not something a strong team with a good strategy can't overcome," Ezren said.

Though her voice was steady, Foster could see the worry lines in her forehead, the way her mouth twitched as she chewed her lip, her fingers tapping incessantly against her leg. Despite her usual positivity, the nerves were getting to her.

And how could they not? This was her first real royale. Ever. And she was going in with a second-rate topsuit. The thought made him want to strangle Harland. He was the chaffing *exec*, wasn't he? After all those rules he tried to enforce, he should be fodding pulling his weight. It wasn't like Calderon Industries didn't have the creds, the team just wasn't a priority.

Foster crowded into the airlock with the others while media, support, and royalers funneled in behind them. "Yeah, well, try not to bust up the suits too bad out there, because this is the best we have. The older models fall apart every other day, and I'd rather not have to start doing day-of-race suit repairs."

Bex snorted. "There's a first time for everything."

"Not a first. You've done that before, right?" Ezren said as she pulled on her helmet, strapping her goggs firmly in place.

Foster shook his head, adjusting the nutrivein rig on his back. "No way. I'm not even sure I could pull off something like that."

Her brows knitted. "But I've seen it in the logs. Did you have someone else fixing up your stuff last year?"

"What logs? Which suit?" Foster asked, adjusting his goggs around his helmet. He'd fixed every one of those suits so often, he knew every inch of them. There was no way he would've missed a weird entry like that.

"That suit you have in the corner of the armory. I was trying to see if I could patch it for a backup, but the code is seriously scrambled. Looks like it was a bad update on a race day, and then someone tried to erase it or something."

Foster froze. Vieve's suit had an update on a race day?

Which race? Had she tried to mod her own suit? Was that why it malfunctioned? Then why hadn't it been reported in the investigation? He was about to ask if she remembered the day of the entry when the porter flung open the airlock door.

Grady stepped out first, his hovercam spinning in front of him. "Oh, stop fritzing, our suits will be just crisp for the next ten minutes. Once the race starts though... no promises."

Foster tried to calm his whirring mind. He'd checked their suits yesterday, and there was no way Ezren, Grady, or Bex had modded their suits this morning. They might be patched and dented, but he knew they would work. Vieve's suit was a problem for another day. He had to focus.

But the Beletheans' optimistic smiles faded as soon as they stepped out in the dirt. Four hundred royalers in the gleaming bright colors of brand-new topsuits turned to look at them, their helmets flashing in the orange glow of the rising sun. Some were familiar, but most weren't.

Although this was a shorter race than the BRR, the qualifier was easily the most chaotic, unpredictable race. Only the top fifty doubles would qualify for the BRR, and although each team could only qualify two doubles, their extra royalers could still knock the competition out of the running. Usually, nearly all the teams had at least one pair in the top fifty... except Belethea, that is. Foster couldn't even remember the last time they qualified.

Then as one, the crowd turned away, some with laughs, others with mutters—all dismissive. Dark navy clouds spiraled and twisted over the towering stone arches and mauve dirt, and Foster's goggs flashed as he got a weather adjustment to their course. The winds would bring rain and lightning with them today, and they would be brutal.

Scanning the starting line again, his gaze caught on a single pair of goggs still staring straight at them. His mother's stare bore into him from across the field as she stood with her full team of eight doubles, their violet and silver top-of-the-line suits glowing tangerine in the sunlight.

She offered a closemouthed smile that didn't reach her eyes and a message popped into his goggs.

Mom: GLAD TO SEE YOU MADE IT TO THE STARTING LINE ON TIME. GOOD LUCK TODAY. HOPE YOU'VE BEEN TRAINING HARD.

Foster wished he could've deleted the message before his eyes involuntarily read it. Although he knew she'd punished Callie and the others for their role at the exhibition, it didn't make up for the rest of their rocky history. It was one of the reasons he'd started to hate the sport he'd once loved. Even on a different team now, he could never get away from her, and no matter what he placed—it would never be enough.

Ezren tugged on his arm. "You okay?"

Shaking away the irritation, he straightened and tried for a half smile. He wasn't here for her today. He was here for Ezren. "Yeah, it's fine. I'm good."

Harland extricated himself from a group of reporters and strode over to them with his usual empty smile and slicked hair.

"Cutting it close, aren't we? I was beginning to worry we had another snafu this morning." Harland leaned in closer, adjusting the circular goggs on his face. "Listen here, Belethea, let's be sure this isn't your last race today, shall we? One qualifying team would be wonderful, but we could use the boost if you could conjure a miracle and make it two."

Grady's face flattened. "Nah, H, we're just here for the picnic."

"Looks like someone has finally realized that this might have an impact on his cushy job," Foster added, crossing his arms.

Grady smirked at him in solidarity, and for the briefest of

moments, it was like before. When they'd been teammates. Friends.

Harland waved them off distractedly. "I'm offering good sense. We put almost our whole budget into those new suit upgrades, and Calderon is breathing down my neck. Which, by extension, means your necks too."

"Well, you know, thanks for having faith in us," Ezren said with a shaky laugh.

"Royalers to your places; this is your five-minute warning," the announcer boomed across the comms.

"Well, *I* believe in you," Sylvia said, squeezing her arm. Her warm gaze swept across each of them in turn, pausing on Foster for just a beat longer. "I always have. And no matter what happens, just remember of all the teams here, you've come the farthest. Grown the most. And no matter what, I'm proud as chaff to be your coach."

Foster's heart suddenly swelled in his throat, and he swallowed it down.

"Now, stay safe out there." She clapped her hands together and shooed them away. "We'll be watching through your goggcams the whole way!"

They shuffled to their place at the end of the long starting line, the spot reserved for the lowest ranking teams. While a little embarrassing maybe, it left them relatively unbothered by the flock of hovercams in the middle of the throng. Not to mention, the center marks reserved for the more competitive teams would turn into a massive scrap at the crack of the gun.

Ezren turned to the others, her brows sloped up with a worried smile. "Good luck."

Bex nodded, and Grady knocked his forearm against Ezren's. "Last one to the finish line buys me a drink."

Ezren laughed. "I like mine with a little umbrella in it."

"What a coincidence, so does Grady," Foster said.

"I'm so glad you remember my order from our last bet," Grady returned.

Foster bit back a smile as the announcer called out, "Two minutes, royalers. All support personnel clear the starting line."

"Heads in," Bex said, and Foster fought to keep the surprise from his face as they pressed their helmets together with a *clack*, their arms automatically lacing around each other's shoulders.

He'd nearly forgotten the tradition. The Belethean team whispered the prayer before every race going back the last seventy years. As a kid, he'd whispered it right along with them as he'd watched on the holopros, dreaming of being at the starting line, of bringing pride back to Belethea.

And now here he was.

Bex's words were quick and soft in their small circle. "Be strong. Be swift. By legs, wheels, and fists, we go into the churn. We race, we fight, and we live to do it again. For ourselves, for Belethea, and for each other. May Casolla keep you safe, the suns keep you warm, and the storm winds blow you to the finish." Her ice-blue gaze met each of theirs, her voice growing stronger. "Belethea, mother of mountains and skies..."

"Protect us," they said together, the finality of it ringing between them.

Foster straightened, the words of Belethea still coursing through him, steadying him against the enormity of the task before them. Beside him, Ezren had stopped fidgeting, brow smooth and stare focused on the path ahead. Yes, they were finally ready.

"One minute, royalers. Good luck, stay safe, and we'll see you on the other side. Into the churn."

"Into the churn," the royalers echoed.

With that, the talk dried up along the starting line, only the wind whistled across the rocky expanse, the distant rumble of thunder promising the kind of dangerous run the fans lived for.

Foster turned to Ezren beside him, his heart drumming with something more intense than his usual pre-race nerves. He looked past her to the team on their right. Pyrrhia Station was the third-lowest ranking team, but they had still brought sixteen racers. And when the race started, they would do one of two things: run straight for the finish or pause to crush the Beletheans while they had the numbers advantage.

From the way Bex was eyeing them, he knew she was thinking the same thing.

He moved to put himself, Bex, and Grady between Ezren and the other team. Grady nodded at him in understanding, his shoulders already tensing as he bounced from foot to foot. Foster wasn't sure when they'd stopped hating each other or if the peace would last, but one thing was certain: no one wanted to see Ezren get hurt.

His stomach clenched. This was her first real race, and their first working together. If it were anyone else, he would've said their qualifying chances were zero, and if she didn't make it, there was no way Harland would let her return next year. If there was even a team next year.

But it was Ezren.

Foster: Remember, everyone here is out to get you, so protect your head. If they crack your helmet and trigger your mayday signal, that's an instant DQ. Your legs will always be your best bet. When that gun goes off, we make a break, straight ahead as fast as you can. Don't stop running, no matter what. I'll be right behind you.

She nodded, shaking her hands out. "It'll be fine. We're going to make it." But she said it more to herself than to him.

The sickening image of Vieve disappearing into a cloud of

dust jumped involuntarily to his mind, and he tapped his helmet gently to Ezren's, wishing he could kiss her again. "Yes. We're going to make it," he breathed, his chest tight with uncertainty.

Then the gun went off.

CHAPTER 24

WITH THE BLAST of the gun, Ezren's legs took on a wild, primal mind of their own, and she sprinted across the dirt. Foster's heavy footfalls thudded close behind her, his long strides matching hers as they followed their weather-tracking path. But behind him... was chaos. A chaos that only made her legs churn faster.

Foster had been right of course. Some of the teams had taken off, same as she had. But many of them were already engaged in the no-rules scraps the royale was known for. And beyond them, the cheers of the fans, both on the surface and projected from the spectator domes, were deafening.

Her legs burning, she risked a glance over her shoulder.

"Don't look back, keep—" A stocky blur barreled into Foster, knocking him clean off his feet.

Ezren skidded to a stop. "Foster!" A green-and-blue royaler rolled in the dirt with him, battering his fist into Foster's helmet again and again.

Ezren raced toward them and kicked the royaler in the goggs, jarring him from Foster, just as something slammed her to the ground. She raised her arms to protect herself as fists and feet collided with her body.

"Ezren!" Foster roared. He tried to tear the racer on top of her away, only as another royaler crashed into him.

Pain sparked behind Ezren's eyes, but her body reacted as Bex had trained her. She bucked her hips, knocking her attacker off balance before twisting and kicking free. She searched the tangle of bodies for Foster before someone tackled her from behind, digging a knee into her back.

"Well, if it isn't the little dark pony," Lucian's familiar voice crowed in her ear. Ezren could twist just enough to see the rock coming down on her head, when the weight suddenly lifted, and a hand yanked her up.

"C'mon, E, keep running!" Simon yelled, pushing her forward and out of the scrap.

"What about Foster?" she called back, her body aching and her heart pounding.

"Bex has got him." He pointed to their left, where the two other teal-and-black Beletheans raced toward them.

FOSTER: YOU OKAY?

Foster's worried gaze looked her over, his suit muddy, but nothing obviously damaged.

EZREN: YEAH. THANKS TO SIMON.

The four of them veered, all gasping for breath as they avoided another cluster of scraps.

BEX: NO ONE WANTS TO LOSE TO BELETHEA. WE'VE GOT A TARGET ON OUR BACKS.

FOSTER: THEN WE STICK TOGETHER AS MUCH AS WE CAN... AND WE DON'T SLOW UP UNTIL IT'S ONLY US AND THE STORMS.

Ezren nodded, pushing the throbbing pain to the back of her mind. They were only bruises—a well-deserved punishment for letting her guard down.

SIMON: RELAX, E, YOU MADE IT THROUGH ONE OF THE

MOST DANGEROUS PARTS OF THE RACE. NOW, ALL YOU HAVE TO DO IS RUN.

EZREN: UNTIL THE NEXT DANGEROUS PART, YOU MEAN.

The knot slowly untwisted in her stomach as she let the run take over, her legs stretching and her mind emptying of everything but the sky and the ground in front of her.

FOSTER: ONE STEP AT A TIME. THIS PART, WE'VE GOT.

Ezren nodded and did what she did best—she ran on.

They closed in on the wheels station nine hours later, the headlights glowing brightly in the dark atop a rise, and Ezren wasn't sure if she'd ever been more tired. The sun had set hours ago, and the blackness stretched out endlessly over the rocky hills, their suit lights only illuminating small pools of the uneven ground under their feet.

It was one thing to run for hours on a sim and quite another to have to deal with actual elements and terrain while avoiding the other royalers. And this was a short race. The actual BRR started with 352 miles—two full days of running—and then piled another day of driving on top of that. Still, at least they hadn't had to deal with weather complications yet, but Ezren wasn't sure if they had their new algorithm to thank for that or luck.

Within sprinting distance of the vehicles, Foster pulled them up short next to a cluster of boulders. "Looks like the topjeeps are already gone, but I see a pair of dunecarts, some quads, and at least a couple jetbikes." He smirked at Ezren, sweat streaking his face under his helmet. "And plenty of terrasails."

She smiled, but it sagged with exhaustion. "Not in this weather." The wind was oddly calm for now... which probably only meant a stronger front building in their future.

"Dunecarts it is," Simon said.

Ezren looked at the two dunecarts, little more than wireframes on four wheels. At least it was better than the jetbikes—she'd never really gotten the hang of the overpowered motorcycles.

"There's at least one team on the right waiting to get the jump on the next double," Bex said, pointing out a flicker of light Ezren hadn't noticed at all.

"Are we sure the vehicles are safe? What if they sabotaged them?" Ezren asked.

"Strictly against the rules," Simon said, shaking out his legs. "They're good, we just need to knock a few heads and get our asses in a seat."

"Remember, it's not worth the fight if you can outrun them." Foster turned to Bex. "If something happens, and we get split up, don't wait for us."

"Same to you." Bex exchanged a quick glance with Simon, her pale eyes hard. "We'll see you at the finish."

Ezren's stomach sank, feeling suddenly vulnerable without Simon and Bex at her back.

Simon clapped Ezren's shoulder. "Remember that umbrella in my drink when you get there."

She slapped him back halfheartedly. "I like mine with extra sugar."

Foster and Simon nodded to each other, something silently passing between them. "You want the right or the left?" Foster asked.

Simon scanned the vehicles. "Right."

"Ready?" Foster's gaze met each of theirs in turn.

Ezren took a deep breath. The first leg had been the easy part... it would only get harder from here. "Yes."

They took off running, Ezren's muscles screaming in protest as they raced for the nearest dunecart. As predicted, four royalers emerged from their cover to meet them. But they weren't on foot. They were on jetbikes, and they were aiming for collision.

"Jump!" Foster yelled.

Ezren dove to one side just as the second racer leapt from the bike to tackle her. But Ezren was ready for this one. She spun the royaler around, landing a knee to their stomach and then a fist to their goggs. Shoving her attacker to the ground, she stumbled to her feet, and looked right into the headlight of another jetbike.

No time to move, she instinctively closed her eyes and braced for impact—frozen in the bright light. The crunch of metal on metal screeched through her ears.

"C'mon!"

She opened her eyes to see Foster in a dunecart, his hand out to her, the broken bike and its squalling rider sprawled fifteen feet in front of it. Grabbing his hand, she leapt into the dune cart, and he peeled out of the lot.

"Wait, what about—" Ezren spun around to see Simon and Bex heading to their own dunecart, their attackers on the ground behind them. "Oh, good, they made it."

"They'll be fine," Foster said. "Just keep an eye on our grav levels and watch for—"

The screech of wheels interrupted him as another dunecart roared out from a cluster of rocks, aiming for their broadside.

"Hold on!" Foster turned the wheel and careened off a slope into the darkness, weaving around rocks as the other dunecart followed behind them.

Ezren adjusted their grav numbers to keep them upright,

her heart banging around her body as she tried to keep herself from falling out while he weaved around the jagged stones. In another lurch, their pursuer took a sudden turn too late, flying off in a different direction.

"I think we've lost them."

"Did they crash?"

"Nope."

"Which way?"

Ezren pointed to the right, thinking Foster would turn in the other direction. Instead, he took a sharp right turn, the dunecart nearly coming up on two wheels before she could increase the grav balance.

"What are we—" Ezren started, just as the dunecart appeared in front of them.

"Brace yourself."

Ezren barely had time to grab the brace bar before Foster slammed the accelerator, broadsiding the other dunecart and sending it rolling into a column of rock. With another sharp turn, they were racing away, the algorithm correcting their track.

Ezren glanced behind them to see one of the racers trying to pull the other from the wreckage, their suitlights flickering in the dark. "Do you think they're okay?"

"If they weren't, their mayday signal would be going off." Foster's shoulders visibly relaxed as they descended into a valley, the terrain open before them. Ezren adjusted their parameters once more, and they practically flew downhill. "Those were enders, spare doubles brought on just to eliminate other teams. If we hadn't taken the initiative, they would've hounded us for the rest of the race."

Ezren swallowed, her gaze scraping the dark rock formations around them for more possible attackers. "So I guess there will be others."

"Maybe. But they usually gather around the checkpoint. So hopefully, unless we get bottlenecked, we should be good for a while."

Ezren couldn't help but notice the baggy smudges under his eyes and the heaviness in his words. It had been a long ten hours, but now they had another six ahead of them. She stifled a yawn just thinking about it. "But we're doing well, right? I didn't count the vehicles, but I'd say it looks like we're in the top fifty."

He gave her a weak half-smile. "Yeah... but we still have four hundred miles left to go." He reached over and squeezed her knee. "You're doing really well, Ezren."

"You're not going to give me the 'assume we're last' line?" Ezren tried a smile, even as her stomach clenched. They *were* doing well... but the real test was still to come. They had to best one of these teams in the brawl or they were out. Clean and simple. And while Foster had been able to get them through the tryout brawl almost single-handedly, he wouldn't be able to handle this one on his own. This would be the real test.

"Always a good policy. You should try to close your eyes though. I'll wake you up at the halfway mark, or if anything exciting happens."

"But I've got to be the lookout, and what about the grav controls?" she said, even as her treacherous eyelids drooped.

"We'll be fine, I promise. You just have to be ready to take the wheel in three hours." He reached over and pulled her head onto his solid shoulder. "Rest on me."

Ezren had no intention of falling asleep. She told herself she would just close her eyes for a few minutes. But despite speeding across an unknown landscape with other racers chasing them down, it only took another blink before she drifted away.

Five hours later, Ezren was behind the wheel as the metal shine of the brawling dome peeked out of the driving downpour. Her stomach untwisted and knotted again. If they were going to fail, it would be here, but it was a pleasant sight with the weather so rapidly deteriorating. The rain had arrived with the dawn, whipping through the roofless frame of the dunecart in sheets that intensified by the minute, and each turn had the vehicle sliding through the thick mud. At least now if they got stuck, they wouldn't have to run very far.

Her hands tight on the steering wheel, she nudged Foster awake where he lay crumpled in the passenger seat. "Hey, Foster, we're almost there."

He jolted upright, his gaze scraping their surroundings through the rain, and Ezren had to envy his instant alertness.

"Any sign of Grady and Bex?"

"None."

"Good, if they're too close, we could end up facing them in the brawl." He swiped a hand over his goggs. "You ready for this?"

Ezren kept her attention on the path ahead, trying to avoid the larger stones while the dunecart's tires bounced over the smaller ones. "Do we need to worry about getting jumped before we get there?"

"There's no scrapping in the brawl dome, but don't be surprised if someone follows us in."

"What, why?"

"Timing is everything here. You only get two losses before you're out, and some teams have better brawlers than others. They'll wait for a weak double to try to get paired for an easy win."

Ezren pulled their dunecart into the temp dome, still wary as she surveyed the cluster of other vehicles parked there—quads, topjeeps, and a few jetbikes—a lot of vehicles. She started to count when Foster pulled her along.

"Shouldn't we wait too?" she asked.

"I've never had that kind of time, but you might want to cross your fingers."

They approached the archway into the arena where a line of royalers lounged on the ground—some dozing, others leaning against the wall, and a few carefully eyeing Foster and Ezren. One pair immediately jumped up and headed into the archway, and a few others got to their feet, eager to follow them in.

Foster laced his fingers with hers, but he didn't look at any of the other teams as he strode up to the race official with the hummingbot perched on her shoulder. "Sterling/Hart, checking in."

"Doubles team number thirty-five, you're on in five minutes in ring two."

Foster pulled Ezren onward at a quick pace, and she tried to slow the racing heart that threatened to climb up her throat and gag her. "Number thirty-five? That's okay, right?"

He didn't meet her gaze. "It's all right, but it definitely means we don't want to waste too much time here."

The crowds in the projected stands cheered as Foster and Ezren stepped into the ring and pulled off their helmets and boots. Ezren flinched at the sudden cacophony. It was easy to forget on the surface that their goggs were streaming for fans across the system. Somewhere, her family and the rest of Belethea were watching. She couldn't let them down.

"Sterling/Hart vs. Brook/Talmadge in arena two," boomed the speaker.

"Talmadge?" Ezren's eyes grew round. They had been on

the road for hours, but everything seemed to be happening too fast now.

Foster's body went rigid beside her as he sucked in a breath of surprise. "It's okay. We've trained for this." But even as he said it, his brow furrowed, and he started to bounce from foot to foot. "They're going to hit us fast, so be ready."

Lucian swaggered into the arena with a smug grin on his face, a confidence reflected in the shoulders of his tall, sharp-faced doubles partner. Ezren's gaze glided over their sleek maroon suits, the muscles bulging from their tall frames, their matching buzz cuts, and their complete absence of surprise. Her drumming heart ratcheted into overdrive, a spike of fear sending a rush of adrenaline to her shaking fingers. They'd been waiting for them. Just like they'd been waiting for Simon and Bex in the exhibition.

"Why do they look so big?" Ezren whispered. Lucian had always been ridiculously tall, but with his new bulk, he stood like a giant.

"It's the Syndali training regimen," Foster said. "But we've been training too. Don't let them get in your head."

"Play fair and be sure to protect yourself," the referee said from the middle of the arena. Ezren's stomach nearly fluttered into her mouth. "Are you ready? Fight!"

And then both teams were charging together. Ezren flew across the sandy arena into a hailstorm of nanite-laced fists. She ducked and turned, immediately on the defensive as Brook's broad frame barreled toward her. Ezren's hands and legs seemed to move of their own accord, the trained reflexes Bex had drilled into her taking over. But it still wasn't enough. Before she knew it, Brook's meaty fist slammed into her cheek and black stars flashed across her vision.

Ezren staggered back, ears ringing and hot liquid pouring over her lips. Somehow she managed to keep to her feet, her arms protecting her face, but someone else lunged at her side. As she braced for the blow, Foster leapt between them, shoving her close to the ring's edge. Still stumbling, she watched him block the first strike, but then Brook took him to the ground, Lucian's fists hammering into his face again and again.

They weren't just trying to win. They were trying to make sure he didn't get back up. *No.* With a cry of desperate rage, Ezren rushed Brook, ramming her foot into the girl's face with a satisfying crunch.

Foster lay on the ground, his face cut and bleeding and his eyelids fluttering as he fought for consciousness. With Foster taken care of, Lucian stalked toward Ezren, huge and grinning, while Brook screamed obscenities somewhere behind her. And Ezren knew she didn't stand a chance.

Her breath coming fast, resolve hardened in her belly. Sometimes they had to play the long game. She sprinted toward Lucian, feigning a punch, before ducking beneath his arms.

She laid her body over Foster's form, wrapping her arms around him, and then rolled them both out of the ring.

"Ring out!" the announcer called. "Winner: Brook/Talmadge!"

But Lucian was still stalking toward them. Ezren turned to face him, fear slicing through her. They were so chaffed. His muscles tensed to lash out when a burly race official stepped in front of him.

"No scraps in the dome. If you want a rematch, you'll have to wait and take it out on the dirt."

Lucian flashed a sharp-toothed smile. "I hope you make it out of this." Stomping into his boots, he picked up his helmet from the ground and tossed the second to Brook. "Because we'll be waiting for you at the finish."

From behind him, Brook spat a bloody glob on the ground and smiled with red teeth. "Don't be late."

They walked off and the announcer blared the next match. "Sterling/Hart vs. Phanik/Phanik in ring three."

The official glanced at the prone Foster and Ezren kneeling beside him. "You have three minutes."

"Three minutes?" Ezren squeaked. She shook Foster's shoulder, his eyelids fluttering on the edge of unconsciousness. "Foster, c'mon, you've got to get up."

Moaning, he turned and retched onto the dirt.

"Oh, suns," Ezren said. If they were disqualified from the next match, they were out. She turned to the official. "Can I compete without him?"

"You can fight as long as he's in the ring." He offered a smile tinged with pity. "Or you could just forfeit the match and go home."

Ezren shook her head fervently even as Foster's eyelids fluttered. She couldn't let this be the end. They'd worked too hard. She thought of Foster training his whole life for this, of Sammy's med scans, of Tuzuno's looming shutdown. There was too much at stake.

She had to try.

"No forfeit." She knew how to take on two at once... as long as it wasn't someone like Lucian, it was worth a shot. "Can you walk?" she asked Foster.

He moaned again, and Ezren huffed out a frustrated breath.

"One-minute warning!" the official blared.

Ezren grabbed Foster by the armpits and hauled him just inside the ring. Then she straightened and faced her opponents. Two nearly identical royalers in silver topsuits, a short blond and a shorter redhead, smirked back at her. With a start, Ezren realized one of them was the girl who had sent her into the storm. *Callie Phanik.* The blond next to her had to be her brother, his hair pulled into a bun that mirrored his sister's.

"Well, I have to say, it really is good to see you this time," Callie said.

"If surprising," her brother chuckled. "But it looks like Sterling got a little tired after carrying her all this way."

Ezren's fists balled, and she remembered what Bex had told her. *If you're outmatched, go with the element of surprise. The longer it goes, the lower your odds.* Ezren breathed deep. She could do this. These two were third string—nothing compared to Bex—and the underestimation would work to her advantage. She just had to use every tool she had at her fingertips, like Simon would.

"Are you ready?" the announcer boomed.

Ezren wiped the blood from her face, trying to ignore the pain radiating through every joint, every bone, every inch of her body. This was the moment where they won or lost. Right here. One brawl and ten miles between her and the finish. That was just another morning at Carmella.

Come at me.

She held up her hands as if ready to block. "L-look, I'm s-sorry if we—"

"Fight!"

And Ezren flew across the stage. Her foot slammed into Callie's face, and the girl's eyes rolled back in her head. With another kick, she was out. One down.

Callie's brother tackled Ezren from behind, cracking her head against the floor with a white flash of pain. Ezren twisted, tightening her hold on the boy before rolling him the last few feet and out of the ring.

The whole thing was over in thirty seconds.

The horn's blare sounded twice with their exit—first for Ezren, then for Phanik. Callie skipped over to them with a sneer. "Wow, I can't believe you actually eliminated your own team. I really didn't think you were *that* stupid."

Ezren flashed a smile before shoving Callie's smirking brother away and climbing to her feet. "Oh, is that what I did?"

"Winner: Sterling/Hart," the announcer boomed.

Callie's grin faded, and she pointed at Belethea's lightning crest on the overhead holopro. "That's a mistake. They—"

Ezren's smile widened, and she gestured to Foster now sitting up in the middle of the arena. "He was down, but not out." Callie gaped at her, still not completely comprehending, even as the official ushered her away. "Honestly, it was good seeing you again. It would've really chaffed if it had been a first-stringer."

As an official led the Phaniks away, Ezren nearly crumpled to the ground, the adrenaline seeping out of her in a nauseating rush. She sucked in a deep breath to try to quell the bile churning in her stomach. Because they still had miles to go, and there was no way she was going to get that lucky again.

CHAPTER 25

HAD Foster told Ezren how fast the brawls went? He couldn't remember. Had they started yet? He was in the ring, so they must be starting at any moment now. Something was wrong with his head though, and his face was strangely wet. But it had been raining. So that must be it. Except they were inside now.

Where was Ezren? He rubbed his eyes, and his hand came away red. Oh, shaft. Where *was* Ezren? Sparks dotted his vision and somewhere far away, the wind howled fiercely, debris slamming against the metal dome, punctuating the roar of the fans.

Fans? He squeezed his eyes shut and finally they focused on the Dreitian royaler yelling from the side of the ring as two figures slugged it out on the ground. Or more like one whaled on the other as they tried to fend off the onslaught. Then Lucian's beatdown came back to him in a painful rush.

He staggered to his feet. Where was Ezren? Had the second match already started? "Ezren," he called out, his voice scratchy.

Then she was suddenly there, dropping his mag-boots in front of him, her steady hand gripping his elbow. "Oh, good, you're back on your feet. We've already spent way too much time here."

"But we still have to fight another round." Foster's head spun and his gut rolled as he shoved on the boots.

Ezren grabbed their helmets from the side of the ring and guided him through the arena with her short, quick steps. "Suns, he really knocked it out of you. Foster, we've made it through the brawls." She pushed his helmet into his hands with a smile. "We're on the last leg."

Foster blinked rapidly, pieces of the last hour coming back to him. Lucian driving him into the floor, and Ezren dragging him into another ring. Fodding chaff, he would have to watch the holos when he got back to figure out what really happened.

"But they just announced we're the 41st to advance, so we've got to—"

"Grady/Gunderson wins," the announcer blared again. "The 43rd team to advance!"

Ezren whooped. "They're here too." Her brows lowered, and her strides lengthened. "C'mon, Foster, we can do this."

She pulled him to the exit and then stopped short before the open metal archway.

He pushed past her, his mind finally starting to clear through the pain pulsing in his temples. "We'd better go then. There's nothing to do but—" And then he looked out into a black, howling maelstrom. Hail, water, and rocks rained down, crashing into the ground through a continuous growl of thunder. Winding cyclones and forks of lightning littered the sky in a deadly greenish haze. "Holy chaff."

"There's no way around it," Ezren said, just as a team brushed past her into the storm. The debris battered against them immediately, blowing them out of sight in a swirl of hail and rock shards.

But Foster was thinking of a different storm at a different qualifier. The dust storm that tore Vieve away forever. And he had been in much better condition. "There's no way we're going out in that, Ezren. It's like you said, no stupid race is worth it."

She looked at him, her dark brows sloped up in worried indecision. "But, Foster—"

Another team passed them in a blur, clapping him on the shoulder. "Pick it up, Sterling, you're cutting it close. See you at the after-party," Grady said with a whoop.

Then, they disappeared into the storm, just like Vieve had. The flash of her last smug smile before she'd chased after Lucian burned through his thoughts. How many times had he wished he could go back and stop her? Foster swallowed. Now Bex and Grady had done the same fodding chaff, and he hadn't even said anything. He should've done something. Called them fodding back. What kind of teammate was he?

"We can't not try." Ezren edged closer to the opening, the wind already blowing her off balance.

"Let's just wait for the update. Please, Ezren." Foster swallowed, anxious sweat cold on his face. "If we get blown off course, we'll just be exhausted and have to travel even farther. It may be faster to wait."

She looked hard at him for a moment and then nodded slowly. "Do you really think so?"

He squeezed her hand with his shaking fingers. "I do."

"Okay," she said with a wobbly smile. "Because I could really use that drink at the finish line."

"I thought you didn't care about this death trap of a race?" he said, trying to distract her as another team tore past them. Team #44.

The audience roared behind them, and her lips flattened. "There's something about it though, isn't there? Something that makes you feel alive?"

"Yes. It's the proximity to death," he deadpanned.

She rolled her eyes, her expression steadying into a genuine smile. "No, it's being in Belethea, I think. I've seen more of it today than I have in the last three years, and even if I have to fight for it, I would gladly do it again."

"You can cross Belethea without the race though."

Ezren shook her head. "This race makes Belethea possible. It keeps us all going—research, terraforming, the dream of something better. And yet there's still so much more we could do. It's worth it for that."

Foster's gaze lingered on her—a bruise purpling her eye and cheek, her lip swollen and bloody, and her eyes gleaming and passionate—and he was sure she'd never looked more beautiful. If this was what she wanted, he would run through a hell-storm for her. But he'd be chaffed if he wouldn't be holding onto her the whole time. "I—"

Their goggs beeped with an update, and Ezren shrieked. "There it is! A path in the storm—we can make it."

Seizing his arm, she backtracked around the rings to a side door. Together, they shoved on their helmets and barreled into the storm.

The path seemed almost nonsensical in the way it looped through the patches of yellow and red, dictating their halting speed as they moved along. If it weren't for Ezren's complete faith in it and the strange pocket of relative calm they seemed to be chasing after, he would've thought the algorithm had malfunctioned. But still, he kept his grip tight on her as he ran, his mind focused on each and every step. His muscles groaned, his body ached, and pain scarred his vision with every jarring step, but he ran as fast as his legs would move.

For Ezren, and her dream of Belethea. He could do this for her. And maybe for himself too—proving what he was capable of, that Belethea had a right to be there, and they were worth fighting for.

This was their year.

A rock banged against Ezren's shoulder, sending her stumbling. He caught her by the arm, keeping her on her feet, and she winced with a pained smile before picking up her pace once more.

Yes. If she could do this, so could he.

The storm whirled by them, and occasionally a streak of color flashed through the sheets of rain and muck. A snatch of a scream caught Foster's ear, but he could see nothing in the lashing water. He glimpsed one royaler carrying their injured partner on their back, and another doubles pair trying to take cover in the lee of a boulder. Maydays blared through their goggs, calling for emergency services to respond—but there was no way they'd be able to reach them in this.

Ezren skidded to an abrupt stop just as the rain whirled into a funnel cloud to their left, smashing into the ground. They cut sharply to the right, but not before he witnessed a lone crimson royaler, arms and legs flailing with panic, tumble up into the twister. Fodding suns. He hoped Bex and Grady hadn't gotten caught in that.

With the storm raging around their patch of safety, the finish line seemed to grow out of the rocky plain—two tall spires surrounded by a field of storm trucks, and a metal dome rising up behind them. It appeared so suddenly, Foster was certain it must be a figment of his battered head until Ezren cheered. "There it is, Foster! We made it!"

"What's the number by the finish? Can you read it?"

"It says sixteen!" she squealed. "I can't believe it. We're going to make it."

The sight lent a surge of hopeful adrenaline through his legs, and he pounded his aching feet into the ground. Half a mile left. At most. And yet it still seemed so far away.

"Wait, wait, wait." Ezren held out a hand to slow him.

"The algorithm just updated. We need to wait another thirty seconds before going forward."

"Do you think it's really that accurate?" Foster asked, gazing wistfully at the cheering crowds practically within arm's reach. Pain throbbed through every cell of his body, his mind screaming at him to let it stop. And they were *so close.* "What difference does thirty seconds make anyway?"

He didn't even realize he was moving forward before Ezren jerked him down into the mud just before a tornado slammed into the ground in front of the finish like it had been shot out of a cannon. The twister scored the ground as it whipped by like a chaotic top, lightning flogging the sky around it while the storm trucks rattled on their chain anchors. Booms of thunder vibrated through Foster as maydays flashed back-to-back in their goggs.

Then as soon as it had come, the tornado whipped out of sight, making the violent sheets of rain seem tame in comparison.

Foster barely had a chance to close his gaping jaw before Ezren yanked him up. "Yes, thirty seconds can make a huge difference."

Foster looked at her in wonder, muddy and serious as she gazed through the downpour at the sky. He still found it hard to believe this girl was for real. "A game-changer," he murmured.

The algorithm updated again, and they took off. They entered the final chute, and still Foster couldn't believe it. Not until they had crossed over the line, and the announcer blared through their goggs.

"Here comes Belethea's very own Sterling/Hart finishing in seventeenth and qualifying for the BRR. That's a new Belethean record!"

And Ezren was screaming, wrapping her arms around his neck. "Seventeenth! We made it!"

Foster stopped, his mouth ajar as Ezren clung to him. His hands moved to her waist, letting her ecstatic shouts of celebration wash over him. They'd actually qualified. A rookie team. Belethea was going to the BRR. He whirled her around, lifting his head back and howling at the sky while the crowd roared.

A fresh gust of stones battered into them. Foster turned, his arms wrapped around Ezren as the volley of sharp gravel pounded into his back like a spray of bullets. He had to laugh at their own ridiculousness. "C'mon, let's get inside before this storm kills us."

And that's when the alarm whined through their goggs.

MAYDAY: Simon Grady, Team Belethea. Emergency teams respond.

Foster froze, his arms still around Ezren as his heart plummeted into his stomach. Foster pulled up the map in his goggs, trying to get a read on the mayday call, but it was all garbled. What about Bex? He checked her position. When they'd last updated, they weren't even two miles from the finish line. Scarcely breathing, he shot her a message.

Foster: What happened? Where are you?

No response.

His heart pumped into overdrive. *Again? How could this be happening* again?

Ezren looked up at him, her eyes wide. "We have to go back for him."

Foster's mind was numb as he stared at Ezren, some part of him agreeing with her. But then there was the other part that saw the storm tearing into her just like Vieve—her mangled face staring up at him. Even the thought of Ezren's crumpled body nearly broke him. His arms tightened around her, more debris beating into his back in the worsening burst. "Ezren, w-we can't." His chest heaved, the panic nearly choking him. "We have to get inside. Let the storm trucks handle it."

She struggled in his grasp, surging toward the finish line. "No, he's out there in this, Foster! We have to go back for him!"

But his grip tightened around her chest as he pulled her up the gravel slope toward the dome airlock, still careful to keep his back to the wind. "I'm sorry, Ezren. I'm sorry."

"No!" She bucked and screamed in his arms, even as a trio of twisting funnel clouds touched down on the flooding plain. "He's still out there!"

Fodding chaff, he hoped Simon was okay. But there was no way he would lose Ezren too. With the wind shrieking and chunks of rock flying past, Foster slammed the airlock button.

With a hiss, the door slid shut, cutting them off from the raging death storm and their lost teammates.

Their friends.

Foster had to plead with Ezren to take a shower and go to the med table, to eat something. He said the same things Sylvia had said to him the year before. The things that were no help at all but needed to be said. There was nothing they could do. Nothing they could've done. The things they knew, but would never really feel in their bones.

Around them, the finishers, staff, and press murmured in subdued knots over the shushing of waves in the beach-style holopro adorning the open dome. More mayday calls came in by the hour, the trainers ferrying in the injured on airstretchers to medics in the side rooms. But Grady and Bex weren't among them.

The hours passed, and Ezren only got more frantic, demanding a storm truck to continue the search herself. But all the storm trucks were already out searching. There was nothing they could do but wait. Exhausted, hurt, and wordless, they paced the edges of the holopro ocean while Sylvia mercifully delayed the media's attempts to wring them for the raw emotions the vampiric fans fed on.

Finally, Ezren tired of her pacing and let him curl an arm around her, her chin dipping toward her chest with the exhaustion she could no longer fight. Still, Foster felt nothing but a hollow fatigue as he returned the stares of the other royalers.

After three hours, word reached them that they'd found Grady—alive but in critical condition. And no one was sure whether to mourn or celebrate. In another four, the suns finally put them out of their misery when the officials announced they'd found Bex, also in critical condition.

Alive.

Foster was sure he'd pass out right there, but doubts cut into his mind. If Bex was in critical condition, why hadn't her mayday gone off with her location? Had her suit malfunctioned? Like Vieve's? Two faulty suits on the same team? The odds had to be slim. Could someone have tampered with them? Was that the race day update Ezren had mentioned?

His questions faded to static as they watched the hovercam footage of Grady's and Bex's prone bodies. Bile rose in his throat as the holopro zoomed in on their cracked helmets and shredded suits, their bodies swollen and bloody. Commentators spewed empty condolences with plastic frowns while the armored emergency storm trucks skirted the storm to Petraskis. They all stared, unable to look away, as Grady coded in the truck, as the responders pumped him full of med nanites to revive him, as precious minutes passed before his weak heart rate pulsed once more.

Sylvia gently pulled their goggs from their heads, silent tears streaking down her face. "I think that's enough of that for now. Our storm truck back to the city will be ready in the morning."

As she left, Ezren finally burst into the sobs that had brimmed in her eyes all day. He gathered her in his arms as she cried, pulling her tightly to his chest, needing to be reassured that she was safe beside him.

Scooping her up in his arms, he carried her from the common area and into a side breakroom, laying her down on a wide couch. But when he tried to pull away, she only laced herself around his neck, burying her face in his chest. He slid next to her on the synleather couch, their bodies knotted together.

"It was my code," she whispered, her voice trembling with fatigue or emotion; he wasn't sure. "It sent them in the wrong direction, I know it."

He kissed her head, wishing he could give her any kind of reassurance that might ease her pain. Or his. But there was none. "We don't know anything, Ezren. Rest now, and we'll know more in the morning."

But the only thing Foster was sure of as they drifted off in a wave of pain and exhaustion was that Ezren had been right from the start.

This stupid race was a fodding death trap.

CHAPTER 26

EZREN OPENED her heavy eyelids to the blinding brightness of the hospital waiting room. She turned her gaze into the firm shoulder her head rested on, trying to block out the harsh sterile smell of the building with Foster's reassuring mango-ginger scent. She pulled Foster's bomber jacket over her against the chill of the room, and his lips brushed against her hair.

She half groaned into his shoulder, before at last gathering the courage to lift her head. "Any updates?"

Across from them, Sylvia shook her head from one of the uncomfortable plastic chairs, her teal nails plucking at her fancy pressed clothes and worry creasing her brow.

"They've put Bex into a med coma, but she's still critical," Foster said, his eyes closed and his head leaning against the holopro on the wall. His hair flattened unnaturally against the blue sky. "And Simon is still in surgery." She hated how Foster said his first name so softly, as if he were too fragile for the usual brusque manner they shared.

Ezren sat up, wiping at her dry lips, and checked her goggs for the time: 0645. What a shafting ungodly hour. She dismissed the latest waves of messages from Micah and her family. They'd been blowing up her goggs with squeals and congratulations ever since she and Foster had finished, especially after they'd gotten an eyeful of the performance bonus she'd received. In what seemed like a true miracle, they finally had enough creds for her mom to schedule Sammy's procedure with the doctor Foster had recommended. But it felt wrong to be celebrating anything while her teammates still fought for their lives down the hall.

She got to her feet with a wince, unfolding her stiff muscles. Spoiled with the team's med tech, she'd nearly forgotten what natural recovery felt like. Walking gingerly, she began her useless circle around the empty waiting room where they'd spent the last forty-eight hours.

She tangled and untangled her sleeves around her fingers while she stretched her legs. It never failed to surprise her how much all hospitals looked the same. Hard white floors and acrid furniture jarred against the wall-holos of sunny, open fields and the soothing sounds of instrumental music. She didn't know if she hated anything like she hated hospitals.

A child limped by with her mother, and a memory spasmed through Ezren. The one of her father screaming for help as he carried Sammy's mangled body into the hospital while she clung to the tail of his jacket, bawling her eyes out.

Blinking away the image, she stumbled to the nurse's station in the hall and folded over onto the desk. Suns, give her darkness and grime any day, it was these sterilized, fluorescent halls that were the place of nightmares. "When's the surgery scheduled to be over, again?" she asked for possibly the third time.

The nurse shook her head, her neon-orange braids swaying with a smile that looked more like a sad frown. "Not for another three hours still. Then he'll be in a med coma for another six. But they're serving breakfast until 0800 in the cafeteria. You should get yourself something to eat." Her face brightened just a smidge. "You deserve some rest. We all saw what you did yesterday. We're so proud of our royalers."

"Um... thank you." Ezren pasted on a fake smile, not really knowing what to say to that. She felt no pride, no elation—just a deep bone-aching worry.

Sylvia set her elbows on the counter beside her. "I know it's hard, Ezren. But we're not doing them a whole lot of good here. We really should take this time to go do a PR round. The BRR is in a week."

Ezren stared at her for a second, wondering how she could be thinking of a PR round. She pointed to the side of her face, still black-and-blue, the pain mercifully blunted by a triple dose of pain-killing nanites. "Do I look like I'm in shape for a PR round, Sylvia?"

"Well, you could use some time in the med tank too." Sylvia rubbed her shadowed eyes with an exasperated sigh, fatigue weighing on her every move. "But I'm just trying to tell you nicely before Harland comes in here and hauls you away kicking and screaming."

"So we're just supposed to leave them here?" Ezren pointed to the double doors that led to the ICU.

"I'm sorry, Ezren. But this is part of royaler life. Their families are in there, not to mention eighteen other injured royalers." She gently rubbed a hand across Ezren's arm, but Ezren's frown only deepened. "Accidents happen."

"But what if it wasn't an accident?" Foster said, lumbering up between them.

Sylvia jolted to life, seizing his wrist and pulling him away from the perked ears of the nurse attendant. "What do you mean?"

"I mean, Bex's suit malfunctioned, Syl," Foster said. "It didn't even send out a mayday signal. Just like Vieve's. Someone must've tampered with it."

"But we were the last ones to update the software." A nervous bubble churned in Ezren's belly. Maybe that was one of the reasons she didn't want to leave the hospital. When they got back, they would have to do a full scan of the storm tracking software. And if it really had led to Bex and Grady getting hurt... Tears swam in her eyes.

"No, it can't be our software," Foster insisted. "The algorithm worked just fine for us." His gray-green gaze flicked from Sylvia to Ezren and back. "Lucian was there at roughly the same time. And he has a grudge. What if he did something to the suits?"

Sylvia shook her head, massaging her temples with her manicured fingers. "You've got to be kidding me, Foster. This sounds like some crazy fan conspiracy theory."

"Look, Sylvia, all I need is their suits after the investigation is over. I'll compare them to Vieve's and see if we're right."

She crossed her arms. "If I do this for you, will you get out of this hospital for a few days?"

"Fine," Foster said, his mouth tight.

Sylvia looked at Ezren. "That means both of you."

Ezren sighed, what little fight she had left going out of her. "Fine, but at least let me get something to eat first."

Sylvia threw up her hands. "Thank the suns." She waved them off as she turned away. "Stuff your faces and meet me in front in twenty minutes."

Not at all hungry, Ezren walked down the hall in the direction of the cafeteria to stall for a little longer. "Did you really just agree to a PR round?"

"Those suits could be important, Ezren. Remember what you said about an update on Vieve's suit the morning of a race?"

"Yeah."

"We've never done something like that before. What if it

happened on the day of the qualifier and someone tried to cover it up?"

Ezren turned, their mag-boots echoing on the reflective linoleum. "That sounds like a big 'what-if.' "

"Two years in a row." Foster shook his head, his brown waves flopping onto his forehead. "That's not a coincidence."

"Well, I guess it should be easy to figure out either way. Once we get the suits back, it should only take a couple days to compare them to Vieve's," Ezren said, her tone souring. "Harland would love that kind of juicy drama before we jump into the BRR."

Foster stopped short. "Wait. You're not still thinking of running the BRR."

Ezren turned around, her brows knitted. "Of course I am. We qualified, didn't we?"

"Ezren, if someone's trying to sabotage Belethea, then there's no way we can race until we get to the bottom of this."

"You must be joking. This is what we've been working for all year. It's practically in our hands." She paused, taking a deep breath, and the tension in her shoulders eased. "I know you're upset about what happened to the others. I'm shattered too. Maybe we can just be more careful if—"

"No, Ezren. It's not worth it. I'm not going to put our lives at risk for some stupid pissing contest."

"Some stupid pissing contest?" Ezren's voice rose. "This is the future of Belethea we're talking, Foster. We could change things. With the terranium rights, we could revitalize our terraforming efforts, not just here, but across the systems. This could change people's lives."

"Oh yeah? And how likely is that? Even in the qualifier, we didn't come in the top ten."

Ezren looked away, her face flushing.

"What makes you think we could win the BRR when that

2% handicap in our suits is going to make an even bigger difference?" She took a step back, and his face softened. "Face it, Ez. It's just not in the cards for us."

"Then why even come this far?" she asked, hating the way her voice shook. "If you really think that, then why didn't you just quit before the tryout?"

His head dipped, and he put his hands on his hips. "I don't know, Ezren." His stormy eyes lifted, measuring hers. "Maybe I should have, and you and Simon could've fed on each other's ridiculous fantasies."

Ezren's ears buzzed, and her stomach sank. Did he really mean that? "I don't know what to say to you right now." She swallowed the tears lodged in her throat, sensing they were entering ground they wouldn't be able to return from. "But I'm running that race, Foster, whether you're coming or not. I'll run it by myself if I have to."

His shoulders fell, and he ran a rough hand across the back of his head. "Look, we're tired. Let's take a break and figure this out later." He blew out a deep breath, and his goggs chimed. "Oh, and also, call your mom, please. She's been trying to reach you all morning." With that, he turned and walked away.

For a moment, Ezren stood there, watching his back until he disappeared around the corner. But he didn't stop, and he didn't wait for her. If he was done racing, then that meant they weren't doubles partners anymore. So what were they, then? If she didn't race, did she just go back home? To a home that wouldn't even be there when Tuzuno shut down in thirty-one days. Directionless, she continued down the hall, not at all sure what she should be doing.

Then she remembered her mom. She opened her goggs inbox, expecting another flurry of "we're so proud of you" and "are you sure you're okay" messages that she'd addressed last night. But there were only the words:

Mom: Waffle is sick, and Sammy is... not good. If you can, please call when you get this.

In an instant, all the sorrow, frustration, and exhaustion that had built up in the last few days fell away, replaced only by an icy cascade of fear. And even though she was still bruised and sore, Ezren took off running down the hall.

CHAPTER 27

FOSTER STRODE out of a backdoor to the hospital, pulling his goggs over his eyes and a cloth surgical mask over his face. He needed to get away from everything. With exhaustion and pain clogging his mind, he knew he wasn't thinking straight, and it only frustrated him more. Stepping into the crowd of the packed downtown district, Foster glanced toward the front of the hospital where reporters bunched outside, waiting for the injured royalers or their teammates to emerge. Sylvia was probably in there somewhere, working her strange magic to overcome his social shortcomings.

He shot her a message.

FOSTER: WALKING. SEE YOU BACK AT CARMELLA.

Weaving through the blur of people, he limped toward Carmella's iron gates, and his eyes widened. Holopros, graffiti, and old-fashioned paper signs coated the stone walls—congratulations, get-well messages, and encouragement stuck to every available surface. A solid, almost pleasant warmth stirred in Foster's chest, and he quickly stomped it out as he wrenched the gate open.

It didn't matter that they'd qualified if they died in the final. What would that gain them? Gain Belethea?

Nothing.

He crossed the strangely silent common room of Carmella's lobby. His temper only burned with the emptiness of it. He passed the kitchen, his footsteps loud in his ears as he climbed the stairs to the armory. There was a part of him that wanted to link into Vieve's suit at that very moment. To tear through the code and check the dates on the last upgrade.

But even as he looked at the metal armory door, his vision blurred, his hand twitching painfully at his side. He couldn't— not without some sleep first. Maybe by the time he woke up, Sylvia would have Grady's and Bex's suits as well, and it would be faster to run a comparison of them at the same time.

With the weak rationale firming in his sleep-deprived mind, Foster dragged himself up the stairs to his room, trying not to look at Ezren's, Bex's, or Grady's doors as he passed them. At one time, he would've rejoiced in the solitude, but now it just made him sick. His door slid open, and he limped into his plain, unadorned room.

It was the closest thing he had to home, but there was nothing comforting about it. He shucked off his jacket, slapped a new pain patch on his arm, sent a quick check-in to Ezren, and let himself collapse onto his bunk.

He didn't gather the motivation to make it downstairs again until the next morning, driven from his cave by the promise of food. The halls and stairs looked exactly like they had when he walked into them eighteen hours earlier. Still quiet, still empty.

At least Sylvia's updates said that Bex and Grady were both in stable condition, although they weren't expected to be brought out of their med comas for another day now. That good news combined with his noticeably less-sore muscles was some-

thing that could be celebrated with at least a bowl of cereal...
even if there was still no one to celebrate with.

Where was Ezren anyway? Was she out with Sylvia on
those PR rounds? He checked his inbox only to find a flood of
Sylvia's PR updates, but nothing from Ezren. He was honestly
surprised Sylvia hadn't dragged him out of bed yesterday. Still,
a surge of guilt ripped through him. He knew how much
Ezren's terraforming lab meant to her—how hard she'd been
trying to get to this race. He grimaced, thinking of the harsh
words that had jumped from his mouth and wishing he could
swallow them back down.

He grabbed a box of cereal and a jug of synmilk, pouring
himself a bowl. Was she avoiding him now? He couldn't blame
her if she was. Maybe even if they didn't race, there was still
something he could do to help Tuzuno.

He looked around the ragged common room of armchairs
and worn-down couches that had once hosted a dozen Blazers
laughing and having a mess. Now it was just a ghost town. He
stopped chewing at the thought of ghosts. That was something
he still had to deal with. Slurping down the rest of his bland
cereal, he started toward the stairs when the front doors hissed
open.

He eagerly turned around, the apology already on his lips.
Maybe they could—

"Hey," Sylvia called to him as she collapsed on one of the
overstuffed couches. "Don't think I forgot about those PR
rounds. We have three interviews this afternoon and one
photoshoot this morning, so you'd better get ready."

He sighed. Should've known that was coming. "What
about Ezren? Do you know where she is? I haven't seen her yet
today."

Sylvia half-sat up and lifted one of her rainbow eyebrows at
him. "She didn't tell you?"

He stilled. "Tell me what?"

"Did you two argue or something?" Sylvia assessed him, a calculating look flashing behind her narrow eyes.

He crossed his arms, unease tightening between his shoulder blades. "Why does that matter?"

"Ezren left yesterday morning. Family emergency."

"Emergency?" Foster started walking toward the door, his face tense. "What happened? Was it her brother? Is he having regen complications?"

"Brakes, kin." Sylvia raised a hand as though to stop him but didn't rise from the couch. "She said not to worry, but she needed some time alone with her family. Besides, even if you do manage to get a storm truck in Belethea's busiest season—doubtful, by the way—you probably won't even get there before she's headed back."

"Then how'd Ezren get a storm truck?" he asked.

Sylvia shrugged, squeezing her temples. "I think she got help from a friend or something."

A friend? In the city? It didn't take Foster five seconds to figure out who that could be. *Davis Banda.* Acid jealousy burned in his stomach, and he turned on his heel, starting toward the stairs again.

"Hey," Sylvia called out, straightening as if suddenly seeing him. "Seriously, are you okay?"

He paused, tapping his fingers against his leg. "I'm fine. When are we going to get Bex and Grady's suits?"

"Oh, yeah." Sylvia propped her elbows on the couch's back. "The race officials said they were too damaged to be repaired, so they've been salvaged for usable parts." She winced. "Which apparently wasn't much."

Foster ground his teeth. "Seriously?" The universe was working against him. It had to be. He turned, striding back up the stairs. "Well, if there's anything left at all, tell them we want it back."

"Sure thing, but before you disappear again, don't forget about the PR appointments."

Foster ignored her as he trudged up the stairs to the armory. The door slid open, and he crossed to the corner where Vieve's suit now hung from one of the pegs on the wall. He didn't allow himself to hesitate as he took it down and tossed it on his workbench. But no matter how fast he moved, he couldn't escape the image of Vieve's cold body lying facedown on the mauve dirt.

He linked his goggs and took a deep breath, diving into the code. Away from the memories into cold hard logic. He only had to search for a moment before he ran across Ezren's note from the last access.

Multiple layers of patches on 4.26.42B. At least one layer corrupted and unreadable. Possible last-minute race day fix? Ask Micah to dissect with Giles.

Who the chaff was Giles? Another ex? Scrolling through the notes, his mind twisted treacherously to the thought of Ezren and Davis together. Davis dropping off her favorite breakfast in those early weeks. Davis and Ezren with their little nicknames outside the club. The jealousy wrenched his gut. So the first time they had an argument, she went running to Davis for help? Or was it because she felt more comfortable with him when everything else started falling apart?

The thought made his shoulders droop, the frustration melting out of him with a strange heaviness. Or was it because whatever had happened to her family had affected Davis too somehow? They did grow up together. But if it wasn't her mother and her brother, who could it be? He knew her dad was long gone, and she hadn't mentioned any other family.

Or maybe it was actually a close friend instead. Like Micah?

Foster pushed the thoughts away as he dug deeper into the code. It really was snarled. One of the patches was a standard race update package, one was totally corrupted, and the other seemed to be a fix for something, but it didn't say what—maybe the corrupted code? But then even below all those layers, there looked to be another file he still couldn't access.

He tapped his fingers on the table, glancing at the clock in his goggs. He didn't have much time before Sylvia carted him off onto her PR nightmare marathon, and who knew when he'd get another chance before the BRR in five days. If he was going to figure this out before the next race, he needed help.

And Ezren had told him exactly where to get it.

Closing out the code, Foster leaned against the workbench. He'd messaged Micah before about Lucian's smear campaign after the tryout, but this time Ezren was angry with him for trying to pull them out of the race... not to mention the whole ex-boyfriend thing. So the odds of Micah being on his side were slim, especially since she was a BRR fangirl. Then again, maybe he could at least find out if Ezren was okay. Even if she didn't want to hear from him, that would untangle at least one of the knots in his stomach.

Sucking in a tense breath, he thought out the message.

Foster: Micah, are you there?

Micah: Why hello, Foster Yunin-Sterling, record-breaking Belethean royaler. How may I help you? :)

Foster: Is Ezren there?

Micah: Not with me, but she's here in Tuzuno with her family.

Foster: Is she okay? She's not answering my messages.

Micah: Yeah, she's probably muted out, but she's doing okay.

Foster: What happened?

Micah: She didn't tell you? Are you two fighting or something? Is it because Davis is here?

Gritting his teeth, Foster raked a hand through his hair. Couldn't she just answer the question?

Foster: We had an argument. But it wasn't about that.

Micah: Oh, well that's good, at least. Not going to lie, I was never a big Sterling/Hart fan, but it was definitely an upgrade from the Banda/Hart.

A strange mix of unease and smugness coursed through Foster. At least she liked him better than Davis.

Micah: Although it's really good for Sammy that he's here.

Foster: What? Why?

Micah: Well... because Waffle is really sick, and Davis and Sammy have always been close.

Foster's stomach dropped. Now it made sense. Ezren loved that not-dog, and he couldn't even imagine how Sammy felt about her. Whatever Ezren had told Sylvia, she obviously wasn't fine, and his heart squeezed at the thought of her going through it by herself. At least her family was there. Still, a small hateful part of him imagined her crying on Davis's shoulder, and he crushed it out. As long as someone was there for her, that's all that mattered. Even if she hadn't chosen him.

Foster: Please tell her that I'm sorry. And... I really wish I could be there for her.

Micah: Sure.

Foster: But I actually called because I need your help on a topsuit.

MICAH: WHAT?! YOU DEFINITELY SHOULD'VE OPENED WITH THAT! WHAT CAN I DO?

FOSTER: LOOK, I THINK SOMEONE HAS BEEN SABOTAGING BELETHEA'S SUITS, BUT I NEED YOUR HELP TO FIND OUT WHO.

Foster's frown eased for the first time in days. Ezren was far away, Bex and Grady were down for the count, but here at least, he could be useful. He could figure this out. Because if someone was responsible for hurting his team, he would make sure everyone and their grandmother knew about it.

And then he would destroy them.

CHAPTER 28

EZREN RAN her hand through Waffle's thick brown fur where the emaciated capybog lay motionless. She traced the rounded tips of the animal's ears, and then the round pink pads of her webbed paws. Waffle snuffled wetly, her short legs twitching, and Ezren rose with a smile. She'd be getting plump off of treats again in no time.

Beside Waffle, her brother snorted out an abrupt snore and buried his face into the capybog's soft fur. Ezren sucked in a deep breath and let it out slowly—the tension, fear, and worry of the week finally seeping out of her. Their little family was going to be okay.

Sammy's door silently closed behind Ezren as she stepped into their small living room. Davis and her mother looked up from where they leaned over the kitchen counter. Both of them nursed steaming cups of hot syncocoa, the sugary aroma coating the air.

Who even thought it was a good idea to keep toxic plants in the dome park anyway? And why in the six suns would Waffle feel the need to eat them? She squeezed her temples. With no veterinarians and no access to canine medications, the last two days had been touch and go, but it seemed like Waffle would pull through. And as horrible as the uncertainty had been, with

Sammy and her mom there, it had been bearable. Nothing like when Sammy got hurt. Nothing like when Dad left.

Ezren, Davis, and Dr. Tanaka had spent a lot of time researching possible treatments and nanite med dosages for small animals, but in the end, there was little they could do but start an IV and hope it would be enough to flush out the remaining toxins she hadn't already vomited up. While Sammy had panicked at first, his tears were dry by the time she arrived, and Ezren was the one who had to put on a brave face. Now her mom sat quietly talking to Davis with soft smiles passing between them—a familiar sight that almost brought her back in time.

Putting her mug down, her mom rose from her stool and wrapped her arms around Ezren. "I'm so glad you were able to come," she murmured. "We've missed you so much."

Ezren returned the tight hug. "I've missed you too."

Her mother pulled back, beaming with a pride that almost brought fresh tears to Ezren's face. "We're so proud of you, Ez. Between what you've done for your brother, the money you've raised for the lab, and how much work you've put into the royale to represent Belethea..." She shook her head, her eyes glistening. "So proud."

The words tingled through Ezren, warming her skin beneath her sweater. She thought of how crushed everyone would be if they didn't even get a chance to compete. "But it's not enough."

"All we can do is our best, my love. I know these steps may seem little when you expect so much of yourself, but great change is built from many little changes." She squeezed her hands. "And building things takes time."

"But Dr. Lutz said we only have a month left before Tuzuno shuts down," Ezren whispered. "What will we do?"

"You don't worry about that. We have plenty of options."

Just no good ones.

"I think I'm going to bed early, but you two stay up as long as you like," her mom continued, smiling at Davis. "I'm so glad things are going well for you, Davis. It's always lovely to see you."

"Goodnight, Ms. Evangeline." Davis flashed his charming trademark grin.

With a parting wave, her mother's door shut with a gentle swish, and Davis and Ezren were alone. A strange, quiet blanket of déjà vu wrapped around them. As if they were colliding with some bizarre alternate universe in which they had stayed together and still ended up in this very room. She squirmed, her skin itching with an awkward self-consciousness —like she was missing something she couldn't quite place.

"I'm sorry for ignoring your messages and then calling when I needed help," she blurted out. He stilled, staring at her, but she forced herself to go on. "But I didn't want to give you the wrong impression." She made herself meet his gaze. "I don't want to be more than friends."

Davis stared at her for a moment before his expression softened with a quiet chuckle. "Relax, Ezren. I get it." He proffered the kettle. "More cocoa?"

Ezren sagged with relief. She wasn't sure what she'd been expecting, but that hadn't been nearly as difficult as she thought it would be. "Sure, thank you." Ezren took her mother's stool, wrapping her hands around the hot metal mug. "And thank you for bringing me here. I really didn't know what to expect when Mom sent me that message, and I went about halfway out of my mind."

"Of course. You know you can always call me for anything." He smirked. "Friends can do that, you know."

"Yeah, yeah, I know." Sitting side by side, they stared off into the nothing in front of them in the oddly comfortable silence. Ezren tapped her fingers on the counter in the midnight quiet. "But it looks like I rushed over here for nothing. Sammy seems weirdly okay. Like he grew up five years while I was gone or something. I must've known they'd be fine on their own, or else I wouldn't have left. Still, I always worked so hard to keep everything together, so it's weird to see it kept running on just the same without me." She chuckled. "Guess I had a super-inflated opinion of myself."

"Nah." Davis shook his head. "They knew how to keep this house going because you showed them. And they're happy partly because they're inspired by you, Ezren. I know you're not into VSoc, but you've inspired all of Belethea. I mean, have you seen this?"

Davis projected one of Micah's hype holos in the air in front of them, but this one was full of fans—packed bars cheering her name, small children with magenta hair dressed in teal costumes, fans with holos that read *Save Terraforming* and *I believe in Ezren's sky*. Uncountable faces flashed in front of them until finally fading into the dim light of the kitchen, ending with the words: *Sterling Hart—bring Belethea home.*

A churn of pride and purpose surged through her in a force wave that stole her breath from her lungs. Could this really be happening? Six terraforming stations had closed in the last year, and Tuzuno was still set to shut down in a month. Did they still have time to save them?

Ezren tried to cover the hopeful tears welling in her eyes and nearly knocked over her drink, sending ripples through its mahogany surface. "All we did was qualify. And Simon and Bex got hurt, so I'm not sure that really counts as a win."

"Every step forward is a win, no matter how small." Davis cocked his head as though thinking. "Isn't that what your mom says?"

Ezren hid her prickling cheeks in her mug, letting the cocoa fill her belly with its warm comfort. "Well, that might be our last step forward. Foster doesn't want to do it anymore."

"Now that you're closer than anyone's ever been?" His brow wrinkled. "Why?"

She shrugged. "He says it's too dangerous."

"Ah." Davis's face suddenly smoothed into a knowing smile.

"What?" Ezren said, confused. "I'm serious."

Davis held up his hands. "I know you are. It's just that I get it is all."

"You do?"

"He's trying to protect you, Ez," Davis said, his voice soft in the quiet.

Ezren's face burned hot. She thought about Foster's sharp words in the hospital... Had they been out of concern? The feel of his arms as he held her after the qualifier wrapped around her once more. Maybe he *was* worried about her... but still, she had to race. "I don't need protection. I can go out there just like everyone else. If he quits, what do I do without a double?"

"Well, the way I see it, you have a couple options." Davis twisted his mug in his hands, observing it closely. "You could throw in the towel, find a different team to race with, or you could race without a double."

"But in all of those options, Belethea loses." She sagged on her stool. "There's no winning here."

He frowned. "Oh, c'mon. It's not like you to give up so easily."

She leveled a glare at him. "Davis, if I can't win, Belethea doesn't get the prize money, Tuzuno disappears with the funding, and terraforming research goes out the airlock shaft."

"Suns, Ez, stop thinking in black and white. You don't have to win the whole thing to make a difference. Look at what Sylvia and Micah can do with a qualifier." His eyes intensified.

"You have a voice now, Ezren, and people are listening. Keep screaming into the void, and eventually, the void will answer."

Ezren snorted into her cup. "Geez, Davey, since when did you get all wisdomous?"

He oozed a dramatic sigh. "You've never appreciated my uncanny insight." He set his cup down and rose from his seat. "But can I tell you one more thing before I go?"

"Is it my fortune?"

Ignoring her gibe, he paused by the door. "I know you're upset with Foster for quitting on you, but his decision will probably turn him into the most-hated person on Belethea." He glanced at her. "And he did it to protect you."

Biting her lip, Ezren pulled on her overlong sleeves. "He could have had other reasons. We don't know he did it for me."

"He did. And I just want you to know, I think that's pretty blime." The door hissed open, and he stepped out. "I know we can't be together, and one day I won't be here for you. But I'm glad someone like that is." With one last smile, Davis turned and walked down the corridor.

Ezren stood, speechless for a moment, feeling like she had both lost and found something at the very same time. Foster's lazy smile flashed through her mind, sending an ache through her chest. Yes, of all the places in the 'verse she could be, she was in the wrong one.

CHAPTER 29

THE NEWS that Bex and Grady had recovered from their med comas and could accept visitors came in the middle of an excruciating interview with *Petraskis Sporting Bulletin,* and Foster literally jumped at the excuse. Leaving Sylvia and Harland to fend off the rest of the questions, he caught the magtrain and made it to the hospital in under nine minutes.

A familiar nurse with a waterfall of vibrant orange braids smiled at him from the front desk. "Foster Sterling here to see Bex Gunderson and Simon Grady, right?"

"That's right."

"They've been asking for you." She craned her head to look around him at the door. "And is Ezren Hart coming too by any chance?"

Foster's lips flattened into a line. "Um... no, not that I know of."

"Aw, maybe later then." The nurse ushered him down the hall projected with a green open field on a bright spring day. "They were actually moved out of the ICU last night and came around this morning. They'd only been awake for about ten minutes before they asked to be put in the same room." She raised a bemused eyebrow. "Little did we know it'd only be the first of many demands."

Foster gave a polite smile, strange nerves tensing between his shoulder blades. "How are they doing?"

"The doctors are expecting a full recovery in another week or two, but their families finally went home for some rest a little while ago, so you should have them all to yourself." She stopped at one of the identical blue-sky doors in the long hallway. "And here we are." The door slid open before her, creating a void in the sunny holopro, and she stepped in. "Good afternoon, you two, we've got a visitor to see you."

"About chaffin' time!" Grady's loud voice echoed from the room.

The nurse gave Foster a *you see what I've been dealing with* look and propped a hand on her hip. "Well, it's only been fifteen minutes since we got the all clear, but I'm sure your fans will be pouring in soon. Anything I can get you in the meantime?"

"Well, we—" Grady started.

"No," Bex finished for him, and the nurse needed no further encouragement.

She patted Foster on the shoulder as she left. "Good luck with this crowd."

Foster swallowed and took a step into the room, squeezing his clammy hands together. Two rolling beds had been placed across the room from one another, privacy curtains peeled back to reveal a stack of medical equipment chirping next to each. For all his talk, Grady's face had hollowed in the past few days, with deep bags underscoring his eyes and his curls falling in a mess across his forehead while nanite medcasts encased his arms and legs.

Bex looked even worse. Her pale skin had turned almost translucent, and her normally bright blue gaze had lost its shine. In addition to the casts on her limbs, she also sported one around her neck as well as a cap that wrapped around her head.

A twist of emotions Foster couldn't begin to sort out trembled through his body. Anger for whoever had done this to them, relief that they would be okay, guilt that he wasn't in here with them... and so many more.

"Hey," he said lamely.

"Hey, yourself," Bex returned, her voice hoarse. She blinked slowly as if having trouble staying awake. "Heard about your finish. Congrats." A weak smile crawled across her pale lips.

"Yeah, where's E?" Grady asked. "I owe her that drink with extra sugar or whatever."

"She's... in Tuzuno. Family emergency." Foster tapped against the rail of Bex's bed. "Nothing too serious though, I think."

"Oh, you two on the rocks?" Grady asked with a smirk.

Foster resisted the urge to roll his eyes. Why did everyone keep asking that? There was nothing abnormal about someone going to visit their family, was there? He decided to ignore the question. "I think someone tampered with your suits."

Grady's face darkened, his hands balling into fists. "I fodding knew it."

"Who was it?" Bex murmured, her eyes closed. "Why are they targeting Belethea?"

"I don't know yet." Foster stuffed his hands into the pockets of his bomber jacket. "I've been running scans on Vieve's suit for clues but haven't come up with anything yet."

"Then they'll be targeting you and Ezren at the BRR." Bex paused, studying him through slitted eyes. "Are you still going to race?"

"Of course they're going to race!" Grady winced, taking in a sharp breath of obvious pain. "They're the best chance we've had in years, and if they quit, they'll be doing exactly what this asschaff wants."

Foster crossed his arms and leaned against the wall of white puffy clouds. "Ezren is still set on it."

A wide grin spread across Grady's face. "I knew there was a reason I liked her."

"Just remember... never let your guard... down." Bex's words slurred as her head sank back into her pillows. "They'll be coming at you... till the end."

"I won't," Foster said, his voice too loud in the quiet room.

Bex nodded, her head slipping to one side before fatigue finally won out.

Foster checked her vitals to make sure she was green before pulling the blanket up over her. He mentally sent the files of the latest holopro games to her goggs so they would be there when she woke up. Clearing his throat, he turned to Grady. "I'll let you both rest, but I brought you the latest Starleaper issues to pass the time." His goggs chirped as Grady received the comic holos. "I'll be—"

"Sterling."

Foster turned to him, tensing for whatever verbal whiplash was coming. He probably deserved it anyway. "Yeah?"

"Vieve's suit... it wasn't an accident, was it?"

"No, it wasn't."

Grady screwed his eyes shut, his casted arm striking out and knocking the cup of water from his tray. Again and again, he lashed against the bed railing. "Suns fodding shaft it." He grimaced and drew back, his cast dented, and the nanites scrambling to reform it.

For a moment, Foster just stood there. Feeling it with him. The rage. The helplessness. The guilt. He should've seen it sooner. "I'm sorry."

"It's not your fault. Someone fodding murdered her." Grady's voice came out rough. "Tried to murder us." His hands tightened in the blankets around him, and he shook his head.

He met Foster's gaze, eyes glistening. "I'm fodding pissed as chaff. But not at you."

Something loosened in Foster, his legs suddenly weakening beneath him. He'd always told himself it didn't matter what Grady thought—what anyone thought. But he'd lied. He rubbed at his damp eyes. "Maybe if I'd looked closer at her suit, we would've realized before..."

Grady held up a hand, his voice low. "Stop. Your ifs are going to kill me, kin. Just make sure you fodding watch your back in the BRR."

Foster took a deep breath, his voice trembling with barely checked emotions. "If we race."

"C'mon, kin," Grady scoffed with a grim smile. "We all know you're not going to let Ezren go it alone. Besides, if these fodders don't want us to race, the best way to shaft it to them is to win the whole chaffing thing." He held out his casted arm. "Make us look good, okay?"

Foster knocked his arm against Grady's, his hazel eyes earnest. "Yeah... we'll do our best."

"You better." Grady winked at him. "Cuz next year, you'll have to deal with Grady/Guns fair and square."

And for the first time since the qualifier, Foster smiled. "You're on, Grady."

CHAPTER 30

EZREN'S heeled boots clicked on the marble floor as she walked into the overflowing ballroom. Royalers from across the system milled under the projected abstract holos of kaleidoscopic artistry coating the high ceiling and walls. Music wafted through the buzz of conversation from a full orchestra on the opposite end, and waiters flitted among the guests, sporting platters of every kind of food imaginable.

Obronians in sheer dresses and open shirts showed off the sun-browned skin of their legs, arms, and even bellies. In Obronian culture, to wear more clothing was to admit shame of your own body. But in all honesty, what they were really showing off was their mild, overcast climate that allowed such things. And you almost couldn't see the clear visors that sat atop their heads.

The Dreitians, on the other hand, were nearly fully clothed in beautiful bright colors. Layers of vibrant patterns—scarfs, saris, and long button coats—draped their bodies, the fabric flowing around them to the floor. And where cloth didn't touch their skin, gold bangles, crowns, necklaces, and earrings glistened instead. Even their half-masks they wore in place of goggs shone with all manner of rare, shimmering stones. On

Dreitis, the more you wore, the more you had. And the more you were protected from the relentless sun.

The spacers, with their one-eyed half-visors, moved through the crowd in their sleek, shapely jumpsuits, projecting subtly shifting patterns they could change with a thought. The swirling landscapes had a way of drawing your eye to wherever they wanted it. Sometimes to quite embarrassing effect.

Finally, there were the Beletheans, if only a sprinkling. They wore their boots, buckles, and top hats, temporary inked designs scrawling along the skin around their eyes in lieu of the goggs perched atop their heads. Combined with the dark three-piece suits, long coats, and ruffled dresses preferred by their largely subterranean society, they seemed less glamorous than the others. A ragtag people, less sure of their place in the system. Or maybe that was just in her head. Ezren ran her fingerless gloves nervously along the silk ruffles of her dress. The corset threatened to suffocate her and yet her chest still felt oddly exposed by the off-the-shoulder sleeves.

Sylvia squeezed her hand. "Don't fidget. You look fantastic."

Ezren smothered the instinct to glare at her. Sylvia was radiant in her high-necked dress with its long sleeves and short skirt showing off her thigh-high boots. Her curls had been teased to their full volume, fanning out from her head in ten different swirling shades of rich brown that seemed to drip into the full-face design of gold ink that adorned Sylvia's face. Ezren might've even envied her if she hadn't known it had taken the better part of the last three hours to achieve the look.

Ezren hadn't even gotten a chance to stop at Carmella before Sylvia kidnapped her from the storm truck station for the prerequisite beautification.

"Is Foster here?" Ezren peered around the whirling bodies for his familiar face.

Sylvia scowled. "He certainly should be. This is the biggest event of the year. If he's not, I swear I'm going to rip off his goggs and beat him with them."

Ezren sagged. Though Foster had sent her a couple of messages asking if she was okay, she hadn't felt like their next conversation should be through goggs. She'd meant to go straight to his room and talk it all out... but she hadn't anticipated Sylvia's abduction.

"Don't worry about him. We'll tell everyone he's probably at the hospital with his teammates or something," Sylvia said. "This is your chance to shine. Everyone who's anyone is here, so if we're going to get a few more sponsors, this is the place."

"What would that do at this point? The race is tomorrow." A spike of panic stung Ezren's chest. The race was *tomorrow*. Was Foster still serious about backing out? Was that why he wasn't here?

"Next year, girl. You have to think of next year. You still have two good seasons ahead of you." Sylvia's face practically glowed as she plucked an entrée from a circling waiter. "Our funding has nearly quadrupled since the beginning of the season. Just think, we might even be able to buy a top-of-the-line suit next year."

"But what if Foster doesn't race, Syl? They'll hate us," Ezren said.

"I think you underestimate how far you've come. You went from being the interloper to being Belethea's favorite underdog."

Which meant she could fall right back at any time, Ezren thought.

"Oh, look, there's Warner Calderon." Sylvia pointed to a stiff man standing at the center of a crowd of dark suits with Harland beside him. Warner Calderon wore a charcoal three-piece suit with a long coat, a bowler above his thick gray hair, and a black cane gripped in his pale hands. His hard dark eyes roamed the ballroom before coming to settle on Ezren. Calderon said something, and Harland waved them over with a jerk of his hand.

Sylvia beamed, pulling Ezren across the room. "C'mon, we have to go say hello." Calderon's gaze followed them as Sylvia dropped into a deep curtsy before him. "Mr. Calderon, I'm not sure you remember me but I'm—"

"Sylvia Long, the former VSoc manager and current stand-in coach for the Belethea royalers." He flashed a white smile, revealing sharp canines, a fad of his generation that always threw Ezren off. "My dear, I may be old, but I'm not so senile as to not recall my own staff."

If this gentle rebuke surprised Sylvia, she didn't show it. "Then you know who this is, but let me at least have the honor of formally introducing you to Ezren Hart."

His smile faded, his eyes softening just a touch as his gaze shifted to her. With a nudge from Sylvia, Ezren dipped into a belated curtsy. "A pleasure to finally meet you, sir."

He returned the curtsy with a stiff bow. "Indeed. I must say, I had my doubts about the open tryout strategy, but it's been pleasant to see such fresh determination on Belethea's team this year. It gives it a more... authentic feel. How're you feeling about the race?"

Ezren offered a smile, hyperaware of the hovercams glowing all around her. "A little nervous if I'm being honest."

"As you should be," he said. "This planet is no less brutal than it was eighty years ago when we first raced across its wild surface."

Ezren raised her chin, her hands tightening. "It may be wild, but it's more beautiful for it."

His sharp-toothed smile returned, crinkling his eyes this time. "Then we agree. We can only hope to preserve Belethea's passion as long as we can." His eye caught on something behind her, and he nodded. "Be safe out there, Ezren Hart. May the winds be at your back, and we'll hope to see you again next year."

With another short bow, he strode off through the crowd, Harland and the rest of his entourage in tow.

"That seemed... strange." Ezren's gaze followed the man out of the tall synwood doors. Why was he already talking about next year? Did he not believe they could do it? Or—her shoulders fell—had Foster already told him he wasn't racing?

Sylvia pulled her away toward another clump of business-like suits. "Yeah, they say he was never the same after that very first race," she whispered. "But, I mean, who can blame him after Carmella died. They say they were madly in love."

"Wait, who was Carmella?"

"How do you not know this?" Sylvia shook her head with a resigned sigh. "Carmella was his partner, of course. She succumbed to her injuries after that first terranium rush. That's why he named Belethea's royale training facility after her."

Ezren faked a smile for a flashing hovercam. "But why would he even establish the race royale when he knew how dangerous it was?"

Sylvia snorted. "Look around you, Ezren. This race rains money and earns the ear of every station in the system. Not to mention averting international war. He had a crisp idea, and he ran with it. Who wouldn't?" Sylvia stopped abruptly, scanning the crowd. "Ugh!"

"What?" Ezren followed her scowl, trying to find what she was seeing.

"All the sponsors are over there lining up for photo ops with the racers," she growled. "Where the fod is Foster? I swear I'm going to kill him for this." She clicked her sparkling nails against her ultra-white teeth. "Okay. You go ahead and get in line while I ask the greeters if he came in."

"Wait! What am I supposed to do when I get there?"

"Smile, be charming, hint that you need better topsuits. Haven't you been paying attention to any of my PR classes—never mind, don't answer that. You'll be fine. Just try to channel Simon and relax."

"Wait, don't leave me." Ezren reached for Sylvia's arm, but she'd already disappeared into the crowd.

"Suns take it," Ezren muttered to herself, briefly considering trailing after Sylvia. But then she noticed all the glances flicking in her direction. All the hovercams high above them recording her every move. If she didn't have the confidence to handle a stupid banquet on her own, there was no way she could take on the BRR without Foster.

She could chaffing do this.

Not meeting any eyes, she stepped into the long line of royale doubles and their coaches. Her gaze still swept the crowd, hoping for a familiar face—Foster, Sylvia... suns, she would've settled for Harland.

"Well, if it isn't the little dust mite."

Ezren's hands tightened into fists before she turned around. She might have settled for Harland, but she certainly would've passed on Lucian. He'd adopted the spacers' glitzy jumpsuit, and his flashing abstract design was even coordinated with Brook and two other royalers at his side, stretching and bouncing from one to another.

"Why hello, Lucian." Ezren pasted on a fake smile. "I'm sorry, am I in the right line? I thought this was for decent kin."

If her comment ruffled him, he didn't show it. "Actually, I'm not sure you are." He leaned in, pointing to the sponsors. "You see, this is for teams that are actually going to race tomorrow."

Ezren's cheeks went cold as the blood drained from her face. "I *am* racing tomorrow. You should know that, right? I think it might have been mentioned on VSoc once or twice," she said lightly, forcing the words through her brittle smile.

Lucian spread out his broad hands, his voice rising. "Then where is your double? Suns, where's your coach, for fod's sake?" People were looking now, and Ezren lifted her chin defiantly. "Has Belethea really sunk so low that they only have one member?" Hesitant laughter sprinkled through the air, the chatter fizzling as Ezren squeezed her clammy hands together behind her back.

"Not that it matters if they have one royaler or two." Brook batted her impossibly long lashes, her ruby lips parting in a lofty sneer. "It's not like they stood a chance of winning anyway."

Ezren opened her mouth to say what she hoped would be something scathingly witty, when a light hand rested on her shoulder. "You would do well to worry about your own team, as I do believe Syndali only qualified one pair this year as well."

Ezren turned to see Greta Sterling at her side. She wore an ink-black jumpsuit with stars exploding in different colors across it, her brown hair coiled into an elegant twist atop her head. She turned to Ezren with a bright, confident smile beneath her gray-green eyes. "Ezren, I'm so sorry to interrupt, but may I steal you for a moment? There's someone I want to introduce you to."

Belatedly, Ezren remembered to close her gaping mouth. "Yes, of course."

Greta Sterling linked her arm in Ezren's and led her swiftly across the empty dance floor. Though eyes still followed them, they were curious rather than condescending, and the chatter renewed with increased fervor.

"First, I wanted to apologize for my behavior toward you. I

honestly thought that you were a fangirl jumping into the royale for your chance in the spotlight. And... after your first showing, I wasn't sure if you'd be good for Foster." Her stormy eyes met Ezren's, the left nearly luminescent behind her green half-visor. "I'm happy to say I was terribly wrong on both counts. With no coaching guidance, your tenacity and talent have impressed, well, everyone, and I have to congratulate you on breaking my qualifier record."

"Oh, um... thank you." Ezren cleared her throat, still trying to adjust to the oddly surreal moment. "Foster's actually the one who's done most of the coaching this year. So it's really all thanks to him."

Greta frowned. "While I am glad to hear that, I suppose his absence this evening means he won't be racing in the final."

Ezren's mouth flopped open again. "How did you know?"

With a flick of her wrist, Greta parted the crowd before them. "Regardless of what my son may say about me, I do know him rather well." Her gaze softened. "I was close by when they announced Simon Grady's mayday... and I could tell he was done. It was the same look he had after Genevieve's accident."

"But he still raced after that," Ezren said.

Greta looked at her with a bemused smile. "Yes, he did, didn't he?" She patted her arm. "Regardless, since he isn't here now, I wanted to make sure you were taken care of. As a talented royaler of Obronian descent, I want you to know there are more opportunities out there for you." She gestured to a man in a gauzy, translucent shirt, and the thigh-baring shorts of the Obronian style. "I've already talked to the Obronian coach about taking you on. If you're interested, now's a good time."

"Racing for Obrone?" Ezren's mind whirled as she tried to catch up.

"Yes, your compensation would be five times what it is now, their training resources and equipment are unmatched, and they've won the royale more times than any other team. Honestly, I'm a little jealous of the opportunity." She turned and squeezed Ezren's hands. "If you really want to win, Obrone is your best shot for next year."

Ezren swallowed. That was what she wanted, wasn't it? This had been the real opportunity that Micah had talked about from the beginning. That's why she was here—to win funding for terraforming, even if she didn't get the terranium prize for Belethea. And honestly, her chances this year were already crushed. There was nothing left for her on Belethea's team. If she and Foster weren't...

She stood there, twisting her hands with indecision, her stomach turning, and her mind coming up blank. What Greta was saying made sense, so why did it feel so wrong? "I... I can't."

Greta chuckled. "You certainly can. I know it's a big step, but honestly, love, there's really only one choice here. You don't have a doubles partner, and—"

"Yes, she does." Foster stepped from the crowd to Ezren's side, lacing his hand in hers.

His touch nearly lit Ezren on fire, heating her from her fingertips to her toes—the relief dizzying and wondrous. *He'd come for her.* Her heart swelled, and she drank in the sight of him.

He wore a long black coat over a vest and tie, and his hair had been styled for once, sweeping away from his forehead. A black swirling design crawled around his green-gray eyes, making them practically pop from his beige skin. Confidence radiated from his broad shoulders and firm grip, and Ezren wanted nothing more than to fall into his arms.

"She can go to Obrone if that's what she wants, but if she wants to race tomorrow for Belethea"—his gaze moved to Ezren, sparking with intensity—"then she has a partner." He raised his voice. "And I think we'll be setting another record tomorrow, even with our three-year-old suits."

The chatter fizzled into silence, a lone violin the only sound drifting through the masses to where all stares pointed at them. Every hovercam in the place recorded their every word, waiting for her answer. *Her voice.* And for once, she didn't cringe away, didn't shrink beneath their red eyes.

This was their moment—*Belethea's moment*—and somehow, Foster had made it happen.

The rush of gratitude nearly floored Ezren, and her vision swam. With a deep breath, she straightened. Because she *did* have something to say, and she had to make it count.

"Belethea is my home, and Foster Sterling is my double. I could never race with anyone else, or for any other team. This planet and the people on it are part of who I am. We work hard, and we dream big, because the dream of Belethea, of living under an open sky, is worth every drop of blood and sweat, every tear that waters our soil. We may not be the richest team or the most advanced planet, and we may still have a terraforming journey ahead of us, but I'd rather build those things together with them, than go anywhere else."

Her gaze scraped over each and every whirring cam, challenging the millions of viewers watching through them. "Tomorrow we will race, drive, and fight to the heart of Belethea. But it's a big heart, and one worth fighting for." She shared a glance with Foster, pride and heat and purpose blazing between them. "We believe in Belethea, and we're racing to win."

The bubble of silence erupted in a din of talk, and the media pressed in on them, abandoning the interviews to pepper them with questions.

Her pulse buzzing and strangely out of breath, Ezren ignored them. She kept her eyes on Greta, waiting for the anger to boil to the surface, for her cam-ready mask and cutting words. But for the first time, a genuine smile lit her face. "Well, Belethea is certainly full of surprises this year. And I'm sure if you ever change your mind, feel free to reach out, Ezren, and I'll help you however I can." She squeezed Foster's arm, her gaze soft. "I'm glad you could make it, Foster, and I'll be proud to watch you..." Her attention flicked to Ezren. "To watch both of you tomorrow."

"Thank you, Ms. Sterling, for your help." A strange suspicion curled in Ezren's gut. Had she somehow planned this?

But still Foster said nothing, his expression unreadable.

Greta offered one more smile. "I know we've had a bit of a rocky time recently, but please know that I wish you fair winds tomorrow. Truly, be safe." With that, she walked away.

Foster turned to Ezren, leaning close to her ear. "Unfortunately, the dance floor is the only place to get some space. So if you'd do me the honor." He held out a hand and Ezren took it, nervous butterflies colliding in her stomach. With one hand on her waist, he took her through the steps of the simplest dance she'd learned in their PR classes while the orchestra swelled into a weave of strings and air. "You really could've gone to Obrone if you wanted to. Micah told me that was the plan," he whispered in her ear.

Doubt flickered behind his dark lashes—a doubt that Ezren wanted desperately to wipe away. Her mouth flattened into a firm line. "I didn't want to. I would've said no even if you hadn't come."

His shoulders seemed to relax under her hand. "I'm sorry I'm late." He pressed his cheek to hers, his lips close to her ear. "And I'm sorry for what I said last time."

"I'm sorry too. I'm just glad you're here now." She pulled back to take him in again, looking impossibly handsome with his three-piece perfectly fitted to his broad shoulders and narrow waist. Catching herself staring, she looked away with a blush that heated her from the inside out. "Did you find out anything about the suits?"

"Not yet. I put Micah on the case and took some precautionary measures." He twirled her slowly before bringing her to his firm chest.

"Then what made you change your mind?"

"When I realized I couldn't stop you from going on your own, I also realized I needed to be there to protect you from what someone once told me was an idiotic, suicidal race."

Ezren pulled away. "You don't have to pro—"

"I do." He held her hand tight, his gaze glinting green in the light. "Because I'm in love with you, Ezren. And people who are in love protect each other with everything they have. They fight for each other, holding on no matter what."

She stopped, her body immobile and on fire under his fingers. Her vision swam, and she started to tremble from the effort of keeping her emotions in check.

His eyes suddenly clouded, worry knitting his brows. "Ezren, are you—"

"I'll fight the whole 'verse before I let go," she breathed, wrapping her arms around him. "I love you too much, Foster Yunin-Sterling. I think it might shatter me."

He smiled, the deep furrow between his brow finally easing. "Then I'll just have to hold you together." With that, he bowed his head and kissed her slow and deep.

And even though a hundred hovercams flashed all around them, Ezren knew this kiss was for her, and her alone.

CHAPTER 31

EVERYTHING ELSE FELL AWAY as Foster savored the sensation of Ezren in his arms. His cheek against her hair, he breathed in the fresh scent of lemon and sage. Taller in her heeled boots, she leaned into his chest, her warm breath tickling his neck. He wished he could pull her gloves off and feel her smooth palms against his. Still, with his hand on the curve of her waist, his worries dissolved with the heady reassurance that he'd made the right choice.

If Ezren believed it was worth it, then he would stand by her, and they would get through the race together. They might not win, but Belethea deserved their best—odds be chaffed. He moved her slowly through the song, and when she drew back to look at him, he couldn't resist closing the distance between their lips. Meeting her soft mouth with his. They said nothing, but they didn't need to. They were in sync again, two people moving as one.

All too soon, the song ended, and Sylvia whisked them away with a glowing smile. On to the never-ending photos, interviews, and networking. Proving to the system that Beletheans were not the backward, primitive dust mites the system believed they were. Proving that they could be as strong and as smart and as fast as the other richer nations. When he thought about it, he knew Ezren was right. As much as he wanted to be selfish, to protect her and himself, this was bigger than them, and they were the only ones who might be able to pull it off.

Might being the problematic word.

At last, hours later, Sylvia released them, and they filed into the magtrain, making their way through the dome's faux night back to Carmella. Then, with a dose of Sylvia's overly cheerful encouragement, and a kiss from Ezren, Foster was in his bunk, staring at the ceiling. But as usual, sleep was impossible with the pre-race nerves coursing through him and the endless possibilities blurring his thoughts. The race wouldn't even start until the next evening, so he had plenty of time to lie awake while thoughts of his mother, Vieve, and even Grady crawled unbidden across his mind.

It was going to be a long night. It always was before a race. And this was the BRR. Even amongst all his misgivings, a thread of excitement rose in goosebumps along his arms. They were the best chance for Belethea in the BRR's history. How was that even possible? But even as he thought it, he knew. It was because of Ezren. Because she'd thrown her whole self into the race without hesitation. Because she believed in it without a flicker of doubt.

If they were going to lose tomorrow, it would be because of him. So he had to show up with everything he had. Even if he didn't believe in the BRR, he believed in Ezren. And for her, he would leave it all in the dirt.

How long he lay there before he drifted off, he wasn't sure, but the quiet knock at his door sliced through his tenuous grasp on sleep. Bleary-eyed with near-dreams, he sent the command to open it, and the door retracted with a hiss, revealing Ezren in a pair of frayed, worn shorts and a loose tank top.

She crossed the room without a word until she stood next to his bed. "I'm so tired, but I can't sleep," she whispered.

On any other night, Foster would've whisked her away on one of their midnight runs until the stress and worry had been burned through her muscles. But not tonight. If they were going to get a good start tomorrow, they needed to rest.

So he did the only thing he could think of. He opened his blanket wide, and she slipped in beside him, curling into his chest as he wrapped his arms around her. Though her skin was cool to the touch, he let her tuck in closer, sharing his heat, her head nestling into his chest and her hands wrapped around his waist.

She clung to him so closely, he imagined their hearts beating against one another, their rhythms syncing together into one song. The steady warmth of her relaxed him, luring him to the edge of sleep.

"I'm scared," she whispered into his chest, her words slow and heavy.

"Of getting hurt?" His hands tightened around her at the thought.

She shook her head against him. "Of letting everyone down."

For a moment, he said nothing while his fuzzy brain tried to pluck the right words from waiting dreams. "It's okay to be scared. That's what makes the royale so great. It's the thrill of the risk—the unknown of the challenge." He rubbed his hand slowly along her back. "But in the end, it'll just be you and me climbing mountains no one has seen, leaving footprints on unmarked dirt. Us and Belethea. Just how you like it."

Even in the dark, he could feel her lips part in a smile on his chest. "Yes... I do like that."

For a moment, the silence stretched between them as he

traced his hand in a slow circle on her back, feeling her muscles relax against him, her breaths evening with his.

"And what happens after the race?" she murmured.

"We go home."

"We?" Ezren's face tilted up toward him, and he could hear the note of hope in her voice. That sliver of uncertainty he wanted to crush out.

He pressed his lips to her forehead. "We."

She tilted her face higher until her mouth found his in the dark, pressing a kiss soft and sweet against his lips. "Have I told you I love you yet?"

"Only the once," he whispered back to her, trailing a line of kisses down her neck.

"That's not enough," she said breathlessly.

"I agree." And he smiled, his lips against her ear. "Tell me again..."

The chirping of Foster's goggs woke him mid-morning, Ezren's body entwined with his under the twist of sheets. He silenced the alarm through his neurochip, pulling her closer. No matter what was on the schedule, it would be worth putting off for a few minutes to savor this. She murmured in her sleep, instinctively burying her face in his chest, and he pressed a kiss to her temple. No matter what happened the rest of the day, he would remember this—that it had begun perfectly.

Her eyes flickered open, still soft with sleep and a smile spread across her face. "I think this is the first time I haven't minded waking up."

Foster opened his mouth to respond when the door swished open.

"Foster, you've got to get up, I've been trying to—" Sylvia stopped dead in the doorway, and Ezren jerked fully awake, her eyes going wide as they met Sylvia's.

"Sylvia, we—"

And then Sylvia burst out laughing, folding over as the honking bray leapt out of her. "Suns, kin, just fodding lock the door next time." She straightened, wiping the tears from her eyes. "But, seriously, get up, I've been messaging you both for the last half hour." She started to walk away when she looked over her shoulder. "Also, I'm totally posting about this on VSoc."

Ezren turned a blazing crimson, and she whipped out of bed, racing after her. "Sylvia! No, you can't!"

"Oh, c'mon, there won't be pictures, and they'll totally..."

Foster chuckled as he fell back into the bed. He grabbed his chirping goggs and projected the notifications to see a scroll of unread messages from Sylvia and Micah. Suns, he must've been sleeping hard. The ones from Sylvia were typical:

SYLVIA: ARE YOU UP?

SYLVIA: HELLO?

SYLVIA: WE'RE GOING TO BE LATE. GET UP!

SYLVIA: OKAY, I'M BUSTING THE DOOR DOWN.

But the messages from Micah had him sitting up.

MICAH: GUESS WHAT! I THINK I FOUND A WAY TO SOLVE OUR PROBLEM.

MICAH: YOU'LL NEVER BELIEVE WHAT JUST HAPPENED!!

MICAH: DID YOU GET MY SURPRISE?!

Surprise? What surprise?

Foster dressed quickly, running some nanite wash through his mouth before rushing out the door. He found Sylvia and Ezren, now dressed in her usual sweater and tights, bickering in the kitchen area of the common room.

Sylvia threw up a dramatic hand. "Tell her I'm allowed to blare whatever happens here in Carmella out to VSoc."

Foster ignored her, offering a reassuring smile to Ezren. Sylvia might talk big, but there was no way she'd post those pictures. As amazing as she was at VSoc-ing, she never posted a picture that someone didn't want public. "Cut to the good stuff. Micah mentioned a surprise. Do you know what that's about?"

Sylvia shrugged, her brown eyes sparkling. "I don't know, guess you'll just have to go outside and see." But even as she said it, she tossed a hovercam into the air, and it came alive with a hum.

"Oh, suns, please tell me it's a gigantic portable vat of coffee." Ezren clutched her hands to her chest as she walked toward the door.

Sylvia raised one of her colorful eyebrows. "Really? It's the morning of the Belethea Race Royale, and you're hoping for coffee?"

"I would also accept something that's first ingredient is sugar," Ezren said. "Candy, pudding, cake, ice cream..."

"Ice cream? Have you even had breakfast yet?" Foster took her hand in his, their fingers lacing together.

"Nah, my bed was too cozy this morning," she said with a mischievous smile. "What surprise do you want the morning of the biggest royale of your career?"

Foster's brows knitted as he tried to think. "A surprise on the morning of the race? Honestly, if we were able to get our suits upgraded that would be—"

The doors hissed open in front of them, and two brand new teal-and-black topsuits glinted from the faux sun of the dome—one tall, one short, and both with the latest generation branding along the side.

Foster's eyes went wide, and he froze, his breath caught in his chest.

Ezren's jaw dropped, and she stepped forward, touching the shining material almost reverently. "Are these for us?"

From the gate across the lawn, a crowd of fans in Belethean teal spotted them and started screaming their names, reaching their hands through the bars.

Sylvia jumped up and down and squealed almost as loud as the gathered fans. "Yes! Aren't they amazing! It's like a Belethean miracle."

Foster's gaze whipped to Sylvia, his heart hammering in disbelief. "Gen XLII suits? Micah did this? But how?"

"Ever since Simon and Bex got hurt with their shoddy suits, Micah started a VSoc fan-funding campaign to get you new gear. Apparently, it was going pretty well, but after last night when you had that big public and oh so adorable, we're racing in-your-face speech, funding exploded." Sylvia's smile widened even farther. "I even managed to sweet-talk one of the race armorers to come check them out and give them the thumbs up on short notice. Not that there was much to check with brand-new, top-of-the-line suits. So these are now your official race look. Drink it in."

"No more 1.5% difference," Ezren whispered.

Foster looked at Sylvia, scarcely allowing himself to believe it. To hope. "This is a game-changer."

"I know. The fans are beside themselves." Sylvia beamed with another squeal and gestured toward the gate where the frenzied mob had begun some sort of swelling, wordless chant. "So get those fodders on and let's go change the game!"

Foster quickly fired off a message to Micah.

FOSTER: THANK YOU.

MICAH: ;) SEE, NOW YOU DON'T HAVE TO WORRY ABOUT SOFTWARE OR SUIT MALFUNCTIONS. AM I GOOD OR WHAT?

FOSTER: BUT HOW DID THE FANS COME UP WITH THAT MUCH MONEY?

MICAH: WELL... DON'T TELL ANYONE, BUT ALMOST HALF OF THE FUNDS ACTUALLY CAME FROM ONE ANONYMOUS DONOR, SHORTLY AFTER YOU DECLARED YOU WERE RACING. I'M GUESSING IT WAS SOMEONE AT THE BANQUET, BUT I DON'T KNOW WHY THEY WOULDN'T JUST PUBLICLY ENDORSE YOU.

Foster's skin tingled.

FOSTER: BUT THE DONOR DIDN'T ACTUALLY BUY THE SUITS, RIGHT?

MICAH: NO, THEY JUST SENT THE CREDS. I'M THE ONE WHO GOT THE SUITS. SERIOUSLY, FOSTER, I SWEAR. THERE'S NOTHING TO WORRY ABOUT HERE. YOU SPOKE AND THE FANS LISTENED... JUST TRY NOT TO LET THEM DOWN.

He looked at Ezren, a smile dominating her face as she pulled on the sleek new topsuit.

FOSTER: I DON'T PLAN TO.

CHAPTER 32

DARK, curling clouds swirled through the sky in a way that sent Ezren's weather algorithm into a panic with wildly different updates every five minutes. In the last few months, she'd spent every spare moment researching the churn belt's weather signature to adapt her algorithm to its unrelenting chaos, but even now, she wasn't sure it'd be enough to get them through. Lightning forked across the distant mountains in pulsing veins of light, and Ezren could see the haze of precipitation and debris crashing into the ground even from a distance.

"So they're not going to postpone for weather this time?" Ezren asked.

Foster stood strangely still, sleek and strong and confident in his new topsuit. "Not this time. In the BRR, it's up to the royalers to determine what kinds of risks they're willing to take. Since it's a multi-day race, the pace is a little slower, with time to make decisions about where to go and when to do what."

Behind them, the goggs cam stream of every royaler peppered the translucent domes of stadium seating, broadcasting to every feed in the system. From the stands, the fans boiled as if baying to be released. Their holopros glowed in the dusky light with the colors of their team—deep crimson, burnished gold, emerald green—and dotted among them were swaths of Belethean teal. Unable to be contained, a swelling chant vibrated from the stands. "To the churn! To the churn!"

Swallowing, Ezren glanced around them at the other doubles clustered in the starting chute. There were fewer racers than in the qualifier, but they were just as packed in, and this time, because of their decent qualifier finish, Ezren and Foster had been lumped in the middle between the Dreitians and Kellen Station. Although Ezren could feel the extra energy humming through her supple new suit, it still didn't feel like adequate protection against their predatory glances.

Foster bent his head toward her, his voice low. "With the storm ahead, there will be more teams than usual looking to scrap at the start."

"But that doesn't make any sense." Ezren tried to lean away from the hulking team beside them. "With such a long race, that kind of delay wouldn't be worth the risk."

"They're not looking to delay us; they're looking to crack our helmets and tear our suits. They want to eliminate us here."

Ezren shifted from foot to foot, the weight of the nutrivein rig built into the back of the suit nearly imperceptible. "But they don't have the big teams to mob us like last time."

"They don't need them," Foster said.

A roll of thunder shook the air as the announcer blared out a warning. "Three minutes until the start. Spectators, please mind the weather conditions and take appropriate precautions."

"The coaches and sponsors negotiate alliances pre-race," Foster continued. "Some are deceitful, but it's all part of the game."

Ezren jumped in place, tucking her knees to her chest to get a feel for the possibilities of the suit. Her muscles moved with ease, the nanites rushing through her and around her in a surge of strength. "So we're going to run for it."

"Look who finally decided to start listening to me." His words held a lightness that didn't reflect in his eyes. "Once we get some distance, hopefully we should be able to swing wide of the storm."

Ezren laughed dryly. "Foster, we're going into the churn belt. There will be no avoiding these things." She looked at him, adrenaline already rushing through her at the thought. "We have to go through."

The wind whipped past them as the announcer blared the one-minute warning to the crowd's deafening cheer. Foster seized her hands, squeezing hard. "Ezren, not all of these teams are going to make it back."

She nodded. "I know that. But we're not going to be one."

He pressed his helmet to hers. "Listen, I just want you to know that I'm glad to be here with you. I'm glad Micah talked you into it. I'm glad you were late to the tryout. And there is no place I'd rather be right now than right here with you."

Ezren sucked in a breath, her cheeks heating beneath her helmet. She had no words to match those, and even if she had, she would never find them through the insistent buzz of nerves and love rushing through her. "Me too," she breathed.

His eyes creased with worry again, and the true meaning of his words dawned on her. Dread pooled in her stomach with the realization. If something happened to him—to them—he didn't want her to feel responsible. She squeezed his hands right back.

"There's no one else I'd rather cross the finish line with." She offered a fierce smile, rising to her tiptoes to meet his gaze. "And if there's cake there, I'm going to eat the whole thing, Sylvia's race diet be shafted."

He turned back to the start with the hint of a smirk in his eyes. "You are an addict."

"On your marks!" the announcer shouted.

All levity dried up between them as a hush fell over the starting line. Ezren tensed, her face hardening. She could do this. All she had to do was run.

"Belethea, mother of mountains and skies..." Foster whispered beside her.

"Protect us," Ezren finished with him.

"Get set."

Just run.

"Go!"

Ezren took two steps before someone barreled into her from the side. But she was ready this time. She grabbed and twisted, using the royaler's momentum to throw them over her hip. She ducked the swing of a second and with another swift jerk, she rolled them over her back. Beside her, Foster dispatched another team with a pair of haymakers, and they were off running again.

Ten heart-pounding seconds later, they were through the scrap. With their new suits, the other doubles fell quickly behind to the roaring cheers of the crowd. But in this race, that wouldn't be the most dangerous part. Still, Ezren allowed herself a tiny smile of relief as she reveled in the ease with which her legs devoured the terrain. While 1.5% didn't sound like much, it was amazing what kind of difference it made.

Her goggs updated with their recommended trajectories. As predicted, there was no way to go but through. Unhelpfully, it also spit out a projected success rate of 61%. Ezren scowled; that had to be an addition from Foster.

FOSTER: ARE YOU SURE YOU WANT TO GO NOW? WE COULD WAIT IT OUT.

EZREN: WE BOTH KNOW IT'S NOT GOING TO GET ANY BETTER.

FOSTER: ...I KNOW.

Foster glanced over his shoulder at a scattering of other

teams keeping a healthy distance from them. They certainly weren't the only ones determined to chance the storm. In fact, Ezren estimated that only a handful of teams had held back. The ones that only aimed to finish had plenty of time to hope for a change in weather.

Not slowing, Foster pulled a tether from his new suit and attached it to hers.

FOSTER: AT LEAST IF WE GET SUCKED UP INTO THE FUNNEL, WE CAN GO TOGETHER.

But Ezren's eyes were still on the clouds, the lightning, and the vortexes flirting with the cliffs and valleys. She compared what she was seeing to the data output in her goggs.

EZREN: I DON'T THINK THE ALGORITHM IS UPDATING FAST ENOUGH TO KEEP UP WITH THE CHANGES IN THE STORM. IF I MAKE A JUDGMENT CALL, WILL YOU FOLLOW ME?

She glanced at him, his irises reflecting the navy of the twisting clouds above.

FOSTER: ANYWHERE.

And that's all she needed. Keeping her gaze on the skies, she pumped her legs, the suit flexing around her muscles—pushing her farther, faster. Foster followed immediately at her side, trying to block the wind as best he could with his broad form.

Her goggs updated with the newest trajectory, and she corrected their course only slightly, the churning funnels glaring down at her like a hundred different eyes in the dark teal sky. Lightning flashed more insistently now, with thunder rolling over the rushing wind. Perhaps Ezren should've felt afraid or intimidated, but she only felt a tingling surge of adrenaline coursing through her, adding its strength to her already empowered suit.

She was out on the surface, in a land few had dared cross,

and she was perhaps closer to death than she'd ever been before. But her blood sang with life. Lightning crashed down onto the peaks in a blinding flash of sparks, the boom making her jump to one side, her feet skidding on the steep slope.

Foster seized her by the wrist and pulled her to safety. "Are you all right?"

And oddly, Ezren began to laugh. "Blime! Totally blime!"

He looked at her with curious eyes edged with a smile. "You must be out of your mind."

"And it's wonderful."

With that, they ran on, the storms only thickening around them. At one point they were forced to veer off course to tack against the merciless wind. At another, they took cover under a rock shelf, dozing in shifts as the hail and debris rained down from the sky. But they saw no other royalers, and Ezren supposed she shouldn't have been surprised. After all, the storm belt was huge, and there were many paths of barren rock by which to reach that steady red dot on her display. She just hoped they had picked the fastest one...

They ran for hours upon relentless hours, their suits feeding them filtered rainwater injected with the tasteless nutrivein concentrate. Ezren's sight began to blur as they started into their thirty-ninth hour, the storms still raging around them. They were getting closer to the checkpoint, but her muscles had begun to scream with pain as she stumbled up and down the mountain range's crests.

Foster paused midway down a steep ridge, the precipitation slowed to a sleet and the wind howling around them. He squeezed her shoulder and pointed to a distant light winking on a shore at the base of the mountain, a dark endless sea spreading beyond it. "There. Do you see it?"

She nearly wilted with relief and dread all at the same time.

She could see it, but it still seemed so far. "How long do you think—"

A sliding on the gravel above them turned her head, and two royalers tumbled down the mountain toward them, their intent fully bared on their faces.

"Run!" Foster yelled, but even as he said it, the first of them collided into him, sending them both rolling down the steep slope.

The cable jerked Ezren down the mountain before suddenly snapping as Foster disconnected it. Ezren rolled, trying to keep herself from tumbling head over foot as a shadow fell over her. She dodged the full-body tackle, sending her attacker sliding down the sharp gravel. Whatever mercy or softness in her had already been crushed out by the long miles, and the dregs of her adrenaline resurged as she pursued her assailant.

Before the royaler could rise, Ezren jammed a knee into their goggs, and her opponent rolled down the incline. Following closely, Ezren grabbed the royaler's helmet and slammed it against the nearest boulder, just like Bex had taught her. A spidery crack whipped across the front of it. With another slam, the mayday call went off with a satisfying whine.

Leaving her assailant, she skidded down the slope in the direction Foster had disappeared, panic already buzzing through her brain. His mayday signal hadn't gone off yet, but that didn't mean he hadn't fallen off the mountain into some crevice. And if they got separated, it could take her ages to find him out here.

She ground herself to a halt, wiping the sleet from her goggs while the erratic gusts tore at her arms and legs.

EZREN: FOSTER, WHERE ARE YOU?

For a beat, there was only the keening of the wind, and Ezren's heart stuttered. What would she do if she couldn't find him? Or worse, if she found him, and he was... She swallowed. "Foster!"

Seconds passed as Ezren staggered about, directionless and heart stuttering with a frantic possibility she refused to accept. She was about to break into a run when finally, a dark shape stumbled out from behind a boulder. Ezren tensed, her hands reflexively snapping up.

"It's okay, it's just me!" Foster called.

Ezren's shoulders slumped with exhausted relief, and she bounded down the ridge toward him. "What about the other?"

Foster's brows drew low over his shadowed eyes. "I honestly don't know. One minute I was throwing him off of me, and then he went over the edge. His mayday signal didn't go off, so he's gotta still be there somewhere."

"Well, his double is out," Ezren said with more weariness than pride.

Foster shook his head. "That doesn't mean they won't come after us. They were Dreitian, which means they have another double out here somewhere. Even if they're officially out of the race, they'll fod us over if they can."

"That's got to be against the rules." Together they started jogging down the mountain once more, the shore looming ever closer.

Foster chuckled. "Ezren, look at where we are." He threw an arm out to the gigantic peaks knifing into the sky, the wild ocean before them, and the shards of serrated islands popping out beneath the forked lightning. "The only rule out here is the first to the finish line wins. That's it. Everything else is just entertainment and creds."

"And politics." Ezren wrinkled her nose, her mind returning to the team they'd left behind, and she frowned. "I thought we were making good time, but it looks like we're still in the thick of it."

"No, we're doing well. The Dreitian teams are always in the top ten. Maybe even top five. The fact that we saw them means we're definitely somewhere in the front of the pack."

"But not in the lead," Ezren whispered.

And the endurance part was supposed to be their greatest strength. Ezren surged forward in the driving sleet, pushing her tired legs as fast as they would go. Her sore muscles screamed at her even as the suit worked overtime to compensate, sucking up the last slops of her energy. She focused her bleary sleep-deprived gaze on the line of vehicles dotting the rocky shore.

In another few hours, they arrived at the checkpoint, and Ezren wanted nothing more than to collapse and never get up again. But as she looked closer at the vehicles, her stomach sank. There were no topjeeps and no dunecarts. Instead, a row of various seacraft stared back at her.

"Um... Foster. I know this may be a bad time to bring this up. But I've never had any real experience driving a jetboat. If this was a real possibility, why didn't we spend more time on this?"

"Well, that's because the BRR doesn't usually cross the Rinaisha Sea. It's happened only once in the last ten races." He nudged her with his elbow. "But you did the sims, didn't you? Think of it as a topjeep on the water, with less chance of rolling. Nothing to worry about."

Ezren eyed the dark, frothing waters, the waves swelling and cresting in angry rushes that echoed the thunder above. "You mean, except all the underwater rocks and those massive towers of water that are threatening to drown us."

"Naturally."

The repair bot scanned their suits, searching for any damage or injuries and refilling their stores of water and nutrivein. It rolled back with a chime, flashing green. "Team Sterling/Hart checking in, healthy status, current place: third."

Ezren's lips twisted as she exchanged a wide-eyed look with Foster.

"What? No squealing? No celebrating? You do realize, this is the best any Belethean team has ever done," he said, jogging out to a small, sleek jetboat at the end of the line.

Third. Ezren tried to wrap her head around it. Objectively, that was fantastic. But they needed better. They would have to make up some time on the sea. "How fast do you think we can push on the water?"

One of the funnel clouds dipped into the waves, drawing the water into a twisting spout as Foster nudged the glossy yellow jetboat into the choppy waves. The word *Churnracer* scrawled across the pristine hull. "Well, the bad news is, seeing as this is my first time, I have no idea. The good news is, this is everyone else's first time on this course too, and the closer we get to the equator, the worse the storms will be. Which means the more of an advantage our algorithm will have." He offered a hand to boost her up. "After you."

Ezren took in the deep bags under his eyes and the slope of his shoulders before clambering into the small recessed cabin. "Are you sure you're in any shape to drive?"

"I'm no legendary street racer, but I'll have you know I have bested one in a race or two. Not that Grady would ever admit it. Besides, I've had plenty of practice this year, running around on no sleep." He gave her a wink before pushing the stream-lined *Churnracer* the last short distance into the water, and she helped him aboard.

"Ah, and here I thought we'd been running away to escape training. I should've known it was part of your plan all along." She laughed, and together they slipped into the tiny cockpit just big enough for two compact seats side by side. Even smaller than a dunecart, but with thicker restraints and more G-padding.

"It was definitely part of my plan... but my plan had nothing to do with training." Foster's goggs projected the controls onto the helm, and the motor rumbled to life. "And since you're sitting here next to me, and I can do this"—he reached over and squeezed the ticklish spot above her knee, startling a yelp out of her—"I think it went rather well."

A sleepy smile lingered on Ezren's lips, but her eyelids were already sliding shut as she leaned against the side of the cockpit. "Are you sure you'll be okay?"

He patted her leg. "Yes. You know I'll always wake you up on time." With that, he punched the throttle forward, and the *Churnracer* lurched into the waves, pressing them back into the plush seats. The small jetboat rose and fell on the swells, water crashing around them and the wind screeching.

Under any other circumstances, it might've been terrifying. Ezren could've reasoned that she fell asleep in the maelstrom because she trusted Foster with every cell of her being. Which was true. More than that, though, she was really just too tired to keep her eyes open even if she wanted to.

But she knew if anyone could get them through the jaws of a hellish sea, it would be Foster Sterling.

CHAPTER 33

FOSTER'S JAW clenched as he fought to keep the *Churnracer* steady. The waves rose and fell in an irregular rhythm, the lights of the jetboat pathetically small in the overpowering gloom of the churn belt. Flashes of lightning illuminated the nightmare of a sky above them—the twisting waterspouts rising out of the sea like angry serpents coiling to strike. Jagged fingers of rocky islands clawed out of the roiling surface, at war with the sky or them, he wasn't sure. But it was all bad.

And yet, despite the looming death from sky, sea, and land, Foster couldn't seem to keep his fodding eyes open. His bleary eyelids drooped, and his head nodded before he jerked awake, slicing the *Churnracer* around another looming rock. He curved around a swelling wave and his treacherous sight blurred again, but this time, a light hand lay across his.

"I've got it, Foster."

"But it's only been an hour," he protested, even as he swapped places with her.

"I'm good. I promise. You know I don't wake up on my own otherwise." Her eyes, surprisingly clear, crinkled behind her goggs. "I'm at least better off than you are."

He opened his mouth to protest, but in his exhaustion, the words slipped from his tongue.

Four rotations later, the hard jerk of the jetboat roused Foster from his sleep once again. A quick glance at his goggs showed he'd been asleep for the better part of two hours, and the hard grimace on Ezren's face brought him to full alert. "What's happening?"

"We just passed someone." She weaved to one side of a rocky spire. "And they aren't happy about it."

He whipped around in his seat, glaring out into the seething darkness. "How close?" But even as he said it, a jetboat careened down the nearest wave. Bigger and heavier than them, it must've been one of the first rides chosen out of the block. Ezren yanked the wheel to the left, finding temporary cover as she curved around another stone pillar.

"What's fodding wrong with them?" Ezren shouted. "If they crash into us, we could both sink out here. Can't they just wait to knock us out in the arena?"

Foster shook his head as their pursuer weaved behind them in the darkness, trying to take advantage of the wave's momentum to get an edge. "The arena would be a fairer shake than this. Their jetboat is heavier than ours. If we collide, they'll probably ride on scot-free."

"Just shaft it. Like it isn't hard enough to dodge the rocks and the storms and the waves without some asschaff trying to take us down in a suicide charge."

Foster's gaze stayed pinned to the jetboat cutting back and forth across the darkness, inching closer with each second. "No, this is definitely personal. It's gotta be Talmadge in there." Which was a little crazy. Talmadge had always been a good royaler, but Foster would never have pegged him as top BRR talent. Solid proof of what could be done with better training and a little motivation, he supposed. "Ezren, they're coming in hot. Can you go any faster?"

Ezren made a wide turn around an aggressive waterspout. "Without getting tumbled by the twisters? Not that I know of."

Foster adjusted their grav levels and projected the map from his goggs. "But look, the shore is only a mile out. What if we did go through the spouts?"

"What?" She didn't take her eyes off the clouds. "Are you crazy?"

Their pursuer powered into the trough of another wave, its bow glancing off their stern with the crunch of metal on metal. The *Churnracer*'s stern skewed to the side, and in a panicked thrash, Ezren managed to regain control.

Foster put a hand on her arm. "If we don't, they're going to sink us, Ezren."

"It sounds like we're going to sink either way!"

"We're strapped in, so even if we skip across the water like a stone, we'll be fine." *Probably.*

"Until we hit the rocks!"

"It's a gamble. Slim odds versus none at all." He glanced at the jetboat coming around, his goggs calculating time to impact. "You have twenty seconds to decide."

Ezren projected the weather algorithm readout from her goggs, her gaze flicking from the wall of graphs to the hellish sky. "Okay. We might have a chance. If we time it perfectly, the funnels might pull us toward the shore." Ahead of them, a trio of tornadic water spires ripped toward them in a furious churn, but the dark curve of land beckoned not far behind them.

Fear curdled into resolve in Foster's chest, his fist clenching the brace bar in front of him. "Ten seconds, Ezren. If you don't turn, they're going to be right on top of us."

"I need twelve." Ezren's stare bore into the tiny window

between the two closest twisters while numbers flashed through her holopro.

The jetboat plowed toward them from one side while the tornadoes raged on the other. "We have to go now! Four seconds!"

"I need more, Foster!"

"Two seconds!" Foster's heart threatened to choke him. "Ezren, TURN!"

"Suns take it." Ezren screwed her eyes shut and veered sharply toward the waterspouts, Talmadge's craft scraping against their hull.

At first, Foster thought the *Churnracer* was heavy enough to cut through the wind... and then the elements decided to put them in their place. He wasn't entirely sure what he was expecting, but one moment they were skimming the water, and the next they were spinning through the air bow over stern. Water and sky flashed before them in equal measures as they hurtled up into the clouds. Ezren screamed in shrill terror while Foster's stomach threatened to give up everything it had ever put down.

But still they tumbled. They hit the water once and were immediately picked up again. Foster lost all sense of direction and distance. Were they even going the right way? Had the other jetboat disappeared? As they jerked up and down, Ezren screamed, tears running down her cheeks. Fighting the crushing Gs, he found her hand and squeezed it. Surely this couldn't go on forever. They had to—

Black flashed in Foster's vision as something tore through the hull in a deafening screech of ripping metal. He wasn't sure what they'd hit, but they hit it fodding hard. The boat broke up into pieces underneath them, the wind greedily ripping through the cockpit. The force wrenched Foster's fingers from Ezren's, throwing her away from him.

"No!" he yelled, images of Vieve disappearing into the dust lancing through the present as his fingers snagged her harness, trying to keep hold. But it was no use. With another wicked gust, the storm callously tossed them apart, and Foster fell to the sea below. His suit managed to absorb most of the impact as his seat hit the surface, quickly sinking into the black water.

Foster tore off his safety belt as his piece of the *Churnracer* sank and he kicked his way to the surface. "Ezren!" he yelled into the dark while the current tugged at his heavy body.

FOSTER: EZREN! WHERE ARE YOU?

Pushing off from the wreckage, he was surprised to find the water only chest deep. He glanced around in the dark and spotted a rocky shore within striking distance. Impossibly, the storm had thrown them in the right direction. *Lucky.* They had been so chaffing lucky.

"Here!" Ezren called, closer than expected. With strong, frantic strokes, Foster swam toward her into the shallows. She had tumbled even closer to land, but something was obviously wrong. Ezren breathed in quick, shallow pants, one side of her strangely still in the jetboat while the other half bobbed in the water. "My arm." Her breath hitched in a low frantic moan. "Stuck."

Foster peered into the cockpit and found Ezren's forearm wedged between the wheel and the crushed dash of the boat. "I think I can get it out, just stay still."

Farther off, the pursuing jetboat whirred, its light cutting through the gloom like a predator's glowing eyes. Foster glanced at it, rage and fear spiraling within him. If it decided to run them over, they were goners. Could he rip Ezren out of the cockpit in time without leaving her arm behind?

"Don't move for a second." His jaw tensed as he pushed her close to the wreckage.

She hissed in pain, but did as instructed, her breathing still labored as the headlights passed over them... and crunched into Foster's abandoned half of the *Churnracer*. Foster tried not to flinch at the grinding of metal, his gaze glued to the jetboat. *Don't turn around. Don't turn around for the other half,* he pleaded.

But the jetboat curved sharply away instead, heading along the coastline to the beacon of the arena shining from the distant cliffside. He sagged with relief. A different coin flip and they would have crushed him and Ezren along with the other half of their maimed craft.

He turned back to Ezren. "Sorry, it's all right. They're gone now." Her eyes were closed, and inside her helmet, her skin had taken on a grayish pallor. "Ezren, are you still with me?"

The boat's wake jarred her where she practically dangled from the *Churnracer* by her trapped arm, and she winced. "It... hurts."

"I know, I know, Ezren." His chest tightened as he tried to keep his voice steady. "Don't worry though, I'm going to get you out." Even as he said it, another, larger wave sloshed over them, and Ezren cried out.

He shoved his head into the cockpit where the crushed exterior held her in. He tried to push it off of her, but there wasn't much room to leverage. He slammed his fist on it, again and again, frantically trying to weaken it. Outside, the seething waterspout howled as it drew closer.

He chanced a look at it as he caught his breath. "Fodding suns." It would be there in less than a minute. "Okay, we can do this, just one more heave," he said with an optimism he absolutely did not feel.

"Okay," Ezren breathed.

"Now!" He rammed his shoulder against the unyielding metal, muscles burning. Ezren strained against the vehicle with him, crying out with the pain of the effort. And still, the tornado of death whirled closer. The *Churnracer* began to shudder under its hungry winds. Soon, it would be sucked up with all the rest of the debris. "C'mon, c'mon, c'mon!" His suit readout pulsed red in his goggs as he gave it everything he had.

With a scream, Ezren yanked her arm back, and at last, it came free.

Foster turned to her with a relieved smile, only to see that her eyes had rolled back in her head, and the fabric of her topsuit over her arm had been shredded. Blood flowed freely, and her elbow bent at an unnatural angle.

Fodding suns.

As bad as it looked, the receding waves reminded him he didn't have time to fix it right now. Lifting her over his shoulder, he ran out of the shallows as quickly as his suit would let him. The vortex tugged at his arms and legs, but it was nothing compared to the motivation that coursed through him. He had to get Ezren to the arena ASAP. Even if their chances in the brawl had fallen to nil, maybe there'd be something they could do to help her.

His desperation turned to rage as he thought of whoever had run over the scraps of the *Churnracer*. Wasn't this race deadly enough without *trying* to kill the other royalers? It had to be Talmadge. His hands tightened around Ezren. If Foster saw him in the arena... that asschaff was fodding dead.

Foster sweated inside his suit, panting under Ezren's weight as he carried her across the rocky shore, doing his best to stick to boulders that might shield them from other would-be murderers. But still, he made it to the arena checkpoint in twenty minutes.

"Sterling/Hart...checking in," he said to the official between heaving breaths. He shifted Ezren from his shoulder to cradle her against his chest, and she groaned. Her ghastly white face scrunched together, blood still splashed across their topsuits. "And I need a medbot, stat."

The robotic health scanner flashed over Foster, chirping in its cheery feminine voice. "No suit breaches, in good health." Then it flashed again over Ezren—yellow this time. "Fracture of both right ulna and radial. Lacerations and substantial bleeding. Suit moderately compromised and repair in progress. Helmet withstood third-degree crack. Current place: second."

The official assessed them with wide eyes and gestured to the chairs that lined the corridor. "Please take a seat and we'll be right with—"

"I need a med room, *now!*" Foster barked, shouldering past him.

"D-downstairs! 3B!" the check-in guy called.

Foster linked to the floor plans and located 3B immediately. He stopped at the elevator and sent an impatient command for it to return for them.

"It's okay," Ezren mumbled, sliding to her feet. She looked around with bleary eyes at the plain gray corridor walls. "Shouldn't we be reporting to the arena?"

Foster's arm curled around her waist as she swayed. "Six teams have to check in before the brawls can start. So the earlier you get here, the more time you have to rest. It's supposed to make the final leg more exciting, but at least it gives us a break from the goggcam stream." He took off his helmet and then helped her remove her own. "Don't worry, they'll give us a thirty-minute warning when they're ready."

The elevator dinged, and they stepped inside. If the situation hadn't been so dire, Foster might've laughed at the mundane sounds of the elevator while they decided the fate of planets amid the raging churn belt.

Ezren didn't say anything else. Which, in itself, worried him. She cradled her arm while the bleeding continued to drip from her elbow, but she didn't even seem to be concerned about it as she stared straight ahead at the nothingness of the elevator. Was she going into shock?

"What are you thinking?" he asked.

"Will they be able to fix my arm?"

"Maybe not entirely on short notice, but enough to go on."

"This doesn't bode well for the brawl, huh?" And even though her tone was light, he could see the despair in her small, dark eyes. "Well, not that we had much of a chance to begin with."

The elevator dinged, but he ignored it, turning to face her full-on. The BRR was a hugely physical race, but the mind always gave up before the body, and he couldn't let her do that. Not when they'd come this far. "That's a load of chaff, Ezren. We're second in the fodding Belethea Race Royale. You can believe we have just as good a chance as any of these shafters. That's why they're out for us. Because they're fodding scared. Of you."

Ezren bit into her pale lower lip. "I don't feel scary. I feel hurt and exhausted and terrified out of my mind."

"So does everyone else. They're just pretending not to be." He raised an eyebrow at her. "Weren't you paying attention in those PR classes?"

She shifted from one foot to the other. "Low blow." But the corner of her mouth twitched up, and Foster straightened with the small victory.

He led her out of the elevator into the fully stocked med room, all manner of machines, metal cabinets, and rolling beds lining the white walls. Though there was no one down there in the minimally staffed outpost, Foster didn't need anyone to show him what he'd gone through many times in training. "C'mon, now, let's get you fixed up so we can blow through that arena and get the chaff out of here. I know it seems far. But there's less than fifteen miles from us to the finish line. This is a speed bump, Ezren, not the end. You just have to believe it."

Ezren's eyelids drooped as he helped her onto a cot and picked up a portable medcast. It flashed with an error, and he nearly threw it across the room. *Of fodding course.* Exhaustion nearly knocked him over. He didn't have the time or energy for intensive debugging—he could barely even think straight. Taking a deep breath, he linked into the code and sagged with relief. The last update had just been faulty. If he rolled it back to an earlier version then it should—

He stopped, frozen in place. That code. He knew that code. It was the same exact style as the faulty patch from Vieve's suit. A cold sweat broke out on his brow that had nothing to do with his exhausted muscles. Was the saboteur here somewhere? He linked into the map of the outpost. The place was fodding huge. What were they *doing* here?

Ezren shifted on the cot with another groan, spurring him back into action. He saved the defective code before wiping it from the medcast. Once done, it hummed in his hands, functional once more.

Her eyelids fluttered open as he clamped her arm in the medcast, and it glowed green with a happy chirp. "Do you believe in us?" she whispered.

His heart twisted with an almost painful love. They were too close to let some asschaff coward stop them here. He leaned down, kissing her forehead and then her lips. "I have never believed in anyone more than I believe in you."

And this time, he wasn't just saying it. He felt it in his bones. They could do this.

He looked at the interlocking squares of the Calderon Industries logo gleaming from the medcast on Ezren's arm.

No matter who tried to stop them.

CHAPTER 34

EZREN WOKE TO A BLARING ALARM, coming up from a basin of sleep so deep she couldn't remember where she was. *Home? No. Carmella?* Was the BRR already over? She blinked her heavy eyelids, taking in the small white-walled room that looked far too much like a hospital for her taste. Machines beeped around her and Foster sat on a cot pulled right next to hers, his face still shadowed with fatigue and a layer of scruff. *Ah... no. Churn Belt... in the arena.*

"How's your arm?" Foster said, his deep voice rough with sleep.

Ezren looked down at where her arm lay in the medcast. The readout projected the scan results—*55% fracture mend. Recommendation: continued rehabilitation.* Not a great prognosis, but at least the pain had eased. The rip of her arm against the crushed metal returned to her with a shudder. "Could be better. Could be worse."

Foster's lips twitched into a frown as his goggs projected four separate holos of messages, code, and what looked like the outpost schematics. "Well, keep it on. The fifth team just came in, so it looks like we've probably got another forty-five minutes until our first match." He rose from the cot with stiff movements and extended a hand to her. "Let's stretch our legs a little."

She gripped his broad palm with her cold fingers and slipped from the cot onto the floor. "Do you know who we're fighting?"

His frown deepened the crease between his brows, but he didn't look at her as he hooked their helmets onto his nutrivein rig. "Ezren, we were the second team in... so there's only one other ahead of us."

"It's Lucian, isn't it?" Her eyes flicked to the cast on her arm again where it had ticked up to 56%. "What are we going to do?"

"I can take care of Talmadge." Foster led her into the metal tube of a hallway lit only with dim overhead lights, still distracted by something scrolling through his goggs. "You just need to stall against Brook until I get there. That's all. Don't fight. Just survive. Run circles around the ring for all I care."

Ezren squeezed his hand with her good one. "Right. Yeah." But still, the nerves threatened to squeeze her throat shut. Even if they lost, they could maybe win the next one. Maybe.

She massaged her temples with one hand, trying to crush out the doubt that threatened to drown her every thought. What was wrong with her? This was no surprise. She'd always known that the brawl would be their hardest trial.

Foster stopped in the spartan corridor and turned to her. "Ezren, we've trained for this, and we're going to give it our all, just like we always do. If you don't step into the arena thinking you can win, then we shouldn't step in at all."

Ezren pressed her lips together. "I... I'm sorry. I don't know what's gotten into me."

"You're exhausted, and hurt, and shook up from almost dying a few hours ago." Foster's stormy gaze bore into hers, sincere and confident. "Of course you're feeling weak. But that's okay. That's normal, and they're feeling it too. This is going to be two tired-ass teams slugging it out. And of all the people I've met, you are by far the best at functioning on no sleep."

She gave him a slim smile. "I'd function better with coffee."

He playfully rolled his eyes. "I'll tell you what, if we win, you can have as much coffee as you want when we get back. I'll fight off Sylvia with my bare hands."

Continuing down the hall, she nudged him with her good elbow. "You make a good coach, you know?"

"Only for you, my first and last student."

Her smile widened. "I guess I kind of like that." She looked around them, trying to get her bearings in the stainless-steel warren of corridors. This place didn't even bother with the fake holopros to make it more pleasant. "Do you know where we're going? I feel like we're going deeper into the ground rather than up."

He shrugged, but it was a tense, almost unnatural gesture. "I figured we could check the place out a little as we walk around. Not many people get to see Kavata Outpost. They leave a skeleton crew of twelve here for the year to research and maintain the place. Other than that, royalers are the only ones who come through."

Ezren nodded, the particulars coming back to her. "This was the first terranium collection outpost before they were able to establish the larger cluster further in. Here they study the correlation between the terranium density and the storms. There's a theory that the terranium itself is what creates all the energy in the churn belt. That if you removed the terranium, Belethea would have survivable storms like everywhere else."

Foster's eyebrows rose. "That research sounds pretty important for only twelve people."

Ezren's thoughts skewed to Tuzuno's shut down date in

only twenty-four days. "On par for Belethea," she responded, her tone flat as she pushed on a pair of heavy, locked doors with the words *Authorized Personnel Only.*

"Shaft." Foster pulled up the schematics in his goggs. "Maybe there's another way."

Ezren considered the access panel for a moment. It looked exactly like the one in Tuzuno. In fact... She linked into the code. "We might be in luck. It looks like they didn't change the standard emergency settings."

She punched in the emergency service access number common to nearly all the terranium labs. A bit of a joke, really, since there were no emergency services within range of more than half of the outposts. But it was a loophole she and Micah had exploited more than once to access high-risk equipment they *technically* didn't have the credentials to operate. Still, it surprised her when the doors opened with an obedient hiss.

Foster glanced at her with a sagging smirk. "Did you really just hack into Kavata Outpost?"

She shrugged with a tiny grin. "*Hack* is a strong word."

The corridor expanded into more open lab space, with holopros and automated bots collecting and testing samples of air quality, belweed, water, and even a luminescent vial of sea-green terranium.

Make that... *a lot* of samples of terranium glowing in large, glass cylinders. Her eyebrows knitted. "There is... quite a bit of terranium here. Is this station also controlled by the winner of the race?"

Foster moved to one of the boxy, industrial-sized centrifugal intensifiers, his goggs projecting three windows of code in front of him. "No, only the main cluster. This one doesn't produce a lot, I guess, so it belongs to Calderon Industries." The furrow between his eyebrows deepened. "But where are the staff?"

"Forget the staff." Ezren strode over to one of the arm-like bots connected to the lab table, her neurochip linking to it. "Where is the terranium supply stored?"

Immediately, the building layout appeared in her goggs with a flashing dot. Down two more floors and nestled further in. She took off with short, fast steps.

"Hey, wait up, Ezren. Where are you going?"

Her brain spun with thoughts she didn't quite want to put words to. "I need to see this."

She stepped out into the wide storage bay, tall ceilings towering above them in an empty room filled with crate upon crate—hundreds, maybe even thousands of metal cubes in neat, towering rows that reached the cavernous ceiling. What were they keeping here? She stepped to the nearest console and fired off another command. "Locate the terranium."

The room lit up green in her goggs, and a small, neat little number appeared at the bottom. 1,043 crates of terranium. Total: 104,300 kg.

Ezren's mouth went dry, and she staggered to one side. The most terranium she'd ever seen in Tuzuno was 20.3 grams. "Who owns this?"

The console's reply was immediate. "Calderon Industries."

"Calderon?" Foster said. "Belethea has never won the BRR terranium rights. And even if we had, why the stockpile? Why wouldn't he sell it?"

"He's Belethean," Ezren whispered, still dumbstruck. "How could he do this? This would be a game-changer for our research. And it's just sitting here—more than one station could use in years. Why would he do this?"

Foster ran his fingers along one of the sleek metal boxes, his jaw flexing. "They're driving up the price to bring more attention to the event. This isn't about national honor, or tradition, or humanity versus the elements..." His face darkened. "It's about money."

The realization slammed into Ezren, punching the air from her lungs. "You were right," Ezren whispered. "You were always right." She let out a bitter chuckle. "I guess that's why Calderon doesn't really want us to win. Why would he when he has all the terranium he needs?"

"He doesn't want us to win." Foster stiffened, eyes wide, as if someone had slapped him. Then, with a sudden jerk, he projected his goggs' message panel to maximum size, poring through the words.

Ezren sat down on the floor, leaning her back against the metal. Did it even matter if they competed now, with what they knew? What would be the point? Even if they won, the terranium stores would probably go to Calderon. And if he wasn't sharing these stores, why would he share anything else?

"It wasn't a *person* sabotaging us, it was the whole fodding company," Foster said. "Chaffing suns. I should've figured it out sooner. The code in your medcast, the equipment here, even the outpost itself looks exactly like the defective updates in Vieve's suit."

"What?"

Foster shook his head, sweat shining on his blanched countenance. "As the race organizer, Calderon Industries does the pre-race suit check. They checked Vieve's suit before the accident. They're the ones that hacked the suit." His breathing hitched in erratic bursts. "She was too good. So they had to take her out. Just like they did to Grady and Bex."

Ezren frowned, trying to wrap her tired brain around what that would mean. "But what about our suits?"

"The new suits were checked in at the last minute. Maybe there wasn't time to adjust and react." He looked at her with round eyes, his jaw slack. "Ezren, this is huge."

She laughed humorlessly, throwing her head back and banging it against the wall. "Well, they should've just told us the terranium reward was a sham in the first place, and then no one would've volunteered to risk their neck for this fodding stupid race. I'm sure they'll be happy to know we're out of the running now."

Foster's lips tightened, the groove between his brows deepening. "What do you mean?"

"If they're not going to give the research outposts the terranium, what's the point, Foster? They'll probably find some excuse to disqualify us before we ever get to the finish line." Ezren swallowed, her throat clogging with tears—of disappointment, of anger, of exhaustion, or perhaps of all three mixing in a well too deep for her to process.

"Chaffing suns." Foster knelt in front of her. "You're telling me, after we worked our asses off for months, for fodding years, that the girl who never gives up is throwing in the towel because some asschaff is trying to rig the game?"

"Some asschaff? Foster, he's the founder of the whole motherfodding race. And he's a shafting murderer." She drove the heel of her mag-boot into the hard metal floor. Stupid. Stupid. Stupid. How could she have been so stupid as to think that she could change anything? She was just some nobody from Tuzuno. "You were right. It's not worth it."

"No," he snapped, "you don't get to say that."

Ezren stilled at his sharp words, and he leaned closer.

"Not after you charged into my life with all that talk of fixing the world and helping Belethea." He stabbed a finger into her knee. "Not after you brought our team, and the city, and the whole fodding planet back to life." His face softened a touch. "Not after you made me believe in you. I won't let you stop believing in yourself." He squeezed her leg, his gaze warm and earnest. "I won't let you give up that easy, Ezren Hart. You deserve more than that. And so does Belethea."

The tears slipped down Ezren's cheeks. Somehow his words only made the finish line seem farther away. She wanted so badly to believe him, to keep going, to hold on to the hope that was so quickly slipping from her fingers. But the problem was too immense. A no-name research intern and a washed-up royaler against Calderon Industries? Even her optimistic imagination couldn't stretch that far.

"But what can we possibly do? They put Simon and Bex in the ICU... and they killed Vieve." She licked her lips, her mind racing. "We can record it with our neurochips, but they're probably monitoring all of our transmissions, and if they find out we know about this..." Her voice lowered to a whisper. "They'll kill us, Foster."

"We're not going to let that happen. We can be smart about this." He reached out and brushed her wet cheeks with a hand. "Why did you enter the race?"

"I wanted to get the terranium to fund our terraforming research." She leaned into his palm, thinking of her talks with Sylvia and Micah—the messages they had been spreading for her on VSoc. "I wanted to have a voice to tell people about Belethea and the progress we were making. Of the possibilities of the technology. I wanted them to see that it wasn't just a dream. That it was worth the price." She sniffed. "I wanted Sam and everyone else to be able to grow up and live under an open sky. Not a false one." The dream seemed more untouchable than ever. Like the stars somewhere high above the storm.

"Ezren, we don't need to win to have a voice." He stroked her cheek with his thumb. "If we make it to the finish, you may not get the terranium, but you'll have the mic to the whole system. At least for a few seconds. The finish line always has a live feed."

Her eyes widened, and she sat up. "Enough to blow the top off of Calderon Industries."

He nodded. "With the right words, I think we can do it."

Misgivings slithered through Ezren's gut. "But do you think people will care? Why would any of the other nations care that Calderon's hamstringing Belethea? We're still nobody."

"BRR fans are purists. Belethea may not be the most popular team, but if Calderon Industries is rigging the race against Belethea, who's to say they haven't rigged it in other ways? And they fodding murdered Vieve." He kneaded one hand with the other. "How could the fans not be furious?"

Ezren took a deep breath and let it out slowly, piecing together the ragged scraps of her resolve. "In any case, we have to try. It's the only way to show them that Belethea is worth more than a race."

"They'll listen to you, Ezren. With this kind of proof, I know they will." Foster straightened and offered his hand to help her up. "Trust me, you're a hard person to ignore."

Ezren swallowed, squeezing his hand and pulling herself upright. She hoped that was true. And she hoped they got the chance to put it to the test.

CHAPTER 35

FOSTER RAN through every swear word he knew and then a few invented ones. They stood on the edge of the circular arena, with virtual fans all around them and a few in-person VIPs lounging in plush armchairs. On the other side, Talmadge and Brook stretched with lazy grins on their faces. He'd known they were going to be their first match, of course, but that still didn't lessen the fodding shaft of it. Although he'd told Ezren they didn't need to win... it would really help if they did.

He hadn't been lying when he said they would have a voice at the finish line, but they would have to squeeze their murder conspiracy theory into roughly twenty seconds. Tops. Plus, if they didn't win, they would most likely come off as a couple of whiny sore losers, and they wouldn't have the celebrity protection status of the winner... the protection that might keep them alive.

But he hadn't really thought that would be an encouraging thing to say, so he'd left it out. And now, they had to beat Talmadge. Which really meant *he* had to beat Talmadge. A feat he had yet to accomplish, even after a year of training together. He'd always been able to best Talmadge on the legs and wheels, but the fodder never let him forget that he would always get his ass handed to him in the brawl.

He was bigger and older, but Foster refused to believe that he was in any way smarter.

Ezren turned to him, her tears dried and replaced with a steady gaze. "I'll keep Brook away from you as long as you need."

His eyes shifted to the discarded cast by the edge of the ring —78% still glowed from the readout. The ember of doubt grew into a flame. "What about your arm?"

She took his hand and squeezed it. "As long as you need." She rose onto her toes and pressed her lips against his. "We can do this."

The crowd cheered as it looked on through the holopro, and the announcer blared across the dome of the arena. "Are you ready?"

Across the ring of mauve sand, Talmadge and Brook tensed, and Foster followed suit—arms up, legs flexed, and a cold sheen of sweat on his brow.

"Fight!"

This time, all four of them advanced to the center cautiously, warily. This was the biggest fight of their lives, and they were exhausted. So they would fall back on the easiest course of action, the most familiar plan, the maneuvers they'd practiced the most.

But their tired muscles didn't do much for their patience. Talmadge lunged forward, and the brief standoff was broken. Foster sidestepped his first tackle, delivering a blow to his side. Talmadge countered with two fast fists, and Foster blocked, leaping back. Foster's gaze zeroed in on his opponent, just as his mother once taught him, everything fading away as he focused on Talmadge's every twitch, carefully measuring the distance between them with every step. Somewhere, time ticked on, but Foster didn't notice as their dance continued. They huffed out ragged breaths, sweat slipping down Foster's shoulder blades and shining on Talmadge's square face.

Talmadge might have beefed up with Syndali's fancy new training regimen, but Foster had long since learned Ezren's secret of a winning underdog. Because even though an underdog might be outmatched in every way, they could still fight harder, fight longer, want it more—and nine times out of ten, that could make all the difference.

Talmadge's shoulders curved in as he wheezed, and Foster couldn't help but smile. He was bleeding and bruised, but he was still on his feet, and he *wanted* this.

He lunged forward again with a quick jab, and a shriek cut through his focus. He paused, his head whipping to where Brook had her knee in Ezren's back, wrenching her broken arm up as Ezren cried out through gritted teeth.

"Ezren!" Foster took a step toward her just as Lucian hurtled into his gut, taking him to the ground. *Shaft it.*

"Gotcha now, you motherfodder," Talmadge said, his teeth red with blood as he put his full weight on top of Foster.

But Foster could barely hear him as he watched Ezren struggle under Brook. He automatically put his arms up to protect himself, his mind scrambling for any scraps of focus. He had to get to Ezren... but he still had to deal with Talmadge first. Talmadge's fist crashed into his face, and Foster captured his arm, trying for a better position. But still, he couldn't keep his attention from Ezren.

Everything seemed to slow as Brook got to her feet, brought up her foot—

"No!" Foster screamed.

But it was too late. Brook's heel crunched down into Ezren's arm, and her bloodcurdling scream ripped through the air.

Seething rage shot through Foster, filling him with the raw energy he thought had been drained. Roaring, he broke free of Talmadge's grip. Flipping him onto his back, Foster smashed his fist into his face over and over again, his hand a bloody blur, until Talmadge's eyes rolled back in his head, and he fell limp to the floor. Foster kicked him across the boundary and turned to where Ezren, still screaming in pain, had somehow managed to entwine herself around Brook's legs, preventing her from helping Talmadge.

Brook's eyes widened as she saw the fury in Foster's gaze. She stumbled back, but there was nowhere for her to go. He feinted high and then buried his fist in her stomach, momentarily stunning her before grabbing her around the middle and tossing her from the ring.

The crowd surged in a bestial cheer that nearly drowned out the announcer's howl of victory, but Foster paid none of it any mind as he rushed to Ezren's side. She lay on the ground, her breath coming in sharp little heaves as she clutched her arm to her chest, her eyes screwed shut.

"Suns, Ezren, I'm so sorry. I should've paid more attention."

"No," she gasped out, shaking her head without opening her eyes. "I'll be fine. My arm, it just... needs some help."

Foster barely needed to glance at it to see that she was right. He clenched his jaw. They would need to reset it. The announcer blared again, "Next match: Brook/Talmadge versus Mahoney/Santiago in five minutes." *Shaft it.* He looked over to where Lucian had already recovered, rage burning in his eyes. They had to get out of here before Talmadge and Brook won their next match, or else they'd be waiting to ambush them as soon as they got outside.

Scooping Ezren up in his arms, he raced her to the side of

the ring where she'd put the programmable cast. Safely on the sidelines, he gently laid her down on the bench next to their other gear. "Ezren... I'm going to put the cast back on you to reset your arm. It'll give you a local anesthetic, but I can't give you the heavier stuff because it'll put you to sleep again." He slid the metal sheath over her arm.

"So... you're saying..." Her body strained with the obvious effort of maintaining consciousness through the all-encompassing agony. Foster winced, nearly feeling the pain with her. Suns, he'd been in her spot before. He knew how bad it was. And yet, he would've given anything to bear this for her—to swap places with her.

"It's going to hurt like shaft." The bot whirred as it calibrated, assessing the damage in her arm.

"O...kay." A bead of sweat trickled down Ezren's cheek, and Foster squeezed her good hand. "Can you make it go... any faster?"

He leaned down and pressed his lips to her hair. "I'm so sorry. Are you hurt anywhere else?"

"Nothing too... bad just glad... we won't have to... go again."

Foster gritted his teeth. Just because they'd won the brawl didn't mean they were done with fighting. The final leg was through the Walibista Channel. A narrow wind-tunnel-like canyon that made the heart of the churn belt survivable... but also had a terrible way of crushing all the royalers together into the worst scraps. While Ezren's arm didn't have to be in fully working condition, it needed to be good enough not to interfere with the rest of her.

The cast started counting down: 3... 2...

Foster squeezed her good hand. "Brace—"

The bot compressed, and Ezren screamed almost as loud as when Brook had broken her arm, except this time, she screamed again and again as the nanites wriggled around, using pressure to rearrange her bones—or what was left of her shattered arm—into just the right spot.

She squeezed his hand, and he bent next to her ear. "It's okay, Ezren. It's fixing you. It's going to be okay."

Still, she screamed. The bot worked while the seconds stretched by, Foster's whole body taut with worry and guilt, until finally it glowed green again. It flashed from its perch on her arm, as if preening. "Set complete, arm heal initiating: 0%."

Ezren's breath still came too fast, but some of the tension fled from her sweaty, pale face, and her teeth clicked shut.

"Ezren, are you okay?" Foster whispered into her ear, kissing her again, even as his gaze wandered over to where Talmadge stood waiting for their second match.

She nodded and struggled to sit up. "Yes... I'm ready to keep going."

And Foster had to clench his hands together to keep from pushing her back down and encouraging her to rest like she needed. Suns, it was way easier to be hurt than to watch the person you loved hurting.

Ezren slid the cast from her arm before rising to her feet. It would have to stay here. She stomped her feet into her boots, slid on her rig, and grabbed her helmet, her bloodshot eyes meeting his. "Let's go."

Foster had to keep his jaw from swinging open at her inhuman strength. Suns, she was beautiful. He really did love her.

He took her good hand and pressed a kiss to the inside of her wrist. "Last leg. We can do this." He shoved on his boots and grabbed his gear, then together they jogged to the exit at the back of the arena, while the crowd cheered around them in a deafening roar. His goggs chirped with a bleak storm update as they approached the airlock, but this was the heart of the churn belt. Although they could still track the intensity of the bursts, there was no waiting out the worst of the storm. Here at the center of the belt, the storm never ended. It forever swirled in a torrent of destruction fueled by the unparalleled energy venting up from the sub-surface terranium.

"It's fifteen miles to the end, Ezren." Foster smiled weakly at her. "We've got this." Did they? They were entering the final leg in first place. Historically, that put their chances of winning at around 82%. He scarcely let himself believe it was possible.

She nodded, tugging on her helmet and stepping into the storm. "Let's do this."

Foster took a step to follow her when a tall figure blocked the way. "I don't think you want to do that." Calderon stepped in front of them, dressed to the nines like all the other wealthy sponsors in a top hat and long coat, his cane planted on the metal floor.

Foster stiffened and grabbed Ezren, pulling her behind him. His gaze combed over the old man, searching for any signs of a weapon. "We just want to race. Let us pass, Mr. Calderon."

"You can't lie to me, boy. I heard all your theories downstairs."

"But how?" Ezren asked in a near whisper. "Our goggs weren't broadcasting."

He snorted. "My dear, of course they weren't. I made sure of it. I have eyes and ears everywhere, and I control when and what gets broadcasted to the system."

Foster's heart pumped harder in his chest. "So what do you want from us?" Would he be so brazen as to kill them outright?

"Belethea cannot win this competition," he said.

"But why not?" Ezren asked in a strange small voice that made Foster want to rip this guy's throat out. "I thought you said you liked us."

"Please don't misunderstand me, my dear. You're not the problem. If you really want to win, please feel free to join the Obronian team next year and give it another go. I'll even be sure to arrange it for you."

"So it's Belethea you hate? You want to see the domes dry up and people leave for the stations?" Foster's hands curled into fists. "But why? You're from Belethea for shaftsakes. You were the original Belethean royaler. Why would you even start this race if you're going to interfere like this? Or is it the money you're after? Aren't you rich enough already?"

The old man chuckled, shaking his head. "It's certainly not the money. It's quite the opposite, really. I love Belethea, you know. Do you have any idea what will happen if you win the race?"

Ezren took a step forward. "Yes. With the annual terranium mining rights, Belethea would finally have the funding and the resources to rejuvenate our dying terraforming research. We're so close to cracking the storm prediction and possible pacification, this could—"

"That. Did you just hear yourself?" Calderon cut her off. "If Belethea gets the terranium they will use it to turn this planet into just another brimming anthill of humanity. They'll suck the planet dry and erase its beauty faster than you can snuff out a candle, crushing any possibility of her own beautiful unique future with their cookie-cutter notion of a livable planet." He scoffed, waving his cane. "Look what they've done to Obrone and Dreitis. Already overflowing with people, overwhelming the native micro life with our own familiar, imported strains."

Foster's mind spun. "But Obrone and Dreitis only had single-celled organisms, and there are huge efforts to conserve them in unadulterated reserves."

The man chuckled. "Oh, come now, boy. You're not stupid.

We've already irrevocably changed the future of life on that planet by our mere presence. Those reserves will continue to shrink until suddenly the native life has been completely wiped out, even in memory."

"But Belethea doesn't have any native life. It was a barren rock when we came here," Ezren countered, her brow furrowing. "If you're so keen on preserving microbiology, then you should be on our side. If we perfect terraforming techniques on lifeless planets, then it could potentially save us from the temptation of colonizing life-bearing systems."

He smiled, the expression cold and stiff. "I do love your optimism, girl. But frankly, I have yet to see humanity resist any temptation that saves money or effort. Furthermore, while I enjoy your forward-thinking, Belethea is first and foremost in my heart. She is wild and free, emotional and open, powerful and godly." His gaze hardened. "As far as I'm concerned, the more research outposts that dry up, the better. They are but blemishes on her beautiful face. Just think, if they were to successfully muzzle her tempestuous spirit, the Belethea Race Royale wouldn't even exist."

Ezren's eyes widened, her jaw going slack. "You... you're the one who's been shutting the outposts down."

Calderon tapped his cane on the floor, flashing his sharp canines. "Perceptive of you."

Foster tried to edge Ezren around the man. "Then why let Belethea compete in the races at all? You're our fodding sponsor. If you're not going to let us win, then just crush the team."

He sighed, his face softening with the wrinkles of his years. "Though an idealist, I'm still a businessman. The race royale gives Calderon Industries a seat on the interplanetary stage. But although I need a pawn to play in the game, how good you are at it makes little difference to me. Influence, power, money. Terranium is shaping our system—fueling sun-arks, building wormgates, shaping environments... the list of applications is endless. This race is our business, and as long as I'm controlling the winner, we have a hand in the fate of the system. Do we want to travel the galaxies in the arks, do we want to ruin other planets like our very first, or do we want to settle into a lovely ring of orbiting self-sustaining stations? With the terranium under my control, these are things I can influence. Not to mention, when you give the winner a little edge, many times they're apt to let you in on the spoils."

"Hence all that terranium," Ezren said, her huge dark eyes glued on Calderon.

"I keep the vultures from completely draining Belethea of her lifeblood. Without the terranium, who knows how her climate would be affected," he said, his voice rising. "But she would not be the same."

"Yeah, I'm sure you tell yourself that's the reason. But I bet it doesn't hurt your intergalaxy cargo trade either." Foster moved Ezren closer to the airlock door. "You're just like every other old man who finally got a taste of power and decided to run his own sick little scam. Well, I have news for you: we're not quitting. We race for Belethea, not for you, you chaff-raking murderer."

"A terrible tragedy, yes. But it is a dangerous race." He held up a placating hand, any trace of emotion wiped away once more. "Far be it from me to stop you from racing. I just wanted to let you know you will *not* be finishing first, so if you want to be safe... I would wait."

Foster bristled at the threat. He couldn't have hacked the suits this time, so what was he referring to? "How many people have you done this to? There's no way you can sweep this under the rug. There are too many coincidences."

"My boy, when you run the show, you get to spin the story."

"Not our story." Ezren straightened, squeezing Foster's

hand as she inched toward the door. "We'll see you at the finish line."

"If that's your choice, you'd best hurry, because Lucian will be right behind you," the man said cheerfully, as if he hadn't just threatened their lives.

"Right behind is still behind." Ezren opened the outer door, throwing herself into the storm, but Foster hesitated, torn between finishing the race and throttling the guy right there.

As if on cue, the interior door opened, and Talmadge and Brook hurtled in.

Talmadge's muscles tightened at the sight of them before shifting to Calderon. He folded in a formal bow. "Have your instructions changed?"

Calderon clucked his tongue and shook his head. "Unfortunately not." His face froze into an icy mask. "They don't finish first. No matter what."

Foster's eyes flicked between the two of them as he put the pieces together. Now it made sense why Talmadge had hopped from team to team. That's why Talmadge was so good but had never won. That had never been his purpose. Calderon was using him to control who won. In fact, he probably had many "Talmadges."

"You mother—" Foster started toward him, but Ezren yanked him through the door, and shut it behind him, tapping a few commands into the panel as Talmadge slammed into the other side.

An alarm blared something about the storm emergency lockdown protocol. "Not now, Foster. Legs are our best defense, remember?"

Reluctantly, he shoved on his helmet and let her pull him from the dome into the storm. He still didn't know what Calderon was going to do, but they could manage a fifteen-mile wind tunnel. They would survive it, and then they would tell everyone what they knew.

But still, he couldn't ignore the bad feeling that he had at last taken on something that was too big for him. After this, he promised himself, he was getting out of the royale game.

If he survived that long.

CHAPTER 36

TOWERING canyon walls rose up on either side of Ezren as she sprinted down the narrow, twisting channel with Foster right behind her. Above them, the storm thrashed in a massive, undulating cyclone, boulders cutting through the air as the winds pressed down on them. Despite all of her close calls and the hundreds of times she'd been battered on the surface, she'd never been scared of a storm before.

Now, even with the canyon protecting them from the raging monster above, she was chaffing terrified.

But it wasn't all the storm. Calderon's words echoed in her ears and pain pounded through her arm as she glanced over her shoulder. With the twisting channel and the dusky light, she couldn't see far behind them. The odds were Lucian would be on them before they had a chance to react, but perhaps they could still outpace him. They only had eleven miles left to go, after all. Swallowing down her thrumming heart, she urged her legs faster, a gust of wind shoving her into Foster.

He wrapped an arm around her but couldn't stop the gust as it blasted them into the canyon wall with a jarring crash and a blaze of white-hot agony. Ezren cried out, clutching her arm to her chest.

He turned his body to shelter her from the storm's pelting debris. "You okay?"

She sucked in a deep breath, sliding along the wall. "Yes, we have to keep going." She chanced a peek behind them and caught a glimpse of Lucian and Brook bent over in the wind, bracing against the wall as they continued their steady trudge toward them.

Foster scowled. "We should just take them out right here, so we have time to handle the storm."

Ezren shook her head, her eyes on her weather readout as she continued to move, staying low to the ground. "If we scrap out here, it's going to come down to chance."

"I don't think we're going to have a choice," Foster replied. "They're getting closer."

Ezren's heart pounded in her chest, her arm throbbing as she tucked it protectively against herself. She'd be no help out here and losing the scrap wouldn't mean being eliminated.

It would mean dying.

The channel curved, and the winds changed suddenly, nearly tearing Ezren from her feet. Foster grabbed her around the waist and attached his storm tether to her. "Stay as close as you can, and I can help weigh you down."

She nodded, and the winds swirled behind them, relentlessly pushing them forward. "Let's go, we have to take advantage of the tailwind."

They ran faster than Ezren thought possible with her tired limbs and broken arm, the wind pressing against their back as they struggled to maneuver around the debris. The exhilaration of the run had almost eased the fear from her shoulders, when Lucian barreled straight between Ezren and Foster, right into the line that bound them together. The force of it dragged them both to the ground.

Ezren's arm screamed with pain, but she barely had time to

register the damage before Brook was nearly on top of her. She kicked out, knocking Brook into a cluster of rocks. The girl lunged forward again, but Ezren kept her feet between them, kicking at the girl's head and stomach and whatever she could reach. With her useless arm, distance was the only thing she had going for her.

The tether yanked her back as Lucian and Foster rolled along the channel, each trying to smash the other into the ground. In another twist of bodies, Lucian grabbed the rope and spun around, flinging them both into the canyon wall.

Stone crunched into Ezren's back, sending sparks through her vision, and still Brook and Lucian stalked toward them.

"Do you have a plan?" she groaned through the pain, darkness edging her peripheries.

Foster staggered to his feet. "Just gotta keep going."

Ezren's goggs beeped as her weather update came in, and her eyes widened. "Foster, we've got to get out of the channel."

He shook his head. "It's okay, we just need to knock them down and make a run for it."

"No!" She grabbed him and dug her mag boots into the wall.

Ezren: That whip squall's going to tear through here like a burst dam. We have to climb out of here. Now!

His eyes twitched as he looked at the weather update before he followed her up the wall with quick hands, the tether pulling Ezren up after him.

Foster: But the surface is a death wish.

From below, Lucian's laugh cut through the howling wind. "If that's how you want to go out, don't let me stop you." With a nudge from Brook, they continued on, running through the channel.

"Ezren, they're gone, we can go back down."

"No, we can't," she said, her attention on the electrified flood of wind and rock spinning directly through the channel, the ground crumbling before it with an ominous crack. She leapt onto the surface and pulled him up after her. "We have to make a run for it."

Following her stare, Foster's brows shot up at the rippling vortex tearing toward them. It clawed hungrily through the channel, the ground splitting before it as it heaved boulders through the air.

The sight jolted Foster into a stumbling run, and together they staggered across the surface. In a blink, the wind changed from a steady push to violently sucking them in with a voracious appetite, and Foster had to press Ezren forward to keep her going.

"We can't make it much farther!" he yelled, fighting the wind.

Ezren pointed to a boulder not far from them. "There, we can tie ourselves to that."

Lurching forward, she managed to wrap their tether around it before collapsing to the ground next to Foster. She flattened herself against the mauve dirt, and Foster followed suit, pressing his body against hers as the wind tried to tear him away from her. The pain in Ezren's arm rattled her bones, but it was nothing compared to the terror-induced adrenaline washing through her.

She wrapped her good arm around Foster, holding him close, just as the tidal wave of air rushed past them. The force ripped them from the ground for a brief moment, stealing the breath from Ezren's lungs before charging by. And though Ezren might have imagined it in the roar of the wind, she thought she could just make out screams whipping away with the burst.

In the brief lull that followed, Ezren let the tension flow

from her body, the pain and exhaustion resurging to the surface. She had to get back up again. They were so close, but they weren't there yet. "It's passed, but we need to hurry. Lucian's mayday didn't go off, and when the wind picks up again, it'll be safer in the channel."

Foster gave her a brief squeeze. "Have I told you how much you impress me?"

She tried for a weary smile as she unwrapped the tether from the boulder and started running toward the channel, her breath ragged.

Ezren: Maybe you need to raise your standards.

Together, they leapt back into the trench.

Foster: In case you didn't notice, we're ten miles from winning the most insane race in the system, and our competition was just washed away in a storm burst. I don't think the standards get much higher.

Ezren's feet pounded into the ground with renewed energy.

Ezren: We can really do this.

His eyes crinkled.

Foster: Yeah we can.

The next eight miles flew by in a blur of elation. The storms had begun to climb again with a new string of cyclones, but they were so close now, Ezren could practically feel the finish line in front of them, and there was no one over her shoulder. After training for months, she could scarcely believe they were almost there, the red dot flashing in her goggs as their destination drew closer.

ETA at current speed: 15 minutes... 10... 5.

They rounded the corner, and a metal archway came into view in the distance, words scrawled across its battered, dented face: *Welcome race royalers! Congratulations!* And then in a less than official-looking script: *Way to kick ass! Storm brawlers for the win!*

Ezren turned to Foster, her legs dragging with exhaustion but a wide grin splitting her face. She chanced one last look behind them—no one. "We made it," she said, exhilarated relief coursing through her.

He squeezed her shoulder. "I can't believe—"

The alarms on Ezren's suit cut through his words in an ear-piercing screech, and the nanite fabric scorched her skin with an agonizing heat, the material constricting all around her.

And with a scream of blistering agony, she fell to the ground.

CHAPTER 37

FOSTER CAREENED TO A STOP, any sense of relief obliterated by the sight of Ezren writhing on the floor of the canyon.

"Get it off! Get it off!" She clawed at the suit that refused to unzip under the panicked fingers of her good arm.

Foster's mind whirled. The oxygen content here was only half of what they needed and taking off her suit would put her at risk of both debris and the wind carrying her away. But they were less than five minutes from the finish; he could carry her.

He knelt, and her back arched as she screamed, wordless and desperate. Then her shrieks abruptly silenced, her hands scrabbling at her throat. Abandoning any semblance of a plan, he ripped the helmet off her head. Her eyes bulged as she gasped for air, and he tore at the seam of her suit, the hot nanites glowing red under his gloved fingers. *Fodding suns.* They were burning her alive.

Not bothering to be gentle, he ripped the fabric at her neck. She gasped as the tear freed her throat, coughing and spluttering before screaming out again. He tore the nanitelattice from her body, ripping through the expensive equipment he had coveted so much until it finally fell away, and he held fast to her bare arms. Dressed only in a sports bra and compression shorts, her skin had already turned an angry red, and a bruised ring started to swell around her throat, but she was free.

"Ezren! Are you okay?" His breath came fast as he wrapped her in his arms, trying to protect her from the shards of debris raining down on them. As a quick afterthought, he shut down his suit's software, racking his brain for how they'd hacked her gear. Then his gaze stilled on her swollen, black-and-blue arm. *The cast. They'd used the cast.*

Ezren dragged in ragged, pained breaths, and Foster remembered that the air quality was still too weak.

"Keep... going," she whispered, her lips tinged blue and her eyelids fluttering. "Need goggs...evid..."

He snatched her goggs from her helmet and rose, cradling her against his chest. "I'm going to get you to the finish. Hang in there."

A sound drew his attention behind them, and he turned to see Talmadge and Brook barreling impossibly fast down the canyon.

Eyes wide, Foster sprinted toward the finish, painfully aware of Talmadge's crashing feet closing in behind him, and Ezren crying out in his arms, sharp bits of rock slicing into her skin as she sucked in useless breaths of air. They were so close now, the doors of the airlock had opened, but Talmadge had drawn up directly beside him with Brook close behind.

They were so close, and he stretched his legs just a little farther. Every muscle screaming in pain, beyond exhaustion, and his heart pumping with rage and desperation. He had to get Ezren safe. Then someone tackled him from the side, and the four of them tumbled forward across the finish line, the door hissing shut behind them.

The wide-open room erupted in a cacophony of shouts and voices, a hundred hovercams flashing around them.

"And Sterling/Hart and Brook/Talmadge have finished with a bang!"

"Closest royale in history!"

"Cams are being consulted to verify the winner!"

"Why doesn't Hart have a topsuit on?"

"Seems like there might be some injury."

Foster shoved the others away, trying to get Ezren some space as she sucked in greedy breaths, her eyes squeezed shut with pain. "Can I get a medbot over here?" he yelled out, his voice cracking. "Ezren, are you still with me?" Afraid to touch her blistering skin, the best he could do was hover over her, trying to keep the others a respectful distance away. He snatched a formal jacket offered by an outstretched hand and draped it over her as gently as he could.

She nodded tightly, taking her goggs from him with her good hand. "Did we... win?"

"I don't know," he said. "But you can be sure we gave it our best chaffing shot."

Beside them, Talmadge dragged Brook up against him and planted an ostentatious victory kiss on her mouth. Then he raised their clasped hands in the air with a whoop. "We won the Belethea Race Royale!"

Another buzz rippled through the crowd as the instant replay slowed on the huge holopros surrounding the dome, clearly showing Talmadge first, then Foster and Ezren, with Brook behind them.

The announcer's booming voice echoed officiously through the dome. "In a stunning finish, the winners of this year's Belethea Race Royale are Belethea's own—"

The announcer stopped, and Foster could see him leaning toward another man. The officiant gestured angrily for a moment before throwing up his hands in resignation. "I stand corrected," he huffed. "Although Sterling/Hart did finish the race, due to Hart's missing topsuit, a breach of safety rule 24.3A, they have been disqualified, so..." He took a deep breath, regaining his professional announcer bravado. "The official winners of this year's race royale are Syndali Station's Brook/Talmadge!"

Another roar exploded from the crowd, but this one was a mixed bag of outrage and excitement. The dome lit up with a holopro of the Syndali starry crest and a close-up of Talmadge and Brook sharing another kiss. Foster's fists curled at his sides. "Fodding robbed," he seethed.

But Ezren rose, and he offered a hand to steady her. She slid her goggs around her head and looked at him with a bitter-sweet smile. "Oh, c'mon, Foster. Calderon was never going to let us actually win, but we both know we did it."

"But he tried to *kill* you," Foster said.

She winced, pulling the oversized suit jacket tight around her shoulders. "You said we didn't have to win to have a voice, right?"

The press swarmed Talmadge and Brook with hovercams and questions as Foster's thoughts sputtered with the injustice of it. Still, there had to be a way to get their attention. His mind spun as Grady's voice echoed in his thoughts: *If you want the spotlight, you gotta be creative.* And the system's spot-light was there, all around them. "We're going to get them to listen."

Holding her hand, he bent down on one knee, and Ezren gasped, her eyes widening with unadulterated shock. Hope-fully, Ezren would forgive him for this later, but still, it was just the two of them amidst a swirling crowd. Maybe it wasn't enough.

Then a high shriek that sounded suspiciously like Sylvia pierced through the rumbling crowd. "Foster Sterling is proposing!"

And suddenly, every single cam in the dome was on them, a hush falling on the crowd as they all listened in.

"Ezren Hart..." Sweat trailed down his cheek, whether because of the whole getting down on one knee thing, or what they were about to do, he wasn't sure. "Would you... please..."

Around them, the crowd seemed to draw in a breath. Even Talmadge and Brook stood still, mouths agape.

"...tell them who murdered Genevieve Navarro?"

Ezren's gaze snapped up as the crowd bubbled in a small murmur, and the words rushed out of her, bold and confident. "Calderon Industries has been rigging the Belethea Race Royale for years, and Warner Calderon is responsible for the topsuit sabotage that killed Genevieve Navarro, and the attempted murder of Bex Gunderson and Simon Grady."

The murmur erupted in a dizzying onslaught of questions and accusations.

"Is this in revenge for your disqualification?"

"How does it feel to turn against your own countryman?"

"Where's your proof?"

Foster shot to his feet beside Ezren, still holding her hand. "Just grab the suit she ditched on the fodding surface." He pointed at her scorched, bruised, and bleeding body, and the rage swelled in him. "Or do you think she did this for the fritz of it?"

Talmadge finally stepped forward. "I don't know, this whole thing just seems like a bitter publicity stunt to steal the limelight that's rightfully ours."

"Says Calderon's favorite podtick thug." Foster lurched forward, ready to scrap right here in the finishing dome, and the crowd jostled for a better position.

Ezren's hand held him back, tightening around his arm. "Forget him. The race is over. Just someone find my suit," she called, limping toward the door.

Calderon stepped in front of the airlock, his entourage blocking her way. "I'm afraid, my dear, that the suit has already been swept away by the elements. We found no trace of it." His dark eyes weighed on her, glinting dangerously. "Unless you have some other proof?"

Foster's mind whirled. By now they almost certainly destroyed the evidence in Vieve's, Grady's, and Bex's suits... and with their topsuit records in Calderon's control, they really didn't have anything else. "You can't believe these people would just swallow the coincidence that *four* Belethean racers have been hurt or killed in the last two years."

"I understand you're still reeling from your loss, but we all know Genevieve Navarro's accident was thoroughly investigated and serves as a testament to this race's dangers. We cannot be held responsible for the reckless software upgrades you've been experimenting with on your own team."

The blood drained from Foster's face, his body going numb as his ears buzzed. He'd played directly into Calderon's hand. But how? The hovercams turned to him.

"Are you responsible for your team's injuries?"

"Is the software the reason behind Belethea's wins this year?"

"Is this all a front to try to protect yourself?"

Ezren straightened. "No! It was my software, and it wasn't faulty."

"So she was a saboteur after all!" someone cried, the crowd drinking in the drama, gorging themselves on it.

"I knew she was no good," said another.

Foster's right hand spasmed with a jolt of pain. Everything was falling apart around them. They'd won, hadn't they? How had it come to this?

"It wasn't her software," another voice boomed. A familiar one, and so close to Foster, he nearly jumped. He turned to see his mother in a battered silver topsuit holding out the torn remains of Ezren's suit. "And the proof is right here." She leaned closer, her chest heaving and sweat pouring down her face as though she'd just sprinted a mile. "You'll have to be quick before Calderon—"

But Foster was already linking into it, projecting the code into his holopro.

"Bigger, Foster," Sylvia said, struggling to get through the crowd.

Sylvia: The finishing dome holopro access point code: 6k+WP`vGFgU^BB]V<!#*

"No! Someone stop him!" Talmadge yelled, surging forward.

Greta threw him to the ground with a deft twist. "Sit your ass down."

Even worn out, Foster flew through the commands. Finding the huge, swarming virus almost instantaneously and projecting it all over the dome. He immediately identified the medcast as the source of the malicious code, but that was too nebulous to pin on Calderon. They needed more.

Ezren: Compare it to this.

Barely pausing to think, Foster projected the Kavata Outpost base code Ezren sent him, and after a tense three seconds, came up with a 99.99% source signature match.

The virus was a product of Calderon Industries.

The press gasped, turning as one to where Calderon had been standing, only to find he had melted into the crowd, leaving a sweaty Harland in his wake. "I apologize, but Mr. Cal—"

A shout cut him off, and the dome's security team nearly ran him over as they barreled past him. The rest of the crowd turned to Talmadge and Brook where they stood with blank expressions.

"Are you working with Calderon?"

"How long has this been going on?"

"Did you kill Genevieve Navarro?"

The pair didn't even flinch when a pair of guards seized them by the elbows. "You're under arrest on the suspicion of conspiracy to commit murder."

Foster turned to where Ezren swayed dangerously beside him. He put an arm around her shoulders to steady her, but she was looking at his mother. "How did you...?"

His mother stood apart from them, leaning heavily on the square med bot. "When Calderon asked me to keep my son off the Belethea team, I was suspicious, especially after your accident. Then after what happened to Simon and Bex, I was only looking for proof. As soon as I saw your suit turn on you in the holopro, I knew I had it."

"And you ran out into the storm to grab it," Foster said. That was no small thing. At his mom's age, it must've wreaked havoc on her body, even if she was out there for only a short time. His throat tightened with a swell of warm emotion, his eyes dampening. "Thank you, Mom."

"I haven't always been the best parent, but I figured I could handle this." She reached out and squeezed his arm. "Now I better go argue that you're the rightful winner before some other rando runs in here."

"I'm right behind you," Sylvia said as she wrapped a huge med blanket around Foster and Ezren's shoulders. "We could not be prouder." She kissed each of them on the cheek before offering her arm to Greta. "Now, let's go sort out those asschaffs."

Greta nodded, tightly gripping Sylvia's arm, and they strode away in the bustling crowd. Foster was left holding Ezren when the rush of reporters seemed to realize that they could be the winners after all.

"How does it feel to be the disputed champions of the Belethea Race Royale?"

"What're you going to do with the prize money?"

"Will you be competing next year?"

"How're you feeling right now?"

Ezren turned at that last question, her smile still a little shaky. "Like I could really use some coffee."

A chuckle flowed through the crowd, and Foster turned to Ezren beside him, her gaze starry and dazed. "Well, is it everything you hoped it would be? You know, besides the lack of coffee and cake raining down on us?"

"It was a little dramatic."

He laughed, a lightness filling his chest. "Well, they had to make it memorable, right?"

"Because the race wasn't memorable enough?" she scoffed.

"Not quite." Then he leaned in close and placed a gentle kiss on her lips. Not for the hovercams, not for the fans, just for them.

Everyone else just happened to be there.

CHAPTER 38

EZREN SQUEEZED THROUGH THE CROWD—FOOD, drink, and music flooding through Tuzuno's main dome in its Casolla Arrival Day celebration. Her mother stood in the corner, laughing with Dr. Lutz and a few other researchers she didn't recognize while her brother and his friends chased after the trilling Waffle in the now toxic-plant-free park. Sam still had nanite wraps around his limbs from his procedure, but they were anticipating full recovery in only another two months.

Across the verdant lawn, Sylvia's brown eyes glinted, her hair piled on her head in a complicated twist as she hobnobbed with the ever-present legion of sponsors and press that followed her now. Even Simon and Bex were there, sipping their umbrella drinks while they posed with the squealing Micah for Simon's hovercam.

The sight of them all filled Ezren's heart near to bursting, but after two hours, she'd had as much as she could take of the crowd. Especially with her goggs whispering of a clear window in the storms. Avoiding eye contact with the never-ending stream of well-wishers, she slipped into the airlock, grabbed her royale suit from her locker, and leapt out into the familiar mauve plains beneath a cloudy teal sky.

Home.

An hour later, Ezren sat on the top of the ridge overlooking Tuzuno outpost, her legs kicking out over the open air beneath her feet. Although storms swirled in the distance, they looked strangely calm after her time in the churn belt. Her brand new topsuit helmet lay beside her, and she breathed in the sweet petrichor of Belethea as the wind whipped through her hair.

She looked out over the new domes under construction around Tuzuno and grinned to herself. She'd joined the royale for the money, but this hadn't even been bought with the winnings or the terranium. After the truth had come out about Calderon Industries, creds had poured in from all over the system to support terraforming.

Although Calderon Industries would be tied up in legal proceedings for the better part of a decade, at least Belethea and terraforming had gotten their justice. Even if a small part of Calderon's argument wriggled in her gut, it could be up to her to preserve the heart of Belethea—her wildness, her beauty. It would be a hard battle, but she could do it—because as a BRR champion, she had a voice now.

And it was loud.

"You know, you really should wear a helmet."

Ezren's heart sputtered, and she turned to see Foster striding toward her. Even as the words escaped his mouth, he pulled off his own helmet, revealing his brown waves, stormy eyes, and lazy half-smile. She rose and launched herself into his arms. "You're early! I thought you were staying for another day."

He chuckled, hugging her tightly. "My mom and her team were able to catch an earlier window through the storms, so I got on the first truck this way."

"Aw, I'm sorry I didn't get to see more of her this time. When will she be back?"

"End of next month."

Ezren's smile broadened, but she didn't say anything. She didn't have to. After so many rocky years, it was nice to see Foster patching things up with his mom, and she could see in his smooth brow that something inside him was healing.

"But how's Tuzuno doing with all the newfound fame?" he continued. "It looks a lot different than the last time I was here."

"Soaking it up like a sponge. They've had resumes from top researchers all over the system wanting to come work, and the expansion efforts have taken off. My mom and Dr. Lutz have already started the third round of their quasiphona experiments that we never thought we'd have the terranium to power. It's all just so unreal." She took a breath, shaking her head. "What about Belethea's race royale team? What will happen to them now that Calderon's no longer the sponsor?"

"Whatever they want, probably. Simon and Bex are beside themselves over getting cheated and will be out for blood next year," Foster said. "They've got loads of other sponsors now to upgrade Carmella and outfit a full roster."

"What about you?" Ezren asked.

"Me?"

Ezren snorted. "Yes, you, Champion Belethea Royale Racer. Racing again? Or coming back as a coach? Sylvia would die to have you."

Foster scrubbed a hand through his hair, eyes gleaming with a barely suppressed grin. "Yeah, but I wouldn't survive Bex and Simon. Besides... after a decade I think I've had my fill of the royale life. I was thinking I'd go back to school." He snuck a nervous side glance at her. "Maybe major in nanite software engineering at Petraskis."

"Have you been talking to my mother?" Ezren raised a brow. "She keeps saying the best way for me to help terraforming is to go off and get my doctorate." And her mom was right. It had taken her some time to realize it, but now that her wings had spread, Tuzuno wasn't quite big enough for her anymore.

Foster's cheeks colored ever so slightly, but he still didn't meet her gaze. "Sounds like a good idea... but I know how much you love Tuzuno, so I didn't, you know—"

She stood up on her toes and kissed him long and hard. When they pulled apart he pressed his forehead to hers, his breath warm on her cheeks. "I'm so glad we'll be going there together, then."

With a broadening smile, he kissed her again, his fingers curving around her back as he pulled her to him, her skin heating as their bodies melded together to the roll of distant thunder.

Then their goggs beeped, alerting them to a shift in the storm, and they reluctantly parted.

"Looks like we've only got seven minutes to get in now."

He cocked a mischievous eyebrow at her. "Want to ra—"

But Ezren pushed away, already three steps ahead of him. "Last one there has to refill Simon's umbrella drink."

"Oh, look who finally decided to show up early for once!" he called as he ran after her.

And together they skidded and weaved and laughed across Belethea's open wilds, the storms swirling over their heads and miles still left to go.

ACKNOWLEDGMENTS

Into the Churn held a lot of firsts for me: my first science fiction novel, my first dual point-of-view story, and my first traditionally published novel. As with all firsts, it required a huge leap of faith that I would not have been able to take if it weren't for a whole village of wonderful, incredible people pushing me off the ledge. (I can make jokes in the acknowledgments, right?)

Seriously though, I want to thank Whimsical Publishing, and specifically Micheline Ryckman, for taking my book and making it unbelievably beautiful. (I mean just look at it! It's so gorgeous, I could cry rainbows just staring at it!) Your talent and passion for creating works of art have amazed and inspired me again and again, and I'm so incredibly honored that you took me and these characters under your wing. Thank you so much for placing your faith in me and this story.

And of course, this book would never have been possible without my family. Thanks so much to my parents, two of my most enthusiastic supporters who are always on hand to throw books at me for a TikTok and keep the neighborhood little free libraries stocked with my stories. Thanks to my husband, Adam, for being my first reader, forever supporter, and caring enforcer of a bedtime that keeps me functional. And of course, most importantly, thanks to my favorite wild boys, Decker and Dashiell, for your endless supply of hugs, joy, and (mis)adventure. I love you all too much for words!

To my beta readers—Mindy, Nick, Rebecca, Benjamin,

Alyssa, Maddy, and Fanna—thank you for helping me whip this book from a spindly rough draft into this enormous adventure. And I want to especially shout out my critique partners: Kayleigh, for always being a positive light, and Caleb, for always pointing out a good hiss in Friday night critiques.

To Cheryl Van Stockum, thank you for capturing my best side in my author photo.

And to all the others who have given their kind encouragement—in person, on social media, in your reviews—thank you so much for both catching me when I stumble and giving me the courage to take this leap. It means the world to me, and this book would never have been possible without you.

ABOUT THE AUTHOR

Author – Hayley Reese Chow is a PowerPoint ranger by day and writer by night. Into the Churn was heavily influenced by her experiences as an All-American collegiate fencer and ultramarathoner. Her first self-published novel won the 2020 YA Florida Author Project and was the 5th place finalist in the 2021 Book Blogger Novel of the Year Awards. She currently dodges hurricanes in Florida with her two wild boys, her long-suffering husband, and a dog that thinks she's a cat. Follow Hayley on her website hayleyreesechow.com or on Instagram @hayleyreesechow